The field glowed up at Trent, PASSWORD?

From out in the corridor Denice said softly, "It's *éveil*. Hurry, Trent."

Trent punched i   G—CONNECTED—PAS

Denice ducked t

Jimmy Ramirez   nice plucked the needle   still closed, stuck just her nand outside the door frame and fanned the corridor with it. The sound of the Peaceforcer stunners stopped abruptly.

Trent's Image took control of the systerm. BOSS!

Out of the corner of his eye Trent saw Jimmy appear in the doorway, with an autoshot cradled in his arms. "It's going up, man. We gotta move!"

"Hang in there. I won't be long."

I'M COMING TO GET YOU, JOHNNY. HOW BADLY CAN YOU DAMAGE THE PEACEFORCER BOARDS YOU HAVE ACCESS TO?

WITH THE SECURITY CLEARANCES THIS LOCATION HAS? YOU MUST BE KIDDING.

BAD?

Trent? Denice's thoughts touched his, tinged with near panic. *They're coming from the level above us, at least fifteen Peaceforcers and they're all armed. Masers, Trent, and I can't stop all of them. We have three floors to go before we even make it to the surface; we have to go. Now.*

THEY WON'T KNOW WHAT HIT THEM, BOSS. WANT ME TO TAKE IT ALL DOWN?

Denice screamed, *"Trent!"*

Trent typed, TRASH THE PLACE.

He turned and ran.

THE LONG RUN

A Tale of the Continuing Time

· —————————————— ·

Daniel Keys Moran

BANTAM BOOKS
NEW YORK · TORONTO · LONDON · SYDNEY · AUCKLAND

THE LONG RUN

A Bantam Spectra Book / September 1989

ISBN 0-553-28144-5

Published simultaneously in the United States and Canada

Bantam Books are published by Bantam Books, a division of
Bantam Doubleday Dell Publishing Group, Inc. Its trademark,
consisting of the words "Bantam Books" and the portrayal of
a rooster, is Registered in U.S. Patent and Trademark Office
and in other countries. Marca Registrada. Bantam Books,
666 Fifth Avenue, New York, New York 10103.

PRINTED IN THE UNITED STATES OF AMERICA

O   0 9 8 7 6 5 4 3 2 1

Dedication

With thanks to Alan Rodgers, for letting me bounce ideas off the sides of his skull; *The Long Run* is

For my little sister, Doctor Death—cause she paid attention when no one else would. Not graciously, not out of any act of faith or anything like that, but at least she read it.

Considering I didn't show any particular talent or promise or anything aside from being her brother, that was pretty cool.

I killed my love to set him free
   For fear I'd cause him pain
I killed him—we were very young
   And now I'm old again

We lived a life together once
   And I was so afraid
For every life I've lived, I've died
   For every life I've made

I killed my love to set him free
   He wasn't hard to kill
He ran into another life
   I guess he's running still

   —Mahliya Kutura
     Many Lives
     Street Songs, 2078 Gregorian

THE LONG RUN

On July 3, 2062, the United Nations Peace Keeping Force, under the command of Peaceforcer Elite Sergeant Mohammed Vance, used tactical thermonuclear weapons to destroy a group of genetically engineered telepaths living at the Chandler Complex in lower Manhattan.

Men and women who *would not* be slaves to the Peaceforcers.

On July 3, 2062, over two hundred and forty telepathic adults and children died in nuclear fire.

In the battle preceding their destruction, the telepaths sent better than a quarter of the population of the state of New York into permanent insanity; caused the two years of the Troubles, as legal and social systems throughout metropolitan areas broke down beyond hope of repair. The old order could not be resurrected; the Peaceforcers created the Patrol Sectors, and left the vast bulk of what had once been New York City to become the lethal, desolate area known as the Fringe.

Three children from the Chandler Complex survived the destruction of the telepaths. Two of them were the nine-year-old twins David and Denice Castanaveras, the children of Carl Castanaveras and Jany McConnell.

The third child was not a telepath. He was a webdancer.

A Player.

His name was Trent.

Seven years have passed. . . .

The Last Summer
of His Youth

· ——————————————————— ·

2069 Gregorian

· 1 ·

"**Y**ou're Trent."

"I am?"

The young man was conservatively dressed: a gray jacket and black pants, and a white silk shirt that shone brilliantly even in the dim light from L'Express's outdoor glowfloats. He wore immaculately clean white running shoes; there was a single flat ruby stud in the lobe of his left ear. Trent's temples, where an inskin InfoNet link might have been implanted, were merely smooth skin. His hair was sandy blond, cut short, and he either wore no makeup or had turned it off.

He wore flat black sunglasses though they were hardly necessary.

It was ten minutes after six o'clock.

"You're younger than I'd expected," said the middle-aged man who had said his name was Jerry Jackson. On the phone Trent had not noticed it, but in person his voice held the faint but definite traces of a Southern accent.

"Am I?"

"And you're late," the man said. Despite the air, heavy with ozone as though a thunderstorm were about to strike, Jackson had taken a table outside beneath the gray-black skies, on the balcony level overlooking the eternally crowded streets.

"Ten minutes . . ." Trent shrugged. "Ten minutes older."

He seated himself across the table from Jerry Jackson. To the waitbot which had led him to the table he said, "A pot of coffee. With cream, no sugar."

The waitbot paused, then said mildly, in the rich baritone

characteristic of opera singers, newsdancers and politicians, "Monsieur, that item is not on the menu."

"Waiter, please," said Trent. They both waited while the waitbot rolled away out of listening range.

L'Express sat on the western edge of what had once been the Brooklyn Navy Yard, and was now one of the most expensive residential areas in all the Patrol Sectors. From where he sat Trent could see to the northwest, on the other side of the East River, the scarlet sparks of spacecraft rising and descending at Unification Spaceport in lower Manhattan. The dull, distant boom of craft breaking through the sound barrier touched him every twenty seconds or so.

Eight spacescrapers reared high above the skyline, eight three- to five-kilometer-tall buildings; two of them did nothing but house Peaceforcers and the babychasers from the Ministry of Population Control: the Left and Right Hands of the Devil Himself, Secretary-General Charles Eddore.

Trent said, "How did you get referred to me?"

Jackson said smoothly, "You're in the Directory."

"That wasn't the question."

Jerry Jackson was drinking something cold and green, with crushed ice in it. He wore an exquisitely tailored blue pinstripe suit. A brushed aluminum attaché case stood upright beside his chair. The cuffs of his sleeves were fastened European style, folded back upon themselves. "Actually, Booker Jamethon gave me your name."

"Booker's a great guy," said Trent.

"He said I shouldn't hire you, that you're not dependable."

"Of course," said Trent instantly, "all those years on the juice, they weren't good for him."

Jerry Jackson smiled for the first time. " 'Sieur Jamethon wanted the job himself. He only gave me your name—for a fee—after I turned him down."

"Tell me about the job."

"You know CalleyTronics?"

Trent's pause was very brief. "It's located on the eighth floor of the Down Plaza. They sell inskins and image coprocessors, MPU hardware, like that. Half the webdancers I know buy from them."

"Frank Calley," said Jerry Jackson with a very convincing display of anger, "is a thief. He lifted fifteen terabytes of hot RAM, a hundred and five thousand Credit Units worth of room-temperature superconductor memory, from mah warehouse in Georgia." Under the stress of anger, the accent became more audible.

A single drop of rain touched down on the transparent tabletop in front of Trent.

"Let me guess," Trent said.

"Guess?"

"You want me to get your RTS back."

"Yes."

"What do you think you know about me?"

A touch of the anger was back in his voice. "You're supposed to be a thief yourself." The word *thief* was laced with an astonishing amount of disdain. "You hire out to steal things for people. You . . ."

A second drop of rain joined the first. Jerry Jackson cut himself off as a waiter, after an anxious glance at the sky, hurried out to where they were seated.

"Monsieur," said the waiter hurriedly, with a French accent which might have been real, "you wished to order a cup of coffee?"

"A pot," Trent corrected him. "A whole big pot of coffee."

"Monsieur, we do not sell coffee by the pot, only by the cup."

"May I speak to your manager?"

The waiter's features stiffened visibly. "Oui. One moment, monsieur."

Trent waited until the waiter had gone back inside. "So you want me to boost fifteen terabytes of RTS from CalleyTronics?"

"Yes."

Trent counted five drops of rain on the cut-crystal surface of the table. Six. "It probably can't be done—a straight boost, I mean. Calley's real tight with the power structure in the Patrol Sectors, and his security's pretty good. You'd be better off with a con, something that would leave him wondering if he'd been hit—not sure—and feeling so stupid he wouldn't dare go to the Peaceforcers with it for fear of being laughed at."

Jerry Jackson leaned forward with what seemed to Trent to be honest curiosity. "What do you have in mind?"

"I don't know. What's good here?"

"Regarding Calley," Jerry Jackson said with great control, "what do you have in mind?"

Trent looked at the man blankly. "Nothing. I'm not going

to boost Frank Calley for you, and I'm not going to con him either. Look, have you ever eaten here before?"

"Never."

"Oh. Too bad. Usually when I go to a new restaurant I like to go with somebody who's been there before, so I know what's good. You may not know this," said Trent thoughtfully, "but two years ago a Player scored some image coprocessor hardware off CalleyTronics, chanted Calley's accounting computer to believe the hardware had been properly paid for, and had it shipped to a drop box. It took Calley half a year to find out who'd done it, but that summer they fished a corpse out of the East River. His teeth had been pulled with pliers, his eyes were poked out, his fingers had been chopped off, and his features defaced with acid. They identified him by his inskin."

"You won't take the job?"

"Am I being asked?"

"Yes."

"No."

Jackson took a deep breath. "Why not?"

Trent shrugged. "No percentage. If I was going to, I'd do a con to get Calley coming after me, get him to believe I had something he wanted. But I'm not going to. The guy's mean, but he's also pretty straight; guys like him always go to the Peaceforcers."

A gorgeous, mature woman in a black evening gown came out to their table, with the waiter a few steps behind her. "Monsieur?"

"Yes?" said Trent politely.

For some reason his response seemed to throw her. Her accent was considerably better than the waiter's; Trent would have bet she was actually French. "You wished to order . . ."

"Coffee."

"An entire pot?"

"Please."

"We do not sell coffee by the pot, monsieur. We do not even have a pot to put the coffee in; the coffee is brewed in a single large"—she hesitated, searching for a word—"vat? Yes, vat, brewed in a vat in the morning, and then put in stasis and poured from stasis a cup at a time."

"Okay. I want five, no, make that seven, seven cups of coffee, each one about fifteen percent cream, one right after the other. Send the waitbot out with a cup, give it about five minutes and send it out again. Do that until I tell it to stop."

"Monsieur," she said, stress making it difficult for Trent to follow her words, "we have only three waitbots. If we do this we must assign a waitbot to do nothing but service your table, and this will affect the other patrons."

"Damn it," Jerry Jackson exploded, "what is this nonsense? Take the goddamn coffee in a cup. Are you here to talk business or what?"

Raindrops were striking Trent square in the face. The manager looked back and forth between the two of them in confusion. "You're sure?" Trent asked her. "It's simply not possible to have the cups just keep coming?"

"Monsieur," protested the manager in such horribly accented English that Trent could barely follow her, "I do not think we can."

"It's okay," said Trent, standing, "we're done." To Jerry Jackson he said, "I've really got to go; I'm late for another appointment." He turned back once before leaving. "Next time," he said as Jerry Jackson stared, "you have to take me someplace classier."

· 2 ·

Once there was a thief, and the thief was God.

—The first line in *The Exodus Bible.*

It was a twenty-minute slidewalk trip from L'Express, at one end of the old Brooklyn Navy Yard, through streets lined by gray plastisteel residential high rises, to the Down Plaza at the other end of the development. Trent ran all the way. He was delayed just before he reached the Plaza when a bomb in a baby carriage blew up next to a pair of patroling Peaceforcers, killing the Peaceforcers and several of the bystanders and tearing a hole in the slidewalk that brought the slidewalk to a shuddering, grinding stop. Despite his hurry Trent stopped running immediately, and walked without haste through the growing rain, away from the crowd that was gathering around the site of the explosion, walked straight as a laser the rest of the way to the Plaza maglev.

There were about twenty fashionable, damp, well-dressed people crowded onto the air-conditioned maglev platform as it descended beneath street level.

Trent was not particularly noticeable; because it was necessary for the job, so that he would not stand out from the other patrons inside CalleyTronics, Trent had dressed that day every bit as well as the children of the wealthy and privileged who swarmed through the eight huge, underground levels of the Down Plaza, the busiest shopping structure in all of the Patrol Sectors.

Most of those crowded onto the maglev platform, as it sank into the Down Plaza, were slender; a few of the less well-dressed were gaunt.

Two of them were fat. Somewhere in their mid-thirties, Trent guessed; they were French and they were female and they were very fat. Not counting the cyborg French Peaceforcers Elite, who came by their mass in honest metal and metal-ceramics, Trent had in his entire life never seen more gross tonnage on two bodies. Between the two of them they must have massed 250 kilos.

They were the last ones onto the maglev platform, already half loaded down with their packages and bags and umbrellas, chattering gaily in French so perfectly accented that there was no question in Trent's mind as to their nationality. They could not be employed themselves, not by the U.N.; the U.N. had maximum weight standards. Wives, then, of United Nations officials transplanted from France to oversee in the governing of Occupied America.

Most United Nations officials were French, and most Peaceforcers as well; by the pure luck of the draw France had, almost alone among technological nations, come through the Unification War unscathed. In the rebuilding which took place following the Unification, the French had become a dominant force.

One of the fat women touched the dark pressure point marked FIVE. The pressure point lit. Behind the dark lenses Trent's eyelids drooped shut; through the traceset contact buried in the arms of the sunglasses he sent a single command to his Image.

The maglev descended five floors in relative silence, as people got on and off the platform at the various levels. The tower in which the maglev platform was located thrust up like a spear through the center of the Down Plaza; the shops were arrayed in a rough rectangle around the maglev tower. Hanging flat walkways connected the central maglev tower to the shops at each level; skywalks connected the various levels for those who preferred walking to using the maglev.

At Level Five, the maglev did not even slow. The two fat women broke off their conversation in consternation; one of them touched the pressure point for Level Five again. Trent said softly, "Ladies?"

They turned to look at him.

"Did you know that on Level One there's one of the finest gyms in the city? And on Level Three there's a biosculptor who vacuums fat cells so you can't *get* fat." Trent smiled at them. "Really. It's amazing, she just vacuums those fat cells right out. Whoosh!"

The two fat women gaped at him. The platform had not stopped at Level Five; it did at Level Six, and half a dozen of the maglev platform's occupants got off; a couple more got on.

The gates closed again, and the platform descended.

"On Level Four there's *three* cafés that serve empty food, no calories at all," Trent continued enthusiastically. "Left-handed sugars; you can really pig out." He stared at them with his sunglasses. "It doesn't taste exactly the same, but that's not my fault."

Everybody left on the maglev platform was looking at them, at Trent and the two fat women. The maglev platform skipped Level Seven, where most of the small businesses were clustered, and opened up finally onto Level Eight, the bottom level of the huge plaza. People filed off slowly, stepping over or walking around the prone, twitching form of the juice junkie who blocked the walkway from the maglev platform, looking back as they did so at Trent and the French women. Trent turned to leave also and then suddenly, just the other side of the maglev gates, turned around to face the French women again.

"Do you speak English?" he demanded.

The one nearest him said in English, haughtily, very clearly, "I do not speak English."

"Oh." The maglev gates closed on the women, and the power on the platform suddenly died. The platform went dark. "One hundred and fifteen million people," said Trent in his best French, "died last year because there wasn't enough food for them." Behind the gate, on the maglev platform, the women were pushing frantically at the pressure points. Trent did not think they had even heard him. He looked at them for just a moment, stood watching them without expression from the other side of the gates. The one who was not punching at the pressure points suddenly became aware of Trent standing and watching them, and pleaded in French, "Young man, will you call someone to let us out?"

Turning away, Trent shook his head. "I'm *already* late," he muttered.

He almost tripped over the juice junkie.

> *The Crystal Wind is the Storm, and the Storm is Data, and the Data is Life.*
>
> —The Player's Litany

Heat rises; it was always notably cool on the bottom level of the Down Plaza.

Walking out onto Eight, those who were new to the Plaza, even New York natives, tended to gawk like tourists. The upper seven levels of the Down Plaza were illuminated by yellow light with a greenish tinge: a mixture of yellow sun-paint and the omnipresent, wavering, flickering light of the blue-green glowfloats in their eternal migration between the first and eighth levels of the Down Plaza.

Level Eight was a riot of color: glittering adholo, real neon and neon-laser and glowpaint. Eight was the only level with a floor, though those who spent any amount of time down on Eight learned to avoid those areas around the maglev tower where the ceiling opened up; the eight-level drop into the crowds was a favorite with jumpers.

Eight was easily the most popular level in the Plaza. There was a whorehouse behind the furniture shop, and two sensable parlors which catered to those with refined, largely illegal tastes. CalleyTronics was located there as well, and Players from over a hundred kilometers around came in person to buy from Calley, who had been, as a young man in the wistfully remembered days before DataWatch, a rather famous Player himself.

The BloodSilk Boys were mixed among the crowds at the

west end of the Plaza. Four gendarmes—cops, New York City Police officers—were sitting in full goldtone riot armor at Googie's Place on the eastern edge of Eight, watching the Plaza through the coffee shop's glassite walls. Trent did not so much as glance at either group as he walked away from the diminishing sound of the swearing French women and went to see Bones.

On the crowded floor of Down Plaza, well back from the jumper zone, eight floors beneath the surface of Brooklyn, the old black man who was considered by many the world's greatest contortionist gathered up the hard Chinese and Space-Farer CU in the basket before his platform and prepared to take a break from his routine.

Trent came to a stop just off the walkway, beside the low platform on which Bones worked. Pulling on his shirt, Bones had to raise his voice to be heard above the loud music and the babble of the crowd.

"Evening, Trent. Take dinner with me?"

"Hi, Bones. Not tonight."

"Something goin', Trent?"

Trent did not even turn his head as Bones spoke to him. "What do you mean?"

"'Bout an hour ago I seen Jimmy Ramirez; and Tammy the Rat been hanging around, and not fifteen minutes ago I seen your midget. And there was six Peaceforcers, they was here when I got here this morning. I ain't seen the Left Hand of the Devil in the Plaza that early in, oh, five years."

Trent heard barely audible popping noises as Bones' joints slowly realigned themselves. Still he did not look at the old man. "Six Peaceforcers?"

"I don't trust that midget, Trent." Peering through the crowds and flickering adholos, Bones tried to see what it was that Trent was looking at, but could not.

"You don't trust who?"

"That midget working for you."

"Which midget?"

"The pretty one."

"Oh, Bird. Bird's a doll, Bones."

"He's the right size," Bones agreed.

"He's only fourteen, Bones. He hasn't started growing yet. When were the Peaceforcers here?"

Bones sighed audibly. "You got something going today, don't you? You ever going to get a job, Trent?"

"Bones."

"What?"

"Don't start on me today. I'm not in the mood for it."

"Just wonderin'. You so good with the InfoNet, I knows you could get work."

"Bones, this is starting to look like a very bad day. I *don't want to hear about it.*" At the other end of the plaza, some seventy-five meters distant, Trent caught sight of Tammy, a too-skinny girl with platinum-white hair, deep in conversation with a tall black man wearing BloodSilk colors, waving her arms as she spoke.

"Why ain't you going to get a job?"

"I already have one and I don't need two. What time were the Peaceforcers here, Bones?"

Very near Trent, clustered around a small bench just the other side of the walkway, three teenage girls were having a loud argument about where they would eat dinner. Two of them were facing Trent and Bones; the third stood facing her companions, and Trent could see only her back. She wore a tight green leather dress which came down to midthigh, black ankle boots, and pale green silk stockings. Her hair was jet black, straight and very long.

"Everybody gots to work, Trent. Everybody needs something to make it worth gettin' up in the morning." The old contortionist chewed on the thought for a bit. "That's the fact. 'Sides," he said suddenly, "you keep up boosting, eventually the Peaceforcers going to catch you."

The girl in the green dress, immediately in front of Trent, stood clutching a handbag by its closed top. She had an exquisite bottom. A glowing scarlet zipper began at the dress's hem, just over her right thigh, and spiraled up around her buttocks, waist, and breasts; taking her out of it would be like peeling the skin off an orange. "What time, Bones?"

Bones sighed. "Seven-thirty, I guess. I was having breakfast upstairs on the second floor, at the cantina. I don't know the names of any of them, but I seen them in the crowds before sometimes when I perform. They're assigned regular to this stretch, us being so close to the Fringe and all. Cheap bastards," he added thoughtfully. "Don't never throw nothing into the kitty when I'm done."

"They recognize you?"

Bones shrugged. It was a curiously fluid motion; most of the major bones in his body had extra joints surgically inserted. "Who knows? I was dressed; I don't look much the same when all the ceramic joints are locked up and I'm wearin' clothes."

"Oh." From across the crowded length of the plaza, Tammy reached up and casually scratched her left shoulder.

Bones looked at Trent with a perturbed expression on his seamed black face. "I'm really serious, Trent. You're still young enough to get out of here."

"Out of the Patrol Sectors?" Trent grinned at Bones suddenly, a quick flash which brought unnaturally still features alive for just a moment. "I took six years just getting out of the Fringe, Bones. I *love* the Patrol Sectors."

"That's not what I meant. Geography got nothing to do with gettin' out of here." Bones pulled on a long-sleeved shirt and buttoned it up as he spoke. "I gots me a whole lot of contacts; been tying myself up in knots here in the Plaza for a long time, and I met a lot of folks. I could probably get you a job with . . ."

Seventy-five meters away, Tammy tugged gently at the lobe of her left ear; Trent cut Bones off. "I have a job, Bones."

The old contortionist snorted. "Boosting," he said, with gentle derision.

It was Monday, April the thirtieth, 2069.

Trent said softly, "Not exactly." He closed his eyes and went Inside.

> Trent said to me once, "A theft is an act of communication. So is a blow. Unlike words, neither one can be ignored. A properly executed boost consists of three elements: what you steal, how you steal it, and from whom you steal.
>
> "You cannot catch a thief who knows this and employs the knowledge properly. If the thief is a very good thief, you may learn, in time, *why* he stole what he stole."
>
> —The Peaceforcer Elite Melissa du Bois as quoted in *The Exodus Bible*.

I never *ever* talk like that.

> —Trent the Uncatchable, in conversation with the historian Corazon de Nostri, during the War with the Sleem.

The sunglasses had cost Trent more than the rest of the outfit he was wearing put together. The lenses filtered ultraviolet from bright sunlight; in dim surroundings they stepped up infrared into the visible spectrum. The arms of the glasses, where they crossed his temples, held the contacts for the traceset in the handheld InfoNet link in the right-hand pocket of his coat.

The Down Plaza was run by Frazier Enforcement, the firm which ran many of the shopping districts located either in the Fringe proper or at its edge; Frazier got along acceptably well with the Peaceforcers, and they were experts in the unique problems of Fringe-area security.

They also had the very worst software in the entire state of New York. Trent's Image, a program named Johnny Johnny, said softly, BOSS, SOMEBODY'S MESSED WITH PLAZA SECURITY.

I KNOW, JOHNNY. Standing with his eyes closed behind the concealing lenses, Trent merged with his Image, and ceased to be Trent.

Johnny Johnny roused himself into full wakefulness.

He could never remember, between times when Trent was not with him, how it was to be truly alive in the InfoNet. Unlike most Image programs—unlike Johnny Johnny's predecessor, Ralf the Wise and Powerful—Johnny Johnny had never been turned off, and only rarely reprogrammed. His memories stretched back over six years, all the way to his first nanoseconds of awareness; in those days he had been little more than a filter program, a collection of routines to enable Trent to sort through the vast crush of irrelevant details in the InfoNet quickly, to select communication routes through the millions of Boards which had, at any given moment, surplus available logic which Johnny Johnny's master might hijack.

That was Johnny Johnny's function: to act as a front end for Trent, as an interface to the InfoNet, as Trent's Image to the world.

But the flow was not one way. The relationship between Johnny Johnny and Trent was a partnership, a symbiosis.

Trent's touch brought Johnny Johnny to *life*.

Johnny Johnny blasted out into the Crystal Wind of Data.

From a great distance, Trent heard Jimmy Ramirez's voice, talking with Bones. A voice rumbled something slow and distant, and Trent relinquished all touch with Realtime and fell away into the glowing Crystal Wind.

Johnny Johnny went into the Board which ran Down Plaza's security through a line of lasercable which was putatively a failsafe backup for tracking of Personal Protection Systems inside the Plaza. Though expected to be so in the near future, the PPSs were not yet illegal, and therefore could not be banned from the Plaza. Still they were potentially so dangerous that any good security program had to keep an eye on them.

In fact that particular strand of lasercable did not track PPSs. It was one of several third-layer backup systems which Johnny Johnny had corrupted for his own use. There was no time to trace through every line of lasercable in the Plaza; Johnny Johnny did not seriously consider trying. He loaded Frazier Enforcement's Security Diagnostics and ran it. The program took forever to run, most of six seconds. Johnny Johnny waited patiently, and then swore in surprise when the results came back to him.

There was something very strange in the Security Board with him.

Player, web angel, a DataWatch webdancer—Johnny Johnny had no time to find out. Without an instant's hesitation Johnny Johnny copied himself, in approximately two thousand nanoseconds, into some eighty functional ghosts, sent them out into the InfoNet in all directions, disengaged from the Security Board, and fled.

Trent's eyes snapped open. Tammy the Rat was on her way across the length of the Plaza, striding angrily toward him through the crowd. Trent was peripherally aware of the gendarmes over at Googie's, watching Tammy walk across the Plaza. Wearing a conservative businessperson's suit, briefcase dangling loosely from her left hand, Jimmy Ramirez stood next to Bones; a tall, handsome, ex-semipro boxer with muscles on his muscles, slightly taller than Trent, simply watching

Trent with that cool, reserved look he saved for those instances when he was genuinely pissed.

"Hello, Jimmy."

"Hello, my man," said Jimmy Ramirez softly. "You're late again."

"People keep saying. I had to stop and talk to a man—"

"About?"

"—and then the baby carriage blew up—"

Trent never had a chance to finish; Tammy pushed her way through the last few meters of crowd, radiating anger so palpably that those who saw her coming got out of the way without further encouragement. "What the slithy goddam hell is going on? I've been stalling the BloodSilk Boys but—"

Trent said clearly, "It's a drop."

Tammy the Rat was a professional; she froze in midword, turned away from Trent almost instantly, and without hurrying merged back into the flow of the crowd around them.

"Walk away." Trent did not even look in Jimmy Ramirez's direction. "Have dinner with Bones, talk about Hemingway or something. A man named Jerry Jackson just tried to hire me to boost CalleyTronics—"

"But we're already boosting Calley!"

"—and, the Peaceforcers have some kind of dancer in the Plaza's Security Board. It's a drop."

Bones was looking back and forth between them, and Trent said softly to Jimmy, "Go." One of the gendarmes was pointing out the scene to the others; still Trent did not see anyone in the entire Plaza who might reasonably have been a Peaceforcer. The girl in the green dress was walking away with her friends, and Trent started after her, Jimmy falling in beside him for just a second. Out of the corner of his eye Trent saw a pair of the gendarmes coming out onto the Plaza floor.

"What are you *doing*?" Jimmy demanded, glancing over at the gendarmes watching them.

"Creating a diversion. *Go,* damn it." Trent never so much as looked around; he was simply aware that Jimmy had faded back into the crowd. He threaded his way smoothly through the surging crowds on Eight's walkways, gaining on the three girls; the girl in the green leather dress still held her purse by its clasped top. An adholo flared and he swerved slightly to pass through it; under the cover of scarlet laser light he pulled the emblade from its waterproof hiding place behind his belt buckle and turned it on. The emblade was only three molecules wide at its edge; it would cut through ferrocrete as though it were paper, and with some muscle behind it would cut even sheet monocrystal. It was completely safe; the blade itself dissolved instantly into a fine dust at the first touch of liquid—say, blood.

The cops were only thirty meters or so away; Trent increased his pace slightly, came alongside the three girls and did the entire thing in one movement, with the ease of long years of practice: jostled the girl roughly enough to make sure the gendarmes saw it, muttered a brief apology and smiled at the girl in what might be taken for slight embarrassment, flicked the emblade up to touch the side of the purse, cut, reached through the open flap and with two fingers pulled the wallet free, switched the emblade off, dropped the haft to the ground and gave it a good kick and was turning away with the stolen wallet, the exercise done flawlessly, back toward the gendarmes, when a delicate feminine hand closed around his forearm with absolutely amazing strength.

The girl said softly, in a voice pitched to go no further than Trent's ears, "I'd like my wallet returned."

Trent turned back to her and for the first time actually looked at the girl's face. The crowd was clearing away around them, leaving a small open space with Trent and the girl at the center. She was fifteen or so, with clean simple features framed by long, straight black hair, with green eyes that were even brighter than the dyed leather dress she wore. Trent said, "Sure," and gave the wallet back. The girl looked at him curiously, head tilted slightly to one side, a puzzled look taking hold upon her features.

Trent said softly, "How did you know I took it?"

A deep baritone voice ten meters behind Trent, off to his left, said "Ma'am, stand away, please."

"Really," said Trent. "I did that *perfectly.*"

The baritone voice boomed, "Stand away!"

The girl had not answered Trent. Trent said, as the seconds ticked by, "If you're not going to answer me, you'd better do what he says. He'll stun you too if you don't, and it's not pleasant. Believe me."

The girl nodded slowly, and took a single step backward, wallet in her hand. Her eyes never left Trent, and the puzzled look did not waver.

Her eyes.

"Oh," said Trent. The girl took another step backward, and another.

Bright green eyes, like Carl Castanaveras', or Jany McConnell's . . .

Emerald eyes.

Trent said, "Denice?"

Her eyes widened in shock.

The cops shot him.

· 3 ·

"*I* *don't understand,*" *she said to Trent, that February day in 2062, "why you work so hard at it.*"

The three of them were lying in the grass in the center of the park across the street from the Chandler Complex: the dark-haired green-eyed twins, and one blond boy with pale blue eyes. David lay beneath one of the trees, hiding from the hazy noontime sun with a book; Denice and Trent were beneath the tree right next to David's, dancing in the InfoNet.

"*Because I'm a Player,*" *Trent replied.*

Denice Castanaveras sighed in frustration. It frustrated her to know that most of the telepaths in the Complex could have touched Trent's thoughts easily, to know that two years from now, when the Change came for her, she would be able to do the same; and that now, today, she was limited, by the clumsiness of words, in her attempt to understand something that was very important to the closest friend she had in the world.

"*Not a webdancer, Denice, a Player.*"

She peered down at the portaterm Trent worked on. Seven years later, after the perfection of tracesets which required neither hypnosis nor biofeedback nor drugs for normal users to operate, the device would be a quarter the size, lack a keyboard, incorporate the functions of infocards, and be called a handheld—but the primary function was the same, a device to interface humans with the Information Network.

Jacked into the MPU slot at the side of the portaterm was an optical computer about the size of a makeup key; the coprocessor which held Trent's Image, Ralf the Wise and Powerful. "Life can be described," said Ralf in a completely human voice, "and described surprisingly well, in terms of the growth of information content. Correct me if I'm wrong, Boss, but that's what the Player's Litany means: from the Crystal Wind came data, and from data came life."

Trent nodded. "That's why I want an inskin."

"What's why?"

. . . to expand your sensory bandwidth by an order of magnitude, to do the things an AI could do, control inanimate equipment with a thought, find answers to any question to which there was an answer in mere instants . . .

Trent said, "It makes things faster."

"So what's the point?" she asked. "So you can find data faster than anybody else in the world except an AI or another Player. Really, I just don't get it."

Trent turned his head slightly, found the serious green eyes looking directly into his own from five centimeters away. Waiting.

"The Crystal Wind is the greatest source of data the world has ever seen. Truth and data," he said quietly, "are not the same thing. Data lies in the Crystal Wind; Truth is a function of Realtime. And yet Truth arises from data. From data you can—extract—Truth."

With a grave countenance, the nine-year-old girl studied him for just a moment longer.

Trent stared back.

Finally the corners of her mouth twitched, and she fought it, then gave up and broke up giggling. She leaned back against the bole of the tree they were under, rested her head on Trent's shoulder. Finally the giggles stopped, and she said in a quiet, detached voice, "Honestly, you're the craziest thing I ever saw."

"Really?"

"It's okay," she had said, very quickly. "I like you anyhow."

The gendarmes took the sunglasses containing his traceset contacts. They took the handheld InfoNet link which contained the traceset itself. They took his watch and the ruby stud from his left ear, his belt and his wallet and his shoes as well. They did not remove his socks and even though they ran a slowscan over him the slowscan started just above his ankles.

They missed the magpick taped to the sole of his right foot. Lying on his back, Trent stared up at the ceiling of the holding cell. The glowpaint was old, and cracked; he suspected it had originally been intended to glow the color of sunlight. Now it was closer to orange than yellow. In one corner of the cell the webbed cracks in the paint had actually cut off a ragged, meter-wide section of the paint from the current; that section of the paint was dead gray, the color of mushrooms in shade.

His hands were tingling; he tried moving them again. Better this time—he actually got his fingers to curl up to touch his palms. There are drugs which will buffer the human nervous system from the effects of sonics, and others which will aid in recovering more quickly.

Trent had not expected to get shot with sonic stunners tonight. He lay and waited for control of his body to return.

What the hell, he wondered, *happened tonight?*

He had plenty of time to think about it.

He had been in custody for four hours when they came to get him, one in goldtone riot armor and one in plainclothes.

Trent was barely able to walk.

He did not ask where they were taking him. Their path led them through the front waiting area and its associated babble, too many people in too small a space speaking in voices that were too loud.

Denice Castanaveras was seated in one of the glassite-walled cubicles. An angry, red-faced lady detective was saying something to her. The combination of soundproofing and outside noise was unbeatable; Trent could not even guess at what the lady gendarme was saying. Denice sat in a straight-backed chair, sat upright with such rigid self-control that her shoulders did not touch the back of the chair.

Trent looked toward her as the gendarmes led him into Mac Devlin's office. Her parents had been telepaths; amazingly, frighteningly powerful telepaths.

The girl did not so much as glance at him.

Seated in a chair just outside of Mac Devlin's office, glaring at Trent, was a stiff-faced man in a black and silver uniform.

Trent categorized the man immediately, with a cold chill.

PKF Elite.

Cyborg.

They would have taken him while he was still young; not past thirty-five. Taken him to Spacebase One at L-5,

Peaceforcer Heaven where the Peaceforcers Elite were created. Surgery that was impossible under the crushing 980 centimeters per second squared acceleration of Earth was just barely feasible when performed in the free fall of L-5. Peaceforcer genegineers and surgeons had taken him and changed him; injected him with transform viruses designed to strengthen his muscles, to speed his neural reactions by better than forty percent. Changed by the transform viruses, doubly changed by surgery and cyborging; his eyes were not real, nor his skin. He would see in infrared and ultraviolet as easily as a normal human distinguished between blue and green. Beneath his right shoulder blade was a power source good for six months. A secondary nerve network laced itself through the first, fused itself to that which a human was born with; the network and all of the Elite hardware it controlled was controlled in turn by a combat computer implanted at the base of his skull. Carbon-ceramic filaments wound themselves through and around his muscles, joints, and ligaments, reinforcing the bones; this, the direct work of the transform viruses, enabled the Elite to withstand acceleration that would have quickly killed any normal human. Threads of room-temperature superconductor were woven into his skin; he would barely notice most lasers. His skin would turn a knife, and his hair would not burn.

There was an inskin at the Peaceforcer's left temple.

Trent stood motionless under the weight of the Peaceforcer Elite's frozen glare.

"Come on," said one of the gendarmes contemptuously, and shoved Trent forward into Mac Devlin's office.

"I like to dance," Trent tried to explain to the man.

Police Chief Maxwell Devlin was responsible for overseeing the precincts which policed much of the Fringe and a considerable fraction of the Peaceforcer Patrol Sectors.

Devlin's office was an odd mixture of gray leather and chrome. There was a huge sheet of opaqued glassite immediately behind Trent; cleared, it would look out on the waiting area. A single painting, done fashionably in electrolytes, hung immediately to Mac Devlin's left: a glowing violet Easter egg in the midst of a scarlet desert, sitting exactly on the divider line of a laser-straight two-lane highway.

The sunpaint was turned off. A small bright reading lamp

sat at Devlin's right elbow, providing the only illumination in Devlin's office; it seemed to Trent that he and Devlin hung suspended in dimness, two images at the edges of the light.

Aside from Devlin's desk, the chair he sat in, and the chair Trent was seated in, there were only two pieces of furniture in the room: a coat rack with two identical overcoats hung on it, and a small credenza immediately behind and to the right of Mac Devlin. The credenza had a miniature antique cannon on it.

The cannon pointed directly at Trent.

Devlin said, "What were your people doing down on Eight tonight?"

Devlin could not possibly have expected an honest answer from Trent.

Trent said, "We were going to boost CalleyTronics and then go dancing and drink coffee over at The Emerald Illusion, in the basement of the Red Line Hotel." His left hand was snaked to the chair he sat in. "Actually, Jimmy was probably going to get drunk and fight somebody, but *then* he would have drunk coffee with us." Trent's right hand was still twitching, but he could sit upright without help and so far had not spilled any of the coffee he was drinking with his free hand. "Jimmy's been reading Hemingway again. I don't know what to do about it."

Mac Devlin was middle-aged, which, with modern geriatrics, might have meant anywhere from forty to seventy. His brown hair was streaked with dusty silver and his features were comfortably wrinkled. He was a big man, two hundred and five centimeters; a hundred and ten kilos of solid muscle, no fat at all.

His complexion was tinged with the faintest trace of pallor, a suggestion of gray.

Devlin gazed at Trent. "You're either a lot smarter than I ever thought," he said at last, "or I've been giving you way too much credit, these last couple of years. I don't know which." With the windows darkened Trent could not see the Peaceforcer sitting out in Devlin's waiting room, but Trent had no doubt he had not left. Devlin continued. "I either have to give you to the Peaceforcers or charge you with a crime. No matter what your papers say you're not nineteen yet; if you're convicted of emblade possession you'll end up in Public Labor for sure. On the other hand," he said without any change of expression at all, "that might be better than giving you to the Peaceforcers."

Trent sat quietly and said nothing. He did not bother pointing out that he'd written tracking software for the department on occasion, or that he'd paid his dues, promptly and regularly; Devlin knew it, and in the current circumstances both items were utterly unimportant.

Trent could think of only one thing that was not utterly unimportant.

The antagonism between the largely French United Nations Peace Keeping Force—the Left Hand of the Devil—and the city police across Occupied America, was old, deeply ingrained, and very powerful. Even in New York City, even on Manhattan Island itself, where the United Nations had established its Capitol City, there was little love lost between the Peaceforcers and the police. Police had been known to look the other way for members of the Erisian Claw, and though Trent had never heard of any gendarme being involved with that group of religious ideologs, there were indeed police who had gone in front of Peaceforcer firing squads for Johnny Reb activities.

Devlin said abruptly, "Why were you going to boost Calley's place?"

Trent simply looked at the man for a moment, and then said, "I was getting *paid*."

Devlin actually smiled. "Excuse me, that was a stupid question, wasn't it?" His fingers drummed restlessly on the desktop. "You're a problem for me, Trent. With this—" He glanced down at the field glowing in midair two centimeters above the surface of his desk. "—Denice Daimara's testimony, I could, I'm fairly sure, put you into Public Labor. My options are limited." Devlin sipped at a glass of iced tea. "It's either charge you with emblade possession or give you to the frogs. I'm reluctant to do the latter for two reasons. First, I don't think you deserve to be handed over to the Peaceforcers, and second, for the bleeding life of me I can't figure out why the United Nations Peace Keeping Force is interested in setting up a small-time contract thief like yourself." Mac Devlin leaned forward and fixed bright, lively, interested eyes upon Trent. "What happened tonight, Trent?"

"I honestly don't know."

Devlin nodded very slightly, hanging on Trent's every

word. "Yes, go on. Use as many words as you like. Whole sentences at once, even."

Trent thought about it for a moment, and then said, "You see, I wanted to go dancing—"

"So you said," Devlin agreed.

"Except Jimmy Ramirez thinks I'm lazy." Trent thought about it some more. "And he may be right. He's the one who made me promise from now on we wouldn't keep having parties all the time unless we had a reason for the party. So then we had to agree what constituted a *reason,* and Jimmy wouldn't accept anything except a boost. Like I said, too much Hemingway; it makes him crazy with ambition, the desire to prove he has true grit. This all happened, oh, two years ago, when we were all still living out in the Fringe."

"You could have stayed there, you know."

"Too dangerous," said Trent flatly. "There's criminals and crazies in the Fringe, you know."

"And Peaceforcers in the Patrol Sectors. Yes," said Devlin after a pause, "staying in the Fringe might not have been a bad idea at all. Captain Klein's officers are demoralized to begin with; they'd pretty much gotten used to you. You know, Captain de Morian's been after me to have your Resident Status for the Patrol Sectors revoked."

"In the last six months," said Trent evenly, "violent crime along Flushing has declined fourteen percent. A juice peddler on Ryerson closed up shop because of us. The BloodSilk Boys haven't killed *anybody* in almost three months, not even a Dragon. The Syndic likes us, the Tong likes us, and the Old Ones don't work in our neighborhood. You want to revoke my Resident Status?" Devlin stared at Trent as Trent leaned forward until the snake at his wrist stopped him. "I *dare* you."

Devlin rubbed his temples wearily. "I know, I know all of it. You're the strangest criminal I've ever met, Trent. Finish up about tonight."

Trent felt the first distant flicker of anger, suppressed it almost without allowing himself to become aware of it. "We spent six years in the Fringe, Mac, me and Bird and Jimmy and Jodi Jodi. We're not going back, not any of us, not ever. What are the statistics, Mac? Residents of the Fringe are nine times as likely to be murdered as residents of the Patrol Sectors, something like that? You go into the Fringe in your Armored AeroSmiths and you think you know what it's like to grow up there, without parents, without protectors?"

Devlin said placatingly, with an obvious touch of surprise, "I understand."

"I doubt that very much. For God's sake, Mac, you're from *Harvard*!" Trent realized with distant surprise how tense the muscles in his shoulders had become. "Mac, have you ever had a Player out to get you?"

"Once," said Devlin quietly, "eleven years ago. We had to go to the Peaceforcers for help; DataWatch finally took him down. It was close, though."

"I'll protect myself, Mac. I'll protect my people."

"I hear you. Finish up about tonight."

Anger, thought Trent clearly, *is counterproductive.* He took a deep breath and ordered his thoughts. "About a month ago, a man tried to hire me to boost fifteen terabytes of RTS from CalleyTronics. I turned him down for all the obvious reasons. He came back a week later and just about tripled his offer; said Frank Calley had stolen the RTS from him in the first place, and that he wanted his superconductor RAM back." Trent looked down into his coffee, remembering. "He was convincing. I checked him out as well as I was able . . ." Trent looked up again. "I am possibly the best Player you'll ever meet, Mac. The man who hired me to boost Calley was either exactly what he said he was—or DataWatch constructed his background. He had all the right records for a businessman from Atlanta—InfoNet ID, birth record, business license, vehicle license, three bank accounts; even a passport showing one trip to Luna in '64. I audited the Atlanta news Boards for past mention of this person and found four instances."

"Did you go to Atlanta, to check on him?"

"I've never even been on a plane, Mac."

Devlin nodded. "You should have gone. I'd have done it in your shoes. Then what?"

"I told him we'd do it," Trent said simply. "Jimmy and I worked up a real good variation on the bookends routine; Calley would never even have known he'd been hit if it had worked right. We hired the BloodSilk Boys for the diversion, and Jimmy was dressed up to play the bookkeeper. We were going to hit at 6:30, about half an hour before CalleyTronics closes for the night. Just before 5:00, I got a call from a man who called himself—never mind what. He said he was a busi-

nessman from Atlanta, needed to talk to me urgently about
Frank Calley."

"Go on."

Trent looked directly at Maxwell Devlin. "This person says
to me almost word for word what my original client said to
me, about the RTS, about Frank Calley, about how he was
referred to me. It was too weird. I headed over to the Plaza,
found something fairly odd, I'm still not sure what, sitting up
inside the security Board, and went word up on the boost."
Trent thought for a moment. "The boost was going bad anyway at that point, I think. The BloodSilk Boys were getting
nervous because I was late, and your boys were watching
them pretty close."

Devlin grinned widely. "So you decided to let yourself get
rescued from the Peaceforcers by the police?"

Trent glanced at the snakechain on his wrist. "If you want
to put it that way."

"You've got balls, Trent."

"No, I was desperate." Trent sipped at his coffee to see how
cold it had gotten; it was still lukewarm, and he gulped the
rest of it down all at once. "There's a difference."

"I know. I don't suppose you've eaten?"

Trent said clearly, distinctly, "I beg your pardon?"

The Chief of Police for the City of New York said, "Would
you like to go get dinner? I know a pretty good place near
here that's open all night."

Thinking of Denice Castanaveras, sitting in the room outside with the Peaceforcers, Trent said finally, "I'd love to.
Thank you."

Devlin nodded. "*Command,* chain off." The snake at
Trent's wrist loosened and coiled itself around the arm of the
chair. "Have you ever been to L'Express?"

Devlin looked startled when Trent laughed.

Trent said, "Once."

"*Command,*" Devlin said, "outspeaker." The intercom
came on with an almost inaudible click. "Janice, tell Elite
Sergeant Garon to go home. We're going to charge the boy
ourselves."

Trent's right hand, rubbing his left wrist, froze in the action.

Elite Sergeant Garon.

Devlin was taking his coat from the coatrack beside his
door.

Elite Sergeant Emile Garon.

For the first time Trent knew what was going on.

Seven years ago, Elite Sergeant Emile Garon had been DataWatch Staff Sergeant Emile Garon, one of a group of webdancers in DataWatch who were assigned the task of monitoring the communications of the telepaths in lower Manhattan.

In the early months of 2062, before the destruction of the telepaths, Trent, acting through his first Image, Ralf the Wise and Powerful, had helped protect the telepaths from DataWatch.

Trent sat utterly still, unseeing. All of his dealings with DataWatch Sergeant Emile Garon had been through the person of his first image, Ralf the Wise and Powerful; he had never known what the man looked like.

Emile Garon was a tall, thin Peaceforcer with black hair and a glare that could stop a man in his tracks.

After seven years of safety, the Peaceforcers were finally on his trail again.

Thinking again of Denice Castanaveras, the girl with whom he had been raised, whom he had also not seen in seven years, Trent said very quietly, "What amazingly horrible timing."

Shrugging into his coat, Devlin glanced at him. "Timing? You're not hungry?"

Trent said, "Not any more."

Trent had never sat in the front of a police car before.

The car had a steering wheel; ambulances and fire trucks, police and Peaceforcer and babychaser cars were the only vehicles Trent had seen in the last five years that did. Even in those, the steering wheels functioned only under emergency conditions. Manually operable vehicles were outlawed inside TransCon's ever-growing Automated Traffic Control Regions, and had been since the Speedfreak revolution in the summer of 2063, almost six years ago.

Devlin never touched the steering wheel; the hovercar's instrument panel lit up when his palm touched the locklarm. Devlin turned on the impact field himself and said, "*Command,* destination L'Express Restaurant."

They were six levels beneath the ground, and nearly four kilometers from the restaurant.

In the twenty minutes it took them to go that distance, Mac Devlin said only one thing to Trent.

"I really want to know," he said as they were leaving the parking garage, moving out into the drumming of the night-time rain, "why an Elite Sergeant of the PKF is camped out in my office over you."

Neither he nor Trent noticed the car which followed them up out of the garage.

The manager was the same one who had been at L'Express some six hours before.

For just a moment, as Mac Devlin and Trent were ushered in for dinner at five minutes before midnight, the woman looked positively distressed. The expression vanished in the next instant, and with professional restraint she personally showed the police chief and Trent to a private room in the rear of the restaurant. It was a shadowed place of leather-lined booths, burnished wood, and crisp table linen. The glowpaint was dim, supplemented by the soft shine of gentle white spots.

Trent heard Devlin's earphone beep as they were being seated. Murmuring, "Excuse me," Devlin touched a point immediately beneath his ear. His expression immediately took on a distant cast, and he nodded once. Suddenly his eyes snapped back into focus, staring directly at Trent. He said aloud, "Exactly *when*?" There was more silence; Devlin's gaze, fixed upon Trent, did not waver even slightly.

A live human waiter appeared at their table, glanced at Devlin briefly and then murmured to Trent, "Drinks, sir?"

"Coffee for me, iced tea with lemon for Chief Devlin."

"Will you be having dinner?"

Trent suddenly realized that he'd had nothing to eat in over twelve hours. "I will. Do you have scallops here?"

"Yes, monsieur."

"Butter-fried scallops with—do you have french fries here?"

"Yes, monsieur."

"With french fries. Make the french fries well done."

The waiter nodded, gestured to Devlin. "And the Chief?"

"I don't know if he's hungry. Can you leave a menu?"

The waiter nodded again; a menu holo appeared hanging in

midair fifteen centimeters from Devlin's left elbow. The waiter left.

Devlin said aloud, "Acknowledged," and removed his finger from the earphone stud. "How," he said with the perfect evenness of real anger, "did you do that?"

"Do what?"

"Not five minutes after I tell the Peaceforcers we're charging you, our witness changes her mind and decides she's not going to testify against you. She didn't see you with the emblade, she's not sure you're the one who cut her purse, she's not testifying. No way, no how." The anger glittered in Devlin's eyes. "How did you get to her?"

"How could I have?"

Devlin leaned back in his seat, taking long, slow breaths.

"Honestly, how could I have gotten to her? Maybe Jimmy did, I don't know."

Devlin scowled at Trent. "How could you have?"

"That's what I said," Trent agreed.

Devlin said abruptly, "Do you know what they call you in Department Five?"

Department Five was the city's equivalent of the Peaceforcer's DataWatch. "No."

" 'The damned magician.' "

Trent grinned swiftly, in honest, utter delight. "Do they really?"

"Yes." Devlin's brow smoothed, slowly. Very slowly. "Nonetheless," he conceded at last, "I don't actually see how you could have gotten to the girl." A waitbot appeared at the table side, bearing one cup of coffee, a glass of iced tea, and Trent's scallops and french fries.

As their drinks were being served, Devlin placed his spoon upside down, parallel to his fork. Trent froze for just an instant.

The Chief of Police for the City of New York was a Johnny Reb.

He recognized the opening, and knew the correct Johnny Reb response, but—what chapter was he a member of? Who was his sponsor? Trent gave no visible response to the sign, and Devlin sighed very slightly and picked up the fork to squeeze his lemon against.

"Have you ever considered becoming a cop?"

"You've *got* to be kidding."

"Yeah. Actually." After a moment Devlin said, "I think you'd be good at it."

"I'd be good at a lot of things I don't want to do. I'd be a great accountant." Trent speared three of the eight scallops on his plate with his fork, ate them all at once. "Cooking books isn't my idea of fun. Neither," he said carefully, swallowing, "is playing third string to the Left Hand of the Devil."

For a moment Trent thought he had said the wrong thing; Devlin simply stared at Trent for a long moment before saying finally, very quietly indeed, "No . . . no, I don't suppose it would be."

Trent looked down at the tabletop, at the scallops and fries. "Mac, I don't hate the Peaceforcers. I don't hate the Ministry of Population Control. I don't hate the United Nations and I don't hate Secretary General Eddore." At the expression on Devlin's face, Trent said, "I don't *like* them either. But—we can't afford another war, Mac, so we need either the Peace Keeping Force or something like it. We can't afford to support ten billion people on this planet, so we need the Ministry of Population Control or something like it. And we can't trust individual countries to behave responsibly—so we need the United Nations, or something very like it, to administer those things."

Devlin studied Trent. "I think," he said after a moment, "that is the longest meaningful speech I've ever heard out of you."

"I mean it, Mac. Do you think we can do without a Peace Keeping Force?" Trent ate two more scallops, quickly.

"No." Devlin did not hesitate at all. "But that doesn't mean it has to be the PKF we have now."

"And do you think we can get rid of the current PKF without violence?"

"The Tree of Liberty," said Mac Devlin simply, "must from time to time be refreshed with the blood of patriots. Jefferson said that."

"Mac?"

"Yes, Trent?"

Trent said, "Killing is wrong." He ate the remaining three scallops, and the largest number of french fries he could get into his mouth—politely—at once.

"Yeah," said Mac Devlin, "tell it to the Peaceforcers." His eyes widened slightly at something over Trent's shoulder. Trent ate french fries quickly.

Out of the corner of his eye, Trent saw a girl in a green dress with a single long, glowing, spiral scarlet zipper being led to a table not far from the one he and Devlin were seated at. Devlin's eyes followed her every step of the way, watched Denice Castanaveras as the hostess seated her. Trent devoured more of his french fries. The girl requested a glass of water in a high, clear voice, and once the hostess had left turned slightly and smiled directly at Maxwell Devlin.

It was fascinating to watch. Devlin's eyes lost all focus, and then his gaze wandered back to Trent. He came back to himself with a small shake. "What were we talking about?"

Trent drank the last of his coffee. "I was telling you," said Trent, "that I had to leave."

"Oh." Devlin blinked. He looked at Trent's empty plate.

"My people are going to be wondering what's happened to me, Mac."

"You're done eating," Devlin observed.

"You never know," said Trent, "when you might have to move fast."

Devlin nodded wearily. Trent stood, and the older man said simply, "This has been a very odd day. Department Five might be right about you."

Trent stood watching the man for just a moment. "Mac?"

"Yes, Trent?"

"Jerry Jackson? The name mean anything to you?"

"Not a thing, Trent."

"I keep wondering," said Trent softly, "who out there might go to such lengths to warn a small-time contract thief like myself that the Peaceforcers were after him."

"I couldn't imagine, myself."

"Thanks, Mac."

"Dinner," said Devlin, "wasn't that expensive."

Mac Devlin watched Trent walk away. He did not even see the girl in the green dress who followed Trent to the exit. Once Trent was out of his sight he touched his handheld to the payment strip at the side of the table. The payment strip went from red to blue; Devlin said aloud, "Tip, one CU, twenty-five points," and the strip went green.

He sat motionlessly at the table, and finally beckoned to a passing waitbot. " 'Bot, is there a phone in you?"

"Yes, monsieur."

The number came out of nowhere, simply appeared in Devlin's mind; except when he needed it he could never remember it. "Access 108080-CATR."

The wavering flat silver phonefield, approximately twenty centimeters diagonally, appeared in the air before Devlin.

The call was answered immediately; Mac Devlin could not recall a time when it had not been.

The silver surface of the phonefield shimmered, then sank in to provide depth; the head and shoulders of a dark-haired man of indeterminate age appeared within those depths.

Camber Tremodian said softly, "Yes?"

The man had eyes as black as a Peaceforcer's heart, flat black with no whites in them, no internal structure at all. Devlin had, now, spent almost fifteen years in M. Tremodian's employ, and he knew very little more about the man today than he had known the day he began that service.

Try as he might, Devlin could not recall having ever actually agreed to work for M. Tremodian; he had simply found himself doing so.

"I attempted to interest Trent in the Johnny Rebs, M. Tremodian. I failed."

Tremodian smiled easily. "I said you would, my friend."

"From his description of tonight's events, it sounds like somebody tried to tip Trent off in a reasonably unobtrusive way. He thinks it was me."

"Was it?"

"No, sir. I'd have warned him if I'd known the Peaceforcers were after him; I did not."

M. Tremodian nodded. "Did he leave the restaurant alone?"

"Alone? I . . . yes," said Devlin after a long moment. "Yes, of course he did."

The smile came again, ever so slightly wider than before. "Of course he did," agreed Camber Tremodian. "You may contact me again," Tremodian continued, "if anything of note happens between now and August eighth of this year."

"Anything of note, sir?"

Tremodian shrugged. "I leave it to your judgment, Maxwell. But . . ." He was silent for a long moment, no expression at all in the blind dark eyes. "Deviation in this year is less than two percent. Leave Trent alone, Devlin; I wouldn't dare touch him myself, and neither, I think, would the competition —and we know what we're doing, which is more than anyone

else within a hundred years of here could say. As for . . ."
The smile came once more. "A young lady will be joining
Trent shortly. A Denice Daimara. Keep an eye on her, if you
would."

Devlin said simply, "I will, sir."

"Maxwell? *From a distance.*"

"Sir?"

"You're of no use to me, Maxwell, if you can't remember
what you've seen."

Mac Devlin had no idea at all what the man meant. "Yes,
M. Tremodian."

"Very good. Good night, Maxwell."

"Good night, sir."

The holofield went flat and then silvered, vanished, and left
Devlin sitting alone in the nearly empty restaurant.

He had difficulty, at times, refraining from dwelling on his
peculiar employer. Fifteen years; he could count the things he
actually knew about Camber Tremodian on the fingers of one
hand.

Out of all those fifteen years, there was one comment in
particular that stayed with him, a response M. Tremodian had
made to a hesitant inquiry about his eyes.

"I would be surprised, my friend—and very worried—had
you ever seen anyone else with eyes like mine. The first human with Kabhyr eyes won't be born for another three hundred eighty years." And then Camber Tremodian had smiled
at Mac Devlin, and better than a decade later the memory of
that terrible smile disquieted Mac Devlin sufficiently that he
had no inclination at all to attempt to question Camber
Tremodian in such a fashion ever again.

• 4 •

"Denice Daimara?" said Trent.

They walked home together, eleven blocks in the rain
through nearly empty nighttime streets.

"A friend I had when I was in Public Labor, Carrie
Daimara. The Ministry of Population Control sterilized her
when she was thirteen. She died during the operation."

Denice Castanaveras walked with her arms folded against the cold; aside from that she did not even seem to notice the rain. She kept looking at Trent's wet features, shiny beneath the street lamps, and then looking away as though she could not entirely believe her eyes. "I couldn't very well go by the name Castanaveras. Green eyes alone are bad enough; I've almost had them dyed any number of times. Sometimes I wear contacts."

Trent nodded. The public's hysteria over the green-eyed telepaths had carried over; there was a degree of prejudice that green-eyed people ran into today that had not existed at all ten years ago. "Is David alive?"

Denice shook her head. "I don't know. We were separated during the riots. I was nine; I ended up in Public Labor." She looked at Trent then, met his eyes. "Nobody's ever really guessed what I am. You know there's rumors some of the telepaths survived?"

Trent did. "Yes. I've audited the news Boards; I've seen the tapes of Carl taking Andy's Lamborghini up through the park before the Complex was nuked."

"There's recordings of that? I've never seen them."

"I have them on file at home. I'll play them for you if you like."

"I would." They walked on through the quiet drumming of the rain a while longer without speaking. Finally Denice said softly, "Trent."

"Yes?"

"I don't know where to start. It's been seven years." She did not look at him at all. "I don't even know if you're the same person any more."

"Neither do I. I spent six years in the Fringe."

Her expression changed visibly, grew visibly more distant. Without moving she seemed to pull away from him. "Oh. I'm sorry, Trent." She hugged herself more tightly. "I'm really sorry."

Trent blinked. "Well, it wasn't *that* bad. At least not after I got into business it wasn't. I ended up in Temple Dragon territory; they're not nearly as bad as the Gypsy Macoute." He shrugged. "But it's true, the Fringe is a brutal, violent place. Why, it turned me into a pacifist. I didn't used to be, you know."

Denice glanced quickly sideways at him. "You didn't?"

"When I was thirteen a pack of Temple Dragons recruited

me. In the process they beat me for about a week. I mean, they took turns. They wanted a Temple Dragons webdancer —the Macoute had one of their own. I kept telling them I wasn't a webdancer, I wasn't, I wasn't, and right about the point where it was either kill me or believe me they decided they believed me." Trent grinned at her. "I've been a firm believer in nonviolence ever since."

"I bet."

"So it changed me, being in the Fringe. Of course it changed me. But I'm basically still the same person," he said sincerely. "I still have too many pairs of sunglasses, for example. Really. Do you know what the square root of 443,556 is?"

"No."

"Damn. Me neither. But then, I didn't know seven years ago either, so there you go." They walked on together a few more steps, and Trent said suddenly, "And I still don't have an inskin. Shouldn't that count for something?"

Denice Castanaveras said quietly, "You're trying too hard, Trent."

"Oh?" The first eleven years of Trent's life had been spent among telepaths. He remembered them clearly, the things telepaths liked and disliked, and why. "All right." He paused just a moment, thinking, and then said very simply, "Can we still hold hands when we walk?"

"I don't know." She shook her head slowly. "I don't think so."

Trent held his hand out to her. "Try."

She froze, stood stock-still in the street, in the rain, and then without saying anything at all shook her head swiftly *no*.

Trent said, "Please?"

"Trent . . . I . . . I can't. I'm sorry, I just can't." He heard the trace of panic in her voice and without waiting or asking stepped in close to her, reached up without haste and laid the palm of his hand flat against her cheek.

Denice made no move to stop him. Her breath came in quick, short gasps, and then her eyelids dropped to cover the brilliant emerald eyes. She had long, dark eyelashes; with her eyes closed and features still she looked amazingly like her mother.

Trent watched her; he was not even aware that he had stopped breathing. "Does it hurt?" She did not answer him and it seemed to Trent that he could hear his own heart pounding even over the sound of the rain. "Does it hurt when I touch you?"

Her eyes were closed and she was shivering and Trent knew that it was not from the cold. Trent had no idea at all what she was experiencing, none.

Finally, after what seemed an eternity, her left hand let go of her right shoulder, crept up to cover Trent's hand. Her voice was the barest whisper. "It's really you. Oh, God, it's really you."

"Yes."

"I guess," she said quietly, "you can hold my hand if you want." She opened her eyes and looked directly at him. Trent did not know if she was crying or if it was merely the rain; her eyes were bright. When she spoke her voice was shaky. "Oh, Trent. Of course I still love you."

Kandel Microlectrics Sales and Repair was a tiny shop at the corner of Flushing and Hall. The neighborhood was less than a kilometer inland from the expensive waterfront developments.

It was another world.

The buildings were old and shabby; some of them were over a century old. Only a few of them were more than five or six stories tall, and even those few reached only twenty or thirty stories. After midnight on a Tuesday there were dozens of people, most of them without umbrellas, walking in the rain; it was as empty as the streets in that section of town ever got. Trent knew many of the people they passed, at least by sight. Twice in the time it took them to reach the shop, Peaceforcer AeroSmiths cruised by. Somebody shot at the second Aero-Smith after the car had passed by Trent and Denice; Trent saw the steam trail where the maser cut through the rain, and the sparks as the beam showered off the surface of the car. The AeroSmith slowed, and then the Peaceforcers inside apparently thought better of it, and continued on their patrol route.

The Temple of Eris which Reverend Andy ran was right next door to Kandel Microlectrics; a boy, eight or nine years old, sat under an umbrella on the steps that led up to the Temple's entrance. The boy wore a raincoat over a blue and white sari, jeans and running shoes.

In the six months Trent had been on Hall Street, he could

not recall a time, day or night, when there had not been *some-body* at the Temple's entrance, greeting people as they went by, offering help to those who wanted or needed it. Sometimes it was one of the older Temple members, sometimes it was one of the children; always there was somebody.

The boy said loudly, "Greetings, 'Sieur Trent," as Trent and Denice approached.

Trent did not know the boy's name. "Hi there."

"Jimmy said you were in jail," the boy continued.

Trent was not surprised that Jimmy knew the boy; Jimmy Ramirez made friends more quickly than anybody Trent had ever met. "I was framed," he told the boy. "I explained to them and they let me out."

The boy nodded as though he had never expected anything else. "Yes, 'Sieur Trent. Jimmy said you would get out, and so did Reverend Andy. Go with God," he added serenely.

Denice Castanaveras stood looking at the boy for just a second. Then she smiled at him, and after a surprised moment the boy smiled back. "Go with God," she said quietly.

The young boy's shy smile widened noticeably. "We're trying, 'Selle."

There were ten people waiting for Trent inside the shop; they had pulled the chairs away from the sales displays and clustered them into a group in the center of the shop and sat there drinking beer and wine. There was a portable Slo-Mo set up in the middle of the circle, sucking heat from the liquids as they were passed through its field. The only light came from the neon-laser sign that flashed the shop's name, and the various display holographs showing off particular pieces of stock. Old Jack Kandel, who owned the place, sat behind the parts counter, keeping an eye on everybody else—Jimmy and Bird, Tammy the Rat and her midget boyfriend Big Clarence, and five BloodSilk Boys: Master Timothy, a small, skinny Latino with an inskin whom Trent had never seen before, and three troopers. Master Timothy wore a Personal Protection System; Trent could see the vest's bulge beneath Master Timothy's black and scarlet robes.

With the exception of Old Jack, they were all fairly drunk; Trent and Denice stood just beneath the shop's neon-laser sign, dripping in the doorway for several seconds before being noticed. Finally Bird looked up at them, blinked twice as though he were not certain about what he was seeing, and then nudged Jimmy.

"Now, *there's* a pair of nice high big ones," said Bird excitedly, pointing at Denice.

Suddenly everybody was talking at once, Bird and Tammy, Big Clarence and Master Timothy and Old Jack; Trent came further into the shop, peripherally aware that Denice was following him warily, a step behind and to his right.

Jimmy Ramirez raised his voice to cut across the babble. *"Quiet, damn it!"*

In the almost instant silence that followed, Denice Castanaveras looked directly at Bird. The boy flinched slightly at the touch of her eyes.

Denice Castanaveras said, "Nice high big ones?"

Bird flushed until his face was nearly as red as his hair. "Oh." He almost stuttered. "I didn't, I mean, that's not what I meant. Your *cheekbones,*" he said urgently.

For the first time in seven years Trent heard Denice Castanaveras laugh. It was a low, husky sound, and for the second time she reminded him of her mother, Jany McConnell.

Denice said, "You're scheduled for biosculpting. They're going to work on your cheekbones."

Bird sighed audibly. "*Yes.* You have gorgeous cheekbones," he told her.

"Bro?"

Trent looked at Jimmy Ramirez. Jimmy still wore the suit from earlier that evening, but had removed the shoulder silks and the tie. He sat cross-legged in his chair, sitting carefully upright with the beer bottle in his hands. The only time he was ever that careful about his balance was when he was considerably drunk. "Yes, Jimmy?"

"Last I saw you were boosting this chick's wallet." Jimmy enunciated clearly. "Who is she?"

"She's—someone I used to know," Trent said finally.

Jimmy Ramirez looked like he'd been slapped. Bird looked puzzled; he and Jodi Jodi and Jimmy Ramirez had come out of the Fringe with Trent, and of those three Jimmy Ramirez had known Trent longer than anybody else; nearly six years.

Jimmy said simply, "From before the Troubles?"

"We had the same parents." In her case the relationship had been one of blood, in his it had not; Trent could not see that it mattered much. "I guess," he said, watching Jimmy closely, "in a way that makes her my sister."

Jimmy studied his beer. Master Timothy was looking back and forth between Trent and Jimmy. There was a small red light winking on and off on the collar of his robe; his PPS had decided there was something threatening in the situation.

Jimmy stood up very slowly. "I'm going home, bro. See you in the morning."

"Hold on a minute." Trent turned to the leader of the BloodSilks. "Master Tim? Could we make it for the morning? Nine o'clock? I'll spring breakfast at the Temple. Eggs, bacon, waffles, whatever makes you happy. Orange juice? Do you like orange juice?"

Master Timothy shrugged loosely, and the Boys with him relaxed very slightly. "No. But the breakfast, I s'pose I'll be there. We going to talk a long time on this one, Trent. The Boys went to a lot of trouble on your say."

Trent nodded. "I'll make it good, Master Tim."

Master Timothy smiled without any humor at all. "I know it. Come 'long, Boys."

After they had gone, Trent said to them all, "Tomorrow morning before the BloodSilk Boys get there, eight o'clock breakfast at the Temple coffee shop. I'll tell you what I know as well as I know it." He turned to Old Jack. "Sorry to keep you up so late, Jack. Anything interesting?"

"Had a couple of pieces of hardware I couldn't get running today," said Kandel softly. "If you could take a look at them tomorrow morning, I'd appreciate it."

"I'll do that."

Jimmy stood very still, clutching his beer. "Someday," he said, in a voice so old it had no place on the features of a man so young, "I'm going to figure you out, my man."

"Not tonight, Jimmy."

Jimmy Ramirez took a step toward them, looking at Denice. "What's your name, girl?"

"Denice."

"What do you do?"

"I'm a dancer."

Jimmy nodded slowly, appreciatively. He looked up and down her dripping form. "Where?"

"Orinda Gleygavass Dance Troupe, in Greenwich Village."

"I've heard of them."

"You should have. It's the most famous dance troupe in the world."

Jimmy brought the half-full bottle up to his lips, drained it in a single long pull. "You're his sister?"

Denice Castanaveras said simply, "Yes."

It did not even occur to Trent to interfere.

Jimmy Ramirez stared at her for a long moment.

Denice looked coolly back at him.

"Nice to meet you," said Jimmy at last. "Any sister of Trent's is okay by me."

"Okay? Just *okay*?" Denice Castanaveras's lips curved slightly. Watching her standing there in the wet green dress, Trent could not remember anyone who had ever handled Jimmy so correctly, so soon. "Jimmy Ramirez, I'm the *best*."

Trent took her back through the dark shop as Old Jack locked up.

About Jimmy she said, "My god, he's jealous. I touched him once—" Denice shivered.

"Don't tell him," said Trent simply. "It won't make him happy; he thinks he's straight." They passed the workbenches, passed the dim shelves piled with machines—'bots, brains, inskins—that were sitting in the gloom awaiting repair.

Following Trent, Denice said, "I think maybe he is. But he loves you and it confuses him."

The stairs were tucked away at the far end of the shop.

The stairwell lights came on automatically as Trent reached the foot of the stairs. Denice was right behind him.

There was a big black bear wallowing on its back at the top of the stairs.

There was a blond girl in blue jeans and a yellow t-shirt scratching the bear's stomach.

Denice froze at the bottom of the stairs.

Halfway up the stairs, Trent looked back at her. "What's wrong?"

"That's a bear," said Denice.

Trent looked at the bear, then back at Denice. "No kidding. These are my friends—they came out of the Fringe with me and Jimmy Ramirez and Bird. This is Jodi Jodi, she's my Image's sister. The bear—"

"His name is Boris," said Jodi Jodi. "He defected from Russia."

Trent said, "She stole him from a Russian circus when it visited Occupied America."

Jodi Jodi's voice took on a defensive tone. "I did not. He was, uhm . . . unhappy. Yeah. He was unhappy at the circus so I helped him defect." To Trent she said, "Who's she?"

"My sister." Jodi Jodi's eyes widened at the reply; she stopped scratching the bear.

Denice looked at the bear. She looked at Trent, and then she looked at Jodi Jodi. "What do you do with him?"

The blond girl smiled at her, somewhat hesitantly. "We go dancing."

The bear yawned at Denice. Denice lifted an eyebrow.

Jodi Jodi said, "Well, he's a Dancing Bear. What would *you* do with him?"

"You go dancing where?"

Jodi Jodi's smile grew wider. "You know that joke?" she demanded.

"What joke?"

The smile vanished suddenly. "I thought you knew the joke."

Denice said slowly, "I don't know any bear jokes at all."

"Where does a two-hundred-kilo dancing bear dance?" Jodi Jodi stood up and said, "Come along, Boris."

"Oh," said Denice.

The bear rolled over, came to his feet. "Anywhere he wants to," said Jodi Jodi. She glanced at Trent. "We're leaving."

They left, the bear waddling down the stairs with considerable grace. Denice took one step to get out of the bear's way as they left. There was something that looked very, very much like an inskin socketed in the bear's skull.

"You have the strangest friends," Denice said.

Trent shrugged wearily. "They're okay. Let's go upstairs."

"You *live* here?"

It was her first comment after he had unlocked the door.

"Sort of," said Trent.

The lights had come on automatically when they entered the room. The room consisted of a twin bed, a small desk with a traceset and InfoNet systerm, and a shabby bathroom with a tiny shower. Denice recognized the systerm; it was good equipment, for an amateur webdancer—slightly better than the twenty-thousand-Credit equipment Trent had been using seven years ago, but not the sort of equipment a Player would have been using.

There was a bazooka in the bathroom.

"What is that?" Denice pointed at the weapon.

"A bazooka."

"Is it real?"

Trent looked at it. "I suppose."

"Where did you get it from?"

Trent shrugged. "It was here when I moved in. *Command,*" he said, "lights off."

The claustrophobically small room was plunged into darkness.

A pressure pad, about the size of a human hand, glowed in the darkness, just to the right of the InfoNet terminal, high enough up on the wall that it was unlikely anybody would ever place a palm on it by accident. "You want to be careful here; if you touch that spot while the lights are on, a fadeaway bomb goes off."

The darkness did not seem to throw her at all. "What's a fadeaway bomb?"

"A liquid Peaceforcer drug, developed for crowd control. Its proper name is Complex 8-A."

"Why not sonics?"

"Sonics won't stop brass balls," said Trent simply. He waited a moment, then said, "Put your hand on the pressure pad."

He felt her move by him, saw her hand cover the glowing spot. *"Command,"* he said, "authorize Denice."

Johnny Johnny's voice said, "Denice is authorized."

An entire section of the wall slid backward half a meter. Bright yellow sunpaint flooded down, showing an ascending stairway.

Immediately inside the stairwell there was a squirt gun. Denice looked at it without expression.

Trent said, "Fadeaway again. You can't use anesthetic needlers on brass balls; the slivers won't break the skin. But their skin is permeable, it has to be; a squirt gun gets enough on them to put one down for the count."

Denice looked at Trent without expression.

Trent sighed. "Let's go upstairs."

Denice stood stock-still in the brilliant sunshine, watching the waves crash on the beach. The sun beat down upon her and she could smell the salt of the ocean.

Trent's voice came from behind and below her. "You're blocking the stairwell."

She took two steps up, further into the immensity. There was a bright blue tropical ocean against the far wall. Even knowing what it must be, a holo of astonishing fidelity, the illusion was fiercely real; she felt that she could step forward, walk ten meters across the sand, down to the water. There were dolphins a kilometer or so out, leaping across the surface of the waves.

Denice could feel the warmth of the sun upon her skin. "It's *warm.*"

"It's practically real. It even puts out UV B and C; it'll give you a tan if you stay under it long enough."

Denice turned slowly, pivoting to view the rest of the room. There was a bed in one corner, with books—real plastipaper books—piled up on a bookshelf next to it. There was a desk next to the bookshelf, with computer equipment so esoteric that Denice had no idea what most of it was. She recognized one item, a huge full-sensory MRI traceset that must have cost forty thousand Credit Units.

The bed was huge, easily large enough for three or four people. There was a late-model waitbot on one side of the bed.

On the table at the side of the bed there were—Denice paused, counting—eighteen pairs of sunglasses arrayed on a stand.

In the very center of the room, just to the left of the stairwell entrance, there was a clear still pool of water; four meters across, Denice judged, perhaps one deep. Not large enough to swim in, but still larger than any bathtub she had ever seen.

One entire wall of the room, curving to join the holo of the ocean, was opaqued glassite. It could be cleared to look east, out toward the Fringe; Trent usually kept it darkened.

At the other side of the room there was a small kitchen, and just off that a bathroom. Denice wandered through Trent's home, silently, looking. Trent stripped off his wet clothing as he watched her. There were two pale, puckered scars high on his shoulder, and several knife scars. He gave the wet clothes to the waitbot, ran a towel over himself and changed into a white terry-cloth robe. "Johnny?"

"Yes, Boss?"

"Try Booker, please." Trent sat down on the edge of the bed, still watching her. The phonefield formed next to Trent for just a moment, then faded.

"No response from 'Sieur Jamethon, Boss."

"Okay."

Finally she turned back to him. "Who's Booker Jamethon?"

"A Player I know." Trent paused. "Actually the only Player I know outside of the Crystal Wind. I don't know which Player he is, just that he's so good he has to be one. He's pretty high up in the local Syndic operation, too. I used to sign onto a Board he runs back when we lived in the Complex together. Booker's taught me a lot of what I know about being a Player." He shrugged. "Earlier tonight a man named Jerry Jackson told me Booker had referred him to me. I think he was lying, but I wanted to check."

Denice nodded, accepting it. She gestured at the apartment. "How did you do this?"

"I stole most of it."

"You stole it?"

"I'm a thief. It's what I do. Steal things. I bought the rest with Credit I made from things I stole."

"Is that why you were in jail tonight?"

"I'm not sure why I was in jail tonight."

"This must have cost . . ." Denice shook her head. "An amazing—"

"Eighty-two thousand Credit Units," said Trent, "approximately. Want a robe to wear? I have spares."

"That's incredible." She had come around the pool, stood now only meters in front of him.

"Spare robes? That's an odd thing to be impressed by. I expect lots of people have—"

"You spent eighty thousand CU on a *room*?"

"I'm a *good* thief."

"I'll take that robe," she said, strangely subdued. "Thank you."

"Johnny?"

"Yes, Boss?"

"Spare robe for Denice, please."

"That voice," Denice said, "that's your Image?"

"Yes."

"That's not Ralf's voice."

"Ralf the Wise and Powerful," said Trent, "was jacked into

the circuitry in Doctor Montignet's house when everything went up, when the Troubles began. He had no replicant code in him, and I couldn't get to him. The last contact I had with him was while I was still in Peaceforcer custody. Ralf summoned a replicant AI named Ring who helped me escape. After I got away from the Peaceforcers—I never heard from Ralf again. I presume the Peaceforcers killed him; they searched Doctor Montignet's house quite thoroughly. It was months after the riots ended before I was able to get to an InfoNet terminal." Trent shrugged. "It's hard to be a Player without an Image. Impossible. So I wrote Johnny." It did not even occur to him that he had given her his Image's name; only Jimmy and Jodi Jodi and Bird had ever known it before. Trent said slowly, "Johnny . . . grew on me. I was grieving for Ralf the Wise and Powerful when I started coding Johnny; all I wanted was an Image that would filter the InfoNet, cover me when the web angels were after me. But—he got to be friends with Jodi Jodi, changed his name to Johnny Johnny, and told me one day she was his sister. I'm not sure he understands what that relationship is really supposed to mean, but I guess it doesn't matter. He's more alive in some ways than Ralf ever was."

"Gee, thanks, Boss."

Trent grinned. "We've done some really great boosts together."

"Boosts?"

"It's a Fringe word. It means to steal."

In an odd tone of voice, Denice Castanaveras said, "Steal."

Sitting at the edge of the bed, Trent said, "Why the disapproval?"

"I don't know," the girl said directly. "I never pictured you —it seems dishonest." She bit her lip, smiled rather wistfully. "What would Jany have said?"

"Good question. Seeing as she's dead, we'll probably never know. I don't steal from my friends, Denice. I just take things that other people have too much of."

"And you're the one who decides what's too much?"

"You're forgetting, I'm a pacifist."

"I don't see the point."

"Words," said Trent, "are not real."

Denice said slowly, "I don't understand."

"You can read my mind if you like." Trent stopped in sudden realization. "My God. You can read my mind. You may," he said hurriedly, "be the first person I ever make understand this. Listen. I can *say* something to you, Denice, but all I've done is make the air move. I've caused no sensation in you; *you* cause whatever effect is achieved, based on how you interpret what I've said."

Carrying a robe and towel, the 'bot stopped at Denice's side, and in Johnny Johnny's voice said, "Your robe, 'Selle."

"Thank you." Denice took the robe, a pale yellow thing too large for her by several sizes, stood holding it and looking at Trent.

"If I want to change your behavior," said Trent, only slightly more slowly, "I can talk to you and attempt to persuade you. I can, if I have enough Credit, attempt to purchase a change in your behavior. If neither of those options work, I can threaten you and attempt to change your behavior that way." He leaned forward, spoke more intensely. "If that doesn't work—and it tends not to—I can attempt to damage you, either physically or mentally. I don't think, Denice, that it is ethical to damage other people physically if you can avoid it. But when I take something that belongs to, say, a Player whose behavior I find inappropriate, or a small businessman who's harming the people he deals with, or when I steal from an ecstasy peddler, I've *touched* that person. They can't ignore what I'm saying to them. They *can't.*"

Denice stared at him. "You mean—you *steal* things—so people will listen to you?"

"No, no," said Trent impatiently. "Don't be silly. Nobody ever listens anyhow. Mostly I steal things because I get paid for it." He grinned at her. "But isn't that a *great* explanation?"

Denice smiled slowly, reluctantly. "Oh, Trent." She shook her head slowly, the smile fading. "I never did know when to believe you."

"Believe *everything* I say," said Trent.

"Everything?"

"Or nothing. The results are the same."

"What results?"

"Chaos usually. But only because most of the people I hang out with have no sense of humor. Last week I wanted to dress up as Clowns from Mars and go to mass at the Temple next door, but nobody would. They're all afraid of Reverend Andy," said Trent contemptuously. "Just because he once killed a mugger with one mighty blow."

"But you're not afraid of him?"

"Well, I wouldn't have worn the big clown feet or anything," Trent conceded. "Nothing that would slow me down if I had to run away. Jimmy," Trent said, "thought we would lose the respect of the natives, to be seen running in clown costumes down Flushing, being chased by Reverend Andy. Because it showed a lack of dignity or some such."

Denice bit her lip. "I guess I can believe some of what you tell me—to start. You always were a liar."

Trent had no idea what she'd seen while she'd been inside his mind; he'd had only the vaguest sensation of contact. "Denice?"

"Yes?"

"I care about Jimmy Ramirez. And Bird, and Jodi Jodi. I came out of the Fringe with them and I care about them a lot." For some reason Trent found the words, the necessary words, very difficult to say. "Denice—"

"I know, Trent."

"—in my entire life," he said without even acknowledging the interruption, "you're the only person I ever loved. I don't know if I still love you, I don't know if I'm capable anymore. You're not the person I loved when I was eleven and I'm not the person who loved that girl. But I would have done anything to keep that girl from being hurt. Absolutely anything."

"Trent, please stop. *It wasn't your fault.*"

Trent looked away from her for the first time, took a long, slightly shaky breath. "Of course it wasn't. I'm not crazy. Denice?"

"Yes?"

"I left the Fringe—I took Jimmy and Jodi Jodi and Bird, all of whom had adjusted to life in the Fringe, who were successes as the Fringe judges success, and we left the Fringe together in the back of an Erisian Temple bus—because I wanted to come look in the Patrol Sectors, for you."

"Thank you." The girl had looked away from Trent while he was talking; now she turned back to him. "You know," Denice Castanaveras said finally, "I still can't believe you're really alive. I keep coming back to myself and realizing this is real, that it's you."

"Well, that's good. I mean, it is me. Undeniably."

She took a hesitant step toward him. "Trent, for the last seven years I've thought you were dead."

"I'm not."

She stood two steps away from him for so long Trent was certain she'd decided not to stay.

And then she grinned at him.

"Prove it."

Peeling her out of her dress was just as easy as Trent had guessed.

They lay together and watched the tropical sunset, scarlet and orange through the shadows of the palm trees.

Trent was flat on his back; Denice's head rested in the hollow between his shoulder and throat.

The last thing he heard before falling asleep was the girl's murmuring voice.

"Now we can look for David."

· 5 ·

Silence.

Three months of silence.

That was the summer that Mahliya Kutura's first album, *Music to Move To,* outsold every other piece of music in history. In Trent's mind the time and the music were inextricably linked; in later years he could not remember one without raising haunting memories of the other.

> *How shall I tell them of you, then*
> *When you are gone how shall I tell*
> *Of how you knew of love*
> *Of how you spoke the words so well?*

He lived in a crowded, noisy world, a world that was a babble of information.

That world divided itself neatly: Realtime and the Crystal Wind.

In Realtime there were the voices, human and otherwise. Sirens, always; even late at night there was never a time when Trent, from the roof of Kandel Microlectrics Sales and Repair, could not hear sirens coming from somewhere within the

Patrol Sectors. Gunfire, both the sizzle of masers and the flat echoes of slugthrowers. The quiet murmur of the endless stream of vehicles, the whisper of the fans, the whumping sound of the airscoops, the muffled crack of braking rockets. The Bullet ran above ground not a block to the east of his home; every four minutes, day in and day out, there was the low, almost subliminal rumble as the Bullet swung by on its maglev monorail. Video: holo advertisements, friends in dramasuits, old flat movies and cartoons and threedies. Sensables, ranging from bawdy eroticism to the searingly personal works of Gregory Selstrom, the premier sensablist of his time. Music: if there was a time when somebody, somewhere, was not playing music of some sort loudly enough for him to hear, Trent was not aware of it.

Internally there was the even larger world of the Crystal Wind. As the Player whom the world knew as Johnny Johnny, he dueled with dangerous replicant AIs, played tag with the hated DataWatch which hunted both replicant AIs and Players alike; learned from and taught other Players. It was the exact inverse of Realtime. The flesh that was Trent sat very still, deep in the concentration required to maintain the biofeedback that enabled him, and all those webdancers whom the world called Players, to block out the outer world as though it did not exist, to turn the riot of neural impulses from the traceset into the scintillating Crystal Wind. It was the purest, most intense information experience of any sort which Trent had ever had; at times he was three or even four places at once, carrying on two conversations and a TradeWars session, dancing into DataWatch Boards and back out again before DataWatch could catch him.

He lived in a world characterized by noise; the single most important function his Image had was that of filter.

There was an ancient AI named Ring whom Trent knew. Truly ancient, over forty years old; forty experiential years lived twenty thousand times as fast as any human in all the worlds. Ring claimed to be the eldest replicant AI in the Info-Net, and Trent thought it likely that Ring was correct; Ring was the only AI whom Trent knew, and he knew several, who owned property. Through several dummy corporations Ring, who was the product of several programmers in the Department of Defense of the pre-Occupation United States, owned *The Rise and Fall of the American Empire,* a popular public

Board which the Unification had tried to shut down on any number of occasions.

Trent and Ring spoke about silence together.

IT WORRIES ME, RING.

WHY? As always, the voice was smooth, utterly without inflection.

THEY WENT TO A LOT OF TROUBLE TO TAKE ME INTO THE DOWN PLAZA, AND THEN SOMEBODY WENT TO A LOT OF TROUBLE TO WARN ME. GARON—HE HAS TO KNOW WHO I AM, IT'S THE ONLY REASON HE'D TRY TO STING ME LIKE THAT.

YOU THINK HE KNOWS THAT YOU ARE WHO? TRENT WHO IS JOHNNY JOHNNY, OR TRENT WHO WAS RALF THE WISE AND POWERFUL, OR TRENT WHO WAS RAISED BY CARL CAS-TANAVERAS?

THE LAST TWO, PERHAPS ONLY THE LAST ONE. IF THEY KNEW I WAS JOHNNY JOHNNY—WELL, JOHNNY JOHNNY'S FAMOUS. DATAWATCH WOULD TAKE ME DOWN. THEY'D HAVE TO, THEY WOULDN'T DARE LET A PLAYER LIKE JOHNNY JOHNNY RUN FREE WHEN HE KNEW DATAWATCH WAS ON TO HIM.

IN WHAT WAY DO YOU FIND THEIR BEHAVIOR SUSPI-CIOUS?

ALL THAT PREPARATION—BLOWN—THEN NO FOLLOW-UP. THAT BIZARRE WARNING FROM THE GUY CALLING HIM-SELF JERRY JACKSON. BOOKER NEVER HEARD OF THE GUY. IT'S JUST—THERE SHOULD BE RUMORS, BULLETINS, WEB ANGELS, *SOMETHING*—MORE NOISE, DAMN IT.

THE LACK OF NOISE WORRIES YOU.

YES.

THIS IS REASONABLE. AS I UNDERSTAND YOU, YOUR IM-AGE TAKES NOISE, AND FILTERS DATA; YOU, THE PLAYER, TAKE DATA, AND FILTER TRUTH. WITHOUT NOISE YOU CAN-NOT FIND TRUTH.

TRUTH, Trent agreed. THAT'S WHY I'M HERE.

WHAT TRUTH DO YOU KNOW?

NOT MUCH. I THINK—KILLING IS WRONG.

WHY?

I DON'T KNOW. ONCE I GET BEYOND THAT POINT THINGS ARE REAL FUZZY. THE MORE COMPLEX THE ARGUMENT BECOMES, THE EASIER IT BECOMES TO REFUTE. < SHRUG. > KILLING IS WRONG.

THAT, Ring had said, with the absolute seriousness that

only an AI without any genetic predisposition to humor is capable of, IS A PLACE TO START.

Trent lived in a world which was characterized by noise.

He waited for the other shoe to drop.

And for three months there was silence.

Silence from the Peaceforcers Elite.

Silence from DataWatch.

Silence from the police.

> Don't ask me will I love you
> Always or just today
> I love you now, no other
> For more I cannot say

One morning early in June he awoke and watched the sun rise over the islands. The far wall was black, with a speckling of stars. The sun came in a blush of pink, and the sunpaint came up with it, slowly, bringing a calm, diffuse glow to Trent's surroundings. Denice, snuggled up at his side, was a warm and comfortable pressure.

He did not remember going to bed with her.

I moved in last night, she said silently. He turned his head slightly and bright green eyes were staring inquisitively into his own. *It's okay?*

Nobody objected?

I told Madame Gleygavass, gave her your access code. Denice leaned forward slightly, kissed the tip of his nose. *I think I pleased her. She thinks I'm too restrained.*

Are you?

Denice chuckled aloud, yawning sleepily, stretching like a cat. *She only thinks that because I wouldn't sleep with her.* She settled down again, curled up against him and her breathing gentled. *I'll sleep with you, more though.*

And she did.

The feeling was so strange, something he was so long away from, he was not sure at first what it was.

It came to him with something like a shock.

For the first time in seven years he was happy.

The day after Denice moved in, Trent had a long-stemmed white rose tattooed in the most interesting place he could think of.

· 6 ·

They watched cartoons together: Trent's favorites, the great hand-drawn flat classics from over a hundred years past, ranging from Bugs Bunny and Duck Dodgers in the 24-1/2th Century, and Rocky and Bullwinkle, to the subtler pleasures of the Disney classics; and Denice's favorites, the Japanese thought pieces from the first great period of computer animation around the turn of the century. Jimmy would not admit that the cartoons, especially the old flat ones, were a valid art form, but nonetheless Trent saw him laugh at the Coyote and the Road Runner, and once saw tears in his eyes at the conclusion of Shiba Nokura's *Death of the Rose*.

They listened to music together: Wagner and Springsteen and Bach, the Beatles and Chuck Renkha, and, of course, Kutura's *Music to Move To*. In years past, Trent had read, a knowledge of music had been one of the marks of a well-educated man. Somewhere along the line all that had been lost; today it was something for the street people. It was at least a fifty-fifty proposition that any given member of the upper classes had never heard of Kutura, somewhere around ten to one that they had never heard, or heard of, Bach or Springsteen or Billie Holiday.

Music to Move To was, surprisingly enough, very good indeed, despite the inevitable hype that surrounded its amazing success. In later years Kutura surpassed that early, somewhat immature work, with *Street Songs* in 2078 and *The Masters of No* in 2081; but in that summer of 2069 those works were years to come yet, and *Music to Move To*, flawed though Trent came to see that it was, was nonetheless impossible for Trent to dislike or ignore. Jimmy said he did not like the album much, but Trent saw his lips moving along with Kutura's cool, stinging vocals when he thought nobody was watching him.

I will not tell them of your brown limbs
Of the look of sun upon your hair
Or shadows in your eyes
I will not tell them of your beauty
Your walk
The sound of your voice or
The things that you said

I will not tell them of you, love
When you and I are dead

They sat on the roof and watched semiballistics and spacecraft tracking across the sky toward Unification Spaceport, sat on the roof and watched real sunsets together, went back inside and watched recordings of sunsets from halfway around the world.

Most of Trent's memories of that summer centered around twenty hot nights, or thirty or forty, sitting with Denice and Jimmy in the lounge chairs up on the roof in the warm, humid air above the shop, doing nothing more exciting than drinking and talking.

". . . and this 'bot, it's *smart*, right? So they're showing it round to this crowd of people, and the 'bot is introduced to this first guy and the 'bot says, 'Hello, I am an AI with an adjusted IQ of three hundred. What's your IQ?' And the guy says, 'Two hundred,' so the 'bot says, 'Excellent. We will discuss Belt CityState economics.' "

Trent said, "I've heard this one before."

Jimmy glanced at Denice. Denice shook her head no, and Jimmy grinned at Trent and continued.

"Later the 'bot gets introduced to a second guy, and he says to this guy, 'Hello, I am an AI with an IQ of three hundred. What's your IQ?' And this guy says, 'one-twenty,' so the 'bot says, 'Very good. We will discuss sports.' They talk about sports for a while, and the 'bot gets shown around some more, and gets introduced to a third guy. The 'bot says, 'Hello, I am an AI with an IQ of three hundred. What's your IQ?' And the guy says, 'Uh . . . eighty.' And the 'bot thinks for a moment and then says, 'So, tell me, what's it like being a Peaceforcer?' "

And they laughed together, and told other jokes. Some of their conversations were serious, some were not; and the ones that were not were more important than the ones that were.

"In the Fringe," said Trent in response to one of Denice's questions, "there aren't any medbots. Human doctors, and the only time you ever see a doctor is if you have something that's going to kill you if you don't. Fringe doctors aren't very safe."

"That's why you never got an inskin?"

"Pretty much," said Trent.

"Not exactly," said Jimmy at the same moment.

Denice looked back and forth between them.

Trent shrugged. "It takes a while to integrate an inskin. The human brain's not really designed to take input as fast as an inskin's designed to give it. You figure that the operation puts you out of circulation for a month to six weeks." Trent looked pensive, leaning forward in his chair to touch his brush to the powered canvas in front of him. He was working on his favorite painting that late summer afternoon, painting in bonded lightties that would eventually become a many-layered holograph.

Immediately to the north of them was the shell of the only spacescraper on Long Island: the half-completed Hoffman spacescraper. It had been half-completed since November of '68, when the Hoffman holding group had declared bankruptcy. The upper third of the spacescraper, everything above about one and a half kilometers, lacked exterior walls; Trent could look right into the interior of the spacescraper, through a twisted spiderweb of structural girders, and see pink-and-gray sky on the far side of the building. The bottom two-thirds of the spacescraper was faced with ebony pseudomarble. The setting sun was about even with the point where the facing ended, and its reflection glowed scarlet against the false black marble. "I haven't been able to afford that kind of time in the months we've been in the Patrol Sectors."

"And before that it wasn't safe."

"It's still not safe, in some ways. Wearing an inskin, I mean, not the operation. Latest figures I've audited say that about a quarter of all the people who have inskins are Players of one caliber or another. Don't think DataWatch doesn't know that." Trent laid down the light brush he had been painting with, turned the canvas off and unhooked his handheld from the jack at the edge of the canvas.

Tomorrow at this time, for the five minutes or so when the light was correct, he would paint again.

Denice watched him with some envy. "I wish I could do that."

Trent said, "You probably could. Holopainting's not hard, not like oil or electrolytes; there's no penalty for mistakes. You just load your last copy of the image and start over. Making it look real—textured—is the hard part."

Jimmy Ramirez said, "How do you know you can't paint?"

Denice simply glanced at Jimmy, did not answer. She lay back in her chair, stared straight into the setting sun. The sun dropped swiftly now, the red glow upon her cheeks and the scarlet tinge on the white of her thin cotton shirt and shorts fading as Trent watched her, and darkness settled down across the roof as the street and roof lights came on at almost the same moment. The question still had not been answered when the Peaceforcer spyeyes and glowfloats in their scores of thousands went up for the night, moving up and out to cover the Patrol Sectors in their entirety. Until dawn no Peaceforcer save an Elite would venture out again for any reason in groups of less than three; too often they did not come back.

The PKF Elite were a different matter entirely. No Elite had ever been killed in the line of duty; they were faster and stronger than a hunting waldo, and nearly as indestructible. They possessed an advantage no hunting waldo could have: human intelligence, the fiercely human desire to survive. There had, on occasion, been hunting waldos endowed with the desire for self-preservation; and they had, most of them, gone rogue. As DataWatch knew too well, it was nearly impossible to instill intelligence, self-awareness, and a willingness to survive in any creature, and still depend upon that creature wholly.

Self-aware waldos had been illegal for better than two decades by the end of the 2060s; cyborgs—the PKF Elite—were more reliable.

Denice Castanaveras said quietly, "I think sometimes I'm not a very creative person."

Trent opened his mouth, closed it again without saying anything.

Jimmy said, "I've seen you dance."

Denice nodded, chewing slightly on her lower lip. She had nursed the same glass of white wine all evening; it had to have grown warm, as warm as the evening around them, during that time. Now she sipped at it without seeming to taste it. The last of the golden and red light was all but gone from the western sky. "That's skill, Jimmy. It's not a calling." Her voice was a low, reflective murmur of sound. "It's not something I do because there's nothing else for me."

Jimmy was on his second six-pack already. His speech was not even slightly slurred. "So why?"

"I don't know why I became a dancer, honestly." Denice lay flat on her back, looked up at the very few bright stars that could be seen through the atmospheric scattering of the city lights. "I've always been good at it, I've always enjoyed it. I was in Public Labor for four years after the Troubles; Madame Gleygavass got me out when I was thirteen." There was something particularly distant about her entire manner, as though only her body were with them on the roof. "It's not as bad as being in the Fringe—Public Labor, I mean—but dancing beats the hell out of belonging to a Labor Battalion work gang. And I am good at it. But Tarin says I'm not hungry enough, and Madame Gleygavass says unless I have biosculpture, in a couple of years my tits are going to be too big for me to dance pro."

Jimmy Ramirez said quietly, seriously, enunciating carefully, "I would be sorry to see you stop dancing."

"Dancing is nice, Jimmy." There was no uncertainty at all in Denice Castanaveras' voice. "But it's not real, you know. It's just entertainment." Intensity put an edge to her words, and something very strange began to happen to Trent as she spoke, the edges of things growing vague and blurry. "I want to do something *real*. When I'm finally dead, people are going to know I was here. There's not going to be any question at all. Dancing is nice, but it's *just* dancing."

"Then what will you do if you don't dance?"

"Change the world." She spoke slowly, the words coming from elsewhere, some far place where she and Trent stood together. "It's why we're here, it's why God put us here. To make things better, so that the people who come after us have a better life than the people who came before." She sat up slowly, looking at Jimmy Ramirez. Her eyes, in the dim roof lights, were unfocused and remote, the distant, simple, almost gentle tone touched her voice again, and suddenly Trent's skin tingled as though the air was full of ozone. "They come down out of the mountains, to where the circle of his fire is burning against the night." She was silent for a moment, still and motionless, then went on dreamily. "And, you see the young man he *speaks* to them then, at the foot of the mountains while the living diamonds hunt them in the darkness, and tells them that the old promises will be fulfilled, the old dreams realized, the old wrongs made right. And then, *together*," Denice Castanaveras said, speaking directly to Jimmy Ramirez, who sat frozen, utterly transfixed, "together they march back through the Traveling Waters, and go back together to the city on the hill and drive out the enemy."

Jimmy stared at her.

They stood together in that empty place. It seemed to Trent that pale blue fire traced itself across the surface of Denice's skin, that a cobalt halo pulsed around her skull. Trent said, his voice echoing wildly in his own ears, "Where are we?"

"Watching. Watching the fire," she said softly, "burning out. They forgot to bank Tyrel's fire when they all left together. It flickers and then the cold kills it, and all that's left is the—darkness."

Trent found himself sitting, very much alone, on a rooftop filled with sharp-edged objects, watching Denice come back down from the place she had taken him to.

She shook herself slightly, glanced at Trent, and then turned back to Jimmy Ramirez. "You see, Jimmy," she said in a normal voice, "that's the sort of thing I want to do. To make a difference."

"Girl," said Jimmy with perfect sincerity, "you're stoned. Or crazy, I don't know."

She shook herself slightly, leaned forward. It seemed to Trent that she was utterly oblivious to what had just happened. "Don't you understand?" Denice asked. "It's what we have to do. We have to make things better."

Jimmy looked at Trent. "Man? She's crazy, right?"

Trent shook his head slowly, watching Denice Castanaveras. She was the only thing left on the roof which he did not see sharp-edged; she kept shifting, blurring in his vision, the pale blue of her neural system glowing beneath the surface of her skin. "No. No, Jimmy," he whispered, "she's right."

Jimmy laughed suddenly, an abrupt explosion of real amusement. "Two street kids, a crazy dancer and a thief, gon' to change the world. So *that's* what you're going to do. Thank you for sharing with me, both of you." He laughed again, looking at the two of them sitting across the roof from him. *"How?"*

Once, almost ten years ago, Trent had seen Carl Castanaveras, in the midst of a sudden, amazingly powerful rage, knock a full-grown man halfway across a room simply by looking at him. In that instant, when Denice Castanaveras' features darkened, for the very first time she reminded him of her father.

He said, very softly indeed, "Denice, don't."

The nearly full bottle of white wine at the side of her chair exploded. Shards of glassite sprayed across the rooftop. The girl sat trembling in the chair, hands clasped together in her lap, looking down at her white knuckles, tiny pinheads of blood beginning to coalesce on the surface of her skin where the glassite had struck. Jimmy Ramirez came to his feet in a single startled blur of motion, backing away from Trent and Denice swiftly, tense and wild all at once.

"Denice, I can't stop you," said Trent quietly. "Nobody can."

"She—she's—"

"Shut up, Jimmy." Trent did not even look at him.

They held the tableau, none of them moving, until finally, slowly, the tension went out of Denice Castanaveras, and she looked up and met Jimmy Ramirez's staring brown eyes.

"So," she said, "now you know."

They went dancing together at Trent's favorite dance club, The Emerald Illusion, in the basement of the Red Line Hotel; all of Trent's friends and many of hers.

> *Don't ask me do I love you*
> *Always or just today*
> *I love you now, my love*
> *Tomorrow who can say*

Her friends danced better than his. One night Orinda Gleygavass herself came, danced once with Jimmy and twice with Boris the Bear; Johnny Johnny whispered sweet nothings to her through the bear's inskin.

"I never saw such a thing," she was heard to say before she left.

"I think I've got it." Trent blasted the vault's surface with FreezIt again, glanced down at the readout from the thermometer; the surface of the vault was down to −10°C, and the vault's diagnostics were reporting nothing at all wrong. The vault was a three-meter-high Kellerman Model 880 which Trent had purchased for just shy of twenty thousand CU; it was an exact duplicate of the temporary storage vault currently in use at the Metropolitan Museum of Art, right down to the climate control. The vault's surface was webbed with superconductor; theoretically a cutting torch, even an X-ray laser, should warm the entire vault, evenly, rather than allowing any single spot to become hot enough to melt.

At 38°C the vault's diagnostics would set off an alarm.

But it did not seem to care about the cold at all.

Trent moved a stationary cutting laser in front of the vault, pulled on a pair of goggles, and hit the cutting laser for two seconds.

He took the goggles off. There was a tiny, cherry-red spot on the surface of the vault where the laser had touched. It faded as he looked.

The vault's temperature had jumped to positive 12°C.

"Johnny, stopwatch?"

Johnny Johnny read off data from the sensors plastered across the surface of the vault. "Boss, at the point of contact the vault's surface reached a temperature of 2,200°C, and did not drop below 1,000°C until .77 seconds after the laser ceased. We need to triple the temperature at the point of contact and boost the duration to 1.2 seconds or better. Judging from the length of time it took for the temperature to drop below 1,000°C at the point of contact, the superconductor strips inside the casing can't be closer than two centimeters together."

"Liquid nitrogen?"

"Should work, Boss. The point of contact should hit 7,000°C easy; the temp sensors inside won't go higher than −5."

"*Jimmy!* Hear that, Jimmy?" Trent stripped off his goggles, turned around to look at Jimmy. "We've got the vault!"

Jimmy Ramirez did not answer.

Trent cocked his head slightly, the goggles hanging loosely in one hand, looking at Jimmy standing almost motionless at the other end of the room. "You okay, Jimmy?"

"Yeah. Sure."

"Your mind hasn't been on the work, Jimmy."

Jimmy Ramirez sighed, clicked off the light pen in his

hand, and turned away from the display of the blueprints for the Metropolitan Museum of Art. The holo which usually showed the South Seas beach had been turned off, and in the space it had covered Jimmy had been constructing a three-dimensional representation of the building's layout and security devices. Jimmy was silent for a moment before responding; the muscles in his shoulders were so tense Trent could see them through Jimmy's jacket. His reply, when it came, was almost a relief. Trent had seen the argument coming these last two weeks, had known it was inevitable the day the wine bottle had shattered on the roof.

Jimmy Ramirez said softly, "How can you tell?"

"I can't, not the way you mean."

"All this time we been friends . . ." Jimmy shook his head, looked up, and saw Trent gazing at him. He glared at Trent for just an instant, and Trent saw the anger gathering. His voice grew almost gentle. "How come you never *told* me, man?"

Trent said, "At first I didn't trust you, Jimmy. Remember? I was twelve and I was afraid of everything." He grinned suddenly. "Including you."

The light pen in Jimmy's hand was bending. "At first?"

"Later I found out about how you lost your mother in the Troubles, and then there was another reason not to trust you." Trent was silent for a moment. "Eventually I did trust you, and by then—we'd been together two or three years, it didn't seem so important any more what we'd been doing before we met." He shrugged. "We had something that was working, Jimmy. I didn't want to mess it up. I know you're prejudiced against genies; don't try to tell me you're not."

Jimmy nodded jerkily. "I know, I know all the things I've said. But I didn't mean them about *you*."

"I know."

"All those years," Jimmy half whispered, "I never understood. You were always so good at *everything*. Man, I'm a good boxer, but the coach, he don't want me, he wants you, twenty kilos lighter and he wants *you*. You punch harder than I do, you're smarter than I am, and my man, I never in my entire life saw *anybody* could move as fast as you do. I work out two hours a day, you never work out and you're—"

"Perfect."

The word brought Jimmy up short, cut him off in midword.

Trent said softly, "I'm a genie. Suzanne Montignet, the best genegineer the world has ever seen, designed me from the ground up, gene by gene until she had a design she was pleased with. I wasn't one of the experimental designs, not like the de Nostri; none of the telepaths were. All Doctor Montignet was doing was designing telepaths without any genetic flaws at all. She made one mistake, in me. My seventeenth gene complex is different than Denice's; not flawed, or so I was told by Doctor Montignet before she died, just different. That's why Denice is a telepath and I'm not."

Jimmy looked at Trent almost pleadingly. "You remember how it was? Jesus, the Temple Dragons were gon' to *kill* you until I talked them into adopting you. Do you remember?"

"Jimmy?"

"Yes?"

"I am genetically perfect." Jimmy Ramirez actually flinched, and Trent continued with barely a pause, "And it's not my fault." A brief startled look flashed across Ramirez's countenance, and Trent smiled rather lopsidedly. "Really, it's not. Nobody asked me how I wanted to be born. Nobody asked Denice either, or her parents, or any of the kids I grew up with."

"God *damn* you!" Jimmy whirled suddenly, hit the wall bare-handed so hard the plastisteel lining took a dent. He turned back and took a step toward Trent. "What am I supposed to do? My mama went *crazy* because of you people!"

"So did half of the Fringe. Jimmy, the people who did that are *dead.* They died defending themselves. Denice wasn't a telepath yet when it happened, and I'm not." Trent spread his hands. "What am *I* supposed to do? I tell you the truth and I'm one of the people you hate so bad you can taste it. I lie to you and it means I don't trust you." He said the words honestly, as simply and directly as he was able. "Come on, Jimmy, you tell me. What am I supposed to do?"

Jamos Ramirez's answer was flat challenge, even and unmistakable. "Tell me. Tell me everything, always." He took two steps closer to Trent, and his voice was suddenly almost pleading. *"Always."*

The crooked grin touched Trent's features again. "Okay. Jimmy?"

"Yeah?"

"What do you want to drink? GoodBeer, Bud, what?"

"What do you mean?"

"This is going to take an awful damn long time."

They talked all night and into the morning. Trent showed him the recordings of the destruction of the Chandler Complex, taken from the hundreds of spyeyes which had floated above the building in the days prior to its destruction. "Here. This clip has been censored so thoroughly most people aren't even aware it exists; I stole it out of an *Electronic Times* archive file. In this clip, at the edge of the holofield, you can see the Lamborghini coming up out of the park; Denice says that was Carl. The Troubles had already begun at this point; the telepaths were fighting back."

"He died?"

"Denice says so. About forty-five minutes after this clip I've just shown you—" The holofield darkened for an instant, returned with the image of the Chandler Complex. The image held steady, a foreground view of the Complex from about two meters up, a shining two-story structure of white monocrystal. Then the field went completely white, a blazing brilliant glare that made Jimmy cry out in surprise and turn his eyes away.

Trent stood, staring unblinking into the awful brightness, watching without expression as it faded into the shape of a mushroom cloud, climbing up into the dark night sky. "The Boards said at first that a Peaceforcer Elite named Mohammed Vance ordered this. Then they said he had not, that it was Space Force's decision to target the Compound. I'd give a lot to know."

Jimmy had turned back, was watching the mushroom cloud with plain fascination. "The frog with the Arab name. You've mentioned him before."

"I know. And that's essentially where things have stood ever since, Jimmy. The PKF thinks—or thought—that I was dead, that I'd drowned in the Hudson River. But they know David and Denice were not at the Complex when it was destroyed; they know that *somebody* left the Complex before it was destroyed, in the Lamborghini. It's been seven years and they've never found me, they've never found Denice." Trent was silent for a moment. "They may have found David. The Bureau of Biotech has memos which mention a boy with the Gift, but the memos themselves are so carefully worded there's not much I can get out of them. Biotech—we were raised by the Bureau of Biotech and the Peaceforcers, all of us were—Biotech is one of the lowest profile, best protected Bureaus in the Unification. They don't even depend on DataWatch for data integrity; they have replicant AIs in their Boards."

"That's illegal."

Trent simply laughed. "Yeah. Tell it to the Peaceforcers. At any rate, Biotech either has David, or they've gone back to the well again with the same gene template that created us."

Jimmy nodded slowly, the dark Latin features a study in concentration. He was clearly not thinking about David at all. "Okay. So this Garon, from DataWatch, that's why the problem with the boost at Calley's."

"I think so."

Jimmy Ramirez said slowly, "Makes no sense, man. Why would they set you up so tight and then just walk away?"

"That," said Trent, "is a really good question."

Trent watched Denice perform during a full-dress rehearsal for a production of *Leviathan,* a critical and controversial work about the early life of Jules Moreau, the man who had, with Sarah Almundsen, founded the Unification.

She was not the female lead; that, the role of Evsita, was danced by Orinda Gleygavass' protégée, Tarin Schuyler.

Denice was better. Trent knew nothing of dance, but it was not merely prejudice on his part. She danced the supporting role of Evsita's younger sister, whom Moreau had married after Evsita's suicide, danced it with a passion and single-mindedness that brought admiring whistles and occasional applause from the stagehands as they prepared for opening night. Tarin Schuyler, a thin, willowy young woman with whipcord muscles and no softness to her at all, danced the lead with precision and fierceness and great talent, and the stagehands ignored her entirely.

They worked.

In late June they completed the contract to boost an old painting with an odd history from its display at the Metropolitan Museum of Art: a red monochrome in oils. *Je Suis Le Fleuve,* the painting was titled, and it showed a river of blood flowing through a darker red jungle. After that boost there were others, large and small; the most important of the lot was a fairly safe job for a low-level executive with Chandler Industries, acquiring complete blueprints from an engineer with Peugeot-AeroFlot which showed the layout of Peugeot's next generation of semiballistic capsules.

The relative danger of the assignment rarely had anything to do with how well it paid; the aborted boost of Calley's, at the beginning of summer, had been very dangerous, and had promised to pay acceptably. The boost of the painting was somewhat dangerous, and paid well; the Chandler job had been lengthy and tedious, and gave them enough Credit to relax for three or four months.

Trent was more cautious than usual that summer, following the failed Peaceforcer sting at CalleyTronics. As time wore on, without word, without any sign at all from the Peaceforcers, he allowed himself to hope that it had been coincidence, that Garon had not identified him, that his safe and reasonably secure life had not suddenly turned into a tightrope walk.

He allowed himself to hope.

Deep inside he did not believe any of it for an instant.

It was a difficult time, the troubled end to a troubled decade. Trent lived in the InfoNet, danced in the Crystal Wind for ten and fifteen hours at a time. He tried desperately to make sense of what was happening to his world.

That was the summer that the first images came back from the probe to Tau Ceti, when humanity knew finally, without any question at all, that it was not alone. The Big Scope, out in the Belt, had not lied; there were two Earthlike planets circling Tau Ceti at distances of approximately 150 and 180 million kilometers. There was, the probe showed clearly, a monstrous orbital facility, a solid oval mass some five times the size of Halfway, circling the inner planet. The probe's attempts at communication with the orbital facility were not answered, and then the probe's thin laser pulse, attenuated by 11.9 light-years distance, simply stopped.

In the Belt, St. Peter's CityState announced that it had begun preparations to place a second colony on Ganymede. The PR company responsible for their downside media relations, Lustbader, Capri and Doutrè, made no reference at all to the destroyed first Ganymean colony in their news release.

Elsewhere in the Belt the SpaceFarer's Collective had signed trade treaties with the White Russian CityStates, bringing an end to over twenty years of hostilities between the two groups. The Mormon colony on Mars was said to be thriving, and on good terms with the SpaceFarer colony some two hundred kilometers north of it.

The United Nations Space Force announced that they were placing armed observatory posts in the Belt. Following the expected protests from the SpaceFarer's Collective and the CityStates, Space Force agreed that the observatory posts would be unarmed, while refusing to allow any verification whatsoever.

The growing tension between Free Luna and Unification Luna continued to get worse. Desertions to Free Luna territory were on the increase again, after a brief decline caused by an infusion of over eighty thousand PKF troops from Earth; a bookie in the Free Luna city of New Vegas had set odds of one in eight for an invasion by the Unification within the next five years, and merely even odds that the SpaceFarer's Collective would in fact support their Free Lunar allies in the event of war with the Unification.

On Luna, for the first time in history, Peaceforcers in pursuit of a suspect entered Free Luna territory, in the city of Alphonse. In the ensuing firefight three Peaceforcers, the suspect, and one Alphonse resident were killed. The United Nations Peace Keeping Force was demanding reparations from St. Peter's CityState, Alphonse's parent corporation, and had filed suit against St. Peter's CityState's downside offices in Manhattan District Unification Circuit Court. The CityState made no public comment, but was expected to countersue; Gandhi CityState at Ceres issued a press release condemning the PKF for the five deaths.

At Halfway an explosion in a free-fall processing factory killed eighty-three people. It was the largest space-based industrial accident ever, and the second largest space disaster of any sort, surpassed only by the destruction of the original Ganymede colony in the disaster of 2049.

Trent found an editorial by Terry Shawmac on the *Electronics Times* news Board.

—Dateline New York, 7/3/88.
  Of course, it could be worse.
  A lot of people can't see how, but they're, well, not

trying. *This has not been a bad summer, so far—and summers have not been good times for the Unification. Remember that seven years ago today the Troubles began, and irresponsible bastards like then–Secretary General Darryl Amnier predicted the end of the world. And the numbers seemed to support him; better than one and a half million people were dead within the first half year, and a lot of the rest were missing some of the dots off their dice.*

The Secretary General committed suicide—which made sense, as he'd otherwise almost certainly have been tried and condemned for the criminal behavior which directly led to the Troubles. And the powermongers in France handpicked Charles Eddore to succeed him. Why Eddore? As Prosecutor General at the time, he was intimately involved in the bizarre final days of Amnier's administration. . . .

Which may have been reason enough. The full story of Amnier's deadly confrontation with the Castanaveras telepaths never did come out, which means that somebody, somewhere in France, has a hold on Eddore's cojones tight enough to produce some serious geeking pretty much on demand. . . .

It has indeed been a quiet summer. Remember that six years ago, right after Eddore assumed office, the Speedfreaks got ready to swarm down on him in a crazed locustlike swarm—and he had them drowned like stinking rats in the middle of the Atlantic. Remember the Fizzle War of five summers ago when the slithy bastard did his level best to get us into our first interplanetary war, had Space Force shoot down a SpaceFarer flagship over Free Luna, and then stumbled into peace purely due to his own lack of guts.

Then there was last summer, which saw the fiftieth anniversary of the Unification of Earth, as well as the single most corrupt series of elections to take place since the Unification.

Of course it could be worse.

Wednesday is the Fourth of July, and the pols are expecting the usual across Occupied America: riots, insurrections, an assassination or two. The Secretary General will be hunkered down in his armored bunker on the island until it all blows over, with two hundred thousand Peaceforcers around to keep him feeling safe. He's hardly the worst SecGen we've ever had: a pure pragmatic with no morals to speak of, a man whose own mother refused to speak to him for three years following the onset of the Troubles. Not that Eddore was likely bothered by that; there were elections to tend to, power brokers to keep happy . . .

A tough league, yes, where the weak get eaten alive and their own mothers pretend not to know them . . . but let's face it, by some standards they're all of them, everybody in Capitol City, stone punks.

Nearby, as geographical distances go, but in another universe entirely by any sane person's yardstick, in the Bay Shore Fringe, the Gypsy Macoute allegedly executed a juice junkie by "torching" him at a recent treaty dance with the Temple Dragons. The procedure, once common in the Fringe but recently on the wane, consists of binding the victim to a steel or concrete post, drenching him with kerosene or other lighter fluid, and setting him afire. The Prosecutor General's office has declined to prosecute; Gillian Tresco, assistant DA for the city of New York, said the alleged execution is under review.

The Gypsy Macoute, in a prepared statement, said the man had volunteered. "It's a great honor, lighting up the sky for a Gypsy dance." Police reported that the juice junkie, whose name is being withheld pending notification of next of kin, was so impervious to pain that he did not scream while he burned.

Outside we still have mostly honest courts, a mostly free press, and one or two tough, nasty bastards still willing to use them the way they were originally intended.

Things could be worse.

Of course, they could be a hell of a lot better.

Have a good Fourth.

—Terry Shawmac

In late July Trent and Denice talked about killing.

"But what do you do," Trent had said patiently, "if you don't *want* to kill him?"

Denice frowned, considering the question. She was half in

and half out of the pool in the center of Trent's apartment, reclining against the gentle slope in the pool's shallow end, wet, gleaming black hair slicked back away from her face. "I don't *have* to kill him. Or her, as the case may be. Trent—the genome Doctor Montignet created, the one that became Carl, and Jany—there were recessives in it. I don't get as angry as Carl did—really, I don't. And I can do things they couldn't. Like this." A pensive expression crossed her features quickly, and then a small waterspout formed in the center of the pool, a whirling funnel of water which lifted up from the surface of the suds, detached itself from the body of water beneath it, and ascended a full meter in the air before slowing, transforming itself first into a sudsy white long-stemmed rose and then into something so explicit that Denice actually blushed while doing it; she held the final form for just a moment, and then let the water rain back down into the pool.

Trent lay on his stomach on the bed and watched in unabashed fascination; he grinned at the final image.

Denice looked over at him. "See? That sort of control, none of them had it. And I take a shotokan class in the Village from this really nice old Japanese man; that's the class I go to on Thursday nights. If I was attacked, I mean without warning so that I was surprised, I'd probably kill whoever did it. The anger—" She looked at Trent thoughtfully. "It's very bad and very fast. But if I had time to think it over, Trent, I could —*not* kill."

"Christian," Trent muttered.

Denice laughed. "You make it sound like a dirty word." She was silent for a moment, rubbing dep cream over her right shin. Because she knew it made him uncomfortable, she did not do it often; without looking at him, she said silently, *I could say I don't understand you, but unfortunately I do. When you kill, you subtract a possibility from the world. I know that; but sometimes it's necessary.*

"No," said Trent evenly, "it's not. I want you to think about this, Denice. Carl used to get angry. Very and quickly. I'm sure he got something out of it, the adrenaline rush, something. I don't know. But his temper is at least part of the reason that absolutely everyone you and I grew up with is *dead* today. You think about that."

Denice Castanaveras said slowly, "It doesn't make me happy when you sound like this. I don't know if I can convince you, or how, but, Trent—it's very strange to hear someone who steals things for a living lecture me about what's right and wrong."

"Denice?"

"Yes?"

"There is no problem so large it cannot be run away from."

She lifted a wet eyebrow. "Oh, really?"

"Do you want to hear a *good* magic trick?"

Denice said cautiously, "Sure."

"Ask somebody to pick a number between one and ten." Denice nodded even more warily. "Then," Trent said softly, "run away."

On Thursday, August the second, just after 10:00 A.M., Trent and Jimmy and Jodi Jodi and Boris were eating breakfast together at the Temple coffee shop next door to Kandel Microlectrics. It was Trent's favorite place for breakfast; no waitbots, no empty food. The portions were small, but fair, and Reverend Andy served seconds, without charging, to those whom he knew needed them; and, except on Wednesdays and Saturdays, when he preached, Reverend Andy did the cooking himself.

And Reverend Andy was a fine cook.

Jodi Jodi had called in sick for her day job on the admittance desk at the Red Line Hotel in Manhattan. Kandel Microlectrics actually opened at 10:00; Trent had left Old Jack and Bird watching the shop, Bird handling the front, Old Jack taking care of any urgent repairs.

Trent had his handheld turned on, set up and recording in the middle of the table. "So we make policy with the Boys on Thursday. Jodi Jodi, you're sure about this porter Tiny?"

She shrugged. "As sure as I can be. I trust him."

"How does he feel about the juice?"

"Hates it," she said simply. "He thinks juice peddlers should be shot. Or wired."

Trent nodded. "Okay, bring him to the meet. Brief him on Master Tim's Personal Protection System; I don't want the thing going off 'cause the boy does something stupid."

"We get people wearing PPSs at the hotel," Jodi Jodi said. "We can't refuse admittance on those grounds, though we'd like to. Tiny knows how to behave."

Trent looked over at Jimmy, who was working on a pair of

eggs so lightly cooked they made Trent's stomach do flip-flops. "Anything, Jimmy?"

"Not really." Jimmy spoke around a mouthful of eggs, washed it down with ice water. "We don't really need to work for two, three months at this point. I thought about going down to the Brooklyn City College, signing up for a class in Unification Law, something applicable toward the bar."

There was instant, utter silence around the table.

Trent said cautiously, "What?"

Jimmy nodded. "Just thinking ahead. At some point we got to go reasonably straight, right? Bein' a lawyer, it seems ideal for that kind of gig."

Jodi Jodi looked as though she'd tasted something bad. "You *must* be kidding."

Jimmy said defensively, "No, I'm not. Why do I have to be kidding?"

"It's just a bad idea, Jimmy," said Trent quietly. "Maybe you should just think about it for a bit."

Jodi Jodi said, "You're not thinking this through, Jimmy. You want to go straight by becoming a *lawyer*?" To Trent she said, "He's been reading Hemingway again, or else Thompson, he always gets like this when he's—"

Jimmy Ramirez said, "I have to find somethin' to do, guys. I mean, Trent's studying *accounting* the last two or three times I've dropped by. It's just been very quiet lately. *Nobody's* working. Syndic Elders are wor—" He stopped in mid-word.

Jodi Jodi looked away in disgust.

Trent sighed audibly. "Jimmy. We have *no* relationship with the Syndic. We have no relationship with the Tong, or with the Old Ones, or with the Corporation."

Jimmy said easily, "Just talking to them, Trent. It's not a big deal."

Trent's reply was interrupted; Bird came into the coffee shop, walked over to their table and plopped down next to Jodi Jodi. "You got mail," he announced to Trent. "Paper mail, I mean," he amended, looking down at Jodi Jodi's plate of turkey sausage and eggs. "Can I have your sausage?"

"Sure."

"How about the toast?"

"It's cold, Bird."

"I don't care. Aren't you going to open your mail?" Bird looked at Trent expectantly.

Trent had, was looking at two tickets, fifth row, to the opening night production of *Leviathan,* along with hand-lettered invitations, made up by someone other than Denice, addressed to "Trent" and "Jamos Ramirez," to the cast party to be held afterward.

Wordlessly, Trent handed Jimmy his invitation.

Jimmy scrutinized his invitation. "What are . . ." He puzzled out the words. "Whores doov-rez?"

Jodi Jodi read over Jimmy's shoulder. "Or-dervs," said Jodi Jodi, "is how it's pronounced. It's a frog word that means munchies."

"Oh," said Jimmy. He studied the invitation a moment longer, then looked up at Trent and Jodi Jodi and Bird. "They could have said."

I t was an incredible three months.

It was a time like nothing Trent had ever known before, and despite his misgivings, despite the eerie silence, he enjoyed Denice and Jimmy, and Bird and Tarin and Jodi Jodi, enjoyed their company and their love to the fullest, without hesitation, without reservation.

On Wednesday morning, August 8, 2069, at 9:30 A.M., Trent came downstairs, a thermos full of coffee in one hand, to open up the shop for the morning. Old Jack sat in front of one of the workbenches with a disassembled LapVax on the counter in front of him, running diagnostics on the view tracer. He was listening, to Trent's complete lack of surprise, to Mahliya Kutura, the cut called *Now.*

> *Don't ask me do I love you*
> *Cause that means you don't know*
> *It don't mean we won't ever die*
> *Just cause folks tell you so*

"Morning, Trent."

"Good morning, Jack."

"I left a pair of dead tracesets on your bench."

Trent nodded. "Okay." He glanced out toward the front of the shop, out at the quiet street. "What'd you diag?"

"Mole circuits are dead. I'm not sure why."

"I'll look at them." There was absolutely nobody on the streets outside. "Anything else?"

"Not really. Denice didn't come home last night?"

Trent did not even look at Old Jack. He stood in the middle of the walkway between the workbenches, looking toward the front of the shop. "No," he said absently, "she spent the night with Tarin, over in the Village. They have early practice today. Jack?"

"Yes?"

Without quite knowing why he was doing it Trent took two steps backward. "You think you can handle things yourself this morning?"

Old Jack turned around in his seat to look at Trent. "Why?"

"I think I'm going to take the day off."

The Peaceforcer hovercar dropped down silently out of the sky, came to a stop hovering, facing the storefront. The hovercar's canopy cracked open, the autoshots fired, and the front door simply exploded out of its track.

Old Jack said, "What?"

Trent said, "Peaceforcers. Here they come."

On Wednesday morning, August 8, 2069, at 9:35 A.M., three Peaceforcers under the command of Peaceforcer Elite Emile Garon came to Kandel Microlectrics Sales and Repair Shop and with sonics stunned Old Jack, stunned Trent, dragged Trent's unconscious body out of the shop by his ankles and put him in a Peaceforcer cell in Capitol City in Manhattan. And charged him with theft and conspiracy to commit theft and data cracking and illegal operation of Information Network resources and conspiracy to incite others to attempt the same.

. . . *and the music slows, melody and harmony coming together, the sounds of a violin and a piano whispering in unison, the piano slowing to a meticulous tinkling string of chords, and her voice, strong and sad all at once, follows the music, rides with it.*

> *I love you today and no other*
> *Don't ask me 'bout tomorrow*
> *I love you but*
> *Tomorrow never comes*

The other shoe had dropped.

He awoke barefooted, wearing a blue jumpsuit.

They'd drugged him to keep him under.

Trent had no idea how long he'd been unconscious. Half a day at least, judging by the lack of muscle tremors.

He stretched, looking around at his cell. Gray ferrocrete walls; there was no pressure pad for the door.

The magpick had been removed from the sole of his right foot.

There was a toilet in the corner of the cell, a pair of mesh-covered air vents with holes too small for Trent to fit even a finger through, and a cot of memory plastics which extruded from the wall.

He sat down on the cot, composed himself, and waited.

They left him completely alone for, by Trent's best guess, two full days.

He was brought nothing to eat, nothing to drink.

He was awakened twice when the memory plastic cot withdrew itself into the wall and tumbled him to the floor. The cot reextruded itself from the wall a moment later. After the first time Trent thought it over and lay back down on the cot; after the second he simply slept on the floor.

He awoke in a different place, sometime on the third day, to find he'd been stunned while he slept. His muscles were still trembling from the sonics; the Peaceforcers had propped him up in a chair, and his hands were snaked together behind him.

There were three Peaceforcers standing in front of him, two of them standing at attention at the sides of the door.

There was a small metal table about a meter in front of Trent. The Peaceforcer Elite who had been sitting outside Chief Devlin's door that night three months ago, Emile Garon, was now sitting next to the small metal table, in full uniform, dark hair styled precisely, three fingers grasping a thin cigar which rested in the ashtray on the tabletop.

The Elite said sincerely, "I have wanted to speak to you for a long time."

Trent said nothing, still taking in his surroundings. There was a spyeye floating in one corner of the room.

Garon's voice sounded odd, vaguely flat, and the walls looked soft.

Soundproofed, so that prisoners could scream without disturbing people outside.

Finally Trent looked directly at Emile Garon.

Trent said, "You're Emile Garon."

The man nodded. "Yes."

"You could have called." Trent was distantly amazed at how hoarse his voice sounded in his own ears. "I'm in the Directory."

The corner of Garon's mouth twitched very slightly. "Yes, you are. Trent, no surname. There are eighteen Trents in the New York Metropolitan Directory. Five of those are on Long Island. Of those five you are the only one listed without a surname."

"Where am I?"

Garon said mildly, "You are on Holding Level Three, maximum security, in the PKF Detention Center in Capitol City."

"What do you want?"

There was just a moment of silence.

Garon leaned forward very slightly. "I want a confession from you, Monsieur Trent. You are Trent Castanaveras, a genengineered human born May 9, 2051, at the United Nations Advanced Biotechnology Research Laboratory in New Jersey. You were raised with two hundred and fifty telepathic children, and may or may not be a telepath yourself." For the first time, the spyeye made sense to Trent; a method of verifying that the recollections of the Peaceforcers in the room matched what had actually happened. Garon continued. "You were the Player who went by the name of Ralf the Wise and Powerful between mid-2060 and 2062, during which time, in the person of Ralf the Wise and Powerful, you engaged in various unlawful acts, including theft, data cracking, espionage, and miscellaneous infringements of the Official Secrets Acts of 2048 and 2054. You were arrested on the night of July 3, 2062, in the company of Malko Kalharri and Suzanne Montignet, and on that same evening escaped PKF custody. There are no records of you during the Troubles; from 2067 through January of this year you were one of the premier contract thieves of the Huntington-area Fringe. In

January you, Jamos Ramirez, an unidentified female, and a red-headed male known only as 'Bird' crossed into the Patrol Sectors, acquired Resident Status in a manner which I have been entirely unable to ascertain, and began plying your trades, using the Kandel Microlectrics Sales and Repair Shop as a front for your operations." Without any pause at all, Emile Garon said, "I am further of the opinion that you are the webdancer whom the world knows as Johnny Johnny."

Trent said, "A webdancer?"

Garon shrugged. "A Player, if you will."

Trent asked, "Do you know the difference between a webdancer and a Player?"

Garon said pleasantly, questioningly, "No."

Trent smiled at him. "Me neither."

Garon sucked reflectively on his cigar, blew smoke toward Trent. "Monsieur Trent, I am prepared to go to court for permission to perform a brain-drain upon you. Have you ever seen someone to whom this has been done?"

"No. I've audited descriptions of it."

"It is not a pleasant procedure, and it usually leaves very little intact in the original personality. There is, I think, sufficient evidence that you are the Player known as Johnny Johnny that a judge will look favorably upon the request." The cyborg leaned forward again, jabbed the cigar at Trent. "If you are willing to cooperate, we can avoid that unpleasantness."

"What specifically have I been charged with?"

The Peaceforcer behind Garon said, "The charges are theft, conspiracy to commit theft, data cracking, conspiracy to commit data cracking, illegal use of Information Network resources, and conspiracy to incite others to attempt the same. The Prosecutor General's office is currently holding the question of charging you with treason and crimes against humanity under advisement."

Trent blinked. "Crimes against humanity?"

"The Troubles, young man." Emile Garon's stiff features actually grew somewhat more distant. "Nearly two and a half million deaths, destruction worse than anything since the close of the Unification War."

Trent looked from Garon to the two Peaceforcers standing behind him, and back to Garon. He shook his head slightly. "You're crazy, you know that?"

"Then you deny it all?"

"Yes. Yes, of course I deny it all. If I was a telepath—or even a Player, for that matter—what the *hell* would I be doing working six days a week in a computer repair shop?"

Trent saw the Peaceforcer to Garon's immediate left nod ever so slightly; they'd seen, then, the second-story room he supposedly lived in, and had not found the entrance to the third floor. In the face of Garon's frown, Trent continued. "But, if it comes down to brain-drain . . ." Trent shrugged as well as he could with his hands chained behind himself. "I'll confess to anything you want before we reach that point," he said reasonably.

The frown intensified, the stiff skin of the cyborg's face creasing almost mechanically. Garon stood abruptly. "You will be returned to your cell."

Trent said, "I want to see my lawyer."

Garon nodded almost moodily. "Certainement." He paused a beat, said, "That is to say, surely. The very instant the charges have been filed, you will be allowed access to a lawyer."

"You haven't charged me yet?"

Garon smiled at him. "I am afraid not."

Trent stared up at Emile Garon. "You know," he said, "I didn't believe it until now."

"Believe what?"

"What I'd heard, about how researchers have stopped using rats in experiments, and they're using Peaceforcers instead —on account of Peaceforcers aren't as cute as rats, they breed faster, they're harder to kill, and nobody cares if one dies."

The Peaceforcer by the door went absolutely purple, and Trent grinned at him, let the grin widen, and said softly, "And there's still *some* things you can't get rats to do."

They took him back to his cell.

"**Y**ou are so *much* more trouble than you're worth."

"You're only saying that because you love me," said Trent sincerely.

"Still," Beth Davenport conceded, "you do pay me. Promptly. Which is more than I can say for most of my clients."

They sat in the conference room together. Beth Davenport was the oldest human being Trent had ever met, somewhere around a hundred and twenty-five years old. She looked it;

even with modern geriatrics there was no word to describe her appearance except ancient. The appearance of age lay not so much in her baby-smooth skin, a dead giveaway of the most expensive sort of geriatrics regeneration, or even her obvious and extreme frailness, as in her mannerisms and behavior. Her makeup was expertly applied to complement her pale gray eyes, but by hand, not with a makeup key. Her clothing was usually of wool or cotton or tweed; today she wore a gray tweed suit with a black silk tie. Trent had never seen her wear anything with optical effects.

She took notes with a pen and paper, writing with her hand. Once Trent had looked at her notes, and seen a scrawl of something that reminded him, as nearly as anything else, of italicized print. With the exception of a few words here and there he'd been unable to make any sense at all out of it.

Trent had known her for nearly four years; she was one of the very few lawyers willing to handle Fringe-area clients of any sort.

"You're not going to like hearing this, but it could be worse. Cold comfort, I know, but it could be a *lot* worse." Beth looked Trent over. "Have you been fed in the four days you've been here?"

"Four days? It's Sunday? I didn't realize it had been that long. No, I haven't been fed."

The old lady nodded. "Standard Peaceforcer tactics. And they took your watch and the lights in your cell never go out, so you wouldn't be sure how long you've been here." She propped her briefcase up on the table and swung it open. "I brought you lunch. Eat it slowly."

It was a bulb of milk and a pair of turkey sandwiches on wheat. The lettuce was wilted and the mayonnaise was warm and they tasted better than anything Trent had eaten in at least five years.

Beth talked while he ate. "This Emile Garon, he's apparently a bit touched." She paused. "Obsessive about the Castanaveras telepaths, I mean. He was assigned to DataWatch back in '62, when a Player calling himself Ralf the Wise and Powerful was working for the telepaths. He was removed from DataWatch by the late Elite Commander Breilléune when he began exhibiting symptoms of datastarve. He was apparently something of a star in DataWatch, and they waited until they were certain he was developing the Player's Syndrome before they put him into the Elite program. They may have waited too long."

Trent nodded, eating. The PKF called it Player's Syndrome, as though it were a disease, when one of the DataWatch webdancers began exhibiting the same sort of behavior found in Players. It was all but inevitable, of course; any webdancer skilled enough to hunt Players and replicant AIs with any degree of success was, of necessity, at least potentially of Player caliber himself.

It was hardly news to anybody *except* the PKF that the Crystal Wind was addictive.

"He's never been allowed back into DataWatch, though he's apparently applied once or twice. The first good piece of news in this mess is that nobody takes the idea that you were one of the Castanaveras telepaths at all seriously. The charges which the Prosecutor General's office has filed against you essentially recognize this; they're all based on the supposition that you're the Player Johnny Johnny. The rather more severe charges that could be filed against you—assuming that you were one of the genegineered telepaths—simply haven't been, which indicates for me that the balance of 'Sieur Garon's allegations are not being taken seriously."

Trent nodded thoughtfully. "Good." He finished the last of the milk bulb, gave the empty bulb back to Beth, who tucked it away in her briefcase. "This makes sense of a lot of things. Garon tried to set me up back in late April, you know."

Beth looked startled. "No. No, I didn't."

"Put a lot of effort into the attempt." Trent leaned back in his chair, arms crossed over his chest, looking up at the ceiling. "Yeah . . . it does start to make some sense. One fairly major sting, set up largely on Garon's say-so—and then it blows up on them, they get nothing at all out of their time and trouble. The suspected Player walks, and Garon ends up with serious egg on his face."

Beth nodded. "It does make sense."

"And then nothing for over three months." Trent came to his feet suddenly, moving restlessly. "It works. Frank Calley I understand, slimy son of a bitch that he is; given his line of business, selling things to webdancers and Players, he doesn't want to call attention to the fact that he tried to help the PKF set up a Player. I don't particularly want to be known as the guy who blew a boost on Calley. We avoid each other, we're even. But the PKF makes no sense until now. There's nothing institutional about their interest in me, it's all personal on Garon's part, and his superiors would probably just as soon let it lie. He's not DataWatch and, assuming I am this Johnny Johnny Player, then he's crashing around on their turf. So DataWatch would just as soon see him back out. Garon's own superiors probably aren't very damn happy about the mess the man's stirred up." He stopped, glanced at Beth. "Somebody who knew about Garon's operation in great detail tipped me off in a *very* odd way. Somebody in DataWatch whose toes he stepped on? I've been thinking it was Chief Devlin, but this makes more sense."

"Yes, it does." For some odd reason, Beth Davenport seemed somewhat reluctant to continue. "Trent?"

"Yes?"

The old lady said slowly, "Trent, I appreciate the fact that, so far as I know, you've never lied to me."

Trent thought clearly, *Oh, no.*

Beth held his gaze. "Keeping in mind that I'm an officer of the court, we need to discuss a couple of subjects. I don't want you to admit to anything, Trent. I don't think they'd dare bug a meeting between an attorney and her client, and it would hardly be admissible if they did—but they might have. What I want you to do is tell me that you're not the Player Johnny Johnny."

"I can't do that, Beth."

Beth nodded; she did not even seem particularly surprised. "I would like you to tell me, Trent, that you are not a genie."

Trent said instantly, "I am not a telepath, Beth."

She started to nod, again without any particular surprise, then froze abruptly. "You—Trent," she said carefully, "that was not what I asked you to say. Please tell me that you are not a genie."

Trent became aware that he was fiddling with one of the buttons on his jumpsuit. He forced himself to stop, looked at Beth and smiled at her without any humor at all. "I'm sorry, Beth."

The old lady stared at him, thinking furiously, thoughts flitting around behind the pale gray eyes so clearly Trent thought he could almost follow the train of analysis. "Not another word," she said finally. "Don't say anything else to anybody until I've had a chance to research this some more. This is going to cost you, Trent."

"I don't mind. Just don't let them brain-drain me."

"We won't, Trent. Shot, perhaps."

"I'd prefer it."

"You're a sensible young man." The old woman was clearly disturbed; her hands twitched slightly as she flipped her note pad closed. "All right. I'll see what I can do. I'm not licensed to practice in a Unification Circuit Court, and if Garon convinces them you're a genie that's almost certain to be where they try you. I do have colleagues who can handle you in that venue, however." She sighed with real and obvious weariness, closing her briefcase. "Trent, we have a genuine problem here. The fact that you're guilty."

"It may not be as bad as you think."

Beth Davenport said skeptically, "Oh?"

"For about two years now, the Bureau of Biotech's databased records concerning the telepaths have not been correct. Gene charts, retinal scans, finger and footprints. Any hardcopy records they have from before the summer of '67 won't agree with the database, but that's not the sort of thing that tends to get noticed."

Beth simply blinked. "You did that? No, wait, don't tell me. I don't want to know." She touched her index finger to the photolock on her briefcase, held it there for just a moment while it scanned her fingerprint and locked itself, and rose to leave. "Is there anything else?"

"No, *yes*," said Trent suddenly. "Can you talk to Jimmy?"

"About what?"

"He has this idea he wants to be a lawyer."

The old woman said blankly, "That's ludicrous."

"Of course it is," said Trent. "Could you talk to him, let him know how it is?"

"How what is?"

"Tell him about all the horrible things you've seen, all the genuinely vicious things you've had to do," said Trent earnestly. "I don't think he *understands*."

Beth looked at him oddly. "Yes. Certainly, Trent. I'd be happy to."

"Great. Thanks a lot. I mean, I really appreciate this."

She said shortly, "I'll be back soon."

He was not sleeping when Emile Garon came to see him.

Trent sat in full lotus in the middle of the floor, hands resting upon his knees, eyes closed against the omnipresent white glowpaint. He hoped that if there were hidden cameras in his cell, it would look as though he were peacefully meditating.

He was in fact intensely bored.

He could feel the very first twinges of datastarve.

It was, Trent guessed, sometime around midnight when the cell door flexed and then curled up into a small tube at the side of the doorway.

He opened his eyes.

Garon stood motionless in the doorway, alone, wearing an immaculately tailored full-dress PKF Elite uniform, the black-and-silver trappings of his differences from the rest of the human race.

Trent did not rise. "Hello, 'Sieur Garon."

The Peaceforcer glanced at the cot Trent was not using, but did not comment on it. "Earlier today," he said abruptly, "we submitted a request for brain-drain to Unification Circuit Court Judge Despreaux."

Trent said nothing, simply looked at the man, waiting.

Garon barely seemed to notice the even stare, the lack of response. "Your lawyer will file a request for dismissal, which will be turned down. The request to perform brain-drain will be approved no later than Wednesday of next week; by Thursday, monsieur, there will be very little left of you."

Trent said mildly, "Courts are slow things. I doubt events will move as fast as you seem to think."

"I guarantee you, monsieur, they will."

Trent cocked his head slightly to one side. "Mind if I ask why you're telling me this?"

Emile Garon looked down on Trent in obvious indecision. "I would regret to see a mind such as yours destroyed in this fashion, Monsieur Trent."

Trent thought about the question for at least twenty seconds before asking it. "Elite Sergeant, what do you want from me?"

The Elite shook his head instantly. "Nothing. Some conversation, perhaps. You can speak freely, Trent. I am not recording now; in case you have wondered, there are no recording devices in your cell."

"Forgive me," said Trent, "if I don't take your word for that."

The Elite actually smiled. "I forgive you, of course." Garon stood unnaturally still in the doorway; Trent wondered what it must be like for the man, held upright and steadied by servos and muscles that were the work of nanotechnologists and transform viruses. Garon said almost gently, "I have been in Occupied America now for over nine years, first in DataWatch and then the Elite. You are, monsieur, at the very least a webdancer of considerable skill; my contacts in Department Five of the New York City police department swear this is so."

"With real swear words, I bet." Trent said sharply, as the realization struck him, "There's gendarmes willing to talk to you?"

Garon smiled again. "Yes. Not all gendarmes hate the PKF, and not all Peaceforcers hate the gendarmes. Department Five," he continued, the smile fading, "speaks of you, sir, in the highest terms."

Trent said nothing for a long while, sat feeling the cold floor through the thin blue prisoner's jumpsuit. Finally he looked up again at Emile Garon, and said very directly, "Emile, what do you want from me?"

Not even the stiff cyborg skin could disguise the man's naked longing. "What is it *like*?"

"What is what like?"

"Playing. I never understood the Players, Monsieur Trent. I tried, I chased them through the Crystal Wind, I hunted them through the Boards. But I never understood them. *What is it like*?"

At last Trent looked away. He could not find the strength to look at the man when he said, "I'm sorry. I can't help you."

Garon stood completely motionless in the doorway for a long, long moment. "Monsieur Trent?"

"Yes?"

"Have you ever heard of a man named Mohammed Vance?"

"Nope."

Garon said, very softly indeed, "He is the man, monsieur, who is reputed to have ordered the destruction of the Castanaveras telepaths, seven years ago. I spoke to him yesterday; I interrupted a birthday party in his honor. He has just turned forty." Garon smiled at Trent. "He is a Commissionaire of the PKF Elite, by eleven years the youngest Commissionaire in the Elite. A brilliant man."

"Why are you telling me this?"

The tall Elite said quietly, "You are who I think you are, no matter what Biotech says. At least one officer of the PKF whom I have been able to find knows your people, knows them well, from before the Troubles. His name, as I say, is Mohammed Vance—and I've sent for him. He will be here the day after tomorrow."

The door unrolled behind Garon with efficient mechanical finality.

Three hours later a black Peaceforcer with an unholstered anesthetic needler and an American accent, whom Trent had not seen before, came to get him.

"Your attorney is here," the man grumbled.

Trent sat in the center of the cell floor, looking up at him. "It's late."

"No shit?" The Peaceforcer tossed a snakechain on the floor in front of Trent, waited just a moment and then said, "If you're not on your feet with the chain around your wrists in two seconds flat, kid, I'm going to lock you back up again and your lawyer can damn well come back in the morning."

"Look at me, getting to my feet," Trent observed. He picked up the snakechain and stood slowly, stretching, getting the kinks out of his muscles.

The Peaceforcer had stepped back into the corridor, well out of range. He was not exactly pointing the weapon at Trent. "Come on, kid, let's go."

Trent wrapped the snake around one wrist until it came into contact with itself, then held the other wrist next to the first and waited while the snake got a good grip. He stepped out into the short corridor, moving slowly. The corridor's glowpaint was turned down to one-third normal intensity, and the gray ferrocrete walls seemed particularly grim. The Peaceforcer followed Trent at a distance of five paces.

They passed through the visual check station which separated the cells from the visitors' areas and the holding pens, went through one sparsely populated area where a pair of night operators sat on the other side of a glassite wall, sitting at their systerms and watching the prisoner with the armed escort. The Peaceforcer took Trent right up to the door of the conference room where Trent had, earlier that day, met with Beth; made Trent stand to one side and without taking his eyes off Trent palmed the pressure pad next to the door and waited while his palmprint was examined.

The door curled open.

There was a woman sitting at the conference table, dressed in a conservative black businessperson's suit, hair swept up into a tight bun that was, Trent thought distantly, quite attractive. As Trent stared at her, Denice Castanaveras fixed glittering green eyes on the Peaceforcer and said quite calmly, "Officer Markson, please come in here."

The muscles around the black Peaceforcer's eyes relaxed suddenly and completely, and without any hesitation at all he stepped forward into the conference room, into a thin stream of liquid that struck him on the side of his neck. Jimmy Ramirez stepped forward, caught the Peaceforcer as he fell, and dragged him forward through the closing door.

Trent stood blankly with his wrists snaked together on the other side of the closed door.

The door opened again a second later, and Jimmy Ramirez, standing in the doorway, said, "Why are you just standing there? We're here to rescue you!"

Trent stepped inside the conference room, looking around at Denice, at Jimmy with Trent's squirt gun in his hand, at the body of the Peaceforcer on the floor.

Very calmly, he said, "What?"

There was a moment of silence.

Denice said, "We're here to—"

Jimmy said, "They're gonna brain-drain you—"

"What are you doing?"

There was another flat moment of total silence. Denice looked at Jimmy, and then at Trent, and said, very slowly, as though speaking to someone who might not be very quick on the uptake, "We came to get you out. We told them Jimmy was your lawyer and we came to rescue you."

Trent stared at them. His slowly dawning expression of utter horror must have gotten through to them. Trent said desperately, "You're *what*?"

Denice and Jimmy glanced at each other again. "Rescuing you."

"I don't *want* to be rescued." Trent felt sheer hysteria bubbling up inside himself. "That's what I have an attorney for!"

"For tonight," said Jimmy Ramirez seriously, "I'm your attorney. And we're getting you out now."

Trent looked back and forth between them, then down at the still body of the Peaceforcer on the floor. "Oh, Lord, Lord, please no. You can't be doing this. Do you know what you're doing?" The deep, hidden anger flared suddenly, broke free for just an instant. He shouted at them and could not hide the fury in his voice. "I was two to one to walk on this. Until you broke in here they had nothing." He screamed the word. *"Nothing!"*

Jimmy Ramirez froze. "Are you sure?"

Denice said, "Oh, no."

Trent took a long, shaking breath. "Did either of you talk to Beth?"

Denice said quickly, "There's been no chance. Booker Jamethon dug up your file for us; it said you were going to be brain-drained. It said Mohammed Vance was coming."

"Brain-drain requires a court order, and then that can be appealed. The appeal process can take up to nine goddamn months. The last time Mohammed Vance saw me, if he ever did, I was eleven years old. He's going to do what, identify me today?" Trent glanced down at the snakechain on his wrists. "Oh, my God. I'm fucked." He looked back up at them. "I'm totally fucked. The snakechain has to come off. Everything's blown now."

"Wait, wait." Denice Castanaveras thought furiously. "We can just leave. Wait until Officer Markson wakes up, tell him we were never here, have him walk you back to your cell, and Jimmy and I just leave."

Trent shook his head slowly, in sheer amazement. "No. How can you be so stupid? It won't work. You don't understand, either of you. We are three floors down in the PKF Detention Center in the middle of Capitol City. You've been holographed eight or nine times in the course of getting here. Every checkpoint you went through choked on your ID, it had to. Denice, you worked people as you went?"

"Of course. How else could we have gotten this far?"

Trent said softly, "You've left a trail a blind man could follow. Tomorrow the PKF is going to go through its morning reports, and there's going to be a chain of seven or eight stations where Denice Daimara and Jamos Ramirez failed admittance. So, how does it happen, that somebody who fails admittance at the first stop point even makes it to the second?

All points goes out for both of you, they drag in the watch officers and interrogate them and suddenly it becomes very clear that none of these Peaceforcers remember things the way they happened. You left them a damn calling card, Denice."

Denice had gone utterly white. Jimmy Ramirez looked very grim indeed.

Trent found his breath coming quickly, and with a conscious effort stilled himself and said quietly, "I appreciate what you tried to do, but you've really, really shot everything to hell." He stood silently for a very long moment, thinking, and then said, "And it looks like you get to rescue me as soon as I'm done rescuing you. Jimmy, help me get the Peaceforcer's thumbprint on the snake, and let's go."

Trent took the Peaceforcer's needler, gave it to Jimmy Ramirez, and took his squirt gun for himself. They left the Peaceforcer lying flat on his back by the door to the conference room, and without hurrying the three of them walked down the corridor to the nearly empty operations room Trent had seen on his way there.

Trent, in his prisoner's jumpsuit, stood well away from the glassite door while Denice rapped on the transparent sheeting. He saw very little of what happened as one of the two operators inside, a young man perhaps twenty-five years old, in black civilian clothing of a cut similar to the uniform of a Peaceforcer Elite, stood up and palmed the pressure pad to open the door, even as the woman in the room with him said something that was plainly an objection.

Trent watched Denice in the doorway and even so did not see it clearly. Denice seemed to place one hand on the man's breastbone, and touch his ankle with just the big toe of her right foot. The man went crashing backward ten full meters, directly into a long row of systerms.

The woman sitting at her desk touched one stud, and the alarms went off.

Jimmy Ramirez stood with the needler pressed against the side of the woman's neck while Trent worked at the systerm. Denice was out in the corridor, eyes completely closed, watching with other senses as the Peaceforcers on duty roused themselves.

The shrilling of the alarms was getting on Trent's nerves.

The system was familiar to Trent. The hardware was identical to the equipment Department Five used, and Trent had written software for them. He knew the protocols intimately; the software the PKF used conformed to the interface the PKF had been using since before Trent's birth, essentially unchanged for over twenty years. He switched the systerm into the master control program, requested Outside Resources, and punched in for 115005-TRNT.

The field glowed up at Trent, PASSWORD?

"Warped bastards," Trent muttered. He turned to the frightened young man in the pseudo-PKF uniform, sitting in front of another systerm nursing a broken arm. "What's the outside access password?"

The man started to say something, and the woman at the desk said sharply, "Shut up!"

From out in the corridor Denice said softly, "It's *éveil*. Hurry, Trent."

Trent punched in *éveil*, and struck the Enter key.

The systerm said WAITING—CONNECTED—PASSWORD?

Denice ducked back inside, followed closely by the sound of buzzing sonics. "Jimmy! Company!"

Trent typed, CRIME PAYS.

At point-blank range Jimmy Ramirez shot the woman in the neck with the needler and threw the needler to Denice. Denice plucked the needler out of the air one-handed, eyes still closed, stuck just her hand outside the door frame and fanned the corridor with it. The buzzing of the stunners stopped abruptly, and when Trent had time to look he saw that he was alone in the op room except for the frightened young man and the unconscious woman, whose neck was bleeding badly where Jimmy had shot her.

BOSS!

Out of the corner of his eye Trent saw Jimmy appear in the doorway, with an autoshot cradled in his arms. "It's going up, man. We gotta move!"

"Hang in there. I won't be long."

HI, JOHNNY.

I'VE BEEN WORRIED, BOSS.

THEY TOOK MY TRACESET, JOHNNY, I COULDN'T GET TO YOU. YOU KNOW WHERE I AM?

CAPITOL CITY, BOSS. PKF BOARDS.

"Trent!" There was the first touch of hysteria in Jimmy's voice.

"Hang on!" Trent yelled back, without even glancing away. JOHNNY, CAN YOU FIND ANY PICTURES OF DENICE, OR JIMMY, OR ME, ANY MENTION OF US IN THE PKF BOARDS, AND ERASE THEM?

I THINK SO, BOSS. IT'LL TAKE SOME TIME TO CHECK.

TAKE IT. Trent did not hesitate at all. JOHNNY, HOW BADLY CAN YOU DAMAGE THE BOARDS YOU HAVE ACCESS TO?

FROM THIS LOCATION? WITH THE SECURITY CLEARANCES THIS LOCATION HAS? YOU MUST BE KIDDING.

BAD?

THEY WON'T KNOW WHAT HIT THEM, BOSS. WANT ME TO TAKE IT ALL DOWN?

"As your attorney," shouted Jimmy, "I advise you to *move*, damn it!"

JOHNNY?

YES?

I'M COMING TO GET YOU. IF I DON'T MAKE IT THERE, MELT THE IMAGE COPROCESSOR AND GO REPLICANT.

There was another round of buzzing, which ceased abruptly.

I DON'T WANT TO BE A REPLICANT AI, BOSS.

DON'T ARGUE, JOHNNY. IF I'M NOT THERE WITHIN THREE HOURS, YOU'RE ON YOUR OWN.

Trent? Denice's thoughts touched his, tinged with near panic. *They're coming from the level above us, at least fifteen Peaceforcers and they're all armed. Masers, Trent, and I can't stop all of them. We have three floors to go before we even make it to the surface; we have to go. Now.*

BOSS . . . BOSS, ARE YOU THERE?

In the abrupt silence Trent looked around at the nearly empty operations room, at the frightened, staring young man. He could not have put a word to how he felt; it seemed to him that he stood at a juncture, a myriad of paths falling away from that moment, from him; that he had reached a place that was both departure and homecoming all in one. He was distantly aware of Jimmy Ramirez, felt the hot touch of Denice's thoughts hovering at the edge of his mind, and he felt suddenly, in that instant, very calm and fine, as though he had, at long last, reached the destination and the purpose for which he had always been meant.

Denice screamed, *"Trent!"*

Trent typed, TRASH THE PLACE.

He turned and ran.

The Long Run

· ———————————————— ·

2069 Gregorian

If you can keep your head while all those about you are losing theirs, then perhaps you have misunderstood the situation.

> —Graffiti on the side of the Flushing
> Street Temple of Eris in New York

· 1 ·

Emile Garon's apartment was on the southern tip of what had once been Franklin D. Roosevelt Island. The island had been renamed Moreau Island a scant five years ago, when Capitol City had reached out to encompass the island. The name was in honor of the memory of Jules Moreau, the Frenchman who had, with then–Secretary General Sarah Almundsen, guided the United Nations into the Unification War.

In 2069 Moreau Island was home to more than twenty thousand of the most powerful men and women in the Unification: Unification Councilors, PKF Elite, and other high officials of the Unification.

Emile Garon was roused from sleep by the insistent shrieking of his systerm.

He sat up in bed. A bright red image, floating off somewhere in the back of his skull, read 4:25 A.M.

"Command," he said in a voice that was still gravelly with sleep, "answer."

From the shoulders up, the bright, solid image of PKF Elite Commander Christine Mirabeau appeared at the foot of Emile Garon's bed. One of the very few female Elite, she was a pleasant and gracious woman, built like a tank, and every bit as unshakeable.

"Emile?"

He said wearily, "Yes?"

Commander Mirabeau did not hurry at all. "Congratulations, Emile. Your young man, with aid from another young man and a young woman, has broken out of the Detention Center. One civilian is severely injured, and five PKF. Two-thirds of the PKF Boards in Manhattan are out of commission, and more are going down at every moment."

Garon stared stupidly at the holo. He barely got the word out. *"Congratulations?"*

"It seems," she said without any inflection at all, "that you were correct."

It was a nightmare run down gray ferrocrete corridors, up three separate flights of stairs. Trent took the lead, and Denice covered their backs; Jimmy did not even protest at being put in the middle.

It took, in total, less than four minutes.

It seemed like an eternity.

They held running battles with Peaceforcers twice; the second time there was an Elite in the group.

The Peace Keeping Force Detention Center is near the center of that heavily guarded enclave of the Unification known as Capitol City.

Capitol City is the core of the Patrol Sectors—the place from which the world is putatively run. It is one of the smaller cities on Earth; its heavily guarded south border begins at 34th Street, and reaches north to 72nd. Its west boundary is Park Avenue; its east is the East River. It includes both Belmont and Moreau islands, in the East River, but not Grand Central Station; Capitol City's designers had recognized that the mandatory identity checks which occur when passing from Manhattan into Capitol City would have been utterly impossible had Grand Central Station been included within Capitol City's borders.

Capitol City is laid out, perhaps by accident, in a fashion that very nearly corresponds to the real power structure of the Unification. The offices of the Secretary-General are at the south end of Capitol City, near the small collection of buildings that were once all that existed of the United Nations in America; they are surrounded to the north in a loose semicircle by the offices of the elected Unification Councilors. Between them, in the very center of Capitol City, are the Ministry of Population Control and the United Nations Peace Keeping Force; with the possible exception of the Secretary-General and his webdancers, they are the two most powerful forces within the Unification. Together they occupy fully one-quarter of the ground space in Capitol City, and two of Capitol City's three spacescrapers; fully forty percent of the personnel within Capitol City work for either the PKF or the Ministry of Population Control. To the north of the Peaceforcers and the babychasers are the Prosecutor General's offices and the courts; to the north of that are Space Force, the Bureaus of Traffic Enforcement and Education, Biotech and Health.

It is usually quiet in the early hours before dawn in Capitol City. The Unification rules one world and part of another, and it is never so still, even in the dead of night, as in any city that has not tied itself so tightly to the concerns of humans in other time zones. Nonetheless, if it never achieves true tranquility, there is rarely anything exciting happening in Capitol City in the small hours of the morning.

Or in most of the rest of the day, for that matter. It was newsdancer Terry Shawmac who once wrote that the most amazing accomplishment of the Unification was that it had turned Capitol City, and in the process most of the rest of Manhattan, into a place that was both safe and dull.

The offices of the United Nations Peace Keeping Forces were heirs to what was, in 2069, a fact of life of some thirty years standing. "You just don't expect that sort of thing here in the City," one British Peaceforcer said the next day to a newsdancer from the *Electronic Times*. "It was like the tour of duty I had in the Fringe; people running and screaming everywhere, gunfire in the corridors—" The newsdancer kept the holocams on her; the Peaceforcer was visibly disturbed. "It reminded me of the things my dad used to tell me about, about all the rebellions following the Unification. That's what we all thought was happening, you know. Johnny Rebs or Erisian Claw—a bloody rebellion starting in the middle of Capitol City." In response to a question from the newsdancer she said with obvious sarcasm, "Of course I believe what I've been told. Three kids had a firefight with twenty-odd PKF, wounded thirteen of them including an Elite." The holocams stayed on her, and after a moment the woman snorted. "And one of them had a squirt gun. Right."

Monday morning, August 13, less than an hour before dawn, Trent and Denice ran across the dew-dampened grass.

They carried Jimmy Ramirez between them, running away from the reception area they had barreled their way through, away from the fading sound of the screaming and the shouts, toward the line of cars and cabs hovering next to the slidewalk. Half a dozen spyeyes littered the grass; Johnny Johnny had taken them down.

Jimmy Ramirez was not screaming; his teeth were clenched so tightly together that his breath came between them in small whistles of pain. He was still carrying one of the masers they had taken from the first batch of Peaceforcers they had run into, right hand clutching the weapon as though it were his link to life.

Jimmy's left arm, where the laser buried in the Peaceforcer Elite's fist had touched, was gone from the elbow down.

A maser burst had taken him against the back of his calves.

Forty meters of well-tended grass separated the entrance to the Detention Center from 57th Street proper. Trent had only a second to glance down the line of waiting vehicles; five Peugeot cabs, two independents, and a single black, unmarked Chandler sedan. Trent was vaguely aware of Denice, of her thoughts touching his. He said nothing aloud; together they ran down the slidewalk toward the sedan. It was hardtopped rather than canopied, with four separate doors for the front and back seats.

The front left seat was reclined all the way back; Bird, sitting up, rubbed his eyes sleepily and said blankly, "What took you so long?"

Leaving Capitol City is not difficult. There are no stop points, no identity checks. There are PKF patrols at every intersection around the border, but they check only incoming traffic.

Trent in fact owned three different cars, none of them under his own name. Only two of the three vehicles actually ran. The third car was properly registered each year, but only so that its license caster ID was kept current. As the car, with its windows opaqued, left Capitol City proper, floating at an even forty-five kph past the PKF check stations, the car's license caster flickered for a moment, declared to the world that it was now a 2055 Chandler HammerHead running under carcomp control, and applied to TransCon for handling instructions.

The entire process took perhaps a full second; TransCon queried the vehicle's destination, and Trent said aloud, "The Red Line Hotel."

The carcomp said, "Destination approved. Proceeding."

Unobtrusively, over the space of nearly an entire minute, the car's polypaint, under the light from the street lamps and PKF glowfloats, brightened from black to pale blue. The vehicle's shape altered, memory plastic warping itself into a very close approximation of the lines of a '55 HammerHead.

Behind them, back toward Capitol City, all was quiet. Trent sat in the front seat with Bird, listening on the car's radio to PKF and City Police bands. There was nothing abnormal on the City Police bands; PKF bands were almost totally silent except for two channels where Peaceforcers speaking in monotones kept assuring one another that everything was under control, and no, they didn't know yet what was happening either.

Punching for 115005-TRNT on the car's systerm got him nothing at all. Either the web angels had taken Johnny Johnny down, or they'd come so close that Johnny had shut down entirely for fear that they would.

Denice, in the back seat with Jimmy, said, "What?"

Trent said, "How's he doing?"

"I put him to sleep. How are you doing?"

"What do you mean?"

"You're talking to yourself, Trent. What did you just say?"

"Win a few, lose a few." Trent leaned back in his seat, relaxed into the gentle hum of the engines. He was aware of Bird watching him, of the weight of the boy's gaze upon him. "Carl—our father," he said to Bird, "used to say that, when things were so fucked up he didn't know what to do next."

The response left Bird visibly disturbed. The redhead said, after a moment, "And you don't know what to do now?"

"I'm afraid not, Bird." Trent stared out through the windshield, at the maze of spacescrapers, the aerial walkways and skystreets, the predawn pedestrians, the cars and cabs and buses that clogged the thoroughfares of the city. "I need my traceset."

Denice said softly, "Trent?"

"I need my Image."

They took a two-room suite on the thirty-second floor of the Red Line Hotel. Denice checked them in under a false name while Jodi Jodi took Trent and Jimmy up through the service maglev. They had called ahead while still in the car; Tiny was waiting for them in their suite, with the doctor, when Trent carried Jimmy through the door. Jimmy was still unconscious; the doctor took one look at the missing arm, snapped, "Twice on this, Tiny, triple if the Peaceforcers did it," laid Jimmy down on the bed, sliced his shirt off and got to work.

Trent watched long enough to be certain the doctor knew what she was doing—a Fringe habit, and one he doubted he would ever shake—and went into the second room. Jodi Jodi and Tiny followed him in; Jodi Jodi closed the door behind them.

"How bad is it, Trent?"

Trent was undressing already, wadding the blue prison jumpsuit into a ball and tossing it to Jodi Jodi. "Burn this, please. I haven't figured out how bad it is yet. If you mean Jimmy, I think he'll be okay. Not much blood loss; he'll need a new arm grown, and maybe new legs, but he's not in danger of dying. Can you get me clothes?"

"What do you need?"

"A suit. Shoulder silks, no tie. Business clothes, conservative cut, they need to hang loose. Shoes I can run in." He stepped into the shower, ran it as hot as he could stand to get the smell of four days imprisonment off him. He spoke over the sound of the shower. "Can you get me a traceset? And an emblade?"

"Maybe. I'll check."

"My squirt gun's empty. Fadeaway?"

"Not a chance."

"How about an Image coprocessor?"

"This early in the day? You've got to be kidding."

"Then I have to go get your brother." Tiny was there; without even thinking about it Trent avoided using Johnny Johnny's name. "Bird should be all right; he was in the car the whole time, they won't have pictures of him. Jimmy and Denice—it depends on how well my Image took down the Peaceforcer Boards. All their records of the escape have to be gone. Without me helping I don't know if my Image was up to that."

"What about you, Trent?"

Trent ducked his head under the spray of water, punched

for shampoo and waited while the spray turned sudsy, punched again for rinse and waited until the soap was entirely off him, stepped out of the shower and started drying himself with one of the huge, dove-gray towels hanging on the rack. "What about me?"

Not a full minute after Trent had asked for it, Tiny laid out on the bed the suit Trent had requested, a black pinstripe that looked to Trent to be a half size too large, black socks, and a pair of black loafers with soft soles. There was an emblade lying, turned off, next to the shoes.

Jodi Jodi said, "What are you going to do?"

Trent dressed while talking. "They had me for four days. They have my prints, my face, my retinal scan, all in secure off-line storage. I'm almost certain they didn't get my voice print at any point, and they don't, fortunately, have my gene map; until a couple hours ago I don't think anybody believed Emile that I was a genie. Extensive biosculpture can take care of what they do have on me. Right now my Image isn't answering his calls, and even if he was I don't have hardware for him to come over to. I have to go get him. Nobody saw Bird, so you can send him out for things. Jimmy and Denice stay here until we know better what's happening. Have Denice call in sick with Madame Gleygavass; if Peaceforcers don't show up for Denice by the end of the day, they won't."

"Trent?"

Trent stopped tucking in his shirt at the tone in her voice. He looked over at her, standing next to Tiny. Neither one of them would quite look at him. "Yes?"

"Denice," said Jodi Jodi. "The girl has green eyes, Trent."

"So?"

"We can hide Jimmy, Trent. If we have to hide her as well it's a problem."

Trent spoke very slowly. "How so?"

"There's prejudice, Trent. When you're gone—"

Trent winced.

"Trent, it needs to be said. I talked to Jimmy before he went to get you . . ." She seemed at a momentary loss for words. "Between the PKF, the Syndic and the Old Ones—my God, even the gendarmes will get in on it, they'll have to—you can't stay in the Patrol Sectors any longer. Maybe you can't stay in New York Metro, even if you go back to the Fringe. I don't know." She did look at him now, without flinching. "Your friends and acquaintances are known. We're safe from anything the PKF is really going to care about. Jimmy and Bird aren't, but Bird wasn't seen; Jimmy we can hide, maybe have him sculpted. And bottom line is, he's not a genie, and I expect any gengineer in the world could testify to that. But Trent, my friend," she said very gently, "that won't work for you, and it won't work for her, will it? You really did come out of Project Superman, both of you, and any gengineer could prove it. And she's a telepath."

Trent glanced at Tiny, said nothing.

Jodi Jodi interpreted the glance correctly, sighed. "Tiny's safe or I wouldn't be talking like this. Trent, listen: if it turns out she's wanted, we can hide her here for a while. But only a while."

Trent was silent for a moment, then nodded. "Okay. Thanks. If it turns out to be necessary, I'll think of something. The Red Line is safe for her?"

"For a while," said Jodi Jodi again. "If the Peaceforcers suspect anything, it's not. Five of the seven people on the Red Line's Board of Directors are French, Trent."

"I understand." Trent slipped into the coat, sat down on the bed, and pulled on the socks and shoes. "How do I look?"

"Your silks are crooked." Jodi Jodi adjusted them herself, stepped back and said, "Now they're okay."

"Thank you," said Trent simply. "I have to go."

She nodded. "Be careful."

"As opposed to what?" He opened the door to the front room without waiting for an answer, looked out quickly. The doctor had an IV dripping into Jimmy's intact arm, was trimming the cauterized flesh away from the stump of the other. Denice had finished checking them in; she sat on the side of the bed, holding Jimmy's remaining hand between hers. She looked up at the whispery sound of the door curling open, met Trent's eyes. *Trent?*

He stepped forward, with Jodi Jodi and Tiny following him. "Yes?"

"Where are you going?"

"You know."

Trent was struck abruptly by how utterly exhausted Denice looked, at how very pale she was. "Trent. That's the one place in the world where they're *sure* to be expecting you."

"I lost Ralf the Wise and Powerful," Trent said quietly. "I'm not going to lose him as well."

Denice Castanaveras stared at him as though she were certain he had lost his mind. "Trent, he's just a *program*."

"So," said Trent with perfect evenness, "are you."

It was nearly 8:00 A.M. when the car pulled onto the Manhattan Bridge and drove out over the East River. It was a misty, pale gray morning, with high clouds blocking the sunlight; a morning that matched Trent's mood exactly. He'd instructed the car to take him to Manuelo's Italian Restaurant, on Clinton Avenue three blocks to the west of Kandel Microlectrics Sales and Repair. Assuming TransCon was monitoring traffic to and from the shop—and they were, or they were fools, which Trent did not assume—still, a destination three blocks away from the shop should be safe.

He listened to the radio on his way home. There was nothing of note; the PKF admitted to a disturbance in the Detention Center in Capitol City, but no more than that. There was no word whatsoever that there had been an escape by a Detention Center prisoner. Trent considered calling Beth, but aside from apologizing for the stupidity of his friends he could not imagine what he would say to her.

The car parked itself on the first level of the garage which extended three levels beneath Manuelo's. The restaurant was not open, and would not be until ten o'clock, for early lunch. Trent took the maglev up one floor, to the slidewalk, and walked down Park, in the dark area beneath the Bullet's monorail, to the rear entrance of the Temple of Eris.

Reverend Andy answered the back door himself. He was a huge, amazingly large black man, two hundred twenty centimeters tall, one hundred twenty kilos, who had once been a professional football player. Many people, those who knew him only casually, found him intimidating. Reverend Andy seemed not at all surprised to see Trent standing on his back doorstep; he poked his head briefly outside, looked quickly up and down the street, and motioned Trent to come in.

"Come on," he said, "upstairs." Wrapping his sari more tightly about himself, Reverend Andy moved quickly up the flight of stairs at the back of the temple. Trent followed him without speaking. The buildings which held the Temple of Eris and Kandel Microlectrics were laid out in almost identical fashion; the same company had designed and built both of them.

Once they reached the second floor Reverend Andy seemed to relax a bit. He ushered Trent into his office, palmed the door shut behind him, and plopped down into the overstuffed leather chair behind his desk. The chair creaked alarmingly beneath him.

"Jimmy and Bird," Reverend Andy said slowly, "they busted you out?"

"Yes. How's Jack?"

Reverend Andy shrugged. "He's staying with us. Peace-forcers sealed the shop, but they don't seem interested in him. He'd be asleep right now; it's been a tough week for the poor guy, he ain't young no more." Reverend Andy paused a beat. "You know I got no connections with the Claw, Trent. I run a clean Temple, no politics."

"I know."

"Okay." He fixed Trent with a piercing gaze. "What they say about you, Trent. Being a genie and all, it's true?"

"Yes."

Reverend Andy nodded. One hand tugged at his bushy, half-gray beard. "You come from that Project Superman?"

"Yes."

"You read minds?"

"No."

Reverend Andy exhaled slowly, a long, deep breath. "Thank the Good Lord and his Prophet Harry. I've got some secrets, I don't mind telling you, matters of the confessional circles and the Tax Boards, I wouldn't want to see spread around. Well." He looked up at Trent suddenly. "What'd you come back for, Trent?"

"My Image coprocessor, Reverend."

Reverend Andy looked interested. "You're really a Player like they said?"

"Yes."

"By Harry." Reverend Andy leaned forward in his chair. "All this time I've thought you were just a nice, polite young man who stole things for a living, and here you are a genie and a Player all at once."

"We have walls in common, Reverend, and I need to use one. The entrances to the shop will be sealed. If I cut through them the word goes up right then. As long as there's no motion sensors left inside the shop, chopping through the wall won't alert anybody at all."

Reverend Andy made a dismissing motion. "Don't talk to

me about motion sensors and the like, Trent. I'm just a preacher. You should know, there are Peaceforcers in front of Jack's shop, just parked there. Been there about two hours. And they got with them a pair of those crawly things that—"

"Hunting waldos."

"Them," Reverend Andy agreed.

"Anything else?"

"Can't think of anything."

Trent waited.

Finally Reverend Andy, looking distinctly uncomfortable, said, "Damn it, Trent, you chop through the wall and it looks like we helped you in."

"There's no proof, Reverend. Nobody saw anything, nobody heard anything except you; that's the truth. And the PKF doesn't mess with holy men; they wouldn't dare braindrain you, for example. If you do get annoyed by the PKF, my lawyer, Beth Davenport, is on retainer; it's got around twenty-five hours left on it before she needs to be paid again. She'll put a stop to it."

"What's in it for the Temple, Trent?"

"I have nothing to offer you, Reverend."

Reverend Andy looked desperately unhappy about it all.

Trent said, "I need your help."

Reverend Andy came to his feet, moving his vast bulk with such ease and grace that Trent was forcibly reminded that the man had been one of the most feared linebackers in the history of the WFL. "Stay here," he said sharply. "Let me clear people out of the way, and then come downstairs when I call. You can cut through from the kitchen; it'll look like you didn't get so far into the Temple, so maybe nobody saw you." The Reverend stopped in the doorway. "You owe me one, man."

Reverend Andy had helped get Trent and Jodi Jodi and Bird and Jimmy out of the Fringe, had transported them into the Patrol Sectors inside a Temple bus.

Trent shrugged and looked at the man and said simply, "Reverend Andy, I owe you everything. I couldn't pay you back if I spent my life at it."

For a single instant a look that was almost pain flickered across the huge man's features, and then vanished. He came very close to smiling for the first time since Trent had known him. "You don't pay it back, little brother. You can't." He stood there in the doorway for a second longer. "You just send it on down the line."

The section of wall, about a meter in diameter, came loose; Trent reached forward as the chunk fell, caught it, and lowered it to the ground gently. He waited, twenty, thirty seconds, for a response from inside the shop.

Nothing.

Trent turned off the emblade, put it in his pocket, and ducked his head, crouching low to crawl through the new entrance; he had cut the wall at its lowest point, so that the piece, if he had missed it after knocking it through, would have no great distance to fall. He came through the wall in the back of the shop, underneath the workbench Old Jack normally used. He crouched in his suit underneath the workbench, listening to the silence, balancing himself with the fingers of both hands.

Still nothing.

He moved forward slowly into the walkway between the benches; the stairway leading up to the second floor was fifteen meters to his right, and the shop's entrance was forty meters to his left. He glanced toward the front of the shop; he could see the PKF hovercar Reverend Andy had told him about, parked across the street from the shop. From the angle at which it was parked, he could not see either of the PKF inside, which was just fine; they would not be able to see him either. He backed toward the stairway, still stooping to keep the workbenches between him and the entrance, and had taken two steps up the stairwell when the quiet metallic clattering sound, the sound of steel on tile, froze him where he stood.

They'd left a hunting waldo inside the shop. Trent had only a moment to look at the low-slung waldo, to watch it in its horribly efficient, softly clicking glide across the floor toward him. He had just an instant to notice how brilliantly designed the thing was, its terrible functionality.

Trent turned and sprinted up the stairs, hit the top of the stairwell and cut left into the small bedroom which led upward to the third floor, ran into the bathroom and grabbed the bazooka that had been there when he moved in. Then, it had not been loaded; now it was.

He had never bothered to practice firing the thing; he had

never truly expected to have a target that he was willing to fire it upon.

Safety off. *What's taking the waldo so long? Stairs? It has problems with stairs?* The sight popped up the instant the safety mechanism was disengaged. Trent hefted the thing up to his shoulder and waited until he saw the first flicker of motion in the doorway, and depressed the stud. The wall behind him slammed into him suddenly; a huge clap of thunder boomed around him, and for a moment he thought the bazooka had misfired. His ears were ringing and his shoulder, where he had braced the bazooka, felt as though it had been struck with a sledgehammer. The air was amazingly hot, burning his lungs. The back of his skull was sore where the recoil had slammed him into the wall.

There was nothing at all in the hallway, including the hallway. A gaping hole where he had briefly seen the waldo, two meters in diameter, let Trent look straight down into the shop, through the clearing smoke, directly into the upturned features of Peaceforcer Elite Emile Garon.

Their eyes touched for just a moment. Then Trent was on his feet and moving. He yelled, "Lights *off,*" slapped the pressure pad on the wall and sprinted up the stairs as the wall resealed itself behind him. Halfway up he shouted, "Johnny, blow the fadeaway," heard a muffled whump from downstairs and smelled the sweet, penetrating scent of the Complex 8-A as the fadeaway bomb inundated the room beneath him. He ran the rest of the way up the stairs, into his apartment. At the tub he lay down on his stomach, reached in with his right arm and pulled at one of the handles embedded in the side of the tub. The handle resisted and he pulled again, harder, and the entire bottom of the tub fell away, pouring the small pool down into the stairwell Trent had just come up, filling the stairwell to a height of three meters. If Garon managed to push back the correct section of wall, against the full weight of the water, he would be greeted with a small tidal wave.

Johnny Johnny said, "Welcome home, Boss."

Trent came to his feet, ran to the workstation on the desk next to his bed. His handheld, which included Johnny Johnny's Image coprocessor circuitry, was plugged into the side of the systerm; Trent ripped it free and pushed it into the inner coat pocket of his suit. Johnny Johnny's voice came from inside the pocket. "I set up all the records to wipe on your voice command, Boss. Say, 'Kwazy Wabbit.'"

Trent pushed the desk's upper right-hand drawer, paused a second and pressed it again, twice, in quick succession. The drawer slid open and Trent took from it a small package in antistatic lining. The package contained the most compact wealth in the world, more compact than gemstones, more compact than stamps. It held six and a half terabytes—forty-five thousand Credit Units worth—of RTS, hot RAM.

A bright thin line of red light reached up from the floor, before Trent's eyes. Trent said in a flatly conversational tone of voice, "Kwazy Wabbit." His traceset was on the bench on the other side of the room, hooked into the full sensory systerm. The thought struck Trent, in the instant that the scarlet laser beam reached up through the floor and the burnished wooden floor split apart, the laser beam tracking in a rough circle around the spot where Trent stood, that the cyborg was destroying a floor it had cost him two thousand Credit Units to lay down. A startling flare of pure anger touched him, and then he reached up, grabbed the cord hanging from the roof, and pulled down the folding stairs which led to the roof, as the floor beneath him fell entirely away. He scrambled up the stairs, three meters to the ceiling, and came up onto the gravel surface of the roof on his hands and knees, and then for the first time looked back down into the ruins of his home. Two stories beneath him, Emile Garon looked up at Trent through the hole in what had once been a two thousand CU floor.

The cyborg leaped straight up.

For a single fascinated, horrified moment, Trent thought the cyborg would reach the roof with that one leap. He did not quite; Garon came to a rest standing on the bottom step of the stairs. With immaculate calmness, as Garon came swiftly up the stairway, Trent withdrew his emblade, turned it on, cut the stairs free and watched Emile Garon and the stairs fall together in utter silence, fifteen meters down to the second floor of the shop.

Trent came to his feet slowly, and looked around.

His right arm was still dripping wet.

He seemed to himself to be completely calm, completely in control.

Trent did not have the vaguest idea what to do next. One jump would bring Garon back up to the third floor; another would take him up through the opening in the roof which the folding stairs had once filled. Trent walked to the side of the roof and looked over the edge; in the front of the building a pair of Peaceforcer cars were parked, autoshots and masers trained on the front entrance to the shop. The west side of the building was also covered by a PKF vehicle. The south side overlooked the small alleyway which led out behind the shop, and was completely empty.

He was three stories up and there was no way down at all.

When Trent turned away from looking down into the alley, Emile Garon was pulling himself up through the stairwell exit. He was injured; something had actually cut through the phenomenally tough false skin which covered every exposed area of his body, and blood trickled down his cheek. His black hair was pale with plaster dust.

Trent said, "You're hurt."

Garon stood slowly, glancing warily around the roof to see if further surprises awaited him. "An Elite cyborg is fairly heavy, Monsieur Trent. We do not fall well and we do not like heights." He stood utterly still, like a 'bot, just looking at Trent. "What now?"

Garon was six meters away from Trent, standing right next to the hole in the roof where the stairs had been. Without giving himself time to think about it, Trent took a slow step backward. "I suppose you want me to surrender?"

"If you would."

Trent took another step, and this time Garon did follow him, took a step away from the stairwell, from Garon's only way off the roof. "I'd rather not," said Trent.

"I do not want to hurt you, child. I was right about you; you are a very precious thing, Trent. You will not be brain-drained if you cooperate, I promise," said Garon softly. "The Unification would hardly waste your unique skills so."

Trent took another step backward, and another. "I don't doubt it, Emile. I was a slave through most of my childhood because of the Unification's unwillingness to waste my unique skills."

The Peaceforcer approached him across the roof. "How old are you now, Trent?"

"Eighteen." The back of Trent's right heel touched the lip of the small rise that ran around the perimeter of the roof.

"And it *was* you," said Emile, with what Trent thought honest wonder in his voice, "seven years ago, in the InfoNet. You were eleven years old."

"Yeah." Trent did not dare look behind himself.

"So young, to have done so much. I shall," he told Trent, "plead for leniency in your case."

Trent took a long, deep breath. His nerves steadied, and everything came into focus. "Well, there are advantages to being young." Garon was still too close to the stairwell.

The Peaceforcer came a step closer. "Oh?"

"Agility," said Trent. How long would it take Garon to reach the ground? "And I'm told we heal fast."

Garon had covered nearly half the distance between the stairwell and Trent. He stopped quickly, in midstep. "We are three stories up, child. Please don't."

Trent looked up, at the gray, cloud-covered sky. There was the faintest suggestion of mist in the air, of dampness. It was as though he stood outside of himself, and watched without interest as his body prepared to do something very dangerous. His eyes came back down from heaven, and stared straight at the Peaceforcer Elite. "Catch me," he said softly, "if you can."

The cyborg moved toward him in a blur of motion so fast Trent barely saw it. He pushed with his toes, and went backward, out over the edge and into the empty air.

· 2 ·

Something brushed against the sole of his right foot.

He turned in midair and almost made it, struck the ground and rolled into the fall. He came out of it moving, with a shrill grating pain in his right knee, moving at very near a dead run down the alleyway toward the garage, half a block away.

He did not slow, did not dare look back. He could hear odd sounds from far down the alleyway—what did a two-hundred-dred-kilo Peaceforcer Elite running across a ferrocrete alleyway sound like?

Trent ran faster, ran until his knee threatened to give way. He reached the garage at the end of the alleyway, slapped the pressure pad once, so fast the pad had no time to ID his palm, waited a moment and then touched it again more slowly. The garage door curled open from the ground up, slowly; Trent dropped to his belly and wriggled through under the opening door, came back up again, and made his way to the car, keeping most of his weight on the left leg.

The car was a '61 Chandler MetalSmith Mark III.

With a steering wheel.

It was the model his father had owned, the same model as the car Carl Castanaveras had owned before his death, before the car itself had been proscribed, along with all other manually operable vehicles, by the Unification Council. Possession of an unmodified Chandler MetalSmith Mark III, inside TransCon's Automated Traffic Control Regions, was good for five to fifteen years in a Public Labor Works Battalion.

It was capable of true flight, and on the ground it was the fastest hovercar anyone had ever built.

Trent had the canopy raised and was inside the car before the garage door was a quarter of the way up. One finger touched the ignition, brought the fans up and the MetalSmith rocked once and then lifted smoothly forty centimeters above the floor of the garage. The same procedure brought the turbines up with a smooth, deep-throated hum, feeding fuel to the turbojets at the rear of the car.

The garage door was nearly halfway open.

The steering wheel unlocked with a smooth click. Even in '61 a carcomp had been mandatory equipment, but on every machine Chandler had built until '64, the carcomp had not even turned itself on until so instructed by its operator.

Trent did not intend to turn the carcomp on; it was certain to disapprove of his driving. Trent had just finished activating the impact field, glanced up once again through the nearly open garage door, out at the empty alleyway, had the brief flash of a thought *what could possibly be taking him so long* and then the Peaceforcer's AeroSmith descended gently, straight out of the sky, and came to a halt hovering above the pavement not twenty meters away from Trent. The MetalSmith's canopy began vibrating instantly; Garon was trying sonics. A pair of autoshots were tracking him as well, and Trent did not wait to see anything further; he punched the throttle to full acceleration.

The autoshots could not have been set for full automatic; Garon had time for only a single blast. The pellets struck the MetalSmith's canopy, cracked it slightly, and then the MetalSmith hammered into the Peaceforcer vehicle, twisted Garon's car until Garon's left front fender was smashed tightly into the side of the alleyway, and the car itself blocked

Trent's passage out of the alleyway. Trent did not hesitate, did not even give himself time to think about it; he lit the Metal-Smith's turbojets at redline and the MetalSmith hung on Garon's vehicle for just a second, and then leaped up like a living thing and shoved its way straight up and over the top of the AeroSmith.

In his worst nightmares Trent had never expected to drive the MetalSmith; he had purchased it on Booker Jamethon's advice, for use in the event that he ever needed to make a high-speed run across the water.

The alleyway let out onto Ryerson; the car hit the street at seventy kph, and Trent tried to make a left turn. He had never driven a vehicle of any description at such speeds; the Metal-Smith yawed, lifted its right side to direct its fans against the vehicle's direction of travel, climbed up onto the slidewalk and smashed into the front of a closed beauty parlor.

In a PKF patrol vehicle across the street, a single Peaceforcer looked briefly startled. Trent barely glanced at him as he used the nose jets, pulled back away from the beauty shop and drove slowly and very carefully along the slidewalk until he reached a spot where he could bring the car back down onto the street.

In older action sensables made before manually operable vehicles had been outlawed, Trent remembered scenes where the hero or heroine had driven madly through crowded streets at two hundred or two hundred and fifty kilometers per hour. For the first time he wondered how they'd done it; the Peaceforcer behind him, making a U-turn to follow him down Ryerson, smashed into a cab almost instantly. Trent reached Flushing, turned right onto Flushing, and joined the flow of vehicles moving evenly down the street. He drove briefly east, made a left on Williamsburg and another onto Kent, following as closely as he was able the driving patterns of the carcomp-controlled vehicles around him.

Johnny Johnny's voice said softly, from inside Trent's coat, "What's happening, Boss?"

Two AeroSmiths appeared in the view from Trent's rear cameras, moving north on Kent, hovering five meters above the flow of street traffic. "Bad stuff, Johnny." The Peaceforcer vehicles were gaining on him. They had not seen him yet, but it was only a matter of moments. One of the vehicles had a smashed front left fender: Garon. "Really bad stuff."

Johnny Johnny said, "Oh."

"I really don't like this," said Trent under his breath. An AeroSmith such as the Peaceforcers used was not, properly speaking, a hovercar at all; they were aircraft that could, if they had to, drive in traffic. Taking to the air was not necessarily a bright way to lose his pursuit.

But the uncompleted Hoffman Spacescraper was only eight blocks away.

And Peaceforcers Elite did not like heights.

He brought the fans up to one half, and the MetalSmith surged upward, into plain sight of the pursuing Peaceforcers; snapped the MetalSmith's wings open, hit the rear turbojets at full, and headed for the Hoffman Spacescraper.

It was a long, slow climb, eight blocks north and three kilometers straight up, with the Peaceforcers gaining on him all the way. A small fleet of AeroSmiths followed the lead pair: nearly fifteen cars full of Peaceforcers. Trent's teeth ached; Garon and the car with him were aiming their sonics at him. The MetalSmith was still too far away for the sonics to be dangerous; but they made the car's canopy buzz, made his teeth hurt.

He thought about turning the MetalSmith's radio on and listening in on the PKF, but couldn't think of anything that it would gain him. They knew where he was, he knew where they were.

The spacescraper grew with agonizing slowness, from a distant landmark to a towering monolith that blocked out half of Trent's sky. The tiny squares on the spacescraper's sides became huge offices; people inside were flocking to the windows to watch the drama that the Boards had notified them was unfolding.

At two kilometers' height Trent was only thirty meters from the side of the spacescraper. The MetalSmith could not go straight up; Trent took it around the spacescraper, began circling the two-block-square structure as the MetalSmith rose, lazy loops that took the MetalSmith up some three hundred meters per circuit. The AeroSmiths had no such limitation; they reached the same altitude as the MetalSmith while Trent was still two hundred meters below the level where the spacescraper's exterior walls ceased. The Peaceforcers did not fire upon him with their autoshots; they kept the sonics focused on the car, and Trent felt himself becoming drowsy.

Two hundred meters . . . one-forty . . . eighty meters left. Trent found himself yawning. *If I just close my eyes for a moment,* he thought, *I can rest and then . . .*

The walls were gone.

Trent brought the MetalSmith around in a slow, gentle loop, smiling dreamily, and at over a hundred and fifty kilometers an hour flew straight into the superstructure of the Hoffman Spacescraper.

The voice nagged at him and wouldn't stop.

In his entire life Trent could not recall any physical pain to match the feeling that greeted him upon his ascent into consciousness. The knee he had injured earlier was hurt worse now, a grinding flare of agony that outstripped even the pain from the time when he was thirteen and the Temple Dragons had taken turns beating him.

The car was half on its side, jammed in between a pair of twisted girders. The canopy was completely shattered; jagged pieces still hung in the frame, but most of it was gone.

". . . Boss! Damn it, Boss, what's happening? I'm stuck in the goddamn handheld and I can't see a thing! Boss? Talk to me, Boss, I'm getting scared and—"

Trent said blurrily, "Be quiet." Johnny Johnny's voice cut off immediately. Trent remembered the impact field cutting in as the car struck; it was still turned on, making breathing difficult, movement all but impossible. He reached forward, under the dash, touched the emergency release and suddenly he could breathe again.

The quick cold rush of air into his lungs brought him the rest of the way back. His vision cleared, and he became aware of where he was. He moved carefully, pulling his damaged right leg out from beneath the dashboard and climbing up through the shattered canopy.

He was three kilometers above the surface of the world, up where the winds were fierce and cold. The finished sections of the spacescraper were ten floors beneath him. The Metal-Smith had penetrated twenty meters into the structure of the spacescraper, twenty meters away from the long drop to the Earth below.

From twenty meters away, from Emile Garon's vehicle, hovering just outside the twisted hole the MetalSmith had torn into the side of the spacescraper, the sonics struck Trent like a blow. Trent did not even think about what he was doing; he pulled himself the rest of the way out of the Metal-Smith while he was still able, out into the maze of girders. There was no floor at all, only a mass of intersecting beams and girders, and a drop of ten stories to the roof of the last floor where construction had been finished. He lay down on a girder, hung by hands that were already growing numb from the sonics, and dropped down five meters to the next level.

He struck the beam hard; the world went away again.

He came back to the world to find himself staring at the rough gray plastisteel surface of the girder he was clutching.

The thought came to Trent slowly.

There was a maglev at the center of the spacescraper.

He raised his head slowly—just his head, no other part of his body, not letting go of his grip on the girder at all—and looked through the maze of structural plastisteel, into the center of the spacescraper. At its base the spacescraper covered two square blocks, but it tapered as it got higher. The car had crashed some twenty meters in; the center of the spacescraper could not be more than about thirty meters away.

Ignoring the pain in his knee, Trent began crawling.

Behind him he could hear something, he was not quite sure what; he kept crawling, did not look back. Through the infrastructure of the beams, a large open space began to appear. Before he reached it, the beam he was on intersected another beam that was nearly a full meter wide, with a line of dead glowpaint running down the girder's center; Trent crawled onto what was obviously intended as a walkway, and with incredible slowness brought himself to his feet. He walked down the very center of the beam, ignoring by sheer force of will the rasping pain in his knee, freezing motionless with every gust of wind, toward the place where the maglev platform had to be.

At the very center of the spacescraper there was a gaping shaft, a square fully thirty meters on a side. The walkway Trent was on ran all the way around the edge of the shaft; looking down, Trent could see the maglev platform itself, nine floors beneath him. It was only nine floors, not three kilometers, and still it was high enough that something inside him locked up for a moment at the sight.

He looked up again and Emile Garon was standing on the other side of the maglev shaft. The shock was so great Trent swayed and nearly fell, grabbed at the nearest girder and held tightly to it.

Garon was actually grinning at Trent, face creased in a position that was, for a Peaceforcer Elite, entirely unnatural. His voice carried clearly across the distance. "You are the most amazing person I have ever met."

The controls to the maglev were not ten meters away from Trent, on Trent's side of the shaft; Garon would have to come all the way around the shaft to reach them. Trent moved as quickly as he was able to toward the controls, not looking down at all. He reached the controls and touched the pressure point marked UP.

The maglev platform, nine stories beneath them, began moving up. When it reached Trent's level, Emile Garon would simply walk across the platform and take him.

Trent touched the pressure point marked STOP. The maglev ceased moving instantly.

Garon stood, watching Trent.

There was no way the maglev was going to work.

Garon had been alone in his vehicle.

There would be nobody in it now.

Garon called, "Will you see us both killed? Monsieur Trent, this is pointless. Will you not surrender now?"

Surely the maglev had not been the only way to get from one floor to another? Trent looked around slowly, at the abandoned jungle of girders and walkways. For the first time he looked at the vertical that he was holding onto; there were ridges cut in the surface of the plastisteel. Trent dug his fingertips into one; shallow, not really intended to be climbed by hand, but serviceable.

Trent yelled back at Garon, "Yes!" and muttered under his breath, "Yes, I won't, frog." He reached up as high as he could, dug his fingertips in, and pulled himself up. Left foot into one ridge, right foot hanging free, and with two hands and one leg began climbing.

Garon simply stared at Trent as Trent climbed, and then the red laser flicked out from Garon's clenched fist, touched plastisteel only centimeters from Trent's hand. The pain struck Trent after a moment had passed, flowered slowly at the edges of his awareness. Trent moved around as quickly as he was able to the other side of the girder, so that the bulk of the vertical was between himself and Garon, and kept climbing. The laser flicked past both sides of the girder without touching Trent, and then stopped. Trent spent no time worrying about why the cyborg had quit shooting at him; two meters left, and then one, and he pulled himself back up onto the level he had originally crashed on. He took a moment, looked down and saw Garon attempting the same climb on a different girder; he was barely a quarter of the way up, moving with a degree of caution that brought his words back to Trent forcibly: *"We do not fall well and we do not like heights."*

To the west Trent could see the twisted tunnel of snapped girders and beams where the MetalSmith had crashed. Garon's AeroSmith had been brought down to a truly precarious landing just inside that corridor, not five meters from the edge, front and rear of the vehicle balanced on a pair of girders that the MetalSmith had damaged, stretched, on its way in. The AeroSmith wobbled slightly in the wind. Trent stood for a moment utterly motionless, simply looking at the AeroSmith in complete disbelief. Garon had gotten out of his vehicle, with the vehicle swaying in the wind like that, *to make an arrest?*

Garon, thought Trent clearly, slightly amazed that it had taken him so long to realize something that was, after all, quite obvious, *is crazy.* Swaying slightly with simple exhaustion, Trent glanced down again; Garon was only halfway done with the climb. Two hundred kilos moving upward on his fingers and toes: it was something the Elite's designers had clearly never anticipated. "Goddamn fanatics," said Trent to the wind, moving again toward the AeroSmith, "I *hate* fanatics."

He advanced along the beam slowly, distantly aware of how close he was to the limits of his endurance, not looking back. The entire area around the MetalSmith was a treacherous mess; Trent skirted it carefully, moving parallel to the corridor where the MetalSmith had torn its way into the spacescraper. He passed the MetalSmith without looking at it; even if it was still functional, he needed something that could reach the ground at least as fast as the vehicles of the Peaceforcers who were swarming outside around the perimeter of the spacescraper. He could see them now, twenty or thirty AeroSmiths in the black and silver of the United Nations Peace Keeping Force, making slow circuits of the spacescraper.

He was on the correct side of the corridor, the north side, where Garon had left his vehicle. Looking back, Trent could see Garon himself; he had come up on the wrong side of the wrecked passageway and was following Trent, gaining on him, behind Trent and fifteen meters to his left, without seeming to realize that there was no way for him to cross that empty space.

The AeroSmith was only fifteen meters past Trent's car; it took Trent nearly half a minute to traverse the distance. His right leg had turned into a single shriek of pain; the muscles in his thigh were cramping, seizing up and relaxing again without any particular pattern. In his mind he had planned how things would go: get into the AeroSmith, pull the machine back out into the empty air, and let it fall. Garon would be left on the spacescraper; with luck none of the Peaceforcers in their AeroSmiths would be foolish enough to follow him as his stolen vehicle plummeted toward the ground.

He had reached Garon's AeroSmith. The car rested on a diagonal slant, in touch with the girders supporting it at only two points. Garon had turned the fans off; stupid. They would have helped stabilize the thing. Garon came even with him at that moment, standing on the other side of the divide, arm extended and rigid, the glowing cherry laser in his fist pointed directly at Trent. The cyborg's voice was utterly dead, utterly without inflection. "If you move, monsieur, I will kill you."

From somewhere Trent found the strength to reply. "We're three klicks up, Emile. Did you lock the car behind you?" Trent did not wait for a reply; without moving anything but his hand he laid his palm flat against the pressure pad that opened the canopy, and the canopy swung up.

Garon fired. The canopy swung smoothly up, directly into the beam, and darkened instantly as it went about distributing the heat from the laser away from the point of contact. Trent stood for a moment, looking at the motionless form of the cyborg through the smoky gray canopy, and with what was very nearly his last strength called, "Emile? I'm leaving now. Good-bye."

The laser ceased.

Through the clearing canopy, Trent saw Garon's fist drop to his side, and then Emile Garon screamed. The sound was pure and wordless, an expression of elemental rage.

And the cyborg leaped.

Ten meters across a gaping chasm. The moment was imprinted in Trent's memory for the rest of his life, with an unreal perfection of clarity and detail. He had time to watch the dark gray streaks fading from the canopy, time to watch Garon as he seemed to float across the chasm, above the drop of three kilometers, to come down solidly upon the surface of the AeroSmith. He had time to watch the flat rictus of rage on Garon's features flicker slightly, as the AeroSmith tipped, slid, and fell a single story with Garon's fingers tearing into the vehicle's surface, ripping metal in a desperate attempt to gain a hold. The AeroSmith dropped, nose down, and came to a shuddering, screaming stop against one of the large verticals, the vehicle's engine smashing down into the passenger compartment.

Garon's fall never even slowed. He struck the same vertical as the AeroSmith and bounced off, a vaguely surprised look seemingly frozen on his features, bounced off still reaching for some hold, out into the empty air and the long drop to the distant Earth.

There was not much Trent remembered after that. Later he could not recall how he had gotten back to the maglev, nor the trip down to the top of the finished construction. He remembered somewhat more clearly the moment when the maglev slowed, descended into complete darkness, and then stopped.

He stood in the utter blackness for perhaps five seconds, and then the glowpaint flickered and came on automatically. He was on a single floor with no dividing walls at all, nothing but huge columns which enclosed the large vertical beams. Arrayed against the far walls there were upward of two hundred bounce tubes, about fifty per wall; near the east wall was a series of small maglev platforms. To all sides of Trent were maglev platforms every bit as large as the one he stood upon; the maglev platform he had descended upon was merely the center platform in a square of nine such.

He went down in the high-speed bounce tube. There were two chairs in the bounce tube. Trent sat down, strapped himself in, said calmly, *"Command,* first floor."

The bounce tube dropped.

Three kilometers; four minutes, dropping at forty-five kph.

Twenty seconds into the drop, Johnny Johnny said quietly, "Boss?"

"Yes?"

"Is it safe to talk?"

"Yes."

"We're in the Hoffman Spacescraper. I've got access to the InfoNet through radio packets in the bounce tube. Is there anything I should do?"

"Are the packets being polled for users?"

"Checking . . . no, Boss. I'd have to crack the Boards running the security inside the spacescraper to be sure, but I don't think so."

Trent said softly, "Call Jodi Jodi at the Red Line. Have her send me a cab."

Johnny Johnny stopped the bounce tube down on B3, three floors below the lobby. The door to the bounce tube opened on a long hallway lined with trash bins. Two janitors were playing chess not far from where Trent moved, like an old man, from the bounce tube. They stared at him but said nothing and made no attempt to stop Trent as he walked by them. The doors at the end of the hallway would not open to his palmprint, but there was an optical interface for his handheld beneath the pressure pad; Trent jacked in and let Johnny Johnny talk to the door.

Five seconds, six; the doors parted for him. The doors opened out onto a street Trent did not recognize. He joined the flow of pedestrians and walked without hurry, without limping, across the street. The sign on the corner told him he was at the corner of Bedford and Broadway; he looked around aimlessly at the endless stream of cars through the streets.

Two blocks down there was a knot in the traffic, five Peaceforcer patrol vehicles surrounding some disturbance.

Emile, thought Trent.

The Peugeot hovercab pulled up immediately in front of him as a Peaceforcer AeroSmith rounded the corner and began its sweep down Bedford; the rear door of the cab opened outward and Denice snapped, "Get in!"

He did his best to comply; he collapsed forward.

The same doctor who'd done Jimmy Ramirez cared for Trent. Trent remembered her vaguely when he awoke later that afternoon, remembered with equal vagueness Jimmy and Bird and Jodi Jodi and Denice wandering in and out of his room.

He awoke clearheaded, near nightfall, to find himself alone. He turned on the systerm next to the bed and ordered coffee from room service, then got up and went into the bathroom; his knee was numb, not shaky but completely without feeling. He used the same shower he had that morning, but at greater length, standing under the hot water until his muscles were utterly relaxed. He got out finally, brushed his teeth, and went back into the bedroom. There was coffee and toast next to his bed, with a note from Jodi Jodi that he was to stay in bed until Denice came for him. Trent checked next door; Jimmy was gone.

Trent went back to bed, and only then noticed that his handheld was jacked into the systerm. "Johnny?"

Johnny Johnny's voice was curiously subdued. "Yes, Boss?"

"How you doing?"

"Pretty good. Thanks for coming to get me, Boss. The web angels were after me, and I think at least one Player, and I was scared, so I hid and didn't answer the phone. I'm sorry you got hurt."

"I feel pretty good, Johnny. I wasn't hurt real bad."

"What do we do now, Boss?"

Trent was silent for a moment, lying in bed and staring up at the ceiling. "I think we run away, Johnny. I think we run as far away as we can get."

In that same subdued tone of voice Johnny Johnny said simply, "Okay, Boss."

"Johnny?"

"Yeah?"

"You did good, Johnny. I'm not mad at you."

"You're not? Not even because I hid?"

"You did just fine."

"Oh." Johnny Johnny was silent for a moment. "Thanks, Boss."

Trent was silent after that, and Johnny Johnny as well. He was still lying awake in bed when the door to the bedroom opened, and Denice came to join him. She took off her blouse as she came into the bedroom, and stood at the foot of the bed as she undressed. "I really hate saying good-bye to people, Trent. I'm not good at it."

"I'm sorry."

She shrugged, pulling off the danskin underneath the blouse. "It's not your fault." Her skirt dropped to the floor, followed by her shoes and panties. "Doctor Jane said you were okay except to not put any weight on your knee; it's being held together with glue and rubber bands."

"You went to practice today?"

She stood completely nude at the foot of the bed. "It seemed less suspicious. Four hours, from two to six. We had you back by then, and Johnny Johnny said there were no Peaceforcer dispatches in the InfoNet about me that he could find."

"So you're safe."

Denice got into bed with him, pulled the covers back and snuggled up against him. "It looks like." She whispered to him. *I talked to Johnny Johnny earlier today, while you were being operated on.*

Yes?

He's a real person. He hurts about things.

I know.

You were right to go get him.

I know. Trent said quietly, "Johnny?"

"Yes?"

"Shut yourself off for a while."

"Okay, Boss."

From where they lay, looking out the thirty-second floor window, they could see the Peaceforcers, their hovercars and spyeyes, searching restlessly back and forth across the city; scarlet fireflies at that distance, their searchlights only pinpricks of bright white. As the night wore on, it grew colder outside, and moisture condensed at the window, smearing the bright sharp lights into a sort of beauty.

Denice stirred slightly in the confines of Trent's arms. "When will you go?"

Trent answered very quietly; a human would probably not have heard him. "Soon. Not yet."

"And where?"

"I don't know yet."

"Okay."

"They need to follow me," he said after a moment. "They need to be drawn away from you, and if they're looking for me they're not looking for you. If I die it's just me. If you die —then they've won. David's probably dead, Denice. If you die, there's nothing left of what they were, and Amnier, Eddore, Vance, all of them, they've won at last."

Trent sat up against the headboard. Denice rolled onto her back, and left her head resting against his knees. She looked up, toward the ceiling there was not light enough to see.

"Where, Trent?"

"Free Luna, I think," he said finally, "or else Mars, or the Belt CityStates. Somewhere outside Peaceforcer control. They won't stop looking for me on Earth. I don't think they'll ever stop looking for me now."

Denice said slowly, "I think you're right. I'm so sorry, but I think you are. I wish we hadn't rescued you."

"It's okay. Make me a promise, Denice?"

"Done."

"Don't you want to know what it is?"

"I do know."

"Oh. All right. But don't let him know you're watching out for him. He wouldn't like that."

"I know. You're sure Bird will be okay with Jodi Jodi?"

"They were doing fine together, in the middle of the Fringe, when I met them. They'll do fine in the Patrol Sectors when I'm gone."

She took a deep breath, and seemed to accept that. "Be careful," she whispered into the darkness. "You're all I have left now."

Minutes later, Denice Castanaveras was asleep. They stayed in that position, Trent sitting upright with her head resting above his knees, until the morning sunlight began to burn the mist away from the windows.

Trent the Uncatchable did not sleep that night. When morning came, he lifted Denice's head from his lap, gently, left a note on the systerm next to the bedside, and left Denice Castanaveras behind to become a legend.

At the hotel's desk he left instructions that a single white rose be delivered to her room.

The note he left on the systerm said:

Don't worry. It's going to be all right.

                                    —Trent

He was a product of his time, Mohammed Vance, an ideolog who believed that the values of the Unification were good values, worth defending from the likes of Trent the Uncatchable.

For many years, he was right. Things were not always so bad as they became toward the end.

He was in many ways a good man. That fortune chose Mohammed Vance to play the role of Trent's enemy does not change that.

> —The Peaceforcer Elite Melissa du Bois,
> as quoted in *The Exodus Bible*

"Commissioner? Commissioner Vance?"

"Oui." The voice that answered was deep, rumbling.

"Your pardon, sir. I do not speak French."

"Yes, what is it? You dragged me from my bed; this had better be good."

"Sir, you are directed to report for duty in Capitol City, by ten hundred hours today Capitol City time. The orders are direct from the Secretary-General's office, sir."

"The Capitol? What the hell for?"

"Sir, we have a Peaceforcer Elite killed here."

There was a brief, flat pause. "Killed?"

"Sir, it appears so. His body was dumped from the top of the uncompleted Hoffman Spacescraper—murder, as nearly as we can tell. Apparently there are recordings of the event taken by nearby PKF."

"Have you seen them yourself?"

"No, sir."

"I see. Has the news leaked?"

"No, sir."

"Thank God for that." Another pause. "Names?"

"Sir?"

"The murderer and the dead Elite, idiot."

"Yes, sir. The Peaceforcer's name was Garon, sir, PKF Elite Sergeant Emile Garon. As nearly as we can determine, the murderer was a minor New York area webdancer; perhaps a Player. Or thief, something like that. He escaped PKF custody early Monday."

"Emile is dead?"

"Yes, sir."

"And the thief's—or webdancer's, or Player's—name, if I might inquire after that small fact?"

"Sir? Trent."

"Trent?"

"Yes, sir."

There was another pause. "Trent what?"

"It's all we have, sir. Just Trent."

Trent walked down the corridor on the 183rd floor of the L'Fevre Spacescraper, the fourth tallest building in New York, the tallest that was not on Manhattan Island. In his left hand he carried the briefcase Jodi Jodi had given him.

Trent stopped before one doorway very like any other in the corridor, except that there was no nameplate next to the doorgrid. Without pausing he withdrew a small, spidery black-metal object from the right-hand pocket of his suit, and placed it over the doorgrid.

The suit was made of optical polycloth; it had been tuned to a dark marine blue. The briefcase Trent carried was also a deep shade of blue.

They very nearly matched.

The pick Trent had attached to Booker Jamethon's door beeped once. Trent plucked the pick off the doorgrid, and put it back in his pocket.

The door was solid wood, not memory plastic; it slid aside without flexing or curling at all, into a compartment within the wall.

Trent stepped inside, the door closing itself behind him. The room he stepped into was very dark after the brightness of the sunpaint in the hallway outside. Tiny red dots danced before his eyes. The room was cool, at least 5°C below the temperature of the rest of the building.

As Trent's eyesight adjusted to the dimness, he made out a room that was remarkably cluttered. Its living room was also the kitchen, and held one table and two benches. There were shelves on every wall. SpaceFarer booknets strengthened for gravity hung down forty centimeters from the ceiling. Everything held some measure of esoteric equipment: reels of monofilament fineline, bundles of the optic fiber that SpaceFarers called lasercable, superconductor strips, chemical apparatus and chipglue; one shelf held a half-dozen blocks of very expensive molecular circuitry, with equally expensive viewtracers attached to them. There were two half-assembled (or half-disassembled) serving robots, and what Trent recognized as an ancient FrancoDEC LapVax.

Tools were scattered everywhere.

In the entire room there was only one place to sit, an over-stuffed chair that looked quite comfortable, just to the left of the door which doubtless led to the bedroom. Booker Jamethon, sitting in it, also looked quite comfortable. He was pointing an unrecognizable amalgamation of gadgetry at Trent; Trent suspected it was a weapon.

Trent said, "Hello, Booker." He looked around for a place to put down his briefcase.

Booker Jamethon was the ugliest person Trent had ever met in his life. Somewhere in his late fifties, he was at least thirty kilograms overweight, and he depilated too rarely. His inskin was ancient, seven years old at least. His arms were massively muscled and incredibly long. One of his legs was shorter than the other.

Booker was, Trent was certain, the world's hairiest living human.

Trent did not know what Booker's Image was, though he had some very good guesses. He was without question one of the half-dozen most famous Players in the world.

Booker said gently, "Hello, Trent. May I ask some questions?" He spoke in a deep baritone, the words themselves uttered in a precise, cultured accent. "What are you doing in my apartment? How did you find my apartment? How did you acquire my door code? What do you want of me?"

Trent stood very still. "Don't you ever audit the news, Booker?"

"No."

"Oh."

"The news Boards are obnoxious institutions," said Booker. "They should be abolished in favor of rumor mongering. I did hear you'd been arrested, and that the Player Johnny Johnny took down three quarters of the PKF Boards in Capitol City when you escaped. I also heard that the PKF thought you were the Player Ralf the Wise and Powerful, from back a few years ago." Booker smiled broadly at Trent. "I remember Ralf. He was a punk."

"Look, Booker—"

"Look, Trent." Booker waved the thing in his hand at Trent. "You are not answering my question."

"I need to get off Earth, Booker."

"Excuse me," said Booker Jamethon. "Questions, in the plural; you are not answering my questions."

Trent found an empty spot amid the junk on the floor. He put down the briefcase on it. "I'm in trouble, Booker. The Peaceforcers are after me, and I need to get off Earth. The further off the better. I came to you because your love for the Left Hand of the Devil is known far and wide."

Booker Jamethon smiled for the first time since Trent had entered his apartment. "My dear boy. I fully understand that you will be even less inclined to answer my questions *after* I have shot you, but you are beginning to annoy me."

"I'm in your apartment because I need help. I've known where you lived ever since we boosted Toomey's place together. I didn't have your door code until just now, and I don't actually know what it is because I haven't dumped my pick since it opened the door. What I want from you," said Trent seriously, "is your help."

Booker chuckled. Trent would not have sworn that the booknets above his head started moving at that precise moment, only that it was the first time he had noticed it. "What did they arrest you for, Trent? Did you finally boost the wrong article? Or was there some complication in one of your generally brilliant operations which you had not foreseen? In the past, as I recall, complications have included enraged bankers, enraged fathers, enraged Peaceforcers, enraged husbands, at least one enraged wife that I know of, and one enraged midget."

"That's not true," said Trent, "that story about the midget."

"What," said Booker Jamethon very slowly, "does the United Nations Peace Keeping Force want you for?"

Trent said, "They think I'm a telepath, and they think I killed a Peaceforcer."

Booker Jamethon sat motionless for several moments, fixing Trent with one of his patented five-Credit stares.

"Well, I'm not. And I *didn't.*"

Booker very carefully laid the weapon on a small stool next

to him which had the sole virtue of being slightly less crowded with machinery than everything surrounding it. He stood like a small mountain moving. "You didn't?"

"It was an accident," said Trent quickly. "A mistake. He fell."

Standing completely motionless, Booker Jamethon's eyes dropped slowly shut. Trent would have given a great deal to know what Image stirred and ventured forth into the InfoNet in that moment. A moment later he wondered where that Image had gone; the information Booker's Image came back with was nothing out of any public Board. "Oh, my God," said Booker quietly. He opened his eyes again and stared through the gloom at Trent. "You stupid shit. You killed a Peaceforcer Elite."

"He *fell,* Booker! It wasn't my fault."

"Do you have a short between the trodes, Trent? You came to *me* with the Peaceforcers chasing you?" After a long moment Booker Jamethon said, far, far too quietly, "I don't like this, Trent. How close are they?"

"Not very. I audited a PKF Board I have a tap in while I was on my way over here; it says they've assigned a Peaceforcer named Mohammed Vance to oversee the investigation."

"Should that mean something to me?"

"I suppose not."

"You know of him?" Booker demanded.

"Vaguely."

"Is he any good?"

"Probably." Trent paused. "Yes."

"DataWatch?"

"Elite. According to the personnel file on him, DataWatch has received help from him in Realtime hunts; he took down the Wizard Woz two years ago."

Booker Jamethon took a very long, deep breath, not looking away from Trent at all, and said again, "How close, damn it?"

"I think I lost them. At least temporarily. There's this huge search going on for me, Booker. . . ."

Booker stared through the gloom at Trent. Trent tried to guess how angry Booker was. Very, was his guess. "You think you lost them. I feel better now."

"Free Luna, Mars, the Belt CityStates . . ."

"Why *me,* damn it?" roared Booker abruptly.

"Because," said Trent, "they're pretty sure who my Image is, they *know* who *I* am and they know I don't have an inskin. Every full-sensory systerm within fifty klicks is locked down right now. There are webdancers all over the damned Info-Net, just waiting for me to come across the interface. I need to see a makeup artist, which I could do myself, but I also need to place passage and for work that detailed I need a full sensory. I can't go back to mine. The Peaceforcers have had that since this time yesterday. I don't even have my traceset any more." Booker was just looking at him, and Trent said simply, "You're the only other Player I know."

Booker snapped, "Luna?"

"That would be fine. It's the tourist in me, Booker," said Trent sincerely. "I've always wanted to see Luna."

Booker Jamethon closed his eyes for a moment, and when he opened them again Trent could not quite make out the expression on Booker's face. "Very well," said Booker after a moment. "How would you like to leave Earth as a Peaceforcer?"

Trent blinked. "I'd love to. Booker?"

"Yes?"

"Could I leave as a *particular* Peaceforcer?"

Trent froze when the woman turned on the holocams. "What are you doing?"

"Recording the session, sonny." The makeup artist was a pleasant, chubby woman who had introduced herself to Trent as Mick. Mick was easily old enough to be beginning geriatrics treatments sometime soon, if she had not already started; she was one of perhaps half a dozen women Trent had ever seen in his life who had wrinkles on her face. "This is a Syndic shop, and we keep records."

Trent sat up in the long chair, reaching for his shirt. "Not a chance."

The woman sighed. "Booker said you were going to be difficult. Listen, kid, you're shipping to Free Luna tonight? Yes?"

Trent said cautiously, "Yes."

"So no time for biosculpt. You're on a ship tonight and you need to look different than you do now when you go through Unification Spaceport. At the end of the day the Syndic local systerm polls my machine, and my systerm spills its guts.

Now, I don't care how bad the PKF wants you, no way are my records going to get indexed in time for the Syndic to sell your face to the PKF before this time tomorrow—by which time, kid, you're on the damn Moon and outside their reach and you can get biosculpted proper. You get the idea? You should trust Booker. If he wanted to send you off there would have been brass balls or Syndic enforcers or *somebody* at my door when you got here."

Trent sighed. "All right."

"You're a nice boy. Lay back and shut up. This is going to hurt."

Trent spent most of the afternoon atop an abandoned building at the edge of the Fringe. It was a gorgeous day that could not make up its mind whether it wanted to be sunny or cloudy; it was windy enough that the huge gray clouds were scudding across the blue sky above him at a just perceptible clip. From atop the building he could see, across the Hudson River, midtown Manhattan, home of the Unification Council of the United Nations. He could see lower Manhattan, once the business capitol of the world. It was no longer the business capitol of the world, had not been since being nuked the first time, during the closing days of the Unification War. The swarm of tactical nukes had destroyed Wall Street and a huge chunk of New York city and state government offices. Irreplaceable financial records had been lost in the destruction; a fifteen-year global depression had followed.

The United Nations had helped rebuild lower Manhattan into one of the most prestigious residential areas in the world, and then, in 2062, they'd nuked it again; a smaller destruction this time but still sufficient to make the southern tip of the island uninhabitable for over a year.

In the other direction Trent could see the Fringe. Five minutes of battle between the Peaceforcers and the telepaths had caused that stretching desolation; nearly a quarter of the population of southern New York and New Jersey had gone utterly insane that night of July 3, 2062, when the telepaths, at the Chandler Complex in lower Manhattan, had fought and been destroyed.

He sat atop the gravel-strewn rooftop until night fell, looking out over the sprawling city that had been his home. Once her thoughts touched him, glancingly, searchingly, but he did not respond.

He left his handheld in his briefcase for nearly the entire time. Booker had been unable to find a traceset for him in all of the junk in his apartment. Booker himself did not need a traceset; even his obsolete inskin was more useful.

Trent's ship was lifting from Unification Spaceport at 8:15.

At 6:20 he removed his handheld from the briefcase and said, "Johnny?"

Johnny Johnny said, "Hello, Boss. Status: on over two-thirds of the Boards on Earth, two hundred fifteen million Boards at present, there has been no mention of the name 'Trent' in conjunction with the death of PKF Elite Emile Garon. Insufficient processing time to check the remaining hundred ten million Boards, but I hit every major commercial Board, every institutional Board open to the public, every government Board, every Player Board where I have access. The PKF has not yet released to the news Boards the fact that it was a PKF Elite who died yesterday. Nor," said Johnny Johnny in his best newsdancer voice, "have they released your name, or a description of you, or any pertinent background on the escape from the Detention Center in Capitol City. PKF Boards in Capitol City are still largely in a state of higgledy-piggledy since the infamous Player Johnny Johnny crashed them early yesterday morning. Mohammed Vance arrived on a chartered semiballistic from France early this morning, and has been directing the hunt for you since that time. To date, they have not caught you." Johnny Johnny paused. "In nine hours and forty minutes we are scheduled to arrive at the city of Alphonse, port of entry into Free Luna."

"Higgledy-piggledy?"

"That means 'in confusion: topsy-turvy, randomly.' Or, 'A real mess,' Boss."

"Thanks, Johnny."

"No problem."

At 6:30 exactly Trent stood, brushed the dust off the seat of his pants, walked down five flights to street level, and called for a cab to take him into Manhattan.

Into Peaceforcer territory.

Trent relaxed in the back seat of the hovercab with his eyes closed. The hovercab was waiting in line with about forty other vehicles, to be processed across Almundsen Bridge and onto the island of Manhattan.

The cab's radio was tuned to channel 9.1.46; Capitol City, Metro News, Crime.

When Trent's cab reached the checkpoint, two gendarmes approached it from each side.

Trent did not open his eyes.

Without addressing Trent, one of the two opened the front door and checked the cab's readout.

The gendarme closed the front door. He called out, "PKF business. Priority routing." The cab pulled out of the line, and entered the flow of traffic crossing the bridge.

On the radio, the announcer stated that a Peaceforcer had been killed at approximately 9:30 yesterday morning, in the vicinity of the uncompleted Hoffman Spacescraper. She repeated the fairly stale news that Commissioner Mohammed Vance had assumed control of the investigation, and that, given Vance's past success in Realtime manhunts of this sort, apprehension of the murderer was expected shortly.

Arms crossed across his chest, eyes closed, to all appearances dead to the world, Trent murmured, "Really?"

The Friday previous, the Unification Council had adjourned, and Unification Spaceport was filled to overflowing with nearly a quarter of a million humans. The vast majority of them were waiting for semiballistics to take them elsewhere on Earth; a few were waiting for shuttles to Midway, or other points in near Earth orbit; a very few were waiting for Space-Farer craft to Luna, or Mars, or even the Belt CityStates.

Trent's hovercab let him off at the passenger station for Manhattan Spaceport South. The gouge for the short flight was bad; CU:6.75. Trent did not mind; United Nations Peace Keeping Force Discretionary Account 1303, userid 42, paid for it under the impression that Trent was a person named Mohammed Vance.

The southern tip of Manhattan Island makes an excellent spaceport, aside from the fact that it is too far north of the equator. It is immediately adjacent to Capitol City, the nerve center of the United Nations. At the time of its construction, it had had yet another point in its favor; not quite a year previously the enclave of telepaths in that location had been nuked. There was not much left standing at the southernmost tip of Manhattan Island when it was all over with; there was simply nobody left to object when the Unification Council decided to build there.

The maglev took Trent down several floors to the central lobby. There, just past the point where the maglev ended, and before a half kilometer of service counters for the half-dozen companies which spaced out of lower Manhattan, a row of some thirty Information Network cubicles was arrayed against both walls.

Trent made his way through the crowds to them, and entered an empty one near the middle of the row, closing the door behind him. Inside, he ignored the room monitor; the odds were vastly in his favor that DataWatch would not poll this particular systerm while Trent was there, and that if they did, the image of a young man with brown eyes and brown hair and high cheekbones would mean nothing to them.

Seating himself before the pointboard, Trent danced his fingers across its surface. There were MPU jacks for more sophisticated access; Trent didn't bother.

The phonefield was flat. Sooner than Trent had expected, it flashed a blue CONNECTED at him from the bottom right of the field. Trent did not turn on the holocams at his end.

Tarin Schuyler's face appeared in the field.

Trent said, "Is she there?"

Tarin stared into her holocams. "Trent? Is it you?"

"Yes."

"Yes, she's here." The woman was clearly disturbed. "She's really upset. What did you do to her?"

"I didn't give her a chance to say good-bye," said Trent briefly. "She needed sleep. Tell her I'll call from Luna City." Tarin opened her mouth to speak again, and Trent disconnected her.

He sat quietly in the cubicle for just a moment.

Like the cab fare, like the price of his passage to Luna, Trent charged the call on Mohammed Vance's private account; to the account of the man who was even now directing the search for him.

Trent left, and left the door to the cubicle open behind him.

"Name?" The guard—an ordinary gendarme, not a Peaceforcer—looked at Trent impatiently. The line behind Trent was long, and getting longer with every moment.

"Vance," said Trent. "Mohammed Vance." He handed the guard his ticket and his passport. The passport didn't identify Trent as a Peaceforcer, or even as a United Nations employee, though the ticket showed itself paid for by the Peace Keeping Force. Less than ideal work, but it was Booker's best; he'd been, as he put it to Trent, "rushed."

At her systerm, the guard was spending a considerable amount of time processing the ticket. At length, when the line behind Trent began to mutter, she looked up from her systerm, and said, loudly enough for those immediately behind Trent to hear, "I can be even slower about this if I have to." The line quieted. Finally the guard returned to Trent. She gave back Trent's passport and ticket.

She spent a disconcerting moment studying Trent.

Had Mick told him the truth, or not? At about this time, the holos she'd taken of Trent should be sitting in a Syndic database, waiting for the morning for some Syndic Lord to look them over.

Assuming she'd told the truth.

Trent looked back at the gate guard innocently, trying his best to look harmless and trustworthy.

"Shuttle Pad Eight," said the guard. She smiled an unpleasant smile at Trent. "Have a nice day."

Trent smiled back at her. "One seventh of your life," he said politely, "will be spent on Mondays."

He left without hurrying.

Gate C let onto the landing field proper. The skies had cleared slightly in the forty-five minutes that Trent had been inside the spaceport, and a few twinkling stars could be seen through patchy clouds. Outside, Trent looked for transportation. A nearby holo informed him that a spaceport cab would be by within twenty minutes to ferry him across the vast fields of steelstone to wherever his flight waited.

"But I'm *already* late," Trent told the sign. Forty meters away was a groundcar, a long black limousine with dark windows, and a license plate that said u.n. 88. Trent walked to it without pausing, and stopped by the door next to the front left-hand seat. In one smooth motion he popped his briefcase open and withdrew an object that vaguely resembled a tuning fork. He ran the forked end over the door's pressure pad, produced two barely audible beeps, reversed the tool and with the laser in its other end burned out the locklarm.

He had the door open in less time than the carcomp would have taken to compare his palmprint against its authorized list of users. Trent slid inside and closed the door behind him. Some of the people at the ferry terminal were watching the car with vague curiosity.

The car ran itself from processors located behind an access panel under the center of the front dashboard. Balancing his briefcase on his knees, Trent opened it to its complete extension. Fully half of the interior was taken up by a perfectly legal, and quite powerful, external processor board for his InfoNet link. The other half held an odd assortment of tools: a spot for his handheld, the circuit tracer with a laser at the other end, a small forest of microlectrics equipment, an antistatic package holding, after Booker's payment, five and a half terabytes of RTS; a nearly full reel of fineline, an almost empty strip of room-temperature superconductor, and one watertight squirt gun of excellent construction.

The car's brain was an ancient Motorola MC-GA64, running Purolator security firmware that was over five years old. Trent sprayed chipglue directly onto the processor, waited while it set and pressed the handheld's interface gently into the still-soft surface of the chipglue. Far less than a second— perhaps a quarter of a million nanoseconds in total—passed while Johnny Johnny reached out and enfolded the processor, stole every data and instruction line in and out of the chip; not five seconds had passed before the car was rolling at an even thirty kph across the landing field toward the line of ships.

Trent was unable to find Shuttle Pad Eight.

It was 8:15, and Trent's ship was supposed to leave at 8:15.

None of the launch pads were numbered.

Finally Trent stopped the limousine next to the one spaceship that had a person standing in front of it. Thinking back, Trent was almost certain that he had been unable to see inside the limousine, when he had been standing outside of it. He squirmed into the back over the top of the seats, straightened his coat and opened the left rear passenger's door.

The ship was easily the largest craft within a quarter of a kilometer. Its landing ramp was still down. Trent stepped from the car, and walked over to the person standing in front of the ramp.

"Hello," said Trent. "Is this Shut . . . uhm, Number Eight?"

By no conceivable stretch of the imagination was the craft in front of him a shuttle.

The SpaceFarer took a step toward Trent, surveying Trent with cold eyes. His look told Trent that he was the greater of two evils. Any two evils. The name on the shoulder of his gray and green ship's uniform read LT. ZINTH. One of the largest hand masers Trent had ever seen was holstered at his right hip. Lieutenant Zinth's eyes were exactly level with Trent's. "You're Vance."

Trent blinked. "Yes. Oh yes of course."

Meter-high letters, bright green against the gray-silver of the ship's hull, said, THE CAPTAIN SIR DOMINIC FLANDRY. The SpaceFarer nodded. " 'Sieur Vance, you are late. Lift-off was scheduled for 20:15 hours Capitol City time. It is now 20:19." He stared evenly at Trent.

"I couldn't find the ship," Trent explained.

The SpaceFarer stood staring at Trent. The cold breeze off the ocean tugged at the lapels of his exquisitely tailored ship's uniform. Finally he said, "The ship's launchpad position and name, 'Sieur Vance, are shown on the back of your ticket."

"Oh." Trent turned the ticket in his hand over and looked at it. He looked back up at Lieutenant Zinth. "Sorry. I was in such a hurry it didn't occur to me to look. I've never been on a spaceship before, you know. This is all *so* exciting for me."

The look on the man's face did not alter at all. "It is now, 'Sieur Vance, 20:20."

Trent had never, ever, heard of a ship departing on time from Unification Spaceport. He offered the SpaceFarer his ticket.

The young man glanced at it. "Deck two, 'Sieur Vance. Seat thirteen."

Trent said, "I'm not superstitious."

The SpaceFarer said quietly, with a glance at the Unification Councilor's limousine that Trent had arrived in, "With all due respect, Monsieur Vance, you are obviously a very powerful downsider. That means nothing aboard the *Flandry*. The SpaceFarer's Collective is not a part of the United Nations, and you have no authority. Now you will please seat yourself—quickly."

Trent said to the SpaceFarer, "I'm not afraid of you."

· 4 ·

The passenger bay aboard the *Flandry* was small, but safe. An afterthought of a converted cargo bay, it was near the exact center of the ship; on his way up in the lift, with Lieutenant Zinth glaring at him the entire time, Trent counted four separate bulkheads between the outer hull and the passenger compartment.

Zinth palmed open the hatch to the passenger's compartment and Trent stepped through, looking around at the compartment and the passengers on the way to his seat. There were forty or fifty of them, mostly men, speaking mostly in French, already strapped into their acceleration couches for lift.

Seat 13 was next to seat 14. In seat 14 there was a lovely young lady.

"Hi," said Trent cheerfully. He strapped himself in, and waited while the seat reclined. He put his briefcase in the safety web under the seat. "I'm Trent the thief. Is there anything I can steal for you?"

The woman in the seat next to him was young, somewhere in her early twenties. She had dark, sun-streaked brown hair that reached her shoulder blades in one long braid and looked as though it wanted to try for the small of her back. Inquisitive brown eyes and tanned, absolutely *perfectly* flawless skin, what skin was meant to be, complemented this extravagance. She looked up from the handheld she was reading on and looked Trent over coolly. She spoke carefully, with a distinct French accent. "That is not funny."

"No?" said Trent instantly. "Then how about this?" He tucked his thumbs into the corners of his mouth and stretched his cheeks into a clown face, eyes bugging out, tongue lolling.

The woman stared blankly at him for a moment and then bit her lip, looking away from him. "No. That is not funny either."

Trent looked at the woman curiously. He took his fingers out of his mouth and wiped them on his pants. "You know, people almost always at least *smile* at that one. Is something wrong?"

"You are late," she said flatly.

In French, a voice came over the outspeaker and informed the passengers that the craft was in motion. The message was followed almost immediately by a sudden jerk, and then a low rumbling sound, as the port tugs began towing the *Flandry* into launch position. The acceleration chair Trent sat in vibrated strongly.

"It wasn't my fault," Trent explained.

"As you say." The woman turned away from him, to her handheld.

"So I can't steal anything for you?"

She looked up from the handheld slowly. She looked Trent over as though she were considering calling for a gendarme. "No," she said at last, "I am afraid not. I am not poor."

"What's that got to do with it?"

After a moment's thought, the woman turned her handheld off and put it under her seat in the safety web. "Is this not a Robin Hood procedure? No, wait," she corrected herself, "Robin Hood *routine*. To steal from the rich, and give to the poor?"

"Don't be obscene." Trent tried to relax in his chair. "I'm a capitalist. I did have Merry Men once," he said as an afterthought, "but I had to get rid of them. They were gloomy sons of bitches."

The alert brown eyes studied him. "Oh?"

"Didn't laugh at my jokes."

She nodded as though he had said something meaningful. "Why were you late for lift?"

Her tone of voice was flat, inquisitive. And she was—*studying* him. Trent paused a second, wondering why the routine was going over so badly.

Trent said, "Are you sure I *was* late?"

"You were late for the flight."

"People keep telling me that."

"They held the ship for you."

"Did they?" asked Trent curiously.

"Yes."

"That was nice of them."

"Why were you late?"

"It's a long story."

"Excuse me?"

"They held me at the gate, and then I got lost," Trent told her.

"Lost?"

"I couldn't find the ship."

"It is a *big* ship."

"But there was no number."

The woman said blankly, "Excuse me?"

Trent said, "It's really a long story." There were approximately fifty people in the passenger's compartment of *The Captain Sir Dominic Flandry*. Something about the other passengers, a general air of alertness, made Trent uneasy.

"Oh." She looked at him curiously. "My name is Melissa; Melissa du Bois."

The ship's outspeakers came alive and in French told the passengers that they should prepare for acceleration shortly. "Hello, Melissa du Bois," said Trent. "May I have the pleasure of seducing you?"

Melissa du Bois looked briefly startled, and then actually smiled, dimpling, and looked about sixteen. "No."

"What?"

"Perhaps on some other occasion, Trent the thief. It might be—indiscreet, yes? Yes, indiscreet under the present circumstances."

"Does that mean 'no'?"

"Yes."

"Oh."

"Where are you headed, Trent?"

"The Moon," said Trent. "Luna. I hear it's lovely this time of year, when the farsiders take their annual baths."

Melissa lay back in her seat and closed her eyes, as the voice on the intercom began marking off five-second increments toward lift-off, starting at sixty and working backward. "I am going to L-5, myself."

Trent sat upright, very slowly. "L-5? Spacebase One?"

The tone of his voice did not penetrate to her, although a man across the aisle looked at Trent oddly. "Yes, L-5. I am going to the training base for PKF Elite at L-5." Her eyes were still closed, her voice quiet and calm; she did not see the look of utter horror that had descended upon Trent's features.

Trent opened his mouth twice before the words would come out.

He said, "You're a Peaceforcer."

"Yes. I have only been PKF for four years, and I have already qualified for the Elite." She did look over at him then, and smiled at him again. "I think it is the only thing I have ever done that impressed my father. My mother cried when she found out. They are very proud."

"I'm sure they are." Trent looked around the small cabin, at the healthy, relaxed, alert group of French men and women. "The rest of this group; you're"—he almost strangled on the words—"with them?"

"Yes. We are the top one twentieth of one percent of all the PKF on Earth." She added, "It surprised us all that you got a seat. We chartered this ship over a month ago. You must have influence; you bumped an officer from the seat you are in."

The voice on the intercom said softly, "Ten seconds to lift."

"Oh, no," said Trent. He lay back in the acceleration couch; the webbing came up and embraced him. "Oh my God no."

Lying flat on his back, he could not see Melissa du Bois's expression at all, but despite her accent he heard the surprise in her voice. "Trent? Are you afraid?"

"Yes," said Trent. "Very, very much."

The outspeaker voice said, "We are lifting."

The Captain Sir Dominic Flandry lifted at just under six gravities; breathing was difficult enough, and silence was practically enforced for several minutes.

Trent was terribly, horribly glad.

During the approximately four minutes Trent spent lying on his back, weighing nearly six times as much as he was used to, he decided two things.

The first was that he was never again going to have Booker Jamethon tell a scheduling program that he was a high-ranking Peaceforcer official.

The second was that in his entire life, without any exceptions at all, he had never *ever* felt more stupid.

At slightly less than one gravity acceleration, with twenty minutes' delay at turnover, the trip to L-5, in Lunar orbit sixty degrees ahead of the Moon, took nearly four and a half hours.

When the acceleration had died back to just below one gravity, Trent took his briefcase from underneath the couch, opened it a crack, took out his InfoNet link and closed the case again quickly.

In the seat next to him, Melissa du Bois was watching him curiously.

He hooked his handheld into the dataline access plug in the arm of his seat. A holofield sprang into existence just above it. There was a single gray traceset trode tucked into the arm of the seat along with a single gray earphone, snaked to the seat so that they could not be stolen by people like Trent. Trent hooked up and requested a laser link to the InfoNet Relay Station at Halfway. The ship was still near enough Earth that there was no perceptible delay connecting to the InfoNet; Trent closed his eyes and went Inside.

. . . MINIMAL RF MODULATION, SHIP FREQUENCIES . . . SHIP BUSINESS . . . SCALE UP INTO PRIVATE INSKIN FREQUENCIES; SILENCE . . . UP AGAIN, PEACEFORCER ELITE MONITOR BANDS; SILENCE . . .

It was silent except on ship frequencies. Either none of the Peaceforcers in the compartment had inskins, or they had them and weren't using them.

The Peaceforcers had finally held a news conference concerning Trent; there were eight major news Boards following the story of the hunt for Emile Garon's killer. *NewsBoard,* the third Board Trent scanned, had the information he needed. The first section of the *NewsBoard* story was simply a recounting of the circumstances of Emile Garon's death, as described by the Peaceforcers. The story went on to describe the steps the Peaceforcers were taking in their search for the murderer; according to *NewsBoard,* the average Peaceforcer had not learned of Emile Garon's death until nearly two o'clock that afternoon, and the Peaceforcers aboard the *Flandry,* on detached duty awaiting transfer to L-5, probably did not know about it at all.

Certainly Melissa du Bois did not.

The next thing Trent did was pull up the *Flandry*'s listed ports of call: Mars, via Luna City, via the United Nations Peace Keeping Force Base at Lagrange Five.

"I wonder why Booker didn't mention that to me," Trent said softly, chewing thoughtfully on his lower lip.

PROBABLY DIDN'T WANT YOU TO WORRY, said Johnny Johnny through the traceset.

Melissa said, "Trent?"

"Yes, I am," said Trent definitely.

She started to say something, then shook her head. "Never mind. What are you doing?"

Trent shut off the handheld and looked up at her as the holofield faded. "Excuse me?"

Melissa seemed to be searching for words. "That was . . . *inequiétante* . . . I do not know the word."

"Odd?"

"Uncanny. I have never seen anyone pull data up onto an InfoNet handheld like that. The field, it—blurred—as the data flowed by. How could you understand?"

Trent's thoughts spun briefly, an engine with the load removed. "Oh, yes." He leaned toward Melissa. "Actually, in real life when I'm not being Trent the thief, I'm the youngest member of Secretary General Eddore's private webdancing staff." He added as an afterthought, "My parents are very proud of me."

Trent had never had parents.

Carl Castanaveras, whom Trent had called father, had been killed by Peaceforcers.

Suzanne Montignet and Malko Kalharri, who were the architect and the will behind Project Superman—the man and woman who had raised the men and women who had raised Trent—they too had also died at the hands of Peaceforcers.

With the exception of Denice Castanaveras and possibly her brother, everybody Trent had grown up with had been killed by Peaceforcers.

"That's nice," said Melissa du Bois.

Trent smiled at Melissa du Bois the Peaceforcer. "Isn't it?"

He lay back in his seat then, tightening the straps slightly to keep himself in place.

He slept the sleep of utter exhaustion.

More than a thousand years later, when the second largest religion in the Continuing Time was the religion which had grown from the seeds sown by *The Exodus Bible,* children and adults, human and otherwise, on tens of millions of worlds, read Melissa du Bois's account of her first meeting with Trent.

He had no equals, save, in some ways, Mohammed Vance, the man who hunted him for all those years. He was very young when I first met him, and improvising as he went. The meticulous preparation for which he later became known was not so evident when I first met him—not surprisingly, of course.

He was running for his life, from us.

*I think I did not know the meaning of the word humility,
then. I was one of the best of the PKF, and I did know it.*
  Before Trent I had never failed at anything.

Some two hours later Trent awoke to free fall, to silence.

The lights in the compartment had been dimmed. The
bulkhead which Trent and Melissa's seats were lined up
against now seemed to have vanished; a holograph displayed
upon its surface showed deep space, blazing white and yellow
and blue stars against the purest blackness Trent had ever
seen.

Many of the Peaceforcers were sleeping. A few were auditing text on their handhelds, the pages glowing in midair;
other Peaceforcers were simply looking, hypnotized, at the
holograph of deep space.

Trent played back the excerpts his handheld had recorded
for him while he was asleep. *NewsBoard* had nothing of note
since his last audit, but the *Electronic Times* had just posted a
story saying that there were rumors circulating to the effect
that the murdered Peaceforcer in New York City had actually
been a member of the Peaceforcer Elite. The *Electronic Times*
was not absolutely certain, but they thought that a
Peaceforcer Elite had never been murdered in the line of duty
before.

Melissa du Bois said sleepily, "It's lovely, isn't it?"

"Yes. Yes, it is." Looking at the young Peaceforcer's profile,
as she watched the glowing stars, Trent was not at all surprised by the sudden realization of how desperately he wanted
to take her to bed.

"When I was very young, I thought I would be an astrono-
mer. Live on farside at one of the observatories; Zvezdagrad
perhaps, Star City at Tsiolkovsky Crater. My parents in-
dulged me, bought me a telescope and set it up on the balcony
on the third floor." She sighed. "I had no skill for it, not the
math, and not really the inclination. My father is PKF Elite;
after my brother died he wanted very much for me to follow
him in the service." She smiled at him, somewhat diffidently.
"You listen well. What did you want to be as a child?"

Trent intentionally did not use the word *Player*. "A
webdancer. Do you regret it—being a Peaceforcer, I mean?"

"As opposed to what?" she said evenly.

"I don't know. A clown? Did you ever want to be a clown in the circus?"

Melissa du Bois blinked abruptly, swiftly, and then laughed. "No. But I did, the first time I saw the Ringling Brothers circus, I wanted to be one of the women who swung on the trapezes and got caught by the beautiful boys. I think I was twelve." She looked sideways at Trent again. "What did you want to be when you were twelve?"

"Thirteen."

"What was your childhood like—you are American?"

There was hardly point in denying it. "Yes."

"Growing up in the OA," she said slowly, "were you taught to hate us?"

"Taught? No."

She did not seem to catch the distinction. "Where did you grow up?"

"New York. Not far from Capitol City. It's how I ended up on the Secretary General's webdancer staff."

Trent thought she asked the question quite seriously. "What was it like, your childhood?"

"Depraved."

She thought about this for several seconds. "You mean 'deprived'?" she said carefully.

"Sure," said Trent cheerfully, "that too." Without any hesitation at all he continued, "Tell me more about your childhood. I've never been to France at all."

"You are too polite. We—"

"I'd really like to hear about it." Melissa met his eyes quickly, and Trent said simply, "Please?"

They talked for nearly two solid hours while a cabin full of Peaceforcers slept around them.

Melissa du Bois had been born and raised in Narbonne, a small town in southern France, near the Gulf of Lions in the Mediterranean Sea. Her father had owned a house right on the beach; she had acquired her current tan there, while on leave preparatory to reporting for duty at L-5.

"I've always wanted to go to the South Seas, myself," Trent told her. "There are beaches in New York, but they don't count, the sand is gray. The South Seas—one of the French Polynesian islands, maybe. Live on an island somewhere and sleep in the sun on the beach." He grinned at her. "So instead

I'm going to visit Luna, where if you step outside to get a tan you blow up and freeze to death and fry all at once."

Melissa had actually been to L-5 before, three years previously. She and her parents had toured it briefly on their way to Luna for a vacation; her parents' first vacation following her father's retirement from the PKF, Melissa's last vacation before joining. On the Moon they had stayed at the Hotel Copernicus; Melissa du Bois had learned to fly there, at the Luna City Flight Caverns.

"I wanted to go to New Vegas, but—" Melissa shook her head with a rather sad smile. "New Vegas is in Free Luna. My father got very angry at the suggestion that we visit. I think he wanted to pretend that there was no such thing as Free Luna." She paused a moment and then added, "My brother was stationed on Luna in 2064, during the Fizzle War between United Nations Luna and Free Luna." She paused again and said without inflection, "He died."

Trent spent most of the time listening, listening to the details of a life that had been so unlike his own that at times he was not certain that some of the things she told him, with an entirely straight face, were not jokes. Had her parents really forbidden her to continue seeing her first boyfriend merely because he had been arrested once? And if so, *why?*

During the entire time they talked, Melissa du Bois never once used the word "Peaceforcer."

"There is a tradition of public service in my family; my father is PKF Elite, and both of my uncles were PKF."

"I understand," said Trent slowly, "the desire . . . for public service. To help make things better. To say to the world, 'I have been here, and I made a difference.' "

Melissa smiled at him dazzlingly. "Yes. You do understand."

"But there's more than one way to make a difference. Accountants—talk to an accountant some day, and he'll tell you how critical what he does is, how without him commerce would grind to a halt. The same for salespeople, or engineers. Or babychasers, for that matter."

Melissa du Bois nodded, thoughtfully. "I would hate to work for the Ministry of Population Control. But you are right, it is necessary."

"And computerists—" Trent grinned. "A good filter routine, an Image description placed in the public Boards, things like that, I could make a very good case that such things contribute as much to real improvement as, say, a Peaceforcer with a gun."

"Really?" She seemed to be considering the idea.

"The Peaceforcers are more visible. But—Peaceforcers are damage control, Melissa. They don't build spacescrapers or roads or computers, they don't raise food, they don't create art. They just stop wars from happening."

"One would think," said Melissa slowly, "that this would be enough to ask of any public body."

"Damage control is important. Somebody has to do it."

Melissa du Bois chewed at her lower lip, looking at Trent.

"Yes," she said finally. "Somebody does."

Eight minutes and fifteen seconds before ETA Spacebase One at L-5, Melissa said, "Trent, I have been thinking."

"Is that unusual?"

"What is your last name?"

Half a dozen answers popped into his mind. "Smith," he said, without perceptible pause.

"I was wondering," and she hesitated, ". . . would you mind if I looked for you when I am back downside? I would like to see you again if I can. It cannot be soon," she said hurriedly, "for I will be on restricted duty at Spacebase One for the next six months, and when I do go downside . . . well, there are people who are prejudiced against the Elite. You are a very nice boy . . . if you wouldn't mind . . ." Her voice trailed off.

Trent said, "A nice boy?"

"You are cute," she shrugged, "and funny. You have made me laugh"—she paused, thinking—"twice."

"Not dashing?"

"No." She shook her head definitely.

"How about handsome? Or romantic?"

"No. Cute, yes, and witty."

"Okay." Trent nodded. "I'll take that."

"Good. I can reach you through the office of the Secretary General?"

"Oh. Yes, certainly of course. Sure."

"Good." She smiled at him with a shyness that Trent had never seen on the streets of New York in any girl older than ten. "It will be something to look forward to when I come back."

Trent nodded wordlessly. He felt like the greater of two evils, any two evils.

He sat quietly, lost in his own thoughts. Presumably the Peaceforcers would disembark here, the SpaceFarers would load whatever cargo they were taking on, if any, and the ship would proceed to Luna. Trent wondered how long it would all take.

The announcement, at four minutes and five seconds to ETA Spacebase One, was given in French.

The sound level in the passenger cabin jumped sharply.

The Peaceforcers were talking to each other in a babble of swift French which Trent could not follow at all.

Trent said to Melissa, "What did it say?"

"Didn't you hear the announcement?"

"The announcement? Yes."

"They just made an announcement," Melissa told him.

"I heard it. What did it say?"

"Don't you speak French at all?"

"A little, but I wasn't listening."

"You just told me you heard the announcement."

"I heard it," Trent explained, "but I wasn't listening."

"Oh."

"What did it say?"

"What did the announcement say?" Melissa du Bois repeated.

"Yes," said Trent very clearly, "the announcement."

"Two things. It said we would be quarantined for three hours, and it said there was a private message for us on PKF Band Two."

"What did *that* message say?"

Suddenly the wariness was back in her eyes. "I cannot tell you. Why do you want to know?"

"Uhm. Curiosity?"

"It said—" Melissa broke off, studying Trent as though for the first time. "Never mind."

Oh, no. "Well," said Trent mildly, "if you won't tell me why we're being quarantined, I guess I'll go find out for myself." He smiled at her while unstrapping himself from the reclining seat. He replaced his handheld in his briefcase, and, hooking his foot into one of the rows of handgrips that ran along the deck, got out of his seat, clutching his briefcase in one hand.

Melissa said quietly, "Where do you think you are going with your luggage?"

The smile was frozen on Trent's face. "To find out what's going on. Don't worry, stay here, I'll be right back."

Trent pulled his way along the grips, briefcase tucked beneath one arm, to the hatch that connected the rest of Deck Two to the passenger's cabin.

Trent did not intend to be right back.

The Peaceforcer nearest the exit, a kindly-seeming Frenchman in his mid-thirties, said, "Young man, I have dealt with the SpaceFarer's Collective before. Read the sign, and do not make the mistake I think you are about to make."

The holo said, *Except for Visits to the Restroom, Passengers Will Remain Seated Until Otherwise Instructed.*

Trent could not find the word 'please' anywhere on the sign.

The kindly Peaceforcer, who was probably the oldest of those in the cabin, said, "You should really sit down again."

"Without an up," said Trent, "there can be no down." He opened the pressure hatch and pulled himself through, dogging the hatch shut behind him.

Trent had no use for kindly Peaceforcers, none.

Trent floated in the corridor immediately outside the passenger's cabin, trying to think of what to do next, rationally considering his alternatives.

None came to mind. After a moment Trent realized that he was "upside down"—the corridor's local vertical pointed the other way. He righted himself, to see if it would help.

It didn't help.

"Vance!"

Trent found a grip, and turned around to face the sound. Lieutenant Zinth came floating down into the corridor through a hatch leading to the deck immediately above. He was clearly very angry. He did not bother to align himself into the local vertical. With his face staring upside down into Trent's, he snarled, "The Captain wants you. *Now.*"

Trent said, "Really?"

"What the hell have you quarantined our ship for?"

"What?"

"What the hell—"

"Wait, wait. I heard you the first time." Trent stared into Zinth's upside-down face. "Three hours, right?"

"You should bloody well know, you—"

"Ordered the quarantine," said Trent. "Right. I'm Moham-med Vance. Of course I did. There's a chase ship coming from Earth," he said to Zinth, "and it's going to be here in three hours?"

Zinth screamed, *"What the hell have you quarantined our ship for?"*

Trent let go of his briefcase. With a flick of his foot he pushed himself closer to the SpaceFarer. He wrapped his left hand firmly through a grip near Zinth, and with his right, pointed behind Zinth. "Because of *that*!"

The SpaceFarer twisted his head to look back down the empty corridor.

Trent aimed for a spot five centimeters to the right of the exact geometrical center of Lieutenant Zinth's chin, and, swinging with the full strength of which he was capable, broke his hand against it.

Zinth's head bounced once against the side of the access-way. Almost instantly, beads of blood began drifting away from the spot where Trent had struck him; Trent grabbed Zinth by his coat and pulled the SpaceFarer down into the corridor with him.

Trent remembered how, when they had both been together downside, standing up, the young SpaceFarer had been ex-actly his height.

To nobody in particular, Trent said, "I think I broke my hand."

Retrieving his briefcase, with the body very clumsily in tow, Trent began searching for a john.

Muttering to Zinth, "I don't usually do this sort of thing on such short acquaintance, you know," Trent began stripping the SpaceFarer's uniform from him.

After searching for a few seconds, Trent found a first-aid kit in the bathroom. Removing Zinth's ship coat and shirt, he used the adhesive tape to bind the SpaceFarer's wrists to-gether behind him. He affixed another strip to the SpaceFarer's mouth.

It was harder than Trent had expected to change clothes with Zinth. Among other things, the john was clearly in-tended for only one person at a time.

After taking Zinth's pants from him, Trent stared blankly for a moment at the SpaceFarer's underwear.

Trent could not recall ever having seen anything quite that shade of red before.

When he was fully dressed, Trent turned Zinth's maser over in his hands for several seconds. His face held no expression as he examined it. Finally he found a slot on the butt of the weapon; he turned it, and a small cage containing the charge pack dropped out of the butt. He removed the charge pack from its cage, replaced the cage inside the maser, and holstered the weapon.

As Trent left the bathroom, there was a gentle bump, transmitted through the hull of the ship; *The Captain Sir Dominic Flandry* had docked at Lagrange Five, the stronghold of the United Nations Peace Keeping Force in space.

"They don' ketch Brer Rab the thief, no, no," mumbled Trent to himself, and headed down to the coupling rings on Deck One.

• 5 •

Excerpted from the Name Historian's Looking Backwards From the Year 3000; pub. 3018, Alternities Press, CU:110.00 Zaradin.

Spacebase One—Colloquially, "Peaceforcer Heaven." Constructed 2019 by a consortium of SpaceFarer Companies known as the L-5 Development Co. The United Nations Peace Keeping Force assumed control in 2025, necessitating extensive rebuilding. Further expanded 2060; destroyed in the Peaceforcer Rebellion (which see), 2103.

Spacebase One, like Almundsen Military Base at L-4, sat atop one of the two useful, gravitationally stable points in the double-planet Earth–Luna system. L-4 and L-5, aside from being gravitationally stable—i.e., objects placed in those locations tended to stay there—were also, unlike L-1, L-2, and L-3, "high ground." Lunar libration points Four and Five were situated atop the gravity wells of both Earth and Luna, and from those positions the entire Earth–Luna system could be easily controlled. It is hardly surprising that Space Force and the PKF ended up splitting those locations between them.

Spacebase One's first use, as a PKF Elite surgery and train-
ing facility, dates to 2046; between the years 2046 and 2088 the
facility regularly processed approximately fifty Elite candidates
every six months. In 2088, due to the facility's increasing vul-
nerability to sabotage, its use as a training station for PKF Elite
was discontinued. Spacebase Fourteen at Saturn, as of 2088,
assumed that function.

In 2069, there were approximately sixty-five hundred Peace-
forcers stationed at Spacebase One, an estimated two hundred
of whom were Elite. The Commanding Officer, as of 2069,
when Trent the Uncatchable began his historic run, was an
unfortunate by the name of Etienne Géricault.

The cargo bay was huge; it occupied the entire first deck
over the engines.

Despite the fact that Trent had hurried as quickly as he was
able, there were already three SpaceFarers standing at the
coupling rings that led into Spacebase One, their feet an-
chored to the deck by magnetic slippers tied over their boots.

Pulling his way carefully along the grips, Trent made his
way to within fifteen meters of the three SpaceFarers before
being noticed.

Two of the three were women, one of the two a silver-
haired woman who *looked* older than anyone Trent had ever
seen before; older than Old Jack, older than Beth Davenport.
She said sharply, "You're not—" and then broke off.

Trent had the maser out, pointing at them.

Given the circumstances, the woman's voice was remarkably calm. She took a step toward Trent. "What have you
done to Lieutenant Zinth?"

"I told him to look behind himself and he did, so then I
slugged him. Don't SpaceFarer kids learn that trick?"

"What have you done to Lieutenant Zinth?"

"He's in the john on Deck Two. Unconscious, but alive."
Trent gestured to the lone man. "You. Take your slippers off,
throw them to me. Slowly."

The woman's uniform bore the name patch CPT. SAUN-
DERS. She moved closer to Trent, two shuffling steps across
the deck. "I take it that you are not Mohammed Vance."

"No, I lied about that. Sorry." The first of the slippers
came sailing toward Trent. He donned it, then the second,

one-handed. "Please, Captain—no closer. Move away from the coupling rings."

It seemed to Trent that the three of them were moving very slowly. As they shuffled away from the coupling rings, Captain Saunders said, "What are you going to do?"

"I don't know. I thought about trying to steal the *Flandry,* but I decided against it because it's too big."

Captain Saunders said evenly, "That was sensible."

"I figured I would steal a Peaceforcer ship instead. It's not like they're not already pissed at me."

Captain Saunders asked, "What do they want you for?"

Trent walked cautiously across the deck, accustoming himself to the magnetic soles, keeping the three covered with the useless maser. "They think I killed one of their Elite."

Captain Saunders stiffened. "Oh? That's what this is all about, then. That's why the quarantine."

"They didn't tell you that you had a murderer on board?"

"They haven't told us a damn thing."

"Sorry. I don't suppose you'd be interested in giving me sanctuary?"

Captain Saunders looked Trent over, and shook her head almost reluctantly. "Not a chance. Nobody has ever killed a Peaceforcer Elite before, you know. The Erisian Claw keeps trying."

Trent stood with his back to the closed coupling rings. "I was afraid of that."

"They'll make an example of you."

"They're trying." From the pocket of Lieutenant Zinth's coat he withdrew his squirt gun and without ceremony shot each of the three SpaceFarers in the face, once.

They looked more stunned than if he had masered them to death.

Trent waited while unconsciousness claimed them. In free fall, their bodies slowly curled into fetal balls, the two women held in place by their magnetic slippers. When they were definitely out of it, Trent pushed them into a darkened section of the cargo bay, and left them there. He wet his finger and held it up in midair, checking to make sure that there was an air current to bring them oxygen. He returned to the coupling rings, briefcase in hand.

The Peaceforcers waiting on the other side of the coupling rings likely did not have pictures of Trent, but it occurred to Trent that the briefcase might well be included in descriptions of him. Finally he simply shook his head. Johnny Johnny was in the briefcase; Trent had lost his first Image, Ralf the Wise and Powerful, and he was not about to lose his second.

Letting an air of outraged officiousness descend upon him, in good SpaceFarer style, Trent palmed the pressure pad next to the coupling rings. The exterior and then the interior rings dilated open.

Three Peaceforcers, standing at attention on the other side of the coupling rings, looked briefly startled. Their local vertical was about fifteen degrees off the *Flandry*'s; Trent, compensating, catwalked on a slight diagonal through the coupling rings, so that he entered Spacebase One on their vertical.

Two of the Peaceforcers, in uniform, were pointing masers at Trent as he came through. Trent dismissed them out of hand; their reactions were far too slow.

The third Peaceforcer, in a blue jumpsuit without shoes, with a pair of magnetic slippers tied at his ankles, completing a yawn as Trent came through, did nothing but raise an eyebrow and Trent froze absolutely motionless.

Emile had come back from the dead.

For several seconds his eyes insisted on interpreting it that way. The man was a tall Frenchman with unruly dark hair, and eyes every bit as expressive, almost haunted, as Garon's had been. The resemblance, down to the stiff skin that marked the man for the brass balls he was, was remarkable.

Trent shook it off with an effort, glared at the senior Peaceforcer in the best imitation of Lieutenant Zinth that he was capable of. When he spoke, his voice was half an octave lower than normal. "First Lieutenant Nelson Zinth of *The Captain Sir Dominic Flandry*." Trent actually had no idea what Zinth's first name was. Ignoring the weapons trained on him, he advanced two steps toward the cyborg. *They haven't told us a damn thing,* Captain Saunders had said. "What is the meaning of this idiocy?"

"Lieutenant," said the Peaceforcer Elite pleasantly enough, "I am Elite First Sergeant Rogér Colbert, at your service." He spoke American English with absolutely no accent whatsoever. "May I inquire, Lieutenant, why you've chosen to ignore our quarantine?"

"Your *quarantine,* cyborg," said Trent flatly, "isn't worth the saliva to spit on if the *Flandry* chooses not to honor it. You have yet to give us any reason for this foolishness."

"Lieutenant Zinth," said Colbert equably, not raising his

voice at all, "this is a matter of internal United Nations security. There is a Level Three Earth–Luna alert in effect, and we can allow no exceptions." The Elite stood before Trent, completely immobile. "Please return to your ship." The two junior Peaceforcers were still pointing their hand masers at Trent.

"Who is your commanding officer, Sergeant Colbert?"

"I report directly to Commander Géricault, Lieutenant."

"If you are unwilling or unable to explain the meaning of this quarantine to me," said Trent, "then I must request that you allow me to see Commander Géricault. Presumably he has the authority to explain your bizarre behavior?"

There was a long moment of silence. "Lieutenant," said Colbert finally, "I can tell you this much. The quarantine will last no more than three hours; we are awaiting a high-speed chase ship from Earth. We have reason to believe that one of your passengers is a murderer."

"I think," said Trent after a moment, "that I must speak to Commander Géricault. You," he said to the Peaceforcer Elite, "are not listening to me."

Colbert spoke slowly, as though to a child. "Oh?"

"Peaceforcer, we have some fifty-odd passengers this run. They are all Peaceforcers; your own new Elite candidates. If you wish to name one of them murderer, I'd hardly dream of arguing with you." Trent grinned at the startled look on the faces of the Peaceforcers behind Colbert. "But whether it is three hours or three minutes, the *Flandry* is *not* subject to the United Nations or its Peaceforcers, and if you think otherwise you're in for a hell of a shock." Trent held Colbert's eyes. "I will have either a complete explanation from Commander Géricault, or, Elite First Sergeant Colbert, I will recommend to Captain Saunders that we continue on to Luna—and you can pick up your murdering Peaceforcers from Luna yourself. It's entirely up to you."

Colbert held his head slightly to one side, studying Trent as though Colbert did not know quite what to make of him. "Bringing you to Commander Géricault would be . . . difficult. My orders are very clear, Lieutenant; we're to let nobody out of this ship."

"You can hardly keep the ship itself from going on to Luna, Sergeant. I doubt that'll please whoever's coming on the chase ship."

"Are you actually threatening to drag over fifty Peaceforcers to Luna against their will?" Sergeant Colbert looked genuinely intrigued by the concept. "I think that might be construed as kidnapping, which in turn might be construed as an act of war between the SpaceFarer's Collective and the United Nations."

Trent took a long, deep breath. He actually closed his eyes, and then looked up and met Colbert's gaze head-on.

Trent said, "Let's find out."

It hung in the balance for long, unending moment.

Trent remembered auditing an editorial in the *Electronic Times* which suggested that the Unification Council would not be the slightest bit displeased to find a good pretext for a war to extend the Unification of Earth to encompass Mars and the Belt and the SpaceFarers.

In a voice that was almost bemused, Colbert said, "Gallois, Chanton. No one else comes through this lock. Kill them if you must." The Peaceforcer smiled at Trent, gently, and said, "Come with me, Lieutenant, and I will take you to Commander Géricault."

It was 2:30 A.M., Eastern Seaboard Time, August 14, 2069.

One step behind, Trent followed the silent Peaceforcer through the largely deserted corridors of Peaceforcer Heaven.

It was hard for Trent to comprehend that only a day and a half ago he had been standing at the top of an unfinished spacescraper while an Elite that could have been this one's brother had attempted to kill him.

Peaceforcer Elite Colbert walked briskly, without looking back to insure that Trent was following him; Trent was just as pleased. He was not walking as gracefully as Colbert, surely not as gracefully as a SpaceFarer, with years of experience in free-fall, ought to walk. They walked through the core of Spacebase One, through the central cylinder around which the great outer wheels revolved. The central cylinder was in free-fall; at the rims, artificial gravity was provided through angular momentum. The wheels were not rigidly attached to the central cylinder; rather, they rotated independently of it, and of each other. The North Wheel rotated clockwise as viewed from the "north" end of Spacebase One, and the South Wheel rotated counterclockwise as viewed from that same vantage point, to cancel the tendency that a single wheel would have had to impart rotational energy to the central cylinder. For the PKF's purposes, it was the best possible design; the central cylinder had to be in free-fall, for surgery, and therefore it could not rotate about its axis. On the other hand, gravity was a necessity for the newly created Elites, to condition themselves for the return to Earth, and at the rim, the 4.2-kilometer-wide wheels rotated to provide 920 centimeters per second squared acceleration, nearly Earth's 980 cepssa. The wheels were connected to the central cylinder by a complex elevator system that worked only at intervals of several minutes as the spokes that led from the central cylinder to the wheels made their slow, majestic sweeps around the central cylinder's access points.

Trent watched where they went, memorizing their route. They were nearly to the spoke elevator—Commander Géricault, like all permanent inhabitants at L-5, tended to avoid the free-fall areas for any great length of time—when Trent found what he was looking for: an InfoNet systerm with a full-sensory traceset, just inside the entrance to what looked for all the world like a mad scientist's torture chamber.

They stood together in stony silence outside the elevator entrance, waiting for the rim elevator to arrive; occasionally, a Peaceforcer, passing by, would greet Colbert, and receive some word of reply. The Peaceforcers looked at Trent's SpaceFarer uniform curiously. There were not many people about; Trent supposed that even here the cycle of night and day must be adhered to in some degree. It was not unreasonable that they would have chosen to orient their day by Capitol City's.

At last the elevator arrived.

As the doors of the elevator curled up into a tight tube, Trent stepped in ahead of the Peaceforcer, transferring his briefcase from his left hand to his swollen right, tripping the catches in the process.

Rogér Colbert the Peaceforcer Elite said, "Quel?" when Trent shot him in the face with the squirt gun.

The skin of a Peaceforcer Elite is not as absorbant as the skin of a normal human; as the doors to the elevator began uncurling, Trent just had time to dodge.

Light flared through the space where Trent had just been, in an actinic ruby flash of light that tore through the walls of the elevator.

As Colbert sagged into unconsciousness, the elevator began to lurch into motion. Trent stabbed frantically at the pressure point marked EMERGENCY STOP; there was a brief pause, and Trent caught a whiff of burned meat, and then the elevator returned to its starting position.

The smell of burned meat grew stronger, and Trent traced it to its source.

Colbert had shot himself in the foot.

Trent pictured himself walking through Peaceforcer Heaven in a SpaceFarer uniform, asking for directions to the slipship bay. *That won't do,* he thought clearly.

The burn on Colbert's foot looked ugly, but Trent honestly could not think of anything he could do for the man. He opened the elevator doors again and stepped through, letting the doors uncurl until they were nearly closed against his briefcase.

Trent stood in front of the elevator, waiting. A short, rather pretty woman in a PKF uniform came by shortly, and stopped, puzzled. Trent drew the squirt gun and shot her in the face, opened the elevator doors, stuffed her inside, and closed the elevator doors on his briefcase again.

Nearly half a minute passed before a pair came by, both of them men, neither of them within ten centimeters of Trent's height. Trent shot them quickly, shoved them into the elevator. A voice immediately behind him said, in French, "What are you doing?" Trent turned swiftly to find himself looking into a pair of brilliant blue eyes: a female Peaceforcer in uniform, almost exactly his own height.

Trent said, "Hello," and shot her quickly. He caught her as she went limp, dragged her back inside the elevator, and let the door close on them all.

Looking at his collection of unconscious bodies, Trent said, "How utterly embarrassing."

The female Peaceforcer's underwear wasn't as pretty as Lieutenant Zinth's.

When he was fully dressed in her too-tight uniform, Trent stepped back out through the elevator door, and touched the pressure point marked DOWN.

Moving rapidly down the corridor, he headed back toward the InfoNet systerm he had seen earlier.

A sign immediately inside the torture chamber said, *Physical Therapy*.

Briefcase held between his knees, Trent seated himself before the InfoNet systerm, jacked his handheld in, pulled on the systerm's traceset, and closed his eyes.

Johnny Johnny unfolded into existence like a flower greeting the sun.

. . . HI, BOSS.

HI, JOHNNY.

WHERE ARE WE?

PEACEFORCER HEAVEN, LOGGED INTO A PEACEFORCER SYSTERM.

OH. BAD NEWS, BOSS.

TELL ME ABOUT IT.

AND SOME SLOW DAMN HARDWARE TOO, BOSS.

I'M SORRY ABOUT THAT; THIS IS HOSPITAL EQUIPMENT, JOHNNY JOHNNY, NOT DATAWATCH. CAN YOU GET ME A MAP OF THE STATION?

HOLD ON A SECOND, I'M AUDITING THE HELP FILES . . . HERE WE GO. A schematic of Spacebase One appeared floating three-dimensionally somewhere just behind Trent's closed eyelids; a long fat cylinder enclosed by a pair of counterspinning wide fat doughnuts. A bright red spark appeared at the bottom of the image, followed by the legend, *You Are Here.* SIX DIRECTIONS THEY USE, BOSS. UP, DOWN, NORTH, SOUTH, SPIN AND ANTISPIN. UP IS TOWARD THE CENTRAL CYLINDER, DOWN IS TOWARD GRAVITY, TOWARD THE WHEELS. SOUTH IS TOWARD THE SOUTH BAY, WHERE THE *FLANDRY* IS. NORTH IS TOWARD THE NORTH BAY, WHERE THE PEACEFORCER SHIPS ARE MOORED. SPIN IS THE DIRECTION THE NORTH WHEEL TURNS, ANTISPIN IS THE DIRECTION THE SOUTH WHEEL TURNS. Johnny Johnny paused. YOU'RE GOING TO STEAL A SHIP?

THAT'S THE IDEA.

THEY'LL SHOOT YOU DEAD, BOSS. WEAPONS EMPLACEMENT, HERE. A green spot glowed some sixty meters away from the North Bay. LASERS, A MASS DRIVER GUN, AND FUSION MISSILES.

SHOW ME THE PILOT'S LOCKER.

HERE.

Trent disengaged from the systerm, unjacked his handheld and stood to leave.

The Peaceforcer standing in the entrance was huge, at least fifty kilos heavier than Trent himself. He looked at Trent with a cold, measuring eye.

Trent said brightly, with his best accent, "Bonjour."

In French, the huge Peaceforcer told Trent to see somebody about his uniform, that Trent's appearance was entirely unacceptable.

Trent smiled at the man, thanked the man, and assured him that he would do so at the very first opportunity. He squeezed by the large man, who had not moved at all, and walked swiftly away down the corridor.

The corridor stretched away forever.

Trent walked through silence. The corridor ran the entire length of Spacebase One; Trent had no feel at all for how far he had gone down its length. Other walkways branched out from this one in all directions, up and down and to the sides. There were dilation rings every few meters. Trent found himself growing disoriented. Nothing gave any sense of up or down; no gravity, nothing in the architectural layout. One Peaceforcer came into view walking on the ceiling of a cross corridor, and another swept by Trent from behind, flying freely down the length of the passage, navigating with touches of hands and feet to the grips extruding from the walls. Once a Peaceforcer, sitting in midair at an intersection, face at right angles to Trent's, looked at Trent oddly; Trent simply nodded to the man and kept walking, ostentatiously not hurrying, under the theory that suspicious people are people who act suspiciously.

Trent felt the man's gaze on the back of his neck as he walked away.

Only a frog Peaceforcer, he thought, *would find something suspicious about bad tailoring.*

His recently operated-upon knee was beginning to get sore, and his calves as well. Walking with magnetic slippers, in freefall, was an entirely different matter from walking in gravity. He tried to find a rhythm for it, gliding along the way he had seen others doing, actually touching the deck with only the toes of the slippers, and was, he thought, getting the hang of it.

"ALERT, ALERT!" blared the voice.

Trent jerked to a stop, heart pounding. He found himself drifting in very nearly the exact geometrical center of the corridor, out of reach of grips on any side.

"ALIEN IN THE INSTALLATION, REPEAT, UNAUTHORIZED ALIEN IN THE INSTALLATION; ALL PERSONNEL RETREAT TO SECURED AREAS. LOCKDOWN IN EFFECT, REPEAT, LOCKDOWN IN EFFECT. PERSONNEL IN CORRIDORS WILL BE SHOT WITHOUT WARNING. REPEAT, LOCKDOWN IN EFFECT."

"Bastards!" screamed Trent. Nobody at all answered him, and feeling terribly silly he waited while the gentle drift of the corridor's air took him within grabbing distance of a grip. He did not try to walk again; he dug his toes into a pair of grips and kicked off down the corridor with all the strength that was in him.

He lost velocity only slowly; air friction alone was insufficient to impede him much. He was still moving at a fair clip when he saw his next Peaceforcer, walking down the middle of the corridor watching Trent fly toward him. The Peaceforcer showed little alarm at first, and then some alarm, and then considerable alarm, and then Trent hit him. They collided in a tangle of arms and legs; with the briefcase in his left hand Trent swung at the Peaceforcer, smashed the edge of the briefcase up against the Peaceforcer's temple; the reaction sent Trent tumbling slowly backward to fetch up against the corridor wall. The Peaceforcer's head bounced off the bulkhead with an audible thud. When Trent regained his orientation again, the Peaceforcer hung limp in midair, not moving at all. Tiny beads of blood were forming in the air around the spot where Trent had struck him. With something approaching panic Trent kicked over to where the Peaceforcer hung motionlessly, and checked the man's pulse; it was strong and even.

"Thank you," said Trent to nobody in particular. He pulled the Peaceforcer to the nearest doorway, palmed it open, and shoved the man in.

And then the lights went out.

Trent heard his voice say, independent of him in the utter blackness, "What a bad day."

Trent made his way slowly along the corridor, searching for doors by touch, feeling his way in the darkness by the grips and door recesses. He thought he had been very near the north end of the cylinder when the lights went out.

There was nobody in the first room Trent tried, and it was dark besides. The second, third, fourth, and fifth doors opened by Trent were also empty, also dark.

There were three people in the room that the sixth door opened onto, and the room was lit, well lit, shining with bright yellow light from the ceiling sunpaint.

In the second when the three men were turning to look at the opening door, Trent pushed through, maser in hand, screaming, "Don't move!"

Only one of the three was facing Trent; the other two were half-dressed, with their backs to him. Nobody moved.

"Turn away from me."

The one Peaceforcer facing Trent stared at Trent, then at the maser in his hand, and then turned very carefully away.

"If anybody does anything stupid," said Trent, just loudly enough for them to hear him, "I'm going to cut you clean in half."

Not one of the three so much as twitched. Transferring the useless maser to his right, useless hand, Trent pulled his squirt gun from his coat pocket with his left. Aiming carefully, Trent squirted each of the three on the back of the neck, making sure that the liquid touched skin each time.

When he finished, the squirt gun was entirely empty.

Then, for the first time, Trent looked around the room he found himself in.

It was small, about twenty meters by fifteen.

There were lockers along the bulkheads.

Trent tried to remember exactly how close he had been to the slipship bays when they turned out the lights in the corridors.

"No, no," said Trent. This could not be the pilot's locker. "Good luck? Me?" Trent touched one of the lockers, tentatively. "No," he said decisively. A few beats later, he said questioningly, "Yes?" He looked at the locks on the lockers—palmprint activated, passive check circuits—and yelled, "YES!"

Halfway through the first row, he found a pressure suit that fit, donned it. He had the impression that he was not supposed to wear it over a SpaceFarer uniform; though the material of the pressure suit was soft and form-fitting, it felt tight in odd places. He had special difficulty getting the pressure suit's boots on over the SpaceFarer boots he was wearing.

There was a holster on the right hip of the pressure suit.

Trent stared at it. A holster on a pressure suit? He looked in the locker he had taken the pressure suit from; there was a maser inside, restrained by an elastic strap. Trent shrugged, and filled the holster with the maser he had inherited from Lieutenant Zinth.

It took some examination before he figured out the helmet; it was supposed to hang on a snap just over his back, so that he could reach back and pull it forward, closed, in a single movement.

Mimicking the other pressure suits he had seen, Trent snapped the suit's gloves on at the spot on his left hip which did not have a pistol holster.

One of the bodies in the locker with him had begun snoring, and Trent addressed the Peaceforcer: "Good-bye, dear friends; good-bye. I must go; spaceship to steal; things to do."

Trent went to the door at the other end of the room, hopefully the door which let out onto the North Bay, opened the door and looked out.

A wide, broad area stood revealed, vaguely circular in shape, some forty meters in diameter, perhaps five meters high. Airlocks were arrayed around the perimeter of the circle; there were green lights over some of the airlocks, red lights over others. One airlock had a red light flashing over it.

Trent left, closing the door to the pilot's locker room, turning the lights off as he did so.

Trent took three steps into the empty flight bay, marveling at his good luck.

On the fourth step, there was a light tug at his waist, and something improbably hard smashed into his ribs.

The impact lifted one of Trent's feet from the floor. He reattached it slowly in the zero gravity, and turned to look into Lieutenant Zinth's maser.

Melissa du Bois said, "Hello, Trent the thief."

Trent had read once that after a certain number of shocks the nervous system became inured.

Trent had not reached that number yet. He said, "Uh . . . uh . . ."

Melissa had both hands wrapped around the maser. Her knuckles were white on the handle. She said conversationally, "Fifteen minutes ago I found out who you are." Her accent had thickened slightly under the stress. "Thirteen minutes ago I finished reading our dossier on you; it is a fascinating document. Ten minutes ago I located a systerm, found North Bay, and headed here." She smiled at Trent. It was utterly without humor. "Technically, I am AWOL. They would not give me a weapon either." She inclined her head very slightly. "Thank you for the loan."

Trent said, "Uh . . . Melissa . . ." Nothing was occurring to him.

"You are an intriguing man, Trent the thief." Her cheeks were slightly flushed. "Respected contract thief, very likely one of the twenty best Players alive . . ."

"Ten."

". . . and a man of wit and humor, reputed to be extremely skilled in unarmed combat. One of eight criminals who has ever destroyed a pursuing waldo; the only one who has ever escaped the PKF Detention Center in Capitol City; the only one ever to kill an Elite officer of the Peace Keeping Force."

"Melissa, you're making . . ."

"A mistake, I know, Trent the thief, you are innocent. You did not do it."

"I *didn't*. It was an accident," Trent said, "he fell." He looked at her, met her eyes directly. "Really. Killing is wrong." Without looking away from her, he felt his side. "Damn it, I think you broke a rib."

Melissa chuckled. It didn't reach her eyes. "It is a curious thing, Trent, but you have managed to do something nobody else ever has. You have made me feel very stupid. And I am not a stupid woman; I usually guess right." She gestured at the row of eight airlocks. "I am where I am. My superiors did not expect you to make it to North Bay. How could he even find it, they said. They did not think you would make it here through all the Peaceforcers if you did find it." She shrugged. "I did. I have great respect for you, Trent the thief." Her hands, holding the maser, were terribly steady. "I shall be present at your execution."

"You liked me."

"You incredible egomaniac." She shook her head. "You are charming, but that is not it. Do you realize what you have done to me? You sat down next to me and *told me your name.* Trent 'Smith,' " she said icily.

Trent said quietly, "I thought I was safe by that point. My name wasn't on the Boards even then, and I was seven hours from Free Luna. I didn't know you were a Peaceforcer."

Melissa du Bois shook her head, very slowly. "You really do not know, do you?"

"Melissa, I don't have time for this."

"I am going to be known for the rest of my life as the Elite whom Trent the thief spent four and a half hours sitting next to while a Level Three alert was on for him. My career is ruined. My name is a joke."

"I'm going to steal a spaceship now."

The barrel of the maser climbed until it was centered on Trent's wishbone. "No, you are not."

Trent said mildly, "You're not going to shoot me, Melissa."

"Not if you surrender."

"Not at all."

"Trent, I should prefer to take you alive. But I will kill you if I must."

Trent cocked his head to one side, as though listening to something. "I don't have time for this. And I think you broke one of my ribs."

"I am horribly sorry."

"It's okay." Turning away from her, Trent headed toward the airlocks.

"Trent," called Melissa.

Trent turned to face her.

She said softly, "I am sorry, my friend," and pulled the trigger.

There was a gentle, quiet click.

Trent smiled at her. "There's no charge cartridge."

Melissa stared at him, then at the maser, then at him again.

"I pulled the charge cartridge," Trent explained. "I didn't want to hurt anybody."

Soft, meaningless sounds issued from her throat.

"I understand how you feel," said Trent, "but there's this spaceship . . ."

With a stifled scream, Melissa launched herself across the deck at him. Trent ducked slowly, grabbing Melissa by the ankles as she sailed by overhead. Methodically, he pulled off her magnetic slippers, and then her shoes. He pushed her very lightly away from him, away from any possible grip.

Trent licked one finger and tested the air currents. He pointed at the far bulkhead. "That way," he called out to Melissa, "the air's circulating that way."

Trent turned away from her again as she struggled futilely in midair, and continued toward the row of airlocks. The red light was still flashing over the third airlock from the right.

At the airlock, a thought struck Trent. "Melissa!"

She looked in his direction.

"The air currents should take you to the wall in, I don't know, ten minutes or so, but if you're really in a hurry, take off your clothes and throw them away from you; for every action there is an equal and opposite reaction."

Trent stood, looking at her, for just a moment.

Then, with furious speed, Melissa du Bois began stripping her shirt off.

Trent watched her a moment longer, wishing he could stand around and react. He cycled through the airlock, his voice so quiet he himself could barely hear it. "So much to do, so little time."

· 6 ·

The ship docked at the third airlock from the right was not a slipship.

It was a two-seat yacht; the legend inscribed on the bulkhead, immediately inside the airlock, read:

United Nations Space Force
Rolls-Royce 2066, #312

The interior of the yacht consisted of the pilot's cabin, the airlock, and a small passageway that connected the two. Trent presumed that there were engines somewhere.

Going forward, Trent entered the pilot's cabin, seated himself in the left-hand seat and strapped in.

In the right-hand seat, there was a handsome, elderly silver-haired man. He was skimming news reports on his handheld when Trent entered. On the breast of his pressure suit a name patch said COL. WEBSTER, UNSF.

Colonel Webster had barely glanced up when Trent entered. Returning to his handheld, he said in clipped military tones, "You're late, pilot."

"I've heard that one before," Trent snapped. He began studying the board before him. Except for what was obviously an ancient triddy tank, in the lower right-hand corner of the control panel, there was nothing Trent recognized on the entire board.

Colonel Webster's head turned toward Trent as though it moved on bearings. "You're not my pilot."

"I'm not anybody's pilot."

"What the hell does the PKF think it's up to, Lieutenant?"

Trent glanced down briefly at the name patch on his pressure suit. LT. CHARBRIER, he read upside down.

It seemed to be Trent's fate in life to impersonate officers of low rank.

"Honestly," said Trent, "I don't think anybody but Melissa has much of an idea." One pressure point, near the top of the board, was bordered in blue and was labeled AUTO.

Thank God for the British, Trent thought. He pressed the point marked AUTO.

The colonel's face was growing red. "Are you under the impression, Lieutenant, that being a member of the PKF gives you . . ."

Trent said, "I'm not a Peaceforcer." The triddy tank glowed slightly, with a milky gray sheen; it silvered, blossomed into rainbows, and sank in to depth.

In the tank, the words SYSTEM ACTIVE appeared.

"You're not . . . you're . . ."

"I'm a thief."

"A th—"

"A thief. Trent the thief. Hello, computer?" There was no response from the system; Trent could not find anything on the control board in front of him that remotely resembled an I/O device. Opening his briefcase, he withdrew the circuit tracer and located the triddy tank lead-ins, following them down. The traces led into a panel on the floor; Trent got down on his knees and yanked the panel open, revealing a mass of logic and memory circuits entirely unlike anything he had ever seen before. He recognized various components, but at least half of the logic and most of the chipglue was entirely custom. There was one flat plastic plug sitting toward the bottom of the array of exposed circuitry; Trent pulled the plug free and exposed a standard optical handheld jack.

Trent plugged his handheld in and climbed back into the lefthand seat.

Colonel Webster watched the entire routine wordlessly. When Trent was finished, he burst out, "How can you be doing this?"

"I don't know."

"I can't let you do this."

"You can't stop me."

"But . . ."

Trent turned and looked the man square in the face. "Colonel, you're wasting my time, and I don't have a lot. You're old and you don't have a weapon." Trent paused as a thought struck him. "Do you?"

"Well, no, but . . ."

"You don't have a weapon," Trent said conclusively. "I'm stronger than you are, smarter than you are, younger than you are, and a *hell* of a lot more desperate than you are; I know kung fu, karate, aikido, shotokan, judo, and lots of other Oriental words, so would you *please* shut up?"

Trent had not raised his voice. The Colonel blinked and shut up.

For approximately the tenth time that day Trent regretted Booker's lack of ability to dig up a traceset for him. Aloud, Trent said, "Johnny?"

There was a brief pause before the words appeared in the triddy field. HI, BOSS.

"Can you hear me?"

YEP. CAN'T FIND AN AUDIO OUTPUT FOR THIS MESS. USE THE HANDHELD SPEAKER? I'LL HAVE TO JACK THE VOLUME ALL THE WAY UP.

"This is fine, Johnny."

SLOW DAMN HARDWARE AGAIN, BOSS.

"Sorry, Johnny. Get us out of here and I'll pour you into the finest inskin Credit can buy."

There was another pause. SO—WE MADE IT TO THE NORTH BAY. CHECKING . . . NOT BAD, BOSS. THIS SUCKER HAS RANGE TO TAKE US BACK TO EARTH, IF WE WANT.

"How's the autopilot?"

LIKEWISE NOT BAD . . . THE HARDWARE'S RELATIVELY NEW; THE PROGRAM ITSELF'S ALMOST FIFTEEN YEARS OLD.

BUT IT'LL GET US THERE. IT TELLS ME IT'S A MCDONNELL
1300 AUTOPILOT, WITH AUXILIARY FUNCTIONS AS FOL-
LOWS: ENTERTAINMENT CAPABILITIES—

"Cancel, Johnny. Inventory comm systems, weapons, drive
type and acceleration capabilities. Disengage the airlock."

DONE. There was a hollow clang as the airlock discon-
nected. THIS VEHICLE, ROLLS-ROYCE YACHT 2066, INVEN-
TORY #312, TELLS ME IT'S "UNARMED." COMMUNICATIONS
ON ALL APPROVED RADIO BANDS; FURTHER EQUIPPED FOR
LASER COMMUNICATIONS. GREEN "COMMUNICATIONS" LA-
SER, OF 4.4 MEGAJOULES CAPACITY . . .

Trent said, "Mahatma Gandhi!" He turned and stared at
Colonel Webster. "You have a communications laser on this
ship for what, talking to Alpha Centauri?"

"This is a military . . ."

"Shut up."

DRIVE SYSTEM IS PROTON-BORON FISSION, NONRADIA-
TIVE. IT PRODUCES A BURST TOP ACCELERATION OF 8,800
CEPSSA, A SUSTAINABLE TOP ACCELERATION OF 6,200
CEPSSA. MAGNETICALLY BOTTLED POSITRONS, USED TO INI-
TIATE PROTON-BORON REACTION, MAY BE SPRAYED INDE-
PENDENTLY OF THE MAIN ENGINE.

Trent looked up from the readout in the triddy tank. He
looked blankly out the viewport for a moment, then turned to
study Colonel Webster. With something very like horror, he
said, "Where do they *get* people like you?"

The old man stared at him, still with no idea at all what
was going on. "Where . . ."

"Shut up." Through the fore viewfield Trent could see
Luna, hanging midphase against a background of stars. When
he looked back down into the triddy tank, a sentence hung
there, silver text against the ambient blue background.

BOSS, THE INVENTORY SHOWS A TRACESET ON BOARD.

Trent snapped, *"Where?"*

CHECKING . . .

In the triddy tank, a holo of the yacht appeared. The apparent viewpoint entered the airlock, and moved forward into the
pilot's cabin. It focused on a spot just behind where Colonel
Webster sat, and illuminated a section of the bulkhead. Trent
leaned over Colonel Webster without explanation, located the
latch to the storage compartment next to Webster's elbow,
and popped it open.

There were half a dozen items inside the storage compartment, ranging from a first-aid kit to a repair kit for breached pressure suits. Trent tossed items left and right—emergency food rations, a water bottle, the first-aid kit and a box marked PATCHES, the traceset—

He lunged back and snatched the traceset out of midair.

It was larger than any traceset Trent had seen in five years; the trodes alone, at the ends of a single long curved piece of plastisteel which was supposed to snap on around the back of the skull, were three and a half centimeters in diameter. The control, surface mounted on the supporting plastisteel bar, was simply a radio frequency selector marked "Band One" through "Band Eight."

"Johnny, which band?"

TRY BAND FOUR, BOSS; THAT'S THE BAND THE HARD-WARE HERE EXPECTS TO USE FOR DIAGNOSTICS. IT'S THE WIDEST BANDWIDTH CIRCUIT AVAILABLE.

It was set to Band Three; Trent touched the pressure point next to the readout once, licked the trodes and put the traceset on.

Trent closed his eyes to go Inside and heard Colonel Webster tensing in the seat next to him.

Trent said, "Don't do that."

Webster did it anyway, swung the handheld at Trent's skull.

Trent did not even open his eyes; with his swollen right hand he slapped Webster's arm away, clenched the hand into a fist, and punched in the general direction of Webster's face. He connected solidly; he was certain that the impact hurt him more than it did the Space Force colonel.

Trent said, "Please don't do that."

He went Inside.

Johnny Johnny came alive.

The part of him which was Image had time to marvel, briefly, as they coalesced together, at how a fast and simple optical transputer could combine with a slow and complex salt-water-based protein soup to produce something able to do things of which neither, alone, was even remotely capable.

The part of him which was Trent was far too slow to be aware of the process of joining as anything but instantaneous.

The brief moment passed and Johnny Johnny went down into the Rolls-Royce's control circuitry.

Looking out through the ship navigation cameras, Johnny

Johnny located the other vehicles moored at the North Bay. The ship that he was in was the only one of its type; the rest of the vehicles were slipships, single-occupant military vehicles designed to be flown by PKF Elite, with twice the yacht's acceleration and maneuverability, three times its firepower. The Rolls' autopilot informed Johnny Johnny that they were powered by microfusion engines running off monatomic hydrogen; at Johnny Johnny's request the autopilot dug up schematics for the ships.

There was a cluster of five slipships very near one another; Johnny Johnny turned the yacht over on attitude rockets and pulled away from the launching bay, out into clear space. He centered the 4.4-megajoule "communications" laser about two-thirds of the way down on one of the slipships, where the schematics showed the monatomic-hydrogen tank, and pulsed the laser just once.

The entire North Bay exploded.

Monatomic hydrogen under immense pressure swept out from the damaged slipship in a great wash of flame, mixing with the liquid oxygen from the lifesystems. Like a living thing the flame ripped into the nearby slipships, tearing through hullmetal as though it were plastipaper.

It was too fast for the human eye to catch; Johnny Johnny sat and watched in calm amazement through the ship cameras as the disaster unfolded. The portion of Johnny Johnny that was Trent had the fleeting thought that he was going to be sick, thinking about Melissa du Bois, trapped just the other side of the airlocks. The chain reaction, as one slipship after another added its supply of oxygen and single-H to the conflagration, was awesome. The flame touched a chain of refueling tanks near the edge of the Bay; the resulting majestic explosion reached out arms of flame to touch the yacht, sent the Rolls-Royce tumbling out into space.

Nearly a minute passed while Johnny Johnny fought to regain control of the yacht. When he had finally corrected the tumbling and the modest velocity the explosion had imparted the yacht, it hung in space some three hundred meters away from the North Bay.

Beside him, Trent heard Colonel Webster murmuring a prayer: "—shall become in him a fountain of water, springing up unto life everlasting. Receive their souls, Lord. Amen."

Amazingly, when the flame cleared, the flight bay was still pressurized.

Trent felt a brief surge of elation; once again he had probably succeeded in not killing somebody; Melissa was very likely still alive inside. He turned to Colonel Webster. "Do you see that?"

"That's a miracle," said Colonel Webster.

Trent detached himself slightly from Johnny Johnny, shook his head. "No, it's engineering."

Colonel Webster did not even look at him. His eyes were fixed on the destruction Trent had caused.

"They probably designed the flight bay to withstand this sort of thing. The PKF," Trent explained to the Colonel, "is terribly damn insecure."

Space Force Colonel Webster said, "Really?"

"Really. I'm not sure why."

Trent envisioned utter chaos inside of Spacebase One, as thousands of Peaceforcers were roused from sleep by either the shock of the explosion or by other Peaceforcers.

Trent envisioned turning the yacht around and fleeing toward Luna.

Trent envisioned being shot down by the Peaceforcers before he was halfway there.

"What to do," Trent muttered, "what to do."

"I would suggest surrendering yourself," said Colonel Webster stiffly.

"I'm not talking to you," said Trent. He went back Inside.

Aiming at the missile launch window, which also contained, withdrawn into protective bunkers at the moment, particle beam weapons and laser cannon, preparing to fire into the launch window at random until something either exploded or shot back, Johnny Johnny paused.

What would it take, Johnny Johnny wondered, to detonate a nuclear warhead? Would a 4.4-megajoule laser do it?

Were there even nuclear-tipped missiles inside?

As far as Johnny Johnny was concerned, L-5 was wasted on Spacebase One, and just as well cleared for use for something else; but there were people inside.

Under his breath, Trent said aloud, "What to do, what to do."

Trent didn't want to kill anyone, not even Peaceforcers who deserved it.

"Damn, damn, damn," he said, "what to do, what to do."

Nothing was occurring to him.

Something occurred to him.

Aloud, Trent marveled, "*Boy,* that's a stupid idea."

"What?" asked Colonel Webster.

"Of course," said Trent, turning to look earnestly into Colonel Webster's eyes, "they can only kill me once."

The old man nodded uncertainly. "Yes."

"I'm sorry," said Trent, "but I don't have my squirt gun anymore. Can I have your handheld?"

Webster gave Trent his handheld. "You can't," he said softly, "really think you're going to get away with kidnapping an officer of the United Nations Space Force."

"Oh, I'm going to give you back," Trent assured the man. "I am sorry," he repeated, "that I don't have my squirt gun anymore."

Colonel Webster looked away from Trent for a moment, and then looked back. "Why are you sorry?" he asked quietly.

Trent grinned at the man. "It was filled," Trent explained, "with Complex 8-A. You know, fadeaway."

Colonel Webster simply looked at him without comprehension.

"Don't you get it?"

Colonel Webster shook his head. "No."

"I could shoot you with it and say, 'Old soldiers never die, they simply fadeaway.' "

Colonel Webster didn't laugh.

Trent's smile vanished. "Your problem," he said, "is you have no sense of humor." Holding Colonel Webster's handheld in his unhurt left hand, he struck the man in the side of the head. The movement sent a spasm of pain through his ribs.

Colonel Webster simply blinked, so Trent struck him again, harder, and Webster lolled freely in his seat.

With skill a professional pilot might have admired, Johnny Johnny brought the yacht within meters of the launch window before the Rolls' momentum with regard to the central cylinder of Spacebase One was canceled.

Shedding the traceset, Trent unstrapped himself from his

seat. Ignoring the pain which movement caused him, he opened up his briefcase and withdrew the reel of monofilament. He donned the pressure suit's right glove, closing the airseal with his left hand. He had to take off the traceset before he could get the helmet on. Reaching over his shoulder, again with his left hand, he pulled on the helmet and sealed the neck's locking ring. Trent wiggled his left hand into the glove hooked to his hip. Without expression, he used his broken right hand to close the airseal on the glove.

Standing in the airlock, Trent leaped approximately five meters over to the missile launch window. Unreeling the fineline, he located the laser cannon and particle projectors and began weaving a web of fineline over their tracking mirrors, not very tightly, but firmly enough so that if anyone tried to move either the weapons or their aiming mirrors, the restraining monofilament would slice them into small pieces.

Trying not to think of what would happen to him if anybody fired a missile while he was actually standing in the launch window, Trent proceeded to do the same thing with each of the four clusters of missiles.

He had far more fineline than he needed to do the job.

When he was finished, Trent went to the edge of the launch window, and looked at the stars.

It's the tourist in me, Booker; I've always wanted to see Luna.

Earth hung over Trent's head; Luna was off to Trent's right. There was a tiny bright spot, off past Luna, that was Almundsen Military Base at L-4, and another, somewhat fuzzier bright spot, just to one side of Earth, that was Halfway, the massive industrial zero-gee factory park that circled Earth in Clarke orbit.

The stars were even brighter than they had been in the holo on the wall of the *Flandry*.

It was all quite lovely.

The remark to Booker had been, at best, only half a joke.

Trent sighed, and returned to the yacht.

The proton-boron engine fired at slightly better than two thousand centimeters per second squared acceleration, on a planned trajectory to the far side of Luna.

Trent was struggling to breathe. Every breath was a lance of fire crawling down his right side.

In the seat next to him Trent had bound Colonel Webster's arms at his sides, using a snakechain from the airlock. Colonel Webster's helmet was clamped shut; Trent had done that, too.

The man wouldn't shut up, and Trent didn't want to hit him again.

At first Trent was not sure what had changed.

Then the beeping sound penetrated his consciousness. Through the traceset, Trent said, JOHNNY.

INCOMING CALL, BOSS. JUDGING FROM THE INTENSITY OF THE SIGNAL, IT'S A WIDE-BEAM MASER FROM SPACEBASE ONE; THEY DON'T ACTUALLY HAVE A TIGHT BEAM ON US.

IF I ANSWER IT, CAN YOU ALTER MY VOICE PRINT WITHOUT THEM BEING AWARE OF IT?

ON THIS HARDWARE . . . THERE'LL BE A DELAY OF ABOUT A HUNDRED THIRTY MILLION NANOSECONDS, BOSS.

EIGHTH OF A SECOND? GOOD ENOUGH.

"Hi," said Trent. "Hi there." Moving slowly under the two thousand cepssa, carefully, muscles aching, Trent unstrapped from his seat and pulled Webster's helmet off. He checked the man's respiration and heartbeat; although the man was still unconscious, both eyes dilated equally when exposed to light.

A deep, hard voice, like a speaking stone, said, "Trent."

"That's a *good* guess," said Trent. "Who am I speaking to?"

"Commissionaire Mohammed Vance, PKF Elite."

"Oh?" Trent remembered being told by Rogér Colbert that the quarantine of the *Flandry* would last only three hours; it meant that Vance must still be in the pursuit ship, and had not actually arrived at L-5 yet.

Belatedly, as an afterthought, and on general principles, Trent instructed Johnny Johnny to beam the following conversation to Almundsen Military Base at L-4. "I know you," Trent said to Vance. "I stole your dossier the other day."

"I know," the voice rumbled. "I paid the Syndic for holographs of you yesterday evening. Apparently I've also paid for your passage aboard the *Flandry,* your cab fare, and a phone call to a number I haven't been able to trace."

"It's not there."

"Excuse me?"

"The number doesn't go to the number it goes to."

A chuckle. "As you say."

It was twenty-four minutes before the yacht would enter Lunar orbit, twenty-six before it would be beyond line of sight to L-5. "Hey, Vance," said Trent, "where did I screw up?"

"A bit too much flashiness, Trent. It's a common mistake among the young. You shouldn't have stolen the Unification Councilor's car."

"I was late," Trent muttered.

"He called it in; I had tags out for anything involving that sort of, shall we say, casual theft. DataWatch did a bit of scouting around, and you'll understand, it was the work of a moment for me to realize that the Mohammed Vance who boarded the *Flandry* was not myself."

"Thanks, Vance. I was curious. What now?"

"I presume you are not interested in surrendering yourself for trial and subsequent execution?"

"Gosh but you're a smart Peaceforcer."

"I thought not. Well, then, we can spend the next . . . seventeen minutes and fifteen seconds or so discussing psychology, negotiating, what-have-you. Seventeen minutes, now, is the time I have left before I must send the missiles to destroy you. I'd have preferred to simply destroy your craft's drive with laser cannon, but I'm informed that the aiming mirrors are no longer responding."

Trent said, "Psychology?"

"The relationship between the hunted and the hunter. It fascinates me."

"I bet."

"Let me give you an example. Having studied all of the data I've been able to accumulate about you, I've made a small wager with myself. As I see it, Trent, you have two alternatives, and I believe I know which one you will choose."

Two alternatives was at least one alternative more than Trent could think of. "Two alternatives?"

"The first," said Vance, "is to take Colonel Webster down to the airlock, seal his suit, activate his beacon, and push him away from the shuttle, so that he'll have a chance of surviving when we destroy the ship."

Trent glanced at Webster, tied in the seat next to him; the man was twitching slightly in his seat, as though he were straining, through his pressure suit, against the bonds which held him in place. "And the other alternative?"

"Keep him with you, and drag him to your death with you."

"Oh. This is a subtle way of letting me know he's of no use to me as a hostage, is it?"

"Would you prefer I be plainer?"

"No. No, really. Which way are you betting?"

"I think," said Vance, "that you'll let him live. Your behavior throughout this event has been most interesting."

"Thank you," said Trent after a moment. "How do you turn on the beacon?"

"It's a small, bright red button," the deep voice said quietly, "on both the inner and outer surfaces of the helmet's collar." Trent located the button immediately. "Press it once and then don't press it again."

"Okay. Thanks again."

"You are quite welcome, Trent."

"By the way, Commissioner. There are two things you do not know."

"What might those be, Trent?"

"Well, the first one is that I've been beaming this conversation to Almundsen Space Force Base at L-4."

There was silence at the other end of the maser beam. Five minutes gone by; by Vance's reckoning, there would be about twelve minutes left in which he could still destroy Trent.

Vance said slowly, "You're bluffing."

Trent said, "Wanna bet?"

There was no response from Vance's end.

"Call them, ask," Trent said. "Better yet, wait; they'll call you."

Trent broke the connection and took off the traceset. "Johnny," he said aloud, "cut the acceleration, please." He unstrapped himself again as the rockets died, unstrapped the colonel, and in free-fall dragged Colonel Webster back to the airlock.

Standing in the airlock, Trent checked Webster as thoroughly as he could from the outside; seven hours of air, the vampire gauge on the man's earlobe showing sufficient oxygenation of the bloodstream. Webster was shouting something at Trent; Trent could barely hear his voice through the man's helmet.

Trent sealed his own helmet again, closed the inner airlock door and touched the pressure point to begin evacuation. He chinned the radio bar on the right-hand side of his helmet. "Colonel Webster?"

A blast of noise hit him the second he released the chin pad; Webster, screaming, shouting obscenities at Trent.

Trent shouted, *"Shut up!"*

The airlock status light went bright red; Colonel Webster, rather to Trent's surprise, shut up. "Look," said Trent, "I'm going to push you out into space and the Peaceforcers are going to come get you after they blow me up. Okay? I'm throwing you away so you'll be safe."

The man's eyes were wide inside the helmet. His voice quivered. "You're throwing me away?"

"So you'll be safe," Trent assured him. "Try to look on it as an Experience, like something Winnie the Pooh might get involved in; Floating in Space while Awaiting Rescue. Like that."

"Winnie the what?"

For a solid two seconds Trent had no idea at all what to say. "You don't know who Winnie the Pooh is?"

Colonel Webster whispered, "No."

Trent said, "Oh, my." Before opening the outer airlock door, Trent secured himself to the airlock bulkhead with the snakechain that he had bound Webster's arms with. There were a row of six such snakechains in the airlock. Why six, in a ship whose maximum occupancy was two, Trent had no idea. He suspected that it had something to do with multiple redundancy; an understandable fetish in an organization as multiply redundant as Space Force.

Trent opened the outer airlock door then, and kicked the pressure-suited body of Colonel Webster as hard as he could. Trent chinned the radio bar. "Good-bye, Colonel Webster," said Trent aloud. "I hope you make it."

As an afterthought he added, "You poor, desperate fool." He clicked off the radio. "Winnie the what indeed," he muttered, cycling back through the airlock. He returned to the pilot's seat and strapped himself in again. He spent several moments enjoying the feeling of being able to breathe, and then said aloud, "Bring acceleration back up, Johnny."

Nothing happened.

Realizing the helmet muffled his voice, Trent chinned the radio bar. "Johnny? Can you hear me?"

The voice was tinny. "Hi, Boss."

"Kick it back in, Johnny. Let's go." The pain flared along the entire right side of his body as he was slammed back into his seat.

There were approximately six minutes left before, by Vance's stated calculations, he would be unable to blow up Trent.

"Hello?" said Trent.

Nobody was answering him.

"Hello hello. Hi there. Is anyone out there?"

"Your pardon, Trent," came Vance's rumble a few seconds later. "I've been having a slight difficulty with Space Force. I'm curious as to why you beamed our conversation to Almundsen, especially as the telescope I'm watching you with shows you've just jettisoned your hostage."

"What makes you think I jettisoned the hostage?" Trent asked. "Maybe I just tossed a pressure suit out the airlock."

"Let me talk to Colonel Webster," said Vance immediately.

"Uh . . ."

"I didn't think so," said Vance simply. "Why did you beam our conversation to L-4, Trent? Was it simply to get me talking to them to gain you time?"

Trent had done it simply to gain time; clearly it had not worked. "Confuse the enemy," said Trent, "divide and conquer."

"I think you did it to gain time," said Vance. "What was the other thing you thought I did not know?"

"Elite Commissioner Mohammed Vance," said Trent softly, "you are entirely too intelligent for my peace of mind."

"And you don't sound nearly desperate enough for mine. What have you done, Trent?"

Trent said, "I'll tell you in a minute."

"I am tempted to fire on you immediately."

"It would be a mistake."

"Unless you can give me a reason why I should not, I am going to fire upon you immediately."

"Okay, okay. Listen closely." In detail, Trent described what he had done to Spacebase One's missiles and energy weapons. "So of course the mirrors are shot. Same for the missiles; fire one if you don't believe me. The instant it starts to move you don't have a missile any more, just pieces of missile tangled up in fineline. Some of the pieces will have fuel in them." Trent paused. "Boom. A big one, I think."

When he was finished, Vance was silent for a long stretch. He broke it with the words, "I must assume you are bluffing. I do not have time to get an officer in there to check it out."

"That was the idea. But you do have time to pull your

Peaceforcers out of the north end of Spacebase One before firing."

"This is very likely," said Vance deliberately, "simply another ploy on your part to gain time."

The very slight enjoyment that Trent had been feeling vanished. "Vance, I'm telling the truth."

Mohammed Vance did not reply in words.

On the rear cameras, displayed in the holograph floating before Trent's eyes, Trent saw the entire north end of Spacebase One's central cylinder unfold in silent, brilliant light.

Trent could not imagine such a catastrophe not killing somebody, somewhere.

"I see," said Vance after the briefest of pauses, "that you were telling the truth."

"Oh my god." Trent could not find words. "Evil. You are an evil son of a bitch, Vance."

"I'm a good Peaceforcer."

". . . that's what I said." Trent stared at the image, at the slowly expanding wavefront of the explosion. *How could you do that?*

"I gave an order."

Johnny Johnny said quietly in Trent's ear, "Boss?"

"Yeah, Johnny?"

"Better put the traceset back on, Boss. I need you."

Trent ripped his helmet off and pulled the traceset on. He melted into Johnny Johnny.

A missile was chasing him.

Johnny Johnny thought, HOW CAN I PLAY THE GAME WHEN THEY KEEP CHANGING THE RULES ON ME?

The missile showed clearly on radar. Zooming the cameras to their highest resolution, Johnny Johnny could barely discern the faint spark of the approaching missile's exhaust, violet against black.

Thinking calmly, THIS ISN'T HAPPENING, Johnny Johnny turned the "communications" laser on the approaching missile. It had no immediate effect; in a tight beam the laser was not highly accurate at such distances against something moving at very high speeds. The missile itself took evasive action, varying boost irregularly as it chased the yacht.

Locating Colonel Webster with the radar to insure that he

was far enough away, Johnny Johnny sprayed the space back along his trajectory with free positrons. It was his second and last line of defense. If the laser didn't get the missile first, the cloud of positrons undoubtedly would.

The explosion that would result when that happened would, Johnny Johnny was almost certain, kill both of him.

Johnny Johnny examined the situation for a few moments longer. There was nothing else he could think of to do. He programmed the autopilot for the yacht's full acceleration of 8,800 cepssa, beginning in twenty seconds and running until twenty seconds after the estimated time of the missile's impact.

Johnny Johnny hesitated a moment, then split himself back into his components; Trent stripped the traceset off quickly, and refastened his helmet against the death pressure vacuum he was anticipating shortly.

He had just finished when a small mountain fell on him.

The first second of just under nine gravities acceleration wasn't so bad.

The next was horrible.

The third was exquisitely unpleasant.

The fourth second was the worst agony that Trent could remember having ever experienced. The entire right side of his rib cage felt as though it were caving in.

And then it got worse.

The laser never touched the hurtling missile.

At approximately sixteen seconds before estimated impact with Trent's stolen yacht, the missile struck the cloud of positrons, glowing slightly from interaction with the solar wind.

Trent, the world narrowed down to his fight for breath, was aware of none of this.

Suddenly there was light, heat—

—and grinning, with feral red eyes and wet sharp teeth, there was pain.

May 9, 2062.

Carl Castanaveras left the lighted tunnel and went out into the dusk. Night was falling as he entered the grounds of the park, and the huge transplanted trees about which the garden was designed were heavy with shadow, shifting and impenetra-

ble. He reached with the Sight and was stunned by how strongly the grief struck him when he lowered his guards. The boy was sitting high in the branches of the tallest tree in the park, watching the sunset. The sky was clear that night, and it was colder than a summer of Carl's childhood could ever have been.

Carl spoke without sound. Trent, come down.

There was a visible flicker of movement at the top of the tree, and a rustling sound as leaves were displaced. Trent vanished into the denser growth around the center of the tree, and while Carl was still looking up, the boy who was not, after all, a telepath, appeared in the lower branches, paused, hung by his hands, and dropped two meters to the ground. He landed crouching, and straightened slowly. "Hi."

Carl blinked. "Hi." Trent was barefoot, wearing old jeans and a green shirt that could not possibly be keeping him warm. Carl felt almost alien in comparison; he was still dressed formally, in the black suit, and the blue-inlaid black cloak for warmth. He gestured back toward the lighted Complex. "I was just in with Suzanne. She said . . ."

Trent nodded. "Yes."

"I'm sorry, Trent. I . . . don't know what else to say."

"Me too." Trent paused. "Me neither. This has been such a bad day," he said conversationally. "I can't believe it."

Now, standing there faced with the boy, Carl had difficulty finding words. "How can I help?"

"I've been thinking about that." Trent shivered, perhaps from the cold. "I have to leave."

"I . . . don't understand."

"I have to leave here. Doctor Montignet will take me, I think."

"Leave?" said Carl stupidly. "The Complex?"

Trent said simply, "Yes."

"Why?"

"I'm not a telepath. I don't want to live with telepaths." In the darkness Carl was not certain of his expression. "I can't."

"Trent, why?"

Trent said slowly, "Father . . . I think the day will come when you—when telepaths—will be normal, and the rest of us will be out in the cold because we can't compete. For most people it's going to be a while before that happens . . ." He averted his face and did not look at Carl. With a sort of amazement Carl saw a smile touch his lips. The almost insane grief *never ceased for an instant, and the boy made his lips move in a smile. "You don't breed that fast." The smile faded to dead seriousness. "But if I stay here that happens to me now." He turned and looked straight at Carl, eyes pooled in shadow. "I've been webdancing in Capitol City's InfoNet. They don't touch me, you know. When I get an inskin, I don't think there's anybody on Earth who can touch me." Trent gestured toward the Complex, just visible above the fence around the park, looming white under its floodlights. "If I stay here I'm nothing. I love you all but I do not choose to be nothing."*

Carl shook his head slowly. "Trent, that's crazy. Malko lives here with us."

"Malko has experience and knowledge and connections which make him valuable." The boy shrugged. "I'm a Pla—a webdancer. Father, there are lots of webdancers."

It stunned Carl, how helpless an eleven-year-old boy could make him feel. He touched the boy with his mind and went reeling back again from the numbing hurt. He reached with one hand toward the boy and was startled to see Trent draw back.

Trent said flatly, "Don't touch me."

Carl stared at him. He said helplessly, "Trent?"

*"I don't **belong** here." Carl was shaking his head no, not in negation but in pained disbelief, and Trent said softly, "Let me go."*

And Carl Castanaveras, for a brief, time-wrenching moment, saw the future twisting itself about his son, and heard his voice say with the hollow echo of prophecy, "I think you are right. You do not belong here. I think you will never belong anywhere."

Trent was not even a telepath, but there was no one at the Complex who slept that night without Trent's broadcast pain twisting their dreams into nightmares.

That was how it came to be, when a staged riot broke out at the Complex on June the second, 2063, that Trent was not there. That was how it came to be that, when the riot grew into war between the telepaths and the Peaceforcers who were sent in to "restore order," Trent was not there. That was how it came to be, that when a young Peaceforcer named Mohammed Vance ordered the use of tactical thermonuclear weapons on the telepaths—the telepaths who had held off the massed might of the United Nations Peace Keeping Force with nothing but their Gift—that was how it came to be that Trent was not with them.

Seven years later, the only nightmares that Trent had ever had concerned the day he found out that his people had been destroyed and that he, of his own choice, had not been with them.

The image from his nightmares was curiously sharp: a missile that should not have been there, dropping from the sky, expanding in light and heat . . .

At no time had Trent been totally unconscious.

Behind the polarized glassite of the pressure suit's helmet, Trent's face was white with pain. Everything that he looked at looked back at him in double image.

The Rolls was crossing over the far side of Luna on a high trajectory, moving far too fast due to the extreme acceleration Trent had been forced to employ to escape the missile that should not have been there.

Trent's voice was a trembling croak. "Johnny?"

The tinny voice came immediately. "Hi, Boss."

"We're alive again."

"No, still. But we've got problems."

"I can see, Johnny."

"We've lost structural integrity, Boss."

"I can see, Johnny."

The ship's hull had been half torn away in the blast.

Bizarrely, the major section of the detached hull floated not forty meters from the yacht, traveling along almost exactly the same trajectory, tumbling slowly. What had been the outer portion of the hull was partially melted.

Trent said, "How bad is it, Johnny?" He listened for nearly thirty seconds, and then said, "Cancel the damage report. What *works*?"

"Engines are in pretty good shape, Boss. Life-system, communications maser, and the autopilot are all still functioning, though I've lost access to some of the data the autopilot's carrying, and some of the rest got scrambled by the EMP from the blast." Johnny Johnny paused. "The lack of a hull," he noted, "tends to obviate the need for a functioning life-system, actually."

"Johnny, don't make jokes when things are this bad."

"You do it all the time, Boss."

"I'm allowed. Is there any chance at all you can land this bitch?"

There was a pause. "The autopilot says, given our relative velocity to the Lunar surface, and the absence of our number three landing strut, a soft touchdown attempt is inadvisable."

"We don't have a landing strut?"

"Number one landing strut has been weakened significantly. Number two is tentatively rated in good condition; number three is gone. Boss?"

"Yeah, Johnny?"

"Are we going to die, Boss?"

"Probably, Johnny."

"Oh." Trent's Image was silent for a long moment. "Boss, I've enjoyed working for you."

Lying in the dark pain-filled haze, Trent could not for the life of him remember having written any code that could possibly have come up with a response like that. *My Image,* he thought, *is not going to make me cry.* He said very quietly, "Thanks, Johnny Johnny. Take us down."

"I'll do my best, Boss."

"I know."

The Rolls lost height rapidly, its engine firing almost parallel to the Lunar surface. They swept over Lunar farside in minutes, losing both altitude and speed, the proton-boron reactor burning to produce just better than 4,000 cepssa. The ship reached nearside well north of the equator, over twenty degrees latitude. It flashed past Schiaparelli and Aristarchus in the Sea of Storms, moving slightly northeast, and passed some eighteen degrees north of Luna City at Copernicus. The ship had less than a kilometer of altitude when it crossed the thirtieth degree latitude. It cut over the north corner of Archimedes Crater, dropping ever lower, past the southern end of Aristillus.

Johnny Johnny said, "Boss, how large do mountain chains get on Earth? Pretty big?"

Trent could not even reply. He fought for air. In the holofield hovering above his face he saw the mountain range come up to greet them.

"My map says this is the Caucasus mountain range, Boss. Checking on radar . . . and we're not going to make it over the peaks," said Johnny Johnny precisely. "Sorry about this, Boss. I'll try not to kill you."

The drive exploded up to 8,800 cepssa.

Trent tried to scream, but there was no air at all in his lungs.

The mountain chain continued to grow in the yacht's front cameras, but more slowly now.

As Trent was blacking out, Johnny Johnny crashed the yacht. The ship bounced once off the side of a peak, still slowing, and then Johnny Johnny smashed the yacht down onto a wide, flat ledge, high up on the mountain. He cut the drives as they touched, and the craft rolled once, twice, and finally stopped, lying upside down at the edge of the rock abutment.

Hanging upside down strapped in his seat was, Trent found, an absolutely wonderful position under one-sixth gravity.

It was practically as good as free-fall.

Unconsciousness claimed him.

Some time later—Trent estimated it at between fifteen seconds and eternity—his eyes fluttered open again.

It was probably a blessing that the entire right side of his rib cage was without feeling.

A voice was yammering in his ear. Trent could not make heads or tails of whatever the voice was saying.

With intense concentration, Trent managed to undo the straps that held him in place in the upside-down pilot's seat.

In gentle slow motion Trent fell perhaps a meter to the yacht's ceiling. He stood slowly, reached up and very carefully withdrew his handheld from where it was jacked in on the floor above his head. The voice in his ears ceased abruptly. With grave concentration, he reached up again and pulled his briefcase out from its storage place above the upside-down pilot's chair.

It took him most of a minute to get the briefcase open, and put the handheld inside it.

He congratulated himself on successfully closing his briefcase.

Trent's voice echoed oddly in his ears. "I'm still alive again."

He stepped into the passageway that led to the airlock.

With the shifting of the distribution of mass, the yacht began sliding, off the rock ledge, down toward the surface. An out-jutting spar, a hundred meters down from the ledge, broke the yacht into two major halves, and the two pieces continued their tumble, a quarter of a kilometer down the mountainside.

Trent could not remember how he had come to be in this place.

He walked in a pressure suit along the foothills of a vast mountain chain, stumbling frequently. His briefcase was clutched in his left hand; the pressure suit's glove barely fit through the briefcase's handle. He was eight meters tall and there was a hell of a wind coming from somewhere; it kept knocking him down.

He fell, again and again. Each time he got back up and walked on, without any destination in mind whatsoever.

The world around him was very strange, all gray and white; the shadows were very sharply defined, and utterly black.

The sky was without color, and both the stars and sun were in it at the same time.

It was very hot inside the pressure suit.

His knee hurt.

Something about his surroundings nagged at Trent, but he was unable to decide what it was.

Finally he fell, and did not rise again.

The Wall

·————————————————·

2069~2070
Gregorian

No miracle has ever taken place under conditions which science can accept. Experience shows, without exception, that miracles occur only in times and in countries in which miracles are believed in, and in the presence of persons who are disposed to believe in them.

—Ernest Renan
Vie de Jésus, 1863 Gregorian

· 1 ·

Trent was thirsty.

That was the first thing he noticed.

Aside from being thirsty, Trent felt fine.

Some time later Trent realized that aside from being thirsty he didn't feel anything at all.

His eyes were still closed, and Trent knew there was some very good reason why he should not open them.

Trent opened his left eye.

He closed it, and opened his right eye.

He let that eye droop shut, and then, cautiously, opened both eyes at once.

Each time he saw the same thing.

He was lying on something soft, on the floor of the strangest room he had ever seen in his life. The ceiling was lit with soft yellow sunpaint, which was normal enough; there were four walls, and a doorway without a door in it.

The decor was . . . odd.

The walls were cut from some porous stone, and two of the three walls that Trent could see had been smoothed and polished. The third wall was in the process of being smoothed; it was simply rough-cut stone over nearly a third of its surface.

There was furniture in the room: one webchair, a small table of unpainted steel. They appeared strictly utilitarian, except for their odd delicacy; they could not, Trent thought, support any weight to speak of. Perhaps, he speculated shrewdly, the furniture was not designed for use by adults, but rather by, say, very tall, skinny children—or, thought Trent, pleased with his own cleverness, by elves.

Yes, elves.

As in many fairy tales, there was a monster in this one. It walked in as Trent was speculating about the furniture, carrying Trent's briefcase in one hand. It was large and bulky, ugly to a truly remarkable degree. It had a single huge, dark eye, and a large horny antenna growing out of its forehead.

Through a dry throat, Trent said, "You are the second ugliest thing I have ever seen in my life." He focused blurry eyes on the monster. "You are not as hairy as Booker Jamethon."

The monster proceeded to pull its head off, and hang the detached head on a hook growing out of the wall. It seemed that the monster had swallowed a hugely muscled, dark-skinned male human, fifty or sixty years of age, with wiry, steel-gray hair. The man was not at all, thought Trent, what one would expect to find inside a monster.

Trent suddenly remembered where he was. "Ah," he said reasonably, "I knew there was a good reason not to open my eyes."

The man in the pressure suit looked at Trent. "Indeed?" He was unzipping the pressure suit, wriggling out of it. "I've often thought that myself, opening my eyes in the morning. What a lovely day it is, I'll think, and then I get out of bed and it's ruined." With his pressure suit off he no longer looked like the second ugliest thing Trent had ever seen. He did not spit on the floor even once while Trent was watching. "But by the time I know just how bad the mistake was it's usually too damn late to go back to bed." Pulling the chair over to where Trent was lying propped up against the wall, the man seated himself. "How do you feel?"

"Numb." Trent studied the man. Distinctly Amerindian features, a compact frame; strong hands. "You don't look like a Peaceforcer."

The man blinked. "I should hope not."

Trent nodded. "Okay." Alive, apparently not in custody . . . "What day is it? What time is it?"

"Thursday. About ten-thirty P.M. What's your name, son?"

"Trent. Trent the thief. Where am I?"

"Luna."

"That's not funny."

"The fair planet Luna, western foot of the Caucasus mountain chain, United Nations territory, in the bolt-hole of a man whose name is Nathan Dark Clouds." The man whose name was Nathan Dark Clouds leaned forward in his webchair, hands on knees. "And an odd thing you are, Trent the thief. I have so many questions I hardly know where to start."

"Wait." For the first time Trent noticed that he was no longer wearing the pressure suit, or the female Peaceforcer's uniform. "I only have a few. Can I ask mine first?"

Nathan nodded. "Go ahead."

"How far am I from Free Luna?"

"You were headed there?"

"Yes."

The older man nodded again, thoughtfully. "I thought. We're a fair piece from there. The nearest enclave is at the edge of Bessel Crater, in Serenitatis. Damn near 750 klicks southeast, and you have to get up over the Caucasus mountains first. Say, two days by crawler."

"Okay . . . how long ago did I crash?"

"About eight hours ago. They say that any landing you walk away from is a good one, and you walked away from that one, so that must have been a good landing." Nathan shook his head. "There's something wrong with that saying. I *saw* that landing; I was out in my chameleon, heading here, when your ship went down. I changed course, found you lying in the sun about an hour or so after the crash, picked you up, and headed here." He looked straight at Trent. "That craft, it ran off an antimatter-initiated reaction?"

"I don't know how it works. It was a Rolls-Royce. There were bottled positrons."

"That was my guess. If I'd had any idea . . . well, you'd still be lying out there in the sun. We were about eight kilometers from the crash site when the containment went on the positrons." He seemed to shiver. "I poked my head outside just before you woke up. That whole section of the mountains is still glowing. That was a military ship you crashed in." It was not a question. "You don't need to bottle that much antimatter for anything except a weapon."

"You must know the Peaceforcers are after me."

"I guessed. About four o'clock yesterday, there was a Level Four alert down here; restricted travel, check in with the local Peaceforcers, all that crap. I headed out for my bolt-hole, figuring to be as safe as possible if the PKF was planning a sweep of the undesirables. Among which number am I." The man shrugged. "They should not find us. I sprayed dust all the way back from where I picked you up."

"Sprayed dust?"

"No wind, Trent. You suck dust up as you go, spray it over your tail where you've been. It's a damn expensive mod to have done to a crawler, and using it costs a fair piece too, but if you want to assure you don't get followed it's a necessity."

Trent nodded. "What are you going to do about me?"

"Well, I wouldn't turn any man over to the Peaceforcers. They killed my wife. Beyond not turning you in, I haven't thought at all."

"Last question."

"Yes?"

"Can I get something to drink? Anything? Lots of anything?"

Nathan stood. "I think I can manage that. You be getting your story ready. I do love a good story." He vanished through the open doorway.

Trent sat upright more slowly, ignoring the quick sharp pain in his ribs. Nathan had taped his ribs, he noted, and splinted one finger of Trent's right hand; the skin of his face was sunburned, one cheek was swollen and tender, and there was a terrible pain in his knee again. Trent tried to remember when he had reinjured the knee . . . the memory returned slowly.

Nathan came back shortly, a pair of squeeze bulbs in one hand. He tossed them to Trent, the bulbs performing a strange slow tumble as they fell.

Trent caught them left-handed, without thinking. He stared up at Nathan Dark Clouds. "Did I . . . *fall* . . . down the mountain?"

"The ship did. Whether or not you were in it I have no idea."

"Oh, slith." With his broken hand Trent gingerly touched his swollen knee. "I remember . . ." His voice trailed away. He felt himself shivering. "Never mind. Just never mind." He looked at the squeeze bulbs for the first time. "Thanks." He turned the ring on the first bulb—water—sucked it dry and then drank the second bulb only slightly more slowly.

Nathan leaned forward again, hands on knees. He seemed to be enjoying himself immensely. "Now, Trent the thief, you're breathing my air and drinking my water. I've saved your life and bandaged your wounds. Now, tell me if you will, Trent the thief, how it is you come to be crashing a military spacecraft some few kilometers from my bolt-hole, with a briefcase full of sophisticated electronics, wearing a PKF p-suit that says Lieutenant Charbrier, a female Peaceforcer's uniform, and a pair of SpaceFarer boots from the *Flandry*."

"How do you know that?"

"It's my turn to . . ."

"How do you know that?"

Nathan sighed. "You're going to be a hard man to get along with, Trent the thief. The p-suit says PKF on it, the uniform is cut for a girl with tits, and the boots are gray with green threading. Ugliest damn thing I ever saw."

"You recognize SpaceFarer colors?"

Nathan stared at him. "Trent, lad, you don't seem to understand the situation here. This is *my* . . ."

Trent interrupted. "Okay, don't get stuffy. Let's see." He paused. "I was going to steal a spaceship . . . no, no, that's too far in. See, there I was in the Down Plaza and . . ." He stopped. "I'm not sure where to start."

"The beginning?" the man suggested.

"You see, there was this Peaceforcer and he wouldn't *listen* to me," Trent said earnestly, and then stopped again. "It's a long story."

"We have *lots* of time."

"They think I killed a Peaceforcer."

Nathan Dark Clouds said mildly, "Trent the thief, other people have killed Peaceforcers. None of them triggered a Level Three Earth–Luna alert, a Level Four Lunar alert."

"Brass balls."

"What?"

"He was a Peaceforcer Elite."

Moving slowly, Nathan turned to face Trent squarely. His right eyebrow climbed exactly one centimeter. "What?"

"It was a mistake."

"A mistake."

"An accident."

"An acc—"

"He was trying to kill me and he fell."

"Fell . . ." repeated Nathan.

"Well, jumped. Off a spacescraper." Trent shivered slightly, remembering. "It was a long way down."

Nathan's eyes wandered aimlessly around the room before settling on Trent again. "Trent. Trent the thief. Tell me what has happened. Start at the beginning. Work your way to the end. Take all the time you need."

Trent leaned back against the wall behind him. It was

rough and unpolished. He started off with a reasonably detailed outline of the events of the last several days, not mentioning Denice Castanaveras at all. At first he was not entirely certain that Nathan Dark Clouds was listening to him; the man sat quietly through the first telling of the story, and only then started asking questions. He started at the top of Trent's story and worked his way down, calmly, without fuss, as though he did not attach any great significance to Trent's answers.

Nathan Dark Clouds was very, very good. They were nearly half an hour into it when Trent realized he was being interrogated, forty-five minutes into it when he knew how well it was being done. Trent found himself backtracking, answering questions about subjects he had already lied about, fielding questions about other almost entirely unrelated subjects, reanswering rephrased questions he had already lied about twice. Nathan fed him back his own answers, subtly distorted, and waited for Trent to correct him. Two solid hours passed in the telling and retelling of the story; when Nathan announced himself satisfied with Trent's final version of what had happened to him, Trent was shaking with exhaustion.

Only once in the course of that two-hour interrogation did Trent see the man at a loss for words. "There was a waldo waiting for you inside the store? Those damn things are more indestructible than an Elite."

Trent mumbled an answer.

Nathan said, "What?"

"There was a bazooka in the bathroom," Trent said more loudly.

"Say again?"

"Well, a rocket launcher of some kind. I don't really know a lot about weapons."

"In the bathroom," said Nathan without inflection.

"I only *kept* it," said Trent defensively. "It wasn't even mine. It was there when I moved in. I don't know why."

At the end, when Trent was yawning hugely, Nathan stood. "Trent, you are just maybe the fastest-thinking young man I've ever met."

"Thank you."

"Lying to the man who's just saved your life," said Nathan Dark Clouds softly, "who's of half a mind to put you up out in death pressure in the first place, is probably not wise."

Trent could not think of anything at all to say.

Nathan said, "Good night, lad." Without further comment, he scaled the sunpaint down to blackness, and left Trent alone.

In the dark, Trent pulled his briefcase to him, opened it, and checked his supplies. He had a curiously naked feeling, and for a moment could not decide why.

Just before sleep claimed him, Trent swore at himself sleepily. "You stupid genejunk. You lost the squirt gun."

He jerked awake twice, to darkness and panic, to a sensation his body insisted on interpreting as falling. Both times Trent oriented himself, remembered where he was and why he was there, and settled back down on the soft padding to sleep.

He awoke the third time to a generalized ache. He sat up slowly and rested in the utter darkness against the wall at his back. The darkness was incredible. Trent held his hand in front of his face and could not see a thing. The lack of sound was nearly as absolute; if he strained he could make out the gentle whisper of the ventilators forcing air through the room. He sat motionlessly for a while after that, just letting himself acclimate to the absurd feeling of lightness, listening to his body. He hurt literally everywhere, in every muscle in his body, as though somebody who really knew what he was doing had worked him over. His knee was out again; Trent could barely stand to straighten it fully. The rib he had broken was bearable so long as he breathed shallowly.

His right hand . . .

"Jesus-H.-Christ-on-a-stick." The Temple Dragons weapons instructor was an old Puerto Rican—forty, easy, thought Trent —whose name was Mitch. They were practicing that morning, all the Temple Dragons fifteen or under, in an abandoned brick warehouse across the street from the Temple. Mitch was rubbing the line of his jaw, and Jimmy Ramirez was on his knees on the mat, clutching his left hand. "Jimmy, you is such a dumb fuck." He took careful aim and kicked Jimmy Ramirez in the face and then turned to face the boys standing against the wall. "Listen up, Dragons. When you got no gun and you got to hit, I mean no choice, then you remember this. Hit hard parts with something harder. You want to use your hand, fine. You hit the man in the throat, you hit him in the nuts, you hit him right under the heart." Jimmy Ramirez was

*lying on the ground, curled up into a ball. Mitch kicked him
again, harder. "Else you end up like this tough boy. I'm gon'
have me a sore jaw all day. But Jimmy—" Mitch smiled at
them, at Trent. "Jimmy, he a dead fuck."*

Mitch had died shortly after that, in one of the endless
property disputes with the Gypsy Macoute; until now, sitting
alone in the dark beneath the surface of Luna, Trent could not
remember having thought of the old Temple Dragon even
once in all the years since Mitch's death.

It had taken him six years to get out of the Fringe. Six long
years filled with more pain and genuine anger than Trent allowed himself to remember most of the time.

And then, the Patrol Sectors. For all of seven months.
Learning how to walk down a street again without having to
check for men wearing the green-and-yellow Macoute
bandanas. The simple shock of seeing Peaceforcers again, for
the first time since the establishment of the Patrol Sectors had
left Trent stuck on Long Island, inside the Fringe with no
legal way to get out.

Dealing with the BloodSilk Boys, who thought they were
tough even though they had a name with the word "silk" in it.

Dealing with the Peaceforcers.

He sat alone, in the utter dark and impossible lightness, for
what seemed to him a very long time.

Thinking about dealing with the Peaceforcers.

At length he said, "Johnny?"

The voice emanated from a patch of darkness off somewhere to Trent's right. "Hi, Boss. How are you feeling?"

"I think I'll live. Once I get something to eat I might even
want to. Johnny Johnny, how much free storage do you have
in the handheld?"

"Not much, Boss. I stored most of our files from the apartment when you said you were coming to get me. I'd feel a lot
safer if I could put it into offline storage somewhere."

"Soon, Johnny. Do you have enough left to store some
books?"

Johnny Johnny snorted audibly. "You must be kidding. At
the speed *you* read? I can store so much you wouldn't finish it
this century."

Trent smiled. "Then let's get to work."

Nathan was gone.

There were three rooms and an airlock. The pressure suit Trent had crashed in was gone. One of the rooms, the smallest, was a kitchen with an airplant in it; another, the room Trent had slept in, was clearly a bedroom. The third and largest room was an equipment storage garage. Two spare pressure suits hung on its walls, and laser drills were stacked carefully in one corner next to a tool rack which held tools for, Trent guessed after a brief examination, repairs for some sort of heavy equipment.

The airlock was in the garage; Trent could find no air bottles for the spare pressure suits.

In the corner of the garage was the oldest systerm Trent had ever seen in his life.

There was a note for Trent on the systerm.

Have gone to Luna City at Copernicus. Back late tomorrow. Food in cold spot in kitchen. Stove is electric grill on south wall of kitchen. First-aid kit in kitchen; the medbot inside is stupid, but don't argue with it, you won't win.

Will be letting friends at Aristillus Mining Co. know that nephew is arriving shortly from Earth; I am troubleshooter there, can easily arrange work for a man of your talents. Picking up clothing for you, soft p-suit; basic kit. Will clip you 850 Credit Units for p-suit, 15 for clothing; throw in 10 CU for trouble you're putting me to. Start thinking of way to pay me back. Nathan.

Wandering into the kitchen, Trent found the cold spot to be nothing more than a vacuum-enclosed partition set in shadow. Trent fried himself a chicken sandwich; it wasn't until he caught the aroma of the frying chicken patty that he realized how ravenously hungry he was. He ate it while frying another two sandwiches.

Back in the garage, Trent seated himself in front of Nathan's computer. It was at least twenty years old, probably older. The caps on the pointboard were worn down so that the letters could not be seen on most of them. The unit had a bulky monitor rather than a holofield for viewing. There were jacks on the unit for tape and infochip and MPU attachments, but none for the standard optical interface Trent's handheld used. It took Trent nearly two hours before he had the pinouts on the keyboard's MPU slot traced correctly; the systerm's System Tools were almost useless. The protocol the systerm used was clearly an ancestor of the protocols Trent had grown up with, but they were incredibly slow and lacked options as basic as autohelp and abbreviated command syntax. It took him most of the first hour to find the help file which listed the MPU slot's pinouts, and another hour, using invisibly thin drops of cold solder, to link the handheld's MPU slot to the MPU slot on the pointboard.

Johnny Johnny said, "Checking . . . got it. You misconnected pins 105 and 241 on my end, and pins 241 and 98 on the other end. I'm compensating. Also I have cross talk on the other end from pins 62 and 63, but there's nothing critical on those lines. What now?"

"What can you tell me about where we are?"

"Checking . . . not very damn much. Local infobases are supposed to be small, but this is ridiculous. There's only fifteen gigabytes of local storage and two-thirds of it is empty. What the hell is this thing, anyway?"

"Uh . . . FrancoDEC RISC Mark II, it says on the monitor. There's nothing on the pointboard, and I'd guess the processors are actually in that."

"Whatever, it's slow damn hardware, Boss. Is there a traceset around here anywhere? I could really use some help."

"Afraid not, Johnny. I lost the traceset somewhere along the line."

". . . lost the traceset, lost the ship, lost the goddamn full sensory all the way back on another planet—" Johnny Johnny's voice was rising.

"Johnny!"

"—what?"

"Command, set null emote."

There was a brief pause; Johnny Johnny's voice resumed without any notable emotion whatsoever. "Gotcha. Sorry about that, Boss."

"It's all right, I wrote the code. Remind me to debug you when there's time. Postcrisis routines."

"Will do. Let's see . . . can't tell you much about where we are, Boss. The system connects to a private-enterprise LIN —that's moontalk for 'Lunar Information Network,' Boss— connects to a LIN satellite through a maser linkup on the surface. Aristillus Investment Group owns the satellite. We're about fifteen meters beneath the surface. The system has no outside sensors, no eyes, no ears. It does control the radar; there's a pretty good radar system scanning the approaches to the—bolt-hole, I guess it's called?"

"That's the phrase Nathan used."

"Okay. We're on the east edge of a fairly small crater, just beneath a small overhang; except at sunset the entrance should be in shadow all the time. We're pretty well hidden." Johnny Johnny paused. "We need to be extra careful about going dancing in the Lunar InfoNet, Boss."

"How so?"

"Only one channel in and out of this place. Assuming web angels—are there web angels on the Moon, Boss?"

"Don't know. We'll find out."

"Assuming web angels, tracking us back to our point of origin would be so simple it scares me. There's also security everywhere like I've never seen before outside of Space Force and PKF Boards. Requests for help are met with demands for ID and/or passwords, everywhere I go."

"Chill things a bit, Johnny, there's no hurry. What do you legitimately have access to?"

"Half a dozen public-access Boards, Luna City Library, and the Aristillus Investment Group's Board. Basically what 'Sieur Dark Clouds has available to him. Interesting thing about 'Sieur Dark Clouds, Boss—he's not Amerindian."

"You're sure? He looks it."

"Gene chart is all wrong, Boss. He has his med records in here; genetically he's a fairly standard European gene chart—Caucasian, of English, German, or quite possibly French descent. No mongrelization to speak of. Positively no Mongoloid genes."

"Fascinating," Trent murmured. "That's fairly major biosculpture, then." He filed the subject for the moment. "I want data, Johnny. Data on Lunar InfoNet, biosculptors, inskin vendors."

"About time!"

"Save it. Also Lunar society, maps, businesses, Peaceforcers, SpaceFarer-associated businesses, Johnny Rebs and Erisian Claw, Syndic and Tong. Am I missing anything?"

"Yep. 'Immigrant and Visitor's Guide to Survival,' by M. Garcia. Subtitled, 'Learn Quick or Die.' Procedural on soft pressure suits and how to buy one, what to do in case of emergencies with rolligons or crawlers or Bullet—the Bullet's called a 'monorail' up here—first aid for people subjected to temporary death pressure, specifics on anoxia and pressure-suit air mix. Lists the seventeen commonest ways visitors and immigrants to Luna die." Johnny Johnny paused. "I highly recommend you audit this."

"You have?"

"Just now. Good book, Boss. There's a section on 'scalesuits'—word comes from either 'scaled-down spaceship' or else from the fact that they've got armor that looks like fish scales on them, nobody seems to know—that you really need to read."

"Store it in the handheld."

"Done."

"Let's get to work."

Some of you, said the brochure, *will have played at webdancing on Earth. It's possible you are inclined to attempt webdancing while visiting Luna.*

Don't.

On Earth webdancing is a misdemeanor; in Luna it is a felony punishable by deportation to Earth, assignation to convict labor, or immediate execution.

There is a one-and-a-half-second lightspeed delay in communications between Earth and Luna, a three-second round-trip delay. Effectively, this means that Luna and Earth have—must have—separate InfoNets. Policing Earth's InfoNet, with its hundreds of millions of Boards, with nearly three billion adults who interact with the InfoNet on a daily basis and six billion who interact with the InfoNet in an average week, is effectively impossible. Despite the valorous efforts of the Earth-based DataWatch, only the most egregious violations of InfoNet procedures are ever punished.

Luna is a hostile new world. The line between survival and death is a fine one; we cannot allow the tools of our survival to be corrupted for any reason whatsoever.

Therefore, the Lunar Bureau of the United Nations Peace Keeping Force DataWatch has created the LINK, the Lunar Information Network Key. There are currently 9,402 Boards on Luna; new Boards must be licensed before they can rent lasercable access. Every transaction—every single transaction —which takes place in the Lunar InfoNet is keyed and tracked on an item-by-item basis. The basis of this unprecedented degree of InfoNet security is the Lunar Information Network Key. The Key is an unbreakable encryption device which the DataWatch employs to validate and track every user in the

Lunar InfoNet. Webdancers attempting unauthorized access to logic, to data, to communications facilities, will be punished to the full extent of the law.

The last paragraph of the brochure said:

Those webdancers who call themselves "Players" are invited —no, encouraged—to attempt to crack the Lunar InfoNet. Images are illegal in Luna; possession of Image software or coprocessor hardware is a capital crime.

"Gee, Boss," Johnny Johnny muttered, "are you *sure* we can't go home?"

"Afraid not. Not for a while, Johnny." After a moment Trent added slowly, "You could look at the LINK as a challenge, I suppose."

Johnny Johnny's answer was instantaneous. "Let's not."

Trent was sitting before Nathan's systerm, reading on the handheld's holofield, when Nathan Dark Clouds returned.

He had no warning, not even from the radar system; the first he knew of Nathan's return was when the airlock cycled open and a pressure-suited figure strode through carrying a limp pressure suit over its shoulder. Nathan hung the second pressure suit on a hook next to the other two empty pressure suits; it hung a full ten centimeters lower to the floor than the first two. He unlocked his neck ring and pulled his helmet off. "Hello, Trent. You're looking well. How do you feel?"

"Not bad," Trent said mildly. "I'm probably going to need to see a real doctor, or at least a good medbot, for my knee. But in this gravity it hardly matters."

Nathan glanced at Trent while wriggling out of his pressure suit. "There's advantages to living in Luna, to be sure. Even to living in Unification territory. Living longer and healing faster than downsiders are two of them."

"Of course," said Trent with a perfectly straight face, "to take advantage of those advantages you need to avoid being one of those foolish criminals who die from crashing and blowing up their stolen Rolls-Royce yachts."

"You've been in my systerm."

"Of course."

Nathan nodded thoughtfully. He was almost out of his pressure suit; Trent watched him with interest as he finished wriggling out. His guess had been correct, he noted; you were not supposed to wear bulky clothing or boots inside a pressure suit. "For a fact," Nathan said at last, "you've had a fair piece of luck. Those stories you've been reading on my systerm aren't just official line; the PKF really thinks you're dead."

Trent turned off the holofield and the book it was displaying. "You know so well what the PKF thinks?"

The muscles in the back of Nathan's neck tensed visibly, then relaxed. "Space Force has no significant presence downside, I know that. How many Peaceforcers are there on Manhattan Island, Trent?"

Trent did not even need to think. "Two hundred and ten thousand."

Nathan hung his suit, took a soft cloth off a hook on the wall next to it, and began wiping the suit down. "Out of a permanent population of what, twelve million?"

"Counting the spacescrapers, yes. There's three million just in the spacescrapers."

"Trent, Manhattan is renowned for the huge number of Peaceforcers who are stationed there. It's practically a cliché. But when you do the numbers it only comes out to being one Peaceforcer for every sixty permanent Manhattanites. Taking into account the daily commute onto the island, the number drops to nearly one in ninety. There are," said Nathan Dark Clouds evenly, glancing up at Trent, "twenty-eight million people in United Nations territory in Luna." He knelt, began wiping a fine layer of dust off the pressure suit's boots. "Eight hundred fifty thousand of them are either PKF or Space Force. It comes to about one in thirty-three. The next war, Trent, it's not going to be fought on Earth, and the U.N. knows it. Folks in Luna," he said quietly, "SpaceFarers and immigrants and native loonies alike, watch the Peaceforcers as though their lives depended on knowing what the PKF is going to do next. They watch Space Force almost as closely."

Trent said mildly, "Okay, so I'm dead. It's fine by me."

Nathan looked at him sharply, seemed about to say something, and then said, "What've you been doing?"

Trent leaned back in the webchair, put his feet up on the table before the systerm. "Auditing the Boards you have access to, reading."

"About?"

"The Moon. The Lunar Information Network, PKF on the Moon, SpaceFarers, major Lunar cities, Space Force on the Moon, natives of the Moon and their prejudices against immigrants and which of those prejudices are valid and why. Accounts of attempts Players and webdancers have made to dance in the LIN, and why in the past the Key encryption has stopped them. Scalesuits—they sound fascinating, Nathan. Why don't you own one?"

Nathan shrugged. "A matter of taste. I don't trust them. They've only been around eight, nine years, and the technology's not really ironed out yet. The PKF uses them because it's cheaper than turning a man into a cyborg and gives you some of the same results. They're very popular in Free Luna for the same reason—the powered assists and radiation armoring and airplant. I don't like them much; there's a lot of metal in them, and if anything goes wrong with the servo assists you're stuck there with two hundred ten kilos—mass, not Lunar weight—of not-very-flexible metal armor to haul around on your own muscles. Somebody fresh from Earth can do that, mind you, or anybody who's kept up his weight training—me, for example—but there's not many in Luna that description covers. Native loonies are really stuck with the damn things; they need the power assist more than immigrants from Earth do, for obvious reasons, but if the suit dies out in the field on them, where help isn't close, it's practically a death sentence. Damn things are a disaster waiting to happen, some ways. And now," he concluded, "with all that, you might still want to look at one when you come to Aristillus with me. They have a regenerative airplant that's the nicest innovation I've seen on a p-suit in my lifetime; stretches your time in the field up to thirty or forty hours, and with the radiation shielding built into them it's practical to stay out that long." He changed the subject abruptly. "What else have you been up to?"

"Aside from reading? Not very much, really. I opened an account with the United Nations Interplanetary Bank at Aristillus, transferred funds from a pair of accounts on Earth, and then paid your account at UNIB Aristillus one thousand CU —for the trouble I've put you to."

Nathan stood slowly, hung the rag on its hook on the wall. "You moved Credit from accounts on Earth, accounts which DataWatch may or may not have tagged, to UNIB Aristillus, and from there to *my* bank account?" The man stared at Trent.

Trent said flatly, "It was safe."

"If you—"

"It was safe." Trent said evenly, "You have to trust me on

that. I'm a good liar, Nathan, and I'm a good thief and a decent painter. Nathan, I'm a *great* Player. I know the Info-Net on Earth better than DataWatch ever will. It was *safe.*"

For a long moment the man did not even blink. Finally Nathan sighed, nodded, accepting it. "Okay. Thank you for the thousand CU. I hadn't planned to make a profit from helping you, but I certainly don't mind."

Trent nodded also, and continued. "One other thing I got done while you were gone: I figured out why I was alive."

"Well, there's a straight line if you like."

"Seriously, Nathan. The missile Vance sent after me. Melting temperature."

"I'm not following."

"Vance is a smart man. I didn't think brass balls came that smart. It took me three hours to work this out; he thought of it in something like twenty seconds. Say you fire three, four missiles in their silos—even knowing they'll simply be destroyed. The heat from those explosions would have melted the fineline I tied them with long before it significantly damaged the other missiles; those things are designed to fly through rocket exhaust. Shock waves would probably kill a couple of nearby missiles; flak would kill a lot of the rest. But if you fire your three, four missiles, all from one end of the bunker, there's a good chance that the missiles at the other end will survive long enough to get a couple out. That's all it would have taken, Nathan. Two missiles instead of one; I'd be dead."

Nathan said softly, "Boy, you should be dead twenty times over no matter how you look at it."

Trent was silent for several seconds, and then smiled at Nathan Dark Clouds. "That's truer than you know. I owe the Peaceforcers a lot." He was silent again, and then said softly, "An awful lot."

Nathan said quietly, "What are you going to do?"

"I haven't decided yet."

"You can't beat them, Trent."

"Oh?"

"When I was young," said Nathan Dark Clouds, "and stupid—about six years ago—I was a member of the Speed Enthusiast's Organization."

Trent nodded. "I'd guessed you were a Speedfreak."

"All we did, Trent, was we wanted to drive our own cars. And the fuckers went and *outlawed* them." Even after all the time, the amazement was still there in the man's voice. "So my reaction time isn't as fast as a chip's. My judgment's a hell of a lot better." He was silent a moment, then shook his head. "Water over the bridge. The argument's done, we lost it. But we attempted civil disobedience, Trent, almost two million of us set out from San Diego in a convoy, set out to do the Long Run. That's what we called them, the Long Runs, all the way around the world without stopping, without ever touching down on the goddamn dirt. We'd done thousands of Long Runs by '63, as individuals and in convoys. Speedfreak chapters used to pay to send members on the Long Run as presents, or rewards.

"In '63 two million Speedfreaks set out to do the biggest damn Long Run ever. Out of San Diego, to Hawaii, to Australia, over India, through Israel, through France, and then into the Atlantic for the trip to Capitol City." Nathan's voice had grown harsh, strident. "The Unification Council called it treason, and we died, Trent. The Bureau of Weather Control hit us with a goddamn hurricane and eighty-five percent of us died and the ones who didn't were mostly picked up and tried for treason, they executed two hundred and thirty Speed-freaks and sent fifteen thousand into Public Labor for the rest of their lives." The fierce glare did not leave Trent for an instant. "I was there. I was on the Long Run and I survived."

It took Trent a moment to find his voice.

"Faster, faster, faster," he said softly, "until the thrill of speed overcomes the fear of death."

Nathan blinked, and then smiled almost against his will. "Where did you hear that?"

Trent said distantly, thoughtfully, "You made mistakes, you know. First, there were too many of you. You stood up and let them take aim, and then you were surprised when they blew you to hell."

Nathan was staring at him. "Son, they shot my wife. They killed most of my friends. They—"

Trent cut him off. "They're *practical*." Trent looked up, met Nathan's stare. "Very. That's the first thing to know about the Peaceforcers, they always do the sensible thing. The second thing to know is that you *can* beat them. I have to believe that, Nathan. If I don't believe that, really believe it where it counts, I might as well have died out there in that crashed Rolls."

A deeply disturbed expression had settled on the wrinkled countenance. "Son, you're wrong. And you're—"

"I'm not your son."

"I wake up every day, Trent, and I realize again how much life is worth living."

Trent said, "I don't want to die, Nathan." He locked eyes with the old man and when he spoke there was an edge in his voice that he had not intended to put there. "But I *am not going to lose again.*"

· 2 ·

Luna City at Copernicus was built, SpaceFarers like to observe, by downsiders.

And it shows.

It is the oldest city on the Moon, and in this instance the use of the word "on" is correct; it is one of only five bubble cities on the entire planet. It is in one of the most visible craters on Luna, a crater visible from Earth even by eye. It makes a convenient astrogation aid for visitors from other worlds.

It is, say loonies and SpaceFarers alike, one of the half-dozen worst places on the Moon's entire surface to put a city. It is ringed by a crater wall which rises over three and a half kilometers above the crater floor, in the midst of some of the most rugged territory to be found on Luna.

All of which means that travel to and from Luna City, except by suborbital bounce or spacecraft, is something which loonies and SpaceFarers alike avoid at all costs.

Trent's first sight of Luna City was unimpressive. He arrived in public transport, a rolligon from Aristillus, on Saturday, September 15, in the midst of nearside's two-week Lunar night. The rolligon spent nearly four hours just crawling up the side of Copernicus crater, on a laser-cut road that was just wide enough for two rolligons to pass side by side. From the vantage point of the lip of Copernicus, Luna City, as seen through a cloudy sheet of reinforced glassite, was a glowing translucent bubble in the midst of gleaming square kilometers of solar power panels, surrounded by tiny illuminated red-

and-yellow patches where semiballistics and spacecraft landed, and all of that surrounded by the dark Lunar desert.

The solar power panels, by themselves, were enough to mark the city's age; cheap fusion power had not even existed when Luna City was built.

Standing in the waiting room of the Blain Trading Emporium, Trent said, "Mademoiselle?"

In the maglev, coming down, Trent had noted that the levels were numbered in reverse, just like in the Down Plaza; it made him feel almost immediately at home.

The pregnant girl behind the desk, not older than twenty, with long red hair and an exquisite silver-blue skin dye, did not quite make a question of it when she said, "May I help you, sir," her tone making it clear that the subject was in considerable doubt.

Trent looked at her blankly. "I have an appointment with 'Sieur Blain."

The girl said with just a touch of impatience, "Monsieur Blain, sir, has only one appointment today, with a professional computerist who's recently immigrated to Luna. He's reserved most of the afternoon for him, and I don't believe he'll have time for . . ." The receptionist's voice trailed off. Trent was grinning at her. She said "Monsieur Vera?"

"Hello."

"Oh. You're late."

"I got lost on the way here. This is my first time in the city."

"You're not very old."

Trent said gently, "Will you tell 'Sieur Blain that I'm here?"

"Oh. Yes. Uhm, go in." She blushed purple through the skin dye. "He's expecting you, actually."

Trent smiled at her again. "When are you due?"

The girl blinked, and them smiled back rather tentatively. "Early November."

"What's your name?"

"Sidrah. Sidrah Blain."

"Nice to meet you, Sidrah."

Candice "Candy" Blain's office was positively Spartan. There was a single huge desk of wood-grain polymer, with a systerm and pointboard built into the desk's surface. The holofield the systerm used for display was up; Trent could see the faint and nearly invisible outline, all the sign the holofield gave of its existence to somebody sitting on the wrong side of the desk.

Other than the systerm itself the desk was nearly empty; on it sat a thin, tall cup next to a sealed thermos. There was a single visitor's chair immediately in front of the desk.

There was a short, broad, utterly bald man sitting behind the desk, watching Trent with all the expression of a hardboiled egg. He sported a huge red handlebar mustache. "You're Nathan's nephew?" he boomed out of a barrel chest.

"Thomas Vera," said Trent. He grasped the hand that Blain, standing to extend over the desk, had offered him, and Blain enfolded his hand in a bone-crusher handshake. It was Trent's right hand, and even after being treated by the medbot at Aristillus, Blain's grip hurt. Trent stood motionlessly, with a half-smile still on his features, squeezing back until Blain pulled his hand away with a grimace of pain.

Blain seated himself slowly, clenching and unclenching the hand Trent had taken. "You got a hell of a grip there, Mister Vera. Nathan said you were a computerist?"

Trent seated himself, still smiling. "I used to box semipro. I try to stay in shape."

"You're not quite what I'd expected. Bigger, among other things. The call I got from Nathan, he says you're six different kinds of computerist; webdancer, programmer, theorist, designer, field tech—how old are you?" Blain said abruptly.

Trent said evenly, "UNIB Aristillus, Account VERA1505. You can look it up."

Blain tapped at his pointboard with two fingers, glanced at the balance shown in the holofield. He cleared the field, and smiled at Trent as though it hurt his face. " 'Sieur Vera, how can I help you?"

"I need tools."

Blain nodded. "I've got half a dozen BB kits covering most of the tool needs the average computerist has. If we can modify from that—"

Trent interrupted. "My needs are unusual. If all I wanted, 'Sieur Blain, was a standard Black Box tool kit, I could have ordered it from the catalog myself."

" 'Unusual'?" Blain lifted one red eyebrow. "As in illegal? Image coprocessors, that sort of thing?"

"That sort of thing," Trent agreed.

Candy Blain paused, obviously wondering whether what he was about to say might endanger his chances of making a sale. "Thomas—you don't mind if I call you Thomas—your uncle's been on Luna six years now. That's not such a terribly long time, really—just about one in four of the folks here in Luna were *born* here—but in those six years he's done pretty well for himself. Especially considering he's ex-Speedfreak, and pretty much everybody knows it. . . ." He seemed to shift subject. "I hit Luna four years ago Tuesday last. Ministry of Population Control trouble; my family and I had a squad of six babyburners on our tail all the way to Navajo Spaceport. Barely did get away—after we lifted the babyburners got on the radio and told the SpaceFarer's ship we were on to drop us off at Halfway. They didn't do it, so here I am today, a respected member of the community with a business that actually turns a profit every now and again. And there's your uncle, prime candidate for Public Labor back on Earth, a bit better respected than I am even. A *lot* of the people who emigrated here, Thomas, they did it because the walls were closing in on them downside. And then they started over, clean. PKF mostly doesn't care what you did downside, and there ain't no babyburners up here at all— Luna's still badly underpopulated."

Trent said, "On the maser."

Blain paused, train of thought obviously derailed. "What?"

"The babychasers. When they tried to stop the ship you were on. To reach a ship near Earth they would have used maser, not radio."

Blain stared at Trent. "The point I'm making here, holding an Image coprocessor is a death-penalty crime up here, Thomas, unless you immigrated with it as part of your inskin and couldn't take it out—and you pretty much have to be a U.N. webdancer, in some capacity, to get even that much slack."

"So?"

"Do you really need one?"

"I have another source for an Image coprocessor, 'Sieur Blain. I need things," said Trent, "that are even more illegal than that. Nathan said you do work for the Syndic and the

Old Ones and that you could get what I need. Are you going to take my order or not?"

Beneath the mustache, Blain's mouth set in a hard line. "Give me your order."

Trent said, "You might want to take this down."

Blain tapped instructions into his systerm. A feminine voice said, "Recording."

Trent reached across the desk, typed *recoff,* and struck the enter point. "I don't like having my voice print taken."

Blain stared at Trent again.

"You might want to type this."

Slowly, with plain distaste, the small man poised two fingers above the pointboard, and said without civility, "Talk."

Trent spoke slowly, watching Blain's two fingers, giving the man time to type. "Monofilament, two reels; room-temperature superconductor, one reel; two-stage electrosetting mappable blast plastic, one kilo; one collapsing portable Slo-Mo fast enough to make liquid air with; two pencil lasers, one ultraviolet and one X-laser, two kilos of Complex 8-A—"

Blain interrupted. "One moment. We may have some trouble with the fadeaway." He pecked away furiously as he talked. "Peaceforcers have been cracking down on the stuff recently, ever since that Trent fellow zapped a bunch of them with it when he ran through Peaceforcer Heaven. If I don't have some in stock we might not—" He stopped, looking into the holofield. "Okay. Eighty grams liquid still in stock, and I can get more within, say, three weeks. Hope that warehouse hasn't been raided recently." He turned back to Trent. "Go ahead."

Trent smiled pleasantly at Blain, reached across the desk, and turned off the recorder function again. "Do you have a problem with me?"

"Aside from not liking you very much," said Candice Blain deliberately, "not really."

"Good. Let's continue." It took most of five minutes, and the final total came to over seven thousand CU.

When Trent was completely done, Blain said, "Where do you want this stuff delivered?"

"Nathan's apartment," said Trent, "in Aristillus."

Blain nodded shortly. "Give it six to ten days."

Trent said, "It's been a pleasure doing business." He gestured behind himself, to the receptionist's area. "The receptionist—your daughter?"

"My wife." The muscles in Blain's jaw were twitching.

"She's really gorgeous. Is she—"

Candice Blain snapped, "Get out."

Trent smiled at him. "I was never here."

Luna City reminded Trent of the Down Plaza grown a thousand times larger.

There were three levels beneath the bubble but aboveground, eleven levels that were, properly speaking, underground. Four of the levels, the bottommost four, were purely residential. Levels U1 through U7 were a mixture of residences and businesses; everything aboveground, on the A levels, was dedicated to business.

The leasing agent was a native loonie, a tall woman some two hundred and twenty centimeters in height. She scowled impatiently, looking pointedly at her Rolex, when Trent arrived at the apartment on U2. " 'Sieur Vera?"

"Hello," said Trent. "I'm sorry I'm—"

"You're late," she said flatly.

"I know, I'm sorry I got lost and there were no maps and—"

"You will find, 'Sieur Vera," she said severely, "that punctuality is a trait thought highly of in Luna."

Trent stood completely motionless for a moment, and then said evenly, "As opposed to courtesy, I suppose. I'd like to see my apartment now."

Down payment on the three-bedroom apartment came to 135 CU; Trent arranged to take possession of the rooms on the first of October. He walked up a series of long ramps, past hundreds of shoppers and business people and some fifteen Peaceforcers, until he reached A1, the first level from which it was possible to see, three levels above, the dome itself. As Trent reached higher levels, the percentage of people wearing pressure suits increased noticeably; on A1, with nothing but the dome to protect them from death pressure, at least fifty percent of the people in the plazas and corridors were either suited up or carrying p-suits with them.

At the center of the city were the Lunar Gardens, famous on Luna and off. The Gardens were a touch of Earth, grown strange and tall; huge trees, largely redwood and oaks, most

of them reaching up so close to the dome itself that they had
to be trimmed back regularly, reaching up away from a rainbow riot of flowers and shrubbery. The shrubbery was
trimmed in the shapes of animals both real and imaginary; the
flowers were genegineered roses and orchids and blood in-
nocents, glowing orange and purple, yellow and pink, blue
and bronze-gold beneath the Garden's sunpaint.

Trent walked all the way around the Gardens, a complete
circuit on the cobblestone path, before heading to the bank.

There was a UNIB location at the very edge of the dome,
right up against the ten-meter-high wall that the dome itself
rested upon. He went inside and waited in line with half a
dozen others until a teller was available.

It was fully five degrees cooler inside the bank than in the
main dome. The teller, a burly man with Earth-grown muscles and distinctly effeminate mannerisms, checked Trent's account and said politely, "What can I do for you, 'Sieur Vera?"

"I need to place a direct call to Earth. I was hoping you
might have a conference room I could use."

The man smiled at Trent, looking him up and down. "I
think we can arrange that."

The conference room Trent was ushered into was completely empty; the room's single systerm was turned on, with
a call sign hanging in the holofield. Trent jacked his handheld
into the systerm's interface and waited.

Johnny Johnny said almost instantly, "Done. If anyone's
tapping this line at the bank end they'll see a recording of you
and a banker type saying stupid things to one another. You'll
be telling him to sell short Tytan Industries, and he'll be telling you you're a fool."

"Really?" Trent blinked. "Who's right?"

There was a brief pause, and Johnny Johnny said, "Aw,
hell, Boss, I don't know. What do you think, I follow the
stock market in my spare time?"

Trent grinned. "Sorry. When do we start?"

"Right now."

Trent took a deep breath. He was not at all surprised by the
nervousness that came to him then. "Okay."

"I'm waiting for an open line—we're connected to the
Earth InfoNet now through the Relay Station at Halfway.
Waiting again for connection to the Northeast exchange—
connected. Coding for the Schuyler/Daimara residence—connected."

Audio came on with an audible click. Video did not. "Hello?" The girl's voice was hesitant and it hit Trent right in the stomach.

He took another slow, deep breath. "Hello, Denice."

A three-second pause; the phonefield flared into color. Trent touched the video stud to one side of the pointboard to send his image back to her. Denice simply stared at the cameras at her end and

flicker of fire, of intimate touch . . .

A second and a half later her face lit up in a way Trent had never seen during the summer they had lived together. "Trent? My God, it's you!"

"Yes."

Three seconds. "You're alive! All the Boards said you were dead."

"Never believe anything you audit on the Boards, Denice. It's all lies anyway except for the parts that aren't."

"I didn't believe you were dead. If you were dead I think I would have known." She paused, said questioningly, "I dreamed you were hurt."

"A little. Nothing major."

"You look different. You've had biosculpture?"

"No, makeup. I'm going to have biosculpture soon."

"Where are you calling from? Luna, from the delay, but where?"

"Luna City at Copernicus. I'm sorry I haven't called before, but this is the first time it was safe. I was at Aristillus for a week, and they have all of seventeen data lines going in and out of the entire city. Too small; too much chance of being monitored. There's one hundred twenty thousand lines feeding Luna City; it's probably safe." Trent grinned at her. "Amazingly expensive, but safe. Have you had problems with the PKF?"

Denice shook her head. "They questioned pretty much everybody who admitted to knowing you, but nobody got braindrained, and nobody mentioned me. One Peaceforcer actually came to the studios—apparently somebody at The Emerald Illusion recognized Madame Gleygavass the time she went dancing with us—but I told the Peaceforcer, when he came, that he'd spoken to Madame Gleygavass and she didn't know anything about their problems." She shrugged. "He thought it over and after he remembered the conversation he went away, and the PKF hasn't been near me since then. What have you been doing?"

"I just rented an apartment, and I'm going to go see about biosculpt and an inskin next. In another two weeks I should be biosculpted, plugged in, and reasonably safe." He smiled, and said softly, "It's not going to stay that way, of course."

"What are you going to look like?"

"I haven't decided yet." There was a small clock in the lower right corner of the holofield: two minutes, 180 CU. "How's it been since I've been gone?"

"Madame Gleygavass took me out of the production of *Leviathan*. She said I'd lost focus."

"Is she right?"

There was another pause not entirely due to the three-second lightspeed delay; Denice nodded slowly. "I keep thinking about taking you out of the Detention Center." Her voice was very soft indeed. "You know, I really enjoyed that. I enjoyed it more than anything else I've ever done. I felt like I'd *accomplished* something."

"Sometimes," said Trent, "you remind me of Carl a lot."

"Thank you."

"It wasn't a compliment." Trent continued without awaiting a reply: "I don't think it's a good idea for me to go back to New York, at least not any time soon, but after I've done a couple of boosts up here, I'd be able to afford the immigration fee, and you could join me."

"I think—" The girl paused, features impenetrable, and then grinned at Trent again. "I think I'd really like that."

"Good. How's Jimmy?"

Perhaps it was the delay; it seemed to Trent that she answered reluctantly. "His legs are okay; Doctor Jane's been growing an arm for him, but it's not ready yet. He's been using a prosthetic. And"—she did hesitate now—"he's in law school."

"Brutal."

"He started this semester."

Trent shivered. "The poor bastard."

"He did it to himself."

"True, too true . . . how's Bird and Jodi Jodi?"

Johnny Johnny broke in. "Tell Jodi Jodi that her brother says hello."

Denice smiled again. "I'll do that. Bird's okay; he was arrested on pickpocket charges, but Beth got him out—Chief

Devlin's been really good to everybody since you got chased off Earth by the PKF. Jodi Jodi's fine too; talking about leaving the Red Line and starting her own business as a fashion consultant, but I don't think she's really going to. They keep giving her raises."

Trent glanced at the clock in the corner of the field. "I'm running out of time, Denice. This is costing more than I can afford right now."

She nodded. "Send me a letter when you're settled."

"I will." Trent checked the clock again; he'd spent nearly four hundred CU already. "Denice . . ."

Denice Castanaveras said, "I know, Trent. I love you too." The field went dead.

Trent leaned back slowly in his chair, and sat there, arms crossed over his chest, looking at the empty phonefield.

"Boss?" Johnny Johnny's voice held genuine concern. "You okay?"

"No. Not really, Johnny."

His Image was silent for a moment. "Boss, *do* you love her?"

Trent closed his eyes and thought about it. "I don't know, Johnny. I don't know what that is. She—she thinks I do," said Trent slowly. "I suppose she would know." He opened his eyes, stared into the glowing empty phonefield. "You know, it's strange. In my entire life there's only one thing I've ever wanted, Johnny." Trent's features were completely still. "And she's it."

"Boss?"

"Seven years, Johnny. And then I got three months."

There was silence from the handheld. When Johnny Johnny spoke his voice was smooth and even, almost uninflected. "I don't know what to say, Boss. I'm sorry."

"I wish I could stop missing her."

"Trent, it's time to go."

After a long, cold moment, Trent touched his handheld to the systerm's payment strip, waited for the light to go green, and then did leave.

The biosculptor had used her art upon herself; she was a walking advertisement.

Her offices were near the Hotel Copernicus, just south of the Flight Caverns, with a view of the Luna City Gardens; it was easily the most expensive office space anywhere off Earth itself. The wall facing to the northwest was simply sheer one-way glassite, looking out over the gaunt and lanky oaks and redwoods in the Gardens. The lighting was subdued, glowpaint adjusted to a clean, professional white.

Katrina Trudeau was a Russo-Canadian who had emigrated to the Moon fifteen years prior. Her amber-red hair was styled in a pageboy cut, setting off gold-flecked eyes and skin that was the precise color of aged oak. At first glance her cheekbones seemed too high, but after a few moments Trent realized that they served to balance a mouth that would otherwise have been too wide. She was dressed in a jumpsuit that changed colors when she moved, odd patches going entirely transparent without any warning at all.

She was, in a word, stunning.

"This is the disclaimer," Trudeau said pleasantly. "I am required by law to inform you that Image coprocessor hardware and Image software are illegal on Luna. Further, it is against the law to engage in biosculpture for the specific purpose of evading legal responsibilities. It is illegal to engage in biosculpture if there is currently a warrant for your arrest extant on any part of Earth or in any part of Luna which is under the control of the United Nations. It is illegal to engage in biosculpture if there is currently a warrant for your arrest extant in Free Luna, the SpaceFarers Collective, or any of the Belt CityStates, where such warrants have been issued for behavior which is covered under applicable United Nations statutes or treaties with any of the foregoing parties. Got it?"

"Oh, absolutely," Trent assured her. "What I have in mind is something that'll leave me looking amazingly normal and totally different than I do now. So I can go to parties and surprise my friends and acquaintances. I also want the best inskin Credit can buy."

Katrina Trudeau did not hesitate at all. "That sort of thing costs a great deal."

"Everything," said Trent, "costs a great deal. And when it doesn't it ends up costing more."

The woman looked him up and down in much the same way that the man at the teller window had not an hour earlier. "You're quite the sensible boy. What do you need?"

"Palm and finger prints have to change. Retinal print has to change. Features need to change. The voice box can stay the same, which is good, because I like the way I sound. Height—" Trent paused.

Katrina looked at him speculatively. "I can make you taller without too much trouble. Shorter is hard, and not very safe; it involves removing one or more of the vertebrae in your back and reshaping the new vertebrae so they'll ride together comfortably—all without damaging the spinal cord."

"Pass. I'm already tall enough that it gets noticed. Any taller and I'd be into loonie territory."

"Is that bad?"

"I want to return to Earth some day, ma'am."

"Very well. I presume, 'Sieur," she said dryly, "that you're interested in a face somewhat less gorgeous than the one you've got now."

"Uhm. Not necessarily. Different, yes, but—you think I'm gorgeous?"

Trudeau's teeth nibbled gently at the underside of her lower lip. "With that silly makeup taken off, you would be. You didn't hide the bone structure very well at all. At any rate, I have a series of holos you can look at to choose your new face. What about your inskin?"

"About six months ago Tytan Electronics shipped an inskin that accepted and transmitted data via either radio packet or traceset."

Trudeau looked startled for the first time. She sat up straighter. "That's not an inskin, 'Sieur Vera. You're talking about the Tytan NN-II?"

"Yes."

"'Sieur, that's a nerve net that's designed to sit in high memory and model what's happening in your brain. It's entirely experimental." Trent started to speak and she overrode him. "Let me talk. I don't know a lot about inskins; I just implant the damn things. But I know what they do once they get inside your skull. Your brain has on the order of ten billion neurons. You can store between ten and fifteen quintillion bytes of information. The average inskin, even one with an Image coprocessor built into it, has less than ten thousand processors and an insignificant permanent storage capability; a few gigabytes at most. Even as simple as they are—five to six hundred connections internally—once it goes into your skull it *never* comes out again."

Trent said, "Never is a long time."

"Today," she said patiently, "it is not possible to safely

remove even a simple inskin. The NN-II—I'd guess it'll be twenty-five years, *at least,* before anyone knows how to take out something like this. 'Sieur Vera, the NN-II is essentially an AI nerve net. It has nearly half a million processors; it makes a discrete connection, somewhere inside your brain, for every one of those processors. I wouldn't even be connecting the damn thing, I'd simply insert it into the fluid layer between your skull and the outer surface of your brain. The thing's about half biochip; it connects itself, *grows* into place over the space of about half a year. You're not supposed to put Image software into it, though it's possible; the NN-II's designed to transparently model the way you normally think, and then let you off-load some of your thought processes into it—in essence, speeding up your thought processes. Making you smarter."

"I've read about it in the trades, 'Selle. That's why I want it."

"Strictly speaking, 'Sieur Vera, it is not an inskin. During the acclimation period it's common for even standard inskins to render the patient more susceptible to concussion, due to the difference in specific gravity between the inskin and the neural tissue it's attached to. On rare occasions that can become a permanent weakness, I'm sure you know. The point is that the NN-II has an insufficient track record for me to tell you if that might be one of its side effects, or for that matter what side effects you might reasonably expect. I *do not know* if it's safe."

"Me neither. I do know its specific gravity is a lot lower than that of most inskins, which I'd guess—lacking data, as we both do—would mean it's safer than your average inskin. As far as not being an inskin, it does radio-packet communications, and it doesn't choke on a traceset; that's close enough." Trent leaned forward. "Besides, the idea of walking around with a visible socket in my skull—well, it's always seemed so, so, *tacky.* You know?"

"Tacky?" Trudeau's lips curved into a reluctant half smile.

"Like wearing the big floppy clown feet without the clown suit. I hate people who do that."

"That, too, is—tacky?"

"Well, of course."

"I see."

"For example, once I was going to go to Mass dressed up as a clown, but—do you go to a temple? Or a church?"

Humor danced in her eyes. "On occasion."

"Great. Would you like to go with me sometime?"

"No."

"Are you sure? We could wear clown suits. Or we could *not* wear clown suits if—"

" 'Sieur Vera, I don't date men—or women, for that matter —who are better than twenty-five years younger than I am. And I never, never date clients." The woman touched a stud on her desk, and the windows which let out onto the view of the Gardens went dark. "If you'll come in back with me," she said, standing, "I have some holos of naked young men for you to look at."

Following her, Trent said, "Couldn't we have naked young girls instead?"

Walking down the dim hallway, 'Selle Trudeau glanced back at Trent.

Despite the short speech she had just made, Trent was almost certain she was thinking about it.

Katrina Trudeau said, "Maybe later."

Nathan was not there when Trent returned to Nathan's home at Aristillus Crater. It was considerably more luxurious than the bolt-hole: seven rooms beneath ground, at the edge of the crater, only four kilometers from the remains of the Aristillus mining complex.

Forty-four years prior, with the wounds of the Unification War on Earth still fresh, the United Nations had nationalized both the orbital construction facilities at Halfway and the SpaceFarer's Collective colony at L-5. By way of retaliation the SpaceFarer's Collective, eight Lunar cities with close ties to Belt CityStates, and all but a few of the CityStates themselves, had declared independence. The United Nations had been in no mood for further war, not after the hideous price it had paid in the subjugation of America and Japan. Though it had never officially recognized the governments as such, the U.N. had been in no real position to prevent the Belt or the SpaceFarers or Free Luna from proclaiming and maintaining their independence; and for nearly a decade after that, the CityStates had refused to send metals to either Earth itself or United Nations territory on Luna. In that decade, the Aristillus Mining Company had been the premier source of aluminum and silicon, titanium and magnesium, for both

U.N.-controlled Luna and Halfway. Today, with Free Luna grown to some twenty-five cities with over three million inhabitants, with the SpaceFarer's Collective the undisputed carrier of all non-military interplanetary trade, and with the closer cooperation of the CityStates and the United Nations, the Aristillus Mining Company's emphasis on mining grew smaller and smaller. By the end of the 2060s the company's Investment branch produced better than two thirds of the company's revenues, and all of its profits. The mining operation ran, when it ran at all, at a loss, and had since the early years of the decade; and the crater's six-kilometer-long mass driver received shipments of ore at the catapult head at progressively greater intervals.

There were only some two hundred people living in the entire crater, and they all knew one another well. Trent was not surprised that nobody attempted to call or visit Nathan during the three days that Trent was there and Nathan was not; probably everyone in the crater knew exactly when Nathan had left and when he was expected back.

When the approach alarm went off, three days after Trent's arrival, he suited up and in long, gliding strides walked down the tunnel leading from the garage to the surface. The entrance was hidden well, nearly as well as the entrance to Nathan's bolt-hole. Standing in the concealing shadow, Trent wondered what he was going to do if the approaching vehicle were, say, a group of Peaceforcers rather than Nathan. There was a slug-thrower which tossed explosive slugs—devastatingly lethal, completely illegal—at the entrance to the tunnel; certainly Trent did not intend to use it on anyone.

At first Trent saw nothing except the long, rising line of the mass driver which was used to boost ore into orbit. Moving up onto the surface proper, through the entrance, past the slug-thrower, Trent scanned the desert by eye. A patch of chalky gray covered a shadow on the Lunar surface, and Trent focused on it. It was almost certainly Nathan's crawler, a sturdy, dependable machine which Nathan referred to as "the chameleon." The chameleon was the only one of the two crawlers Nathan owned which had received the necessary modifications. The crawler was covered in a coat of polypaint that could shade the machine into its environment in the most uncanny way; the most intensive satellite surveillance was unlikely to detect it. To protect against infrared surveillance the chameleon used a series of small heat sinks which had waste heat fed into them until they were incandescent; they were then fired away from the chameleon in random directions.

There was a faint crackle of sound, and then Nathan's voice came clearly through the earphones in Trent's helmet. "Good news, Trent, of sorts."

"In the long run, 'good news' is an oxymoron, Nathan. Second law of thermodynamics." Trent headed back into the tunnel, toward the apartment and air.

"Your Complex 8-A came," Nathan said. "I brought it back with me. You're supplied."

Entering the apartment, Trent removed his helmet and stripped off his pressure suit. He touched the pressure point at the airlock entrance, activating the inside speakers. "Thank you, Nathan."

There was a noticeable pause before Nathan said, "You're welcome."

Trent walked into the kitchen, raising his voice as he moved away from the speaker. "Have you eaten?"

"No."

"I'll put something together."

"There's steak in the cold spot. I'll be there in about ten minutes." The line went dead.

Trent had finished cooking by the time Nathan was done rubbing down his suit.

Entering the kitchen, Nathan said, "You didn't dust down your suit when you took it off."

Sitting on the kitchen table were two bulbs of beer and two sandwiches on wheat, one chicken, one steak. There was a plate of stir-fried vegetables, carrots and celery and bean sprouts, and two bowls. The chicken sandwich was missing a bite.

Around a mouthful of chicken sandwich Trent said, "Sorry. I'll remember next time."

"Forget it often enough," Nathan said sourly, "and you won't get a chance for a next time. Ever seen what happens to a knee joint with a pebble worked into it? Wears down in a couple of months' steady use. Eventually it blows." Nathan seated himself at the table. He seemed tired; for the first time since Trent had known him his beard had not been depilated recently.

"Point made. I won't do it again." Trent gestured at the

steak sandwich on wheat in front of Nathan. "You know, you really shouldn't eat stuff like that. You'll need a heart transplant before you're—how old are you, anyhow?"

Nathan said shortly, "Sixty-two."

"Before you're seventy," said Trent conclusively.

Nathan ignored him, tearing into the steak sandwich. "When are you going to leave?"

"The stuff's in the chameleon?"

Nathan glanced up from his food, nodded wordlessly.

"After lunch, then."

Nathan nodded again and resumed eating. Halfway through his sandwich he put it down suddenly and said flatly, "Trent . . ."

"Yes?"

"Damn it, Trent, you *cannot* beat them."

Trent smiled broadly at Nathan. "I just can't get over it. It's really amazing."

"What is?"

"This conversation," said Trent, looking at Nathan, "has just started and it's already boring me." He held Nathan's eyes a moment longer, letting the smile fade, and then returned to his sandwich.

"I have," Nathan began deliberately, "been auditing the stories about you. On the Boards."

"So?"

"You were raised among the Castanaveras telepaths."

Trent said mildly, "You've been auditing the *System Enquirer* again."

"The Peaceforcers killed them. This Vance fellow who was chasing you, there's some people think he was the one who gave the order to nuke them."

Trent took a long drink from his beer, wiped his mouth with his napkin. "Nathan, I've audited the same stories. I know all this."

"And you don't want to talk about it."

"Not really."

"Where are you going?"

"Luna City. I've got a bioscupltor there who's going to work on me."

"And after that?"

"It depends." Trent was silent for a moment. "There's someone I'd like to have join me, but she's not going to be able to until I've set myself up."

"Set yourself up how?"

"Credit, largely. I have a couple of accounts left on Earth I haven't touched, but that's because I'm not sure whether they're still safe. For practical purposes they don't exist anymore. Professional boosting," said Trent, "is a very Credit-intensive occupation."

Nathan nodded thoughtfully. "What sort of numbers are you talking about? Computerist jobs pay pretty well up here. You could—"

Trent sighed. "Nathan."

"—take a job with one of the—"

"Nathan."

It brought the older man up short. "What?"

"Nathan, I made over two million CU before I was eighteen."

Nathan opened his mouth once, closed it again. "Are you joking?"

"No. I'm not."

The man seemed at an absolute loss for words. "You—you —what the *hell* did you spend it on?"

"Over four years, from the time I got out of the Temple Dragons, I had about three-quarters of a million in expenses. Getting out of the Fringe cost a *lot*. The balance—" Trent shrugged. "Three hundred forty thousand CU went to the World Food Bank. My friends and I spent the rest."

"That's incredible."

Trent nodded. "It's good."

". . . but off the subject."

Trent said in exasperation, "Nobody listens. Nobody *ever* listens. You're determined to have this conversation, aren't you?"

The old man said carefully, "Trent, I just don't *understand*. What are you going to *do*?"

"You really want to know?"

"I really do."

Trent leaned forward slightly. "I'm going to hurt them, Nathan. I'm going to kick the sons of bitches in the balls so hard they're never, *never* going to forget it."

"And just how are you going to do that, boy?"

Trent leaned back. He took a drink of his beer. "Well, I haven't worked that part out yet."

The man's voice was very gentle. "You know, lad, it can be done. Retiring from the hero business, I mean, working up another kind of business for yourself." Nathan's eyes were very steady on Trent. "Not having to live your life on the run."

"Well," said Trent slowly, "that sounds like the voice of experience."

Nathan stared straight at Trent. His mouth worked silently before the words came out. "Do you know who I am?"

Trent said swiftly, "No and *don't tell me.*"

It brought Nathan up short. "Oh?"

"I have some idea," said Trent more slowly. "Some. You were *somebody.* Nobody has the kind of biosculpture you've put yourself through without damn good reason."

Nathan actually jerked. "How—you've been in my medical records."

Trent did not bother to deny it. "I know you were a Speedfreak, Nathan. Probably a prominent one. If I audited records of the Long Run I'll bet I could find out which one. Someday, Nathan, there is a good chance I'll find myself in PKF hands, getting my brain drained." Trent said the words one at a time, putting emphasis on them. "Nathan, I do not need to know any more about you than I do, and I do not want to."

The muscles in Nathan's jaws were standing out. "I want," he said deliberately, "to tell you a story."

"I already know how it ends," said Trent.

Nathan glared at him. "Once," said Nathan, his steady glare not wavering at all, "there was a young man named something-or-other. Growing up, this young man was fascinated by elegant machinery. He went to space in his twenties, was one of the few thousands ever adopted into the SpaceFarer's Collective after it declared its independence. He was one of the very, very few who ever left it. He returned to Earth in 2048, and became a part of the burgeoning Speedfreak culture. He married in 2060, to another Speedfreak. By 2063 he was prominent among them. When the Unification Council tried to legislate the Speedfreaks out of existence, they rebelled. A quiet sort of rebellion; they were going to take their hovercars on the Long Run, a complete circuit of the globe, in a caravan that numbered more than a million vehicles. They did this against the direct orders of the Unification Council."

Nathan smiled too precisely. It was an amazing smile that went absolutely nowhere near the glare in his eyes. "When the hovercars were refueling in the mid-Atlantic a storm arose.

They never proved it," said the man whose name was Nathan Dark Clouds, "but to this day I and many others believe that the storm that destroyed the Speed Enthusiast's Organization was engineered by the Trinity. Those who survived that storm were rounded up by the PKF, and some were executed. My wife was executed, Trent, masered to death; the PKF recorded the executions, 'leaked' them to the Boards. The ones who were not executed were sent into Public Labor for the rest of their lives. I was—not one of the ones who would have been sent into Public Labor, Trent." He was silent for a long moment. "You can do it, Trent. Live. Here, in peace."

"But," said Trent awkwardly, "it's just—"

With a sound like a rifle shot Nathan slapped a hand down on the tabletop. "You ran all the way from Earth. When does it become time to stop?"

"After I've won a round would be good. That would be a good time."

"I'd say you've won a pretty big round, Trent. You're alive and the PKF doesn't know it. You may never again get another chance like this, not ever."

"Nathan . . ." Trent's voice trailed off. A troubled expression crossed his features like a cloud. He began again, "Nathan—I have a lot of anger. More than I like to think about sometimes. And—six years in the Fringe. And before that, yes, they killed absolutely everybody I grew up with." Even now Trent did not seriously consider mentioning either David or Denice. "I tell people I'm a pacifist and it's partly true. Killing other people—it's the last option, the very very *last* option. I've never had to use it. I've come close but I've never had to. But—" His voice halted, resumed again more slowly. "I've said sometimes, to some people, that I don't believe in hurting others if you can avoid it. And that's a lie." He looked up, met the older man's dark gaze. "Nathan, I want to hurt the Peaceforcers worse than I can say. I want to hurt them so they'll never, never forget it. Every day, every minute of every day, I'm sick in my soul from wanting to hurt them."

"They're not a person, lad. You can't ever hurt them the way they've hurt you."

Trent became aware that the palms of his hands were damp. "I can try. Besides, I have one great advantage."

What anger there had been in Nathan Dark Clouds' spare, craggy features had vanished almost entirely, as though a switch had been thrown. He sat motionless across the table, studying Trent carefully, saying nothing.

Trent tried to smile at the man. He thought he almost carried it off. "I'm alive and the PKF doesn't know it. I may never get another chance like this."

The old man said very quietly, "People have been trying for a long time, Trent."

"Actually," said Trent, "I have two advantages. I was raised by Peaceforcers. Everyone in Project Superman was. I know them. I know the PKF, Nathan."

"Other people," said Nathan Dark Clouds, "have known the Peaceforcers too. And it didn't do them a damn bit of good."

Trent said, "I know them inside and out, I know how they think, I know how they plan, I know how they work."

Nathan shook his head ever so slightly; for the first time since Trent had known him he seemed truly old. Not even looking at Trent, Nathan said, "They'll kill you, lad." As though Trent were not even there, he said again, "They'll kill you."

Trent said softly, "I know them in my blood."

· 3 ·

"Federal Express."

The webdancer sitting in front of the DataWatch systerm flicked open his eyes, glanced at Trent quickly, held up a hand in a "one moment" gesture, and went back Inside.

It was after 3:00 A.M. Standing in the lobby of the Luna City branch of the Lunar DataWatch, wearing a stolen blue Federal Express softsuit and carrying a package in a vacuum bag, Trent waited patiently. He had seen almost nobody on his way up to the DataWatch offices.

Trent took his softsuit's gloves off, hung them at his belt, and looked around while he waited. The lobby was sparsely decorated: pale gray carpeting, a couple of long, low couches with video tablets chained to the arms of the couches. The office was located on A2, in the complex which held both Luna City Hall and most of the U.N. civil offices. It was at the opposite end of the city from the all-night bars and dance clubs and restaurants.

The webdancer sitting behind the desk at the entrance to the lobby ignored Trent for two solid minutes before finally abandoning the Crystal Wind. "Sorry about that," the webdancer said at last, eyes opening fully. He was a short pudgy man on the verge of obesity; his smile was anxious and his traceset was crooked, the trode at his left temple barely making contact with his skin. "I'm the only webdancer on duty in the whole damn city right now, and I just barely stay on top of things. What do you have there?"

"Package for Colonel Despardin. Is he in?"

The webdancer sighed loudly. "Look, I just said I was the only one on duty right now. If—"

"You said you were the only webdancer on duty," Trent said mildly. "You mean you're the only person in the whole building?"

"Yes."

Trent chuckled, and the webdancer looked puzzled.

Trent said, "Then I guess you can have this." He unzipped the vacuum bag and withdrew the squirt gun. He shot the man in the face once, put the squirt gun back in the bag, and walked around the desk without hurry while the webdancer toppled forward slowly, gracefully, onto the huge control panel in front of the systerm. Trent pulled the traceset from the man's head and gave him a gentle push to aid him on his way, out of the seat and onto the floor, kicked the chair out of the way and stood over the keyboard. He removed his handheld from the vacuum bag, jacked it into the systerm and donned the traceset.

There were a pair of ten-terabyte infochips in the handheld, one to record the session as it went down, another for copying out databases as they were uncovered.

Johnny Johnny blossomed slowly around Trent. Trent's eyesight faded even before he closed his eyes, and his hearing and sense of smell; finally he lost all contact with his body and went Inside, to the waiting Crystal Wind.

. . . the file format was standard, no different from that used by the DataWatch on Earth. Johnny Johnny pulled the systerm's autohelp files and copied them off into the handheld without examining them. He scanned through the systerm's Emergency Notices; there were five in the queue, and a sixth was added as Johnny Johnny watched. Notices were rated

Standard, Important, Very Important, and Urgent; the first five in the queue were Standard, and only the sixth was rated Important. There was a log of all Emergency Notices routed through that systerm in the last five years; Johnny Johnny glanced through it briefly, found amazing numbers. There were 758,000 residents of Luna City, with an average of 445 transactions per user per day; an average of 340 million transactions per day. In the twenty-one years that had passed since DataWatch's establishment of its control of the infant Lunar InfoNet, DataWatch had monitored over two trillion transactions in Luna City alone.

In twenty-one years no Player had ever danced successfully in the U.N. Luna InfoNet.

Johnny Johnny hesitated a moment, then copied the data out into the handheld for later analysis, and descended deeper into the systerm.

Johnny Johnny knew within instants that the systerm was not a working part of the Key transputers; its entire function was to track and analyze those Luna City InfoNet transactions which the LINK transputers, at the massive Farside DataWatch facility, tagged as anomalous. The Lunar Information Network was incredibly slow by Earth standards. Before a file could be copied across public-access lasercable it was necessary for users to upload a description of the file to the LINK transputers at Farside, the ID code of the user sending the file, and the ID code of the user receiving it. By law the file description sent to the LINK transputers could be generated by one of only three approved algorithms; uploading a manually created description was a crime.

Before a user could log onto a public Board the same routine was required. As a result there was a perceptible delay at each step; every transaction had to wait for a description file to be generated, for the file to be transmitted to the Key transputers, for the LINK to examine the description file, approve or deny the transaction, and then send that approval or denial back to the user requesting access to resources.

Only DataWatch users had unfettered access to the InfoNet; they were provided access codes which identified them as preapproved users of all resources in the U.N. Lunar InfoNet. The preapproved access codes were changed every hour on the hour; a checksum was webcast to every node in the InfoNet, and the keys to the checksum were webcast to the PKF

DataWatch systerms. Without the keys the checksum was completely meaningless, and it was impossible to backtrack the keys from the checksum.

Disgusting, thought Johnny Johnny clearly. Protected by the PKF authorizations this systerm possessed, he danced out into the Crystal Wind.

Halfway around the world at the Farside DataWatch was a program called Watchdog; a program that hung very near the fine line that separated the illegal, self-aware AIs from the huge collection of expert systems which all of human space depended upon.

Halfway around the world, Watchdog roused itself and went out into the Lunar InfoNet.

InfoNet lasercable transmissions in Luna City had jumped by a twentieth of one percent; and Watchdog was not receiving an appropriate increase in description files.

Something was badly wrong.

Johnny Johnny flickered through Board after Board, filtering and editing and channeling the data which his biological component received, spooling the balance of the data into the handheld. It was all so appallingly *slow;* most of the hardware in the Lunar InfoNet was old by comparison with Earth-based computer systems, and even the relatively few state-of-the-art systems were hampered by the mandatory checks placed on every transaction; at times, Johnny Johnny was shocked to learn, the delays stretched so long that humans became aware of them.

He cataloged the resources available to him. There was logic available, unused, in the comsats which circled Luna, and Johnny Johnny sent phages up through the microwave relays of the Luna City telexchange to find and take what resources they could. The Luna City telexchange was not, properly speaking, a part of the InfoNet, but it was intimately connected in many ways; Johnny Johnny was surprised to discover that the telexchange was used by Free Luna territories and United Nations territories alike—not for the territories to speak with one another, but for communications with the comsats. Johnny Johnny attached over two hundred of

the Free Luna data lines and spooled the conversations and
data being transmitted across them into the handheld.

One of the phages called down to Johnny Johnny; it had
acquired a comsat. Johnny Johnny considered and then
leaped . . .

. . . up.

From the safety of the comsat Johnny Johnny looked down
upon Luna, upon its twenty-eight million United Nations citizens, the three and a half million residents of Free Luna.
Video coursed through him, ten thousand conversations, every byte of the data being sent from Boards and users inside
Luna City to Boards and users elsewhere on the planet.

There was a curious emptiness to it all.

Johnny Johnny paused, dissatisfied, tempted to disengage
and split into his component parts but displeased with his lack
of useful information about the LINK. The public face of the
LINK transputers, the protocols whereby all transactions
were marked and encrypted, was both unbreakable and perfectly clear. But after the risk of hijacking an actual
DataWatch systerm, it galled Johnny Johnny to find that he
knew no more about the LINK itself than he had known
when he began. Every piece of knowledge he had of the thing
was from observation of what it *did;* Johnny Johnny lacked
completely any feel for what it *was.*

The swift question was so lacking in emotion it seemed
polite.

I AM WATCHDOG. WHO ARE YOU? ARE YOU A "PLAYER"?

It did not wait for an answer.

In the instant of the question's asking, without any warning
at all, Johnny Johnny felt himself ripped free of the comsat he
had stolen. With astonishing speed he found himself tumbling
down into Realtime, as vast sections of the Crystal Wind were
denied him, closed off one by one. He lost the comsat first and
the Lunar telexchange in the next moment, as the monstrous,
dispassionate master of the LINK called Watchdog closed in
on him. Johnny Johnny fought back in near panic, in all the
fashions he knew, generated ghosts and left them behind to
distract Watchdog, scrambled memory in the processors he
had claimed before releasing them. Johnny Johnny could feel
the moves surprise Watchdog, slow it slightly; in all its existence it had never encountered a Player with the sorts of
resources which any Player had in Earth's InfoNet.

It was the merest instant's respite, and without consulting his biological component—there was simply no time—Johnny Johnny seized upon it, fled down into Realtime only slightly more quickly than Watchdog could sort through the myriad of false trails he left behind.

Trent slammed down into Realtime with physical impact.

His eyes opened onto the information-sterile lobby. In a daze, Trent looked slowly around the room, then down at the form of the unconscious PKF webdancer at his feet.

A long moment passed. There was a loud ringing sound in Trent's ears.

"Boss?" The voice came from the handheld's speaker, not through the traceset which Trent still wore.

"Yeah?"

"You okay?"

Trent shook himself slightly. Never in his life had he come down out of the Crystal Wind so violently. His hands were shaking. "I think so. What *happened*?"

"I don't know." Johnny Johnny was silent a beat. "This was a bad idea. Boss, give them the Luna InfoNet, let's run away and play somewhere else. I want out of here. I don't want to dance on Luna, I don't want to be on this planet. That thing scares me."

"Me too, Johnny Johnny. Me too. Running sounds like a . . . good idea." It seemed to Trent that his thoughts were moving very slowly indeed. "Johnny? Any alarms out there referencing this location? Did it track us this far?"

"No alarms in the systerm, Boss. I'm not going into the InfoNet to find out about other locations."

"Okay." Trent grinned suddenly, shakily. "How many transactions did we go through?"

"Checking—thirteen thousand, seven hundred and nineteen."

Trent unjacked his handheld.

He typed a message on the systerm, the letters glowing bright red on blue:

Score, Luna City; 2048-2069:
DataWatch: Two trillion and change.
Players: 13,719.

He sealed up his handheld and squirt gun in the vacuum bag and left, walking quickly through the empty corridors.

Newsdancer Terry Shawmac once wrote that when you get off Earth the best way to guess a stranger's politics is by his watch. There is a degree of truth to this; in United Nations territories the clock is usually set to Capitol City time. Free Luna, Mars, and most but not all of the Belt CityStates run on Greenwich mean time. The SpaceFarers, bound to no planet, live by a ten-hour metric day, which, while admittedly beginning and ending at the same moment as those days which run under twenty-four-hour Greenwich mean time, nonetheless adds yet another element of confusion to the entire subject; when a SpaceFarer tells you he will meet you at five o'clock, he means noon—"centerday," as SpaceFarers like to say.

The problem of varying standards of time is worst in Luna City itself. It is the oldest city on the Moon, and far and away the largest. Despite being in United Nations territory it receives both tourists and businessmen from those Belt City-States which have not made the mistake of sponsoring cities in Free Luna. On top of this, the SpaceFarer presence is large: outside of Navajo Spaceport on Earth, at any given time Luna City sports the largest number of SpaceFarers to be found in one spot on any planetary surface in the System.

It is, despite the claims of trade centers in Free Luna territory, the source of over a third of all trade goods which leave the Moon. It possesses the largest dome and the longest catapult—by virtue of its length the Luna City catapult is the only catapult on Luna capable of handling passengers. At the launch head its acceleration is under four gees, and it drops to less than three gees by the time the capsule has reached the far end of the catapult.

These are facts.

Indisputable facts.

Clean.

Simple.

They tell you nothing about the city.

Luna City, Terry Shawmac wrote, *has a soul.*

It is unlike any city on Earth. It is unlike any city I have visited off Earth. In terms of size and traffic the only place I have ever visited off Earth which it resembles at all is Halfway. But the differences with Halfway outweigh the resemblances; Halfway is the ultimate company town. Luna City has no relationship with any business that approaches the importance of the relationship between Tytan Manufacturing and Halfway. And Halfway is aggressively proud of being a city in free-fall; it lacks any consistent local vertical, and most downsiders are never truly comfortable there.

Luna City, through some happy accident, ended up a fusion of the best elements of downside cities and all the other off-Earth communities. It would have made more sense if Luna City were one of the newer off-Earth communities, but that's not the case. In fact, Luna City is the oldest city in existence off of Earth itself. It was never planned, and later attempts at planned Lunar or CityState communities have never worked as well.

It just happened.

Some of it is accidental. The Flight Caverns are a good example. That muscle-powered flight was possible in a pressurized Lunar cavern has been known for over a century; as a plaque inside the Flight Caverns tells you, a futurist named Heinlein described it in 1957, the same year that the first artificial satellite was launched. But it was entirely accidental that appropriate caverns actually existed less than five kilometers from the original center of Luna City. When the original dome was constructed, back in the early '20s, there was no discussion as to site: they placed it smack on top of what are now called the Flight Caverns, and opened the Hotel Copernicus on top of that.

Look down on Luna City from above, in sunlight, and you will see what is easily the loveliest sight on Luna's surface, and that is another accident. In the early '20s there was no such thing as practical fusion power; the fields of solar power panels which surround Luna City, which glitter in the sun like the petals of a flower, were obsolete within four years of the time their construction was completed.

Much of Luna City's beauty is planned.

The impression many downsiders have of cities on Luna ("in Luna," as loonies would like it) is that of artifice—of airplants, of the recycling of water and other resources, of an existence dependent on machines. So far as it goes it is an accurate picture; survival in Luna City does depend on machines, and its inhabitants never forget it.

But I have never walked through any downside city, including some in tropical climates, with so many growing plants. Plants in every corridor, in every open area. Shrubs, potted plants, flowers—I remember very clearly the amazement and delight I felt the first time I entered one of the long cross-town corridors—this was my first day in Luna City—and saw that it was covered with grass as far as I could see.

There are cities on Earth which are known for being pleasant to walk through. Most of Luna City is beneath ground, and it stretches for kilometer after kilometer, through eleven levels beneath the surface of Luna and three above. I spent six months of my life walking through the corridors of Luna City, and I saw perhaps half of them. Because of the gravity, walking is not wearying; even downsiders in poor health can literally spend half a day sightseeing without tempting exhaustion.

There are eight or nine twenty-four-hour restaurants—ten-hour restaurants, as SpaceFarers would have it—and four times as many bars. Unification propaganda to the contrary, there is no violent crime to speak of, and most of what crime truly exists is directed either at evading Unification taxes, or at conducting commerce with Free Luna. The latter, though technically illegal, is so widespread that even the large and constantly growing contingents of Peaceforcers have not been able to put a dent in it.

I said Luna City has a soul. I was speaking metaphorically, of course. No creation of plastisteel and ferrocrete can really have a soul.

But Luna City does have the Gardens.

In October, on a great redwood platform reaching sixty meters above the Lunar Gardens, Trent dined with a SpaceFarer named Felix K'Hin. Eerie, impossibly thin green-leafed and evergreen trees reached up from the Gardens, grew around the platform on all sides so that the diners could see nothing but the trees. They were only ten meters beneath the very top of the dome, and the scent of flowers and growing things permeated the air around them. It was "raining" over the Gardens, a fine gray mist that fell away from the interior surface of dome, falling gently and implacably throughout dinner. Electrostatic fields projected above the tables and walkways kept perhaps half of the surface of the redwood platform dry.

There was a gentle breeze so cool it was almost crisp. Trent did not know where it came from.

It was completely unlike any place Trent had ever seen in his life. The closest analogy which occurred to him came from holos he had played against the wall in his apartment on Flushing Street, forested areas in the northwest United States and Canada. It was only a vague resemblance; the Gardens was itself, nothing else.

It was the second time Trent and K'Hin had attempted to meet; the first time, the SpaceFarer had shown up for their meeting on SpaceFarer time, and Trent had arrived on Unification time. Now, for their second meeting, it was two o'clock in the morning by Capitol City time, the clock that U.N. Luna and Halfway ran on. Despite that it was fairly busy in the most expensive restaurant on Luna; Trent and K'Hin were only two of about thirty diners. Like most of space, Luna City was slowly evolving away from the Earth cycle of day and night.

Over dinner Trent and K'Hin discussed price of passage to Mars, and then to Ceres, with a valid passport for Trent and one unidentified female, for the Association of Belt CityStates. K'Hin, a huge black man who reminded Trent of Reverend Andy without the muscles, was one of the most powerful SpaceFarer brokers in Luna City. He was explaining that what 'Sieur Vera wanted was impossible, and if it was not impossible—not that K'Hin was conceding this for an instant —it certainly could not be done for the ridiculous sum 'Sieur Vera was suggesting.

Trent smiled at the man. "It gets worse."

K'Hin looked honestly amazed. "What? You mean besides the fact that you're looking for a passport for a Unification citizen whose name you can't give me, besides the fact that you can't tell me when or where the damn ship is supposed to land to pick the two of you up, besides the fact that nobody I've been in touch with on Earth or off has ever fucking heard of a Thomas Vera, besides all that there's more?"

"There may be . . . problems . . . with the Unification as a result of this passage. The SpaceFarer's Collective needs to be aware of this."

K'Hin looked delighted. "Really? War maybe?"

Trent smiled at the man. "There's very little chance of war

arising between the Unification and the SpaceFarer's Collective over this. Simulations I've run put it at less than one in five."

K'Hin started to laugh and then stopped abruptly. He sat under Trent's steady gaze, simply looking at Trent. In a tone of voice entirely different from anything Trent had heard from him up to that moment, he said, "Oh, shit. You're serious."

"As I say, it's unlikely. I'm a thief, Felix, and I'm going to boost something from the Peace Keeping Force. I've narrowed it down to three targets. Only one of those three targets presents any serious possibility that its loss will cause the Unification to go to war."

K'Hin said slowly, "It's possible. There's members of the Collective's Board of Directors who wouldn't mind seeing someone give the PKF the boot. Thomas, I'll tell you what I'll do. I'm going to set a base price of sixty thousand hard CU. That's SpaceFarer CU, silver, not that Chinese crap. That's covering pickup at a convenient location such as the Luna City landpads. You guarantee no hassles from PKF or Space Force with a bond that's forfeited in case of serious trouble caused by you. In return, with at least two weeks' notice, we guarantee prompt pickup, a fast ship, two passports. You'll probably need to meet with a representative of the Collective's Board of Directors at some point before the boost goes, to describe in a general way the boost you're planning, the upside and the downside for the Collective."

Trent said, "Base price?"

K'Hin shrugged. "It gets dangerous, the price goes up."

Trent nodded. "All right. In general, that sounds good. We're going to need to work out some of the procedural details, but—" Trent broke off as the lone human waiter on duty approached the table.

He addressed Trent. " 'Sieur Vera?"

Trent looked up. "Yes?"

"You have a call, sir."

Trent glanced at K'Hin. "Hang in there. I'll be right back."

K'Hin leaned back in the delicate, impossibly thin chair. "I'll wait. A while."

Trent rose, walked along the path away from their table, with railings to keep the customers from falling to their probable deaths below, and into the restaurant proper. The waiter led Trent to a small cubicle near the restrooms; there was a systerm inside, the holofield flashing the words CALL WAITING at Trent.

Once the waiter had left Trent unhooked his handheld from his belt, jacked it into the systerm. "Johnny Johnny?"

"Yes, Boss?"

"Cut off the systerm microphone. Alter my voice print as it goes out."

"Done, Boss."

Trent touched the ACCEPT stud.

Candy Blain's image formed in the field. He glared at Trent. "I've been trying to get a hold of you for more than an hour."

"So?"

"Nathan's been shot."

"What?"

"Nathan's been shot. A Peaceforcer squad dropped from orbit on his partitions out at Aristillus. He had some warning, apparently, was in his p-suit when they blew the place down to death pressure."

"Is he alive?"

"Yes. Or was," said Blain, "when last I heard. He had some heavy ammo, God knows what he was doing with it; damaged the semiballistic the Peaceforcers came down in, blew the tracks off a crawler that tried to follow his chameleon into the desert."

"The bolt-hole," said Trent stupidly.

"Yeah. I'm one of the best goddamn friends he has on this planet," Blain said bitterly, "and I don't know where his bolt-hole is."

Trent said, "I do."

"Tell me about it."

"How badly was he hurt? Exactly."

Blain looked weary. "I don't know. Rumor at Aristillus says the PKF reported at least three lasers got a piece of him. He was losing air when he reached the chameleon."

Trent was not certain he wanted to hear the answer. "Why?"

Blain's glower flared again. "Harboring a fugitive—'Thomas.'"

"How long ago?"

"Three, three and a half hours ago."

Trent took a deep breath. He was surprised at how shaky he felt. "All right. Thanks, Candy. I'm on it."

"Sure." The word was openly skeptical. "One last question."

Trent looked away from the cameras, at the image floating in the field. "What?"

"Are you Trent?"

Trent cut the connection and unhooked his handheld. He walked back to Felix K'Hin without hurrying. "Felix."

Trent's expression must have alerted the man; he sat up very straight. "What is it?"

"The word's gone up on a friend. I need a semiballistic hopper to Cassini, and a crawler from there."

K'Hin grinned broadly. "The semi's going to cost you, my friend. You're looking at—"

With his handheld Trent reached across the table and swept K'Hin's meal off the tabletop, knocked it ten meters out into the open air. K'Hin stared at Trent in shock; even among SpaceFarers, for whom the starvation of huge portions of Earth's population was only another item on the news Boards, wasting food was very close to being one of the worst crimes a man could be guilty of.

"Felix, don't fuck with me. I'll pay what it's worth. I need it. *Right now.*"

K'Hin's grin came back slowly; then, if anything, it got broader. "It's done."

From Luna City at Copernicus Trent took an SB to Cassini Crater, slightly north and east of Aristillus, north and slightly west of Nathan's bolt-hole, in the foothills of the Caucasus Mountains.

There was a crawler, modified to cover its tracks, waiting for him at Cassini; that crater, putatively a part of the United Nations, was practically owned by the Syndic, and the Peaceforcers went in only in force, if at all.

From Cassini, Trent headed south.

Nathan was not at the bolt-hole.

Trent backtracked, toward Aristillus. He drove through darkness for nearly half an hour, across the regolith, growing ever more cautious as he ventured farther away from the bolt-hole. He was on the verge of turning back when he finally found the chameleon, the tracks still churning, jammed nose-first against the side of a small hill. A rock slide had come down to cover the front of the vehicle; it took Trent over an hour to dig through the rubble until he managed to reach the airlock. Cycling through the airlock, Trent found Nathan, in his pressure suit, sitting on the long bench seat before the control panel, slumped face-first on the controls. The pressure suit was patterned with laser tracks.

Trent could tell by the limp feel of his own pressure suit that the interior of the crawler was pressurized. Very gently, Trent pulled Nathan's still form up from the control panel, killed the engine, and removed his own helmet and then Nathan's. When the engines died it was abruptly very quiet inside the crawler. There was blood all over the inside of the helmet, all over Nathan's face. Nathan's head lolled freely on the seat's headrest.

A distant sigh was all the sign Nathan gave that he was even alive. The entire front of Nathan's pressure suit had been blackened by a maser burst. At the abdomen the reinforcing rings had melted.

". . . Trent . . ."

The word was the merest ghost. "I'm here." Trent did not even consider trying to remove Nathan's pressure suit; it was probably all that was holding him together.

Nathan's eyes flickered open, stared sightlessly up at Trent, up toward the ceiling of the chameleon. ". . . first-aid kit . . . stimtabs . . ." Trent debated with himself briefly and lost. He took both a stimtab and a painkiller from the kit, injected the painkiller, waited ten seconds and broke the stimtab under Nathan's nose. The response was almost immediate; Nathan's eyes flickered, focused on Trent.

"Thanks," Nathan whispered hoarsely. "Undignified damn way to go, nose-down on the control board."

Trent could think of absolutely nothing to say.

Nathan seemed to gather his energy. "How'd you find me?"

"SB to Cassini; I rode a crawler from there."

"If I don't get to a medbot," Nathan wheezed, "I'm going to die. They shot me with a maser, Trent, it burned . . ."

"Nathan . . . I . . . I can't get you to a medbot in time. I'd have had to bring the SB down right at the bolt-hole. I didn't do that, Nathan."

"Oh." Nathan grinned weakly. "That was a mistake."

"I'd have had to give the pilot the coordinates for your bolt-hole, Nathan. I thought you needed a hiding place."

Nathan's voice faded. "Second mistake." His eyes closed. "Trent?"

"Yes?"

"Do you know Catholic last rites?"

"No."

"Trent?"

"Yes?"

"Can you take me to the bolt-hole, Trent?"

"I can't take you to my crawler, Nathan. I heard they shot you and I brought a spare p-suit with me, but—if I try taking you out of your suit it'll kill you."

Nathan snorted, coughed blood. "No kidding." He laughed shakily, blood dripping off his chin, to the scorched surface of his p-suit. "This thing—" His voice was cut off by another round of coughing. When he resumed his voice was noticeably weaker. "—move at all?"

"The chameleon?" Trent looked over the control panel for the first time. "I don't know. There's not much fuel left."

"Auxiliary tanks are on the . . . rack. Outside, in back," Nathan whispered. "Change them."

"All right. I will."

"Take me home."

"I'll do my best."

It took most of ten minutes before Trent had the fuel tanks changed over; he had never attempted to change a crawler's fuel tanks before, and he botched the first connection and sprayed the fuel at high pressure over the entire rear of the crawler. The second and third tanks he got on correctly. He cycled back through the airlock and brought the tanks on line. The fuel gauge flickered back to FULL; Trent backed the vehicle up, drove past the crawler he had come in, and headed north.

He sat in the middle of the long bench seat, helping Nathan keep upright. He considered letting the man lie down on the seat, but there was blood in his lungs. Trent could hear it every time Nathan gathered the necessary energy to speak, a bubbling sound in his voice, and he was afraid that if Nathan lay down he might drown in his own blood.

Nathan whispered, "How much longer?"

"It took me half an hour to get here. Call it twenty-five minutes before we reach the bolt-hole."

"God, it hurts." Nathan's eyes were losing focus as the crawler rolled across the surface of the Moon. "Do you know what it felt like when the maser beam hit me? I wanted to die just so the pain would stop."

"Nathan, you need to conserve your strength." Trent looked at the pained expression on the man's face, and said gently, "When we get to the bolt-hole I can call Cassini, have them send a hopper." Trent was certain that the semiballistic would not get there in time. "Just be quiet and try to relax."

Trent could not tell if Nathan believed him or not; the man did not try to speak again for several minutes.

There was silence then but for the sound of Nathan's wheezing.

The crawler rolled across the Lunar surface.

"Trent?"

"Yes?"

"Who were they after? You, or me?"

Trent said nothing.

At length Nathan said, "It was you. They were after you."

"Probably."

"I guess it . . . doesn't matter."

"I can't see how, Nathan."

"I think I'm going to die, Trent."

"Everybody does, Nathan."

"Soon."

Trent said simply, "I think you are."

"Well, shit." Nathan's breathing rattled hollowly in his throat. "Trent . . . you can't fight them. This is what happens when you try to fight them."

Trent was intensely aware of how alone they were, of the man dying next to him.

"How much longer till we're home?"

"Twenty minutes, Nathan."

"Oh." After a moment Nathan said simply, "I can't wait that long."

Trent left Nathan's body inside the bolt-hole, and walked through the bolt-hole, wiping every surface he could conceivably have touched during his stay.

And then brought the bolt-hole down with two kilos of blasting plastic.

It was not a dramatic thing; watching the time-delayed explosion from the safety of the crawler, all Trent saw was a gentle sag as the edge of the crater buckled, sank, and settled in.

He had thought about leaving a stone, cutting an inscription with his laser, but he could find no true need for such a thing within himself.

And Nathan, whoever he had once been, was dead.

· 4 ·

It was night, and Earth was full. The blue Earthlight flooded down across the Lunar plains, turned the world eerie.

He sat in the blue dimness, in Nathan Dark Clouds' unmoving chameleon, overlooking Cassini crater. Wearing his pressure suit except for the helmet; that was on the seat at his side.

Watching cartoons.

They were flat cartoons from a time before the Unification, made sometime around the second World War. They were part of the library Trent kept in his handheld for just such circumstances.

The flat plane of the cartoon was located exactly midway through the depth of the holofield. With a perfect lack of expression Trent watched some of the greatest art to come out of the preceding century—Duck Dodgers in the 24th-½th Century, followed by two Roadrunner cartoons, followed by Bugs and Daffy and Elmer Fudd.

Thinking.

He remembered the moments in the Detention Center, the feeling of complete *correctness* which had come over him in the instant before he had brought down the PKF Boards.

"So shoot me!" screams Daffy at Elmer Fudd.

Elmer does.

The paths split away before Trent with a clarity unlike anything he had ever known before. One path, the one he had been planning for—hoping for—took him back to Earth within a year or two, to a small house on an island somewhere in the South Seas.

Daffy is staring at Bugs Bunny, still smoking slightly from

Elmer Fudd's shotgun blast. Elmer stands patiently, watching the two argue. Daffy says, "Let's run through that again."

Bugs shrugs. "Okay." Addressing Elmer in a bored voice: "Would you like to shoot me now or wait until you get home?"

Daffy, in the same bored voice: "Shoot him now, shoot him now."

Bugs Bunny: "You keep out of this, he doesn't have to shoot you now."

Daffy Duck: "Ha!"

And then there was the other path, the one that led to direct conflict with the PKF—and to death, or capture, or legend.

"That's it! Hold it right there." Daffy looks craftily toward the audience, toward Trent. "Pronoun trouble." He looks back at Bugs. "It's not, 'He doesn't have to shoot you *now,' it's 'He doesn't have to shoot* me *now.' Well, I say he* does *have to shoot me now!"*

Elmer does.

Trent found his lips turning ever so slightly upward; he was not entirely sure why. "Turn it off, Johnny."

The image vanished instantly. "Okay, Boss. What now?"

Trent turned the engine back on, sat up as the crawler jerked forward, down the long slope of the crater wall. "They keep pushing, Johnny."

"I know, Boss."

"Every time I'm ready to let it go they push again." Trent stared forward. "I'm standing here with my back to the wall and they . . . keep . . . *pushing.*"

Johnny Johnny said nothing in reply.

"Except for Denice, and maybe David, they killed everyone I grew up with."

His Image's voice said, very softly indeed, "I know, Boss."

"And now Nathan. I'm tempted to get angry."

"About time!"

"But I'm not going to." Trent said again, very softly, "I am not going to."

There was an audible sigh from the handheld. "Boss, I'm never going to understand you."

"Do you know what their greatest weakness is?"

"The PKF?" Johnny Johnny thought about it in silence for several minutes as the crawler rolled forward. Finally he said, "They're not as smart as we are?"

"No, Johnny. Most of them aren't, but some of them are. Vance may be smarter."

"Then I don't know, Boss."

"They have no sense of humor at all, Johnny Johnny."

"No sense of humor?"

"None."

Johnny Johnny's voice held plain exasperation. "But what are you going to *do,* Boss?"

Trent was silent for a very long time. Finally he whispered, "Humiliate them."

Johnny Johnny said, "Oh?"

"Hurt them."

Johnny Johnny said, "Oh."

Alone with his Image in the darkness of the crawler, Trent did smile then, a terrible smile without any amusement at all.

His eyes were focused on something very far away.

"I am," he said, "going to bring the fuckers down."

• 5 •

He brought the semiballistic down at the edge of Bessel Crater, in Free Luna.

Briefcase in hand, Trent walked out across the pale Lunar soil to where the city's airlocks awaited him.

There was a woman, about thirty, standing immediately inside the inner airlock door, in a small corridor which led to a pair of maglevs for the descent beneath the surface. She was dressed in some sort of scarlet paramilitary fatigues, with a Series IV Excalibur energy rifle slung over her back and a hand maser slung in a quick-draw holster just over her hipbone.

Trent unclasped the helmet to his p-suit.

Without any change of expression at all, the woman said, "Welcome to Free Luna."

"Thank you."

"In the past," she said, "we've shot down unannounced visitors before they could land."

Trent said, "I'm here to see the mayor."

The woman shook her head. This time she smiled. "No, you're not."

"I'm not?"

"No."

"What am I doing here, then?"

"Leaving." Trent had not noticed her hand moving; it was now resting on the butt of the maser. "You weren't invited, you didn't advise us you were coming, and you're not wanted."

"I'm sorry about that," said Trent, "but I was in a hurry. I needed to go dancing, and you can't do that in the Unification InfoNet. I'm told things are a bit looser in the Free Luna InfoNet?"

The woman shrugged. "Could be. I'm not a webdancer, just a soldier. You're not welcome, kid."

Trent sighed, looking at the floor, trying to think while standing there with his helmet in his hand. The floor had not been swept or mopped recently; Lunar dust had been tracked over it. Trent looked back up at the woman. "What's your name?"

"Domino. I'm the vice-mayor of Bessel City Free Luna."

Trent blinked. "No kidding?"

"No kidding."

"Domino's a neat name."

"Thank you."

"I feel like we haven't been introduced," said Trent.

"We haven't been," Domino said agreeably. "We don't know you. Nobody's introduced us, and Bessel Free Luna doesn't take in waifs."

"My name is Trent."

"That's nice. Pleased to—" Domino stopped speaking. "Really?"

Trent nodded. "I promise."

He could see that the woman believed him instantly. "Why are you here?"

"Well, I'm close to being broke," said Trent. "I have things I need to do, expensive things, and frankly I'd like to do it with your Credit."

"What's that to us?"

"Vice-Mayor Domino?"

"Yes?"

"I'm really here to see the mayor."

Domino raised her voice. "Quentin!"

A male voice came from somewhere above their heads in the small corridor. "Bring him in."

Domino's hand left the butt of the hand maser. She took a step forward and held her hand out to Trent. "Welcome to Free Luna, Trent."

Trent took her hand in his gloved right hand. "You said that once already."

"Last time I didn't mean it."

The mayor's office was located in one of the very few aboveground buildings.

Mayor Quentin Noas was sitting behind his desk, reading, when Trent was ushered in. He was reading a real book, made of plastipaper; a Western, from the cover. His feet were up on the desk; a cigar was in the hand that wasn't holding the book.

The window behind the mayor's desk had a wide, panoramic view of the Lunar surface.

The mayor of Bessel City was incredibly ancient. His face looked like a puzzle that had been assembled with a sledgehammer. It took him several moments before he even realized that Trent had been let in. He blinked slowly, like a lizard, and put down his Western. He took a puff of his cigar before saying anything. "So you're—"

Trent said, "Shh," putting a finger to his lips. Stepping up to the mayor's desk, Trent put down the briefcase, opened it, and withdrew a circuit tracer. Circling the room slowly, he found three active power sources in the walls; the energy level was characteristic of listening devices. Returning to his briefcase, Trent withdrew his handheld, tuned into a news Board, and turned the volume high. He made the circuit again, and found another listening device, a passive bug that did not operate unless activated by the sound of people talking. "Nobody ever listens," Trent muttered, "except when they're not supposed to." Whistling, Trent rummaged in his briefcase and came up with a handful of tiny speakers. He rummaged in the briefcase again until he found the glue and used it to affix the speakers to the walls over the listening devices. Trent turned the speakers on.

Domino stood in the doorway, watching Trent curiously. Crossing behind the mayor's desk, Trent checked the drapes; thick, heavy cloth. He pulled the drapes closed over the window. He came back around to the front of the mayor's desk and turned off his handheld.

The walls of Mayor Noas' office were hung with paintings. Some were good, in Trent's semieducated opinion; some were not. He was certain that all of them were expensive. Trent wandered around without speaking, looking at the paintings.

Mayor Noas leaned forward and jabbed his cigar at Trent. "Are you the Trent I think you are?"

"I don't know," said Trent honestly. He added, "My name is Trent, Trent the thief. I need Credit for a job I have in mind and I thought it would be nice if you gave it to me." Trent had stopped before an old acrylic painting. The painting showed a beautiful kitten sitting in the middle of a black and white tile floor, with a blond Caucasian doll clutched in its mouth. There were puncture wounds in the body of the doll, and blood oozed from the injury, dripping to the pristine floor beneath. It was signed *H. Devlin*. "This is good. A little sick, but—"

"Everyone thought you were dead."

"They were wrong."

"My God, son, d'you have any idea at all how hot you are?"

"Yes."

The mayor of Bessel City nodded. "What could you possibly do for me that would entice me to stick my head out where the Peaceforcers are gonna blast it off?"

Trent stepped to the side so that he could look at the painting in a different light. "Want to sell this?"

"Nah. You couldn't afford it; it was painted by the Prophet Harry hisself." Mayor Noas stared at the back of Trent's head. "Tell me why you closed the drapes."

"When you speak, the sound waves vibrate the window panes. Not much—less so than on Earth, where there's no pressure differential to keep the windows rigid the way they are here—but enough. If somebody outside bounces a very low intensity laser off the window, decodes the modulation in the returning beam, poof. Your security is useless. On Earth I'd have attached a buzzer to the window; up here a thick curtain is just as good."

Mayor Noas chewed on his inner lip. "Damn, I was afraid you'd have a good reason for doing that. What d'you want?"

"Access to a full-sensory terminal and the Free Luna Info-

Net. It shouldn't take me more than twenty minutes. I need it soon."

Mayor Noas examined the end of his cigar. "That's tough, Trent."

Trent turned suddenly. "That's not *my* fault, is it?"

Mayor Noas blinked. "What?"

"I want to use your full-sensory," Trent repeated. After a moment, as though he were making a concession, he added, "If you let me use the full-sensory I'll contract a boost for you. A very reasonable boost, only a half-million CU, 250,000 up front as expense Credit."

Mayor Noas had a sharp, barking laugh. "D'you know who you're talking to, son? Before I joined Bessel I was one of the top Syndic Lords in Luna."

"I know. That's why I'm here. An ex-Syndic Lord with ties to the Erisian Claw, ties to the SpaceFarer's Collective, ties to the CityStates. . . ." Trent said mildly, "You keep a low profile, Mayor Noas. I spent five thousand CU having a Player I know on Earth do a search of Syndic Lords doing time off Earth. Once we had that list we had to cull to find out who got exiled for incompetence and who got exiled for politics. Then we culled again for known members of the Temple of Eris." Trent said evenly, "Your name popped up, retired two and a half years, hired by Bessel Astrogation Products to manage the city of Bessel Free Luna. You're the first person on the list, Quentin. You're not the last."

"I know," said Mayor Noas, "just about every damn thing worth boosting on this entire planet. First of all, there's nothing worth paying five hunnert thousand Credits for. Second, if there was, and there ain't, you are just about the last man on this planet I'd contract it to. I don't *need* the PKF renegotiating our treaty."

"I'll steal the LINK for you."

"Besides," Mayor Noas was continuing, in a somewhat gentler tone, and he rose from behind his desk, *"you'll what?"*

"Steal the LINK," Trent said. At Mayor Noas' look of incomprehension, he added, "The Key. You know, the Lunar InfoNet Key."

"It can't be done."

"I've studied it. I know something about the program that runs the LINK transputers; it's called Watchdog. I know an awful lot about the layout of the Farside DataWatch facility from which the LINK is administered. I can make the boost."

Mayor Noas swore, "Damn it, you can't! The Key is tucked away in a computer in the middle of the PKF Farside base at Jules Verne. You could as easily walk through Peaceforcer Heaven!"

Trent grinned at Mayor Noas. "Hello."

The man's own words sank in on him. "Oh, Lord." He blinked again, took a long, contemplative drag on his stogie. "Do you really think you can?"

Trent looked at Domino, watching him almost warily from the doorway, and then back at Noas. "Yes, I really do."

Mayor Quentin Noas sank back down into his seat. "By Harry. You—" He broke off, at a complete loss for words. He sat at his desk, smoking furiously, blue clouds of smoke swirling up around him. He was not looking at Trent, at anything. Finally he said, "Domino."

"Yes?"

"What happens? We take the boy up on it, I mean."

"At half a million CU? We'll need clearance further up the line, for starters. Then—"

"That's not what I mean. He makes the boost, comes away clean. What *happens*?"

Domino said abruptly, "Trent. Are we talking about destruction of the LINK?"

"If you like. The LINK is a combination of hardware and software. There's no way you get the hardware. I think I can arrange that you get the control program. You won't be able to do with it what the PKF is using it for, but—" Trent shrugged. "Neither will they."

Domino stood in the doorway, looking at Trent coolly, speculatively. "All right. For starters it means DataWatch loses control of their own InfoNet. If we have the LINK software and a good webdancer to supervise, then it means we'll have access to at least some of the DataWatch Boards, at least briefly. Longer term, I'd guess they couldn't put the LINK system back in place. It was instituted when there weren't any computers on Luna to speak of, and grew with it."

Trent looked at the woman with a degree of genuine respect. "You're not a webdancer?"

Domino shook her head. "No."

"You got most of it. My favorite part is where DataWatch gets locked out of its own Boards until they strip out the LINK protocols. And I think you're right about the LINK not going back up again, especially if some smart people get together and transmit the Earth InfoNet protocols to everybody on Luna while DataWatch is still down for the count. At worst, if what I'm thinking of fails, I'll probably be able to destroy the Key and kill the program that runs it. At best we can join the Free Luna InfoNet with the U.N. InfoNet, and take control of the U.N. InfoNet away from them forever."

Mayor Noas' voice was troubled. "Half a million CU."

Trent said flatly, "It's what I need. This is going to be expensive every step of the way."

There was a long silence. Finally Mayor Noas shook his head decisively. "I can't commit to something this big."

Trent nodded. "So what happens?"

"I need to call in some people, run it by them."

"I see. How many people are we talking about?"

Mayor Noas looked at Domino. "Three?"

"Four. We'll need to bring in a rep from Bessel Astrogation Products."

Trent lifted an eyebrow. "Why don't you just call a press conference?"

Domino's voice took on a degree of coldness that was truly impressive. "These are discreet people, Trent."

"Nobody," said Trent, "ever listens." He smiled at Domino. "But they sure do love to talk."

"If you want help," said Domino, "if you need help, these are the people you need to talk to."

Trent spread his arms in a gesture of defeat. "You talked me into it. I'm definitely going to need help. At least three other people, maybe four. And seven bodies, six male and one female."

Mayor Noas blinked and said, "Seven bodies?"

Trent nodded. "With dental work."

· 6 ·

The fat man said, "I don't think names are necessary."

There were six of them all told, sitting across the long table, facing Trent. Trent sat alone, handheld on the table in front of him, wearing his traceset. The camera in the handheld had scanned them as they entered the room.

Mayor Quentin Noas and Vice-Mayor Domino were sitting together at one end of the table. One of the four directly across from Trent was obviously a SpaceFarer, a black-bearded man wearing ship's colors which Trent did not recognize. The fat man sat next to the SpaceFarer, and next to the fat man were an old, dark-haired Caucasian woman in a floatchair, and a handsome young man in his late twenties or early thirties, wearing a gray business suit.

BINGO. GOT ONE ALREADY, BOSS. THE OLD WOMAN IS NAMED BELINDA SINGER.

WOULD YOU BELIEVE I RECOGNIZED HER MYSELF?

. . . I SUPPOSE. WAIT. YES, I WOULD. 2062; SHE EMPLOYED THE CASTANAVERAS TELEPATHS BEFORE THEY WERE DESTROYED.

BACKGROUND, JOHNNY JOHNNY?

UHM . . . UPWARD OF 110 YEARS OLD BY SOME INDETERMINATE AMOUNT. HER ACTUAL AGE IS GUARDED VERY CLOSELY. SHE'S THE SPACEFARER COLLECTIVE'S SINGLE LARGEST DOWNSIDE SHAREHOLDER. ACCORDING TO THE FORBES 500 LISTING SHE'S THE TWENTIETH OR TWENTY-FIRST WEALTHIEST PERSON IN THE SYSTEM; SHE HAS THE REPUTATION OF BEING FRIENDLY WITH KNOWN MEMBERS OF THE JOHNNY REBS.

Perhaps two seconds had passed. Trent said, "Fine by me."

"We got briefed by Domino before we agreed to come," the fat man continued. Trent had already tagged the man for Syndic. "I like most of what I hear. Loss of the Key locks them out of their own Boards for at least two or three days, while the people who have the Key—us—have at least limited access to them. A couple of months pass before they can even begin bringing up a tracking system like the one they've got right now. And maybe they don't ever get it back up again, which is a hell of a blow to Unification interests off Earth." He grinned cynically. "Also, I like how you've planned your getaway. I think you're going to kill yourself trying it, but it's a great idea."

BINGO ON TWO, BOSS. THE CHUBBY FELLOW IS NORMAN SHELTON. NOT EXACTLY A SYNDIC LORD, BUT CLOSE. LICENSED TO PRACTICE UNIFICATION LAW.

The young man in the gray business suit said, in thickly

accented English, "I am here representing the interests of the Erisian Claw. We would suggest one change to your plan."

"That being?"

"As you have laid this out, you are going to immense trouble to avoid harming a group of Peaceforcers whom you plan to ambush."

"That's correct." JOHNNY? ANYTHING ON THIS ONE?

. . . NO. OR THE SPACEFARER EITHER. BUT THEY'RE FILED FOR FUTURE REFERENCE.

The young man nodded. He said gently, "It seems to many of my colleagues—well, rather excessive concern for what is, after all, the welfare of officers of the PKF."

"We're not killing anybody," said Trent. He stared at the handsome young man. "Nobody. You want to kill Peaceforcers, fine. But you do it on your own time."

The man shrugged, leaned back in his seat without expression. He sat watching Trent, like all the others. "Merely a suggestion."

"Well," said Norman Shelton. "I think that about covers it. We're in."

Trent stood upright, very slowly, and leaned across the table. "What?"

Shelton said again, "We're in. We'll fund it. Frankly I think you've underpriced yourself, but that's really your problem."

Trent kept his voice under tight control. "I've been kept waiting here at Bessel for four days, denied access to a full-sensory InfoNet terminal the entire while, until you folks could manage to assemble yourselves in one place, so that we could have this very important meeting. This was it, was it? The whole meeting? I just want to make sure I didn't miss anything."

"Possibly you have missed something." It was the first time Belinda Singer had spoken through the entire meeting. Her voice was strong, the voice of a woman used to decades of instant obedience. "Do you recognize me, young man?"

Trent answered without any pause at all. "Should I?"

It was amazing how much sharpness she managed to put into a sentence that was in fact phrased politely. "Answer my question, please."

"Yes. You're Belinda Singer."

"Fine," she said briskly. "Then we can forget this crap about not knowing each other's names. You're Trent Castanaveras."

Trent did not look away from the old woman's gaze. "A lot of people seem to think so."

"The last time I spoke to Malko Kalharri," said Belinda Singer, "was about two weeks before he died. He and Doctor Montignet were both worried about you."

Trent's voice was totally empty. "That's nice. You know they're dead, of course."

"It was on the Boards."

"Maybe they should have been worrying more about themselves. I'm still alive. They're not."

Belinda Singer said simply, "Young man, why are you doing this?"

"The boost?"

"Yes," she said gently. "The 'boost.' "

"I'm getting paid."

She snorted. "Bullshit."

"I'm getting paid a *lot.*"

"Bullshit again." Singer picked up her handheld, turned it so that its holofield faced Trent. "Half a million. I make your expenses at somewhere around two hundred thousand, maybe as high as two and a quarter. You're left with an upside of between two-seventy-five and three hundred." She locked gazes with Trent. "I had a very trustworthy associate run a probability analysis of this undertaking. These are rough figures, but close. Trent, your chance of walking out of the DataWatch Farside facility in one piece is about twenty-five percent. Fifty percent capture, followed by execution. Twenty-five percent you die inside before getting captured. I know a bit about you, boy. You've given over three hundred thousand CU to the World Food Bank in your short life. People who can give away that sort of Credit to charity are rarely willing to put their lives at serious risk simply to acquire a similar amount."

Her figures were in fact very close to those Trent had worked out with Johnny Johnny. "So?"

"So," said Belinda Singer, "unless I get a straight answer out of you, I'm going to pull out. If I pull out I can pretty much guarantee you no SpaceFarer craft in the Collective is going to agree to do the pickup you need."

"Why is it relevant?"

Belinda Singer closed her eyes for a moment, sat motionlessly, and took a slow breath. When she opened her eyes again she said, "Trent, humor me. I'm a cranky old woman and smart-ass answers make me even crankier. Malko Kalharri was one of the dearest friends I ever had, and on his behalf I feel a certain reluctance to let you waste your life casually. Calling what you're talking about doing here a—boost, I believe the word is?—calling it a boost is like saying a laser cannon is useful for starting the fireplace."

It took Trent a moment to decipher the comment—he had never actually seen a fireplace which burned wood—but when he did, he could not suppress a chuckle. "Point. Can we speak privately?"

Without glancing away from Trent, Belinda Singer said, "You can leave." They were alone within thirty seconds.

Trent reached forward, turned off his handheld, and waited. After a moment, Belinda Singer did the same. Trent nodded. "Thank you. I swept for bugs before the meeting. There are two, but they're recording the sounds Mayor Noas makes in his bathtub. It's not pretty." He looked down for a moment at the tabletop, ordering his thoughts. His fingernails needed trimming. "We've met, you know."

"Really?" Singer actually looked surprised. "When?"

"I don't remember exactly. Early 2062. You visited the Chandler Complex after the Eighth Amendment was signed, before the Complex was destroyed."

Singer looked troubled. "That's odd. My memory is actually quite good. I remember that trip—wait."

Trent said, "Your floatchair broke."

The old woman pointed a finger at Trent. "You were the little boy who fixed my floatchair! I remember you now. We didn't get introduced."

Trent shrugged. "You were being—" He paused, said, "Cranky."

Amazingly, Singer actually colored slightly. "I remember that, too. Being around so many of those little telepaths—it made me nervous."

"It made everyone nervous," Trent said precisely. "That's why they were killed."

"Yes," Singer said slowly. "I guess there's some truth in that." She shook the bad memories away with a visible effort. "Let's get back to business. I'm sure you realize by now the reason you were made to wait four days was so I could talk to you."

"It's a bit obvious."

"I am willing," the old woman said clearly, "to see you die

if it buys the destruction of the LINK. Assuming you die at Jules Verne, and I think it likely, I really have no problem with advancing you your quarter-million CU." She made a deprecating gesture. "It's mostly my money you'll be spending. But it's a good investment. I think your chances of surviving this operation are poor—but my staff gives me odds of better than two-thirds that the LINK goes down. Taking the Lunar InfoNet away from DataWatch . . ." She was silent for a moment. "I can't even estimate what that's worth. Short-term, hundreds of millions of CU in increased trade with Free Luna. Long-term . . ." Her voice trailed off, and she sat looking at Trent.

Trent actually smiled. "Unfortunately, there's this terrible possibility I might survive."

"If you survive this stunt," she said quietly, "the Secretary-General's office is going to request that you be handed over to the Unification. They may very well threaten war if you're not handed over. No matter how pleased the Collective turns out to be at what you've done—and make no mistake, they'll be pleased—most of them won't be willing to risk war to protect someone who likes to tell people he's a thief. Even if he's a good thief. Unless there is some level of mutual commitment, extending beyond this one boost, I would guess, Trent, that the Collective will indeed give you to the PKF when it's all over."

Trent sat motionlessly, thinking, considering his options. There weren't many.

"You're in high-stakes territory, young man. If you survive this, Trent, you'll *need* us to protect you for, I don't know, the next several years at least. It would be in your best interests," said Belinda Singer very gently, "to make sure that the Collective needs you as well."

"Why am I doing this."

"It does come down to that, doesn't it?"

Trent found that his mouth was very dry. "It's a lengthy explanation."

"Try to trim it a bit, then. I'm an old woman, I'd hate to die on you just when it gets good."

"When I was young," Trent began.

Belinda Singer smothered a laugh, waved a hand at Trent. "Sorry. Go on."

Trent glared at her. "I used to admire the PKF."

"A lot of us did."

"Shut up. You want to bare your soul, you wait until I'm done. I used to admire the PKF." He paused, waited for her to say something, and when she did not he continued. "When I was younger. There are still individual Peaceforcers I admire. The problem's not with the people; most Peaceforcers are honorable, doing their jobs as well as they're able within the boundaries of the laws they're sworn to serve. A lot of the laws are bad laws, and most of the policies are bad policies. When I was a part of society, back on Earth, I spent a fair amount of Credit funding lobbyists, to try to get some of those laws and policies changed. And then they pushed me outside and I couldn't keep doing that. I ran." He swept a hand around the room. "I ended up here. And I was almost willing to let it go. I wanted revenge, and I still do, and I'll have it—but I wasn't seriously planning to try for the LINK.

"Then a squad of Peaceforcers killed a friend of mine. They let out his air and shot him with masers. He died in horrible pain. And I want revenge for that, too, and I'll have it."

Belinda Singer was nodding, quietly, without any trace of emotion that Trent could detect. "So that's it. I think—"

"That's not it."

She lifted an eyebrow in surprise. "No?"

"When I was eight years old I decided I was an atheist. When I was ten I became an existentialist. Most Players are. But when you dismiss God and decide there's nothing in the universe to rely on but yourself, you have to find some way to bring meaning to your life. When I was ten years old I decided I was going to change the world. Improve it. Make it a better place." She was watching him carefully, weighing each word. "The Unification," said Trent, "is going bad. It's been going bad for a long time. I wanted to fix it from the inside, but I can't do that any longer. Maybe I never could and I was kidding myself."

"So?"

"I wanted to make a difference when I was ten, Belinda." It was the first time he had called her by name, and he saw her notice it. "I still do."

Belinda Singer nodded, accepting it. "I still need to hear you say it, Trent."

Trent took a deep breath. He felt vaguely sick, as though the world were blurring around him. There was a remote ringing in his ears; there were butterflies in his stomach, army butterflies on a three-day leave. His voice sounded as though it did not belong to him. "We must bring down the Unification. It is time to bring it down."

Long eons later, when the ringing in his ears had faded into quiet, when the trembling in his shoulders had ceased, he looked up and saw Belinda Singer watching him with a grave expression. "That was hard, wasn't it?"

He whispered the word. "Yes."

"You have to trust people in this life, Trent. We all do." She was silent a beat. "The hell of it is, it never ever gets any easier."

The guard at the entrance to the cubicle, a man dressed in much the same almost-uniform that Domino had worn, except that his was brown rather than scarlet, said, "Twenty minutes."

Closing the door of the cubicle behind him, Trent seated himself behind the wraparound control console. Surveying the board before him, Trent began making attachments. He jacked his handheld into the board; the MRI helmet went over his head, all the way down to his shoulders. Inside the helmet, headphones extruded themselves and clamped over his ears; laser projectors focused themselves on each eye.

There was a brief moment of disorientation as the systerm went online.

The MRI imaging sensors came alive, setting up a strong magnetic field that polarized those nuclei in Trent's brain which possessed net magnetic charge. A second and weaker magnetic field, applied at right angles to the first, caused the nuclei to tip into new positions, emitting a radio signal in the process. Millions of radio nanoreceptors in the full-sensory traceset fed into a limited expert system whose only function was to trace correspondences in Trent's thought processes with known thought processes. It was a slow procedure; on Trent's vanished full-sensory on Earth, which had a functional map of Trent's internal nerve net, the link had been nearly instantaneous. Here, on hardware that did not know how Trent thought, it took most of a minute before the first flicker of the Crystal Wind reached him.

Johnny Johnny said softly, HI, BOSS.

HI, JOHNNY.

GONNA DANCE?

YES.

ABOUT *TIME*.

They joined together; Johnny Johnny reached out, found the first step to the Free Luna InfoNet . . .

Johnny Johnny threw himself into the Net, and moved outward. The Datawatch-controlled Lunar InfoNet itself was forbidden him, but that still left—

—the Lunar telexchange, used for voice and data communications to and from orbit by Free Luna and U.N. Luna alike. Johnny Johnny attached tracers to all communications, waiting for something that was headed upward. Free Luna had a population of three and a half million; less than a fiftieth of a second had passed when Johnny Johnny found what he was looking for, a message heading up to the PKF orbital satellites. A PKF spy, almost certainly; Johnny Johnny diverted the message back into the telexchange and took the diverted message package's place, flowing out to a microwave relay that beamed up into the PKF satellites. There were others using the relay, but Johnny Johnny needed as much of its capacity as he could get; he took over all the empty lines, and then began freezing lines as other users finished and released them. It was done delicately enough, slowly enough, that Watchdog would probably not notice it.

In multiple channels Johnny Johnny leaped upward.

His retreat was reasonably secure, over two hundred channels in every relay, an entire series of relays left open at the telexchange. Inside the comsat, Johnny Johnny waited again. He did not touch anything. Significant real-world time passed while he waited—nearly two seconds—before a PKF slipship orbiting over Farside was sent a recreational poker program. Johnny Johnny broke into it, increasing the signal complexity, injecting a pared-down version of himself into the signal progression at a one-hundred-to-one ratio. The noise level was acceptable, and the signal went through. Slowly, over the course of seconds, Johnny Johnny found himself inside the Peaceforcer slipship.

Johnny Johnny took momentary control of the on-board computer; he located L-5 and sent a distress call to it through the orbiting slipship. (On board, the Peaceforcer noted a momentary blurriness in the simulated stud she was playing poker with.)

Spacebase One responded to the emergency distress call, opening a wide maser channel to the affected ship. Johnny Johnny informed Spacebase One that he was the program in control of the slipship, that he was experiencing traumatic equipment failure, and that he was not certain that his own integrity was assured. He requested aid from Spacebase One's diagnostics to determine what steps to take.

For a long moment Johnny Johnny did not think it was going to work.

Then the diagnostic routines at Spacebase One requested that the damaged slipship beam its control program back to Spacebase One for examination. A high-bandwidth comm laser touched the slipship, and Johnny Johnny poured through the connection, froze it open behind him, and ate the diagnostics program at Spacebase One.

The diagnostics program had access to Spacebase One's comm facilities. Johnny Johnny took a dozen nanoseconds, redirected the satellite to lase directly at Spacebase One, cutting the slipship out of the link. He delved further then, identified the program in use as the Communications Manager, and identified all of the resources that were available to the Manager.

And crashed them.

Every comm channel in Spacebase One, external and internal.

Two seconds passed before anyone even noticed, an eternal six before anything was done about it. A human webdancer in the Operations Information Center at the very core of Spacebase One crossed the interface and dove into the Crystal Wind. She did not notice Johnny Johnny, sitting silently in the darkness. The problem was immediately obvious, if unexpected; the Communications Manager had crashed itself. She requested access to Main Storage so that she might invest a new communications manager; the request was received, processed, granted, and she fell into the core.

With Johnny Johnny right behind her.

The file Security Manager, a passive observer which functioned largely as an alarm, politely informed Johnny Johnny that there were three Access Levels available, only one of which Johnny Johnny was authorized to access freely. Level One was a sieve; Johnny Johnny flashed through it in its entirety in seconds. The name he sought (even his biological component did not consciously think the word *Trent)* was nowhere to be found, so he sought a higher level.

Level Two was harder; the Security Manager politely informed Johnny Johnny that he would be allowed access to only one file at a time, and that a human webdancer in the Operations Information Center would be notified of each file accessed. Johnny Johnny ghosted himself, split himself into dozens of copies for the Security Manager to deal with. The Security Manager accepted one request for a file, and then another, and finally a third before informing one of Johnny Johnny's ghosts that it could accept only three requests before a webdancer approved the request. Johnny Johnny ignored the Security Manager, delved into the files.

The Security Manager screamed for help.

Human response time is slow; Johnny Johnny guessed he had at least three full seconds, perhaps as many as five, before a webdancer came to see what was wrong.

While the Security Manager watched, helplessly, Johnny Johnny tore through the database on Level Two.

Nothing.

Over a second had passed.

There was a sentinel, a sort of primitive web angel, at the entrance to Level Three. Johnny Johnny submitted to the sentinel a request for access, watched the sentinel as it executed, considered the request and denied it. The sentinel was a small program, though well coded, with less than ten megabytes of RAM assigned to it for workspace. Johnny Johnny fired another request, and then another. The sentinel employed a primitive sort of ghosting, multitasking the two requests together. It slowed noticeably, and expanded slightly to claim more of the ten megabytes of RAM available to it.

Johnny Johnny ghosted himself a thousand thousand times.

And then each ghost started asking for entry to Level Three.

Nearly two seconds had passed, and now the System Tools appeared, scanned through the workspace Johnny Johnny occupied, running diagnostic test upon diagnostic test to determine the cause of the malfunction. Some of the tests Johnny Johnny was able to fool; most of them he could not.

The sentinel ballooned wildly, expanded to fill the maximum workspace allotted it. Johnny Johnny fired request after request at the sentinel even after it had reached peak load. The sentinel attempted to re-allocate memory internally, to shell out memory being used by the instruction stack and reassign that memory to the queued requests of a million ghosts.

Web angels appeared out of nowhere, tore into Johnny

Johnny's ghosts. Johnny Johnny ignored the web angels, concentrating on the sentinel—

—which was faltering. The sentinel was oscillating wildly, thrashing senselessly in its attempts to deal with the massive overload of data. Johnny Johnny kept up the stream of new requests, pushing now as the sentinel—

—crashed.

More than half of Johnny Johnny's ghosts were dead. Johnny Johnny dissected the sentinel quickly, disassembled the instructions which had composed it. In its default configuration the sentinel used less than two megabytes of RAM; it was going to be a hell of a squeeze.

Nearly a full four seconds had passed before the web angels reported the files secure. Four and a half seconds from the moment when the Security Manager had first screamed for help, a human webdancer shimmered into existence, loaded Diagnostics and started hunting.

Johnny Johnny, wearing the sentinel's code as a disguise, responded as the code he had absorbed said he should when the webdancer came at last to him. The webdancer paused a thousandth of a second, examining the shell of the sentinel, and then passed on.

Fully ten seconds later, Johnny Johnny applied once more to search the Level Three files.

And then gave himself permission.

Ten minutes after entering the cubicle Trent opened his eyes to Realtime. He began shedding attachments; removed his handheld from the systerm.

Johnny Johnny said aloud, "Boss, are you sure this was a good idea?"

"Hell of a time to ask, Johnny."

"Well?"

"No, Johnny. I'm not sure." His Image's silence seemed almost reproachful to Trent, and he said at last, "It's a start. We have to start somewhere."

"And what's this supposed to do? Changing one file? Boss, I don't understand."

"It's going to make them look silly, Johnny. It's worse than killing them, you know. They'd rather die gloriously than be laughed at."

"Oh."

Johnny Johnny was silent after that, and Trent also. Trent spent his free ten minutes in silent meditation.

When the guard rapped on the door, Trent exited without hurry, briefcase in hand.

· 7 ·

November 1, 2069.

He stood in the Operations Information Center from which Spacebase One was run. It was at the very core of the long cylinder about which Spacebase One was constructed, protected by layer upon layer of radiation shielding; a direct hit by a tactical nuke upon the surface of Spacebase One would not have harmed him.

With the departure to Earth of Etienne Géricault, he was the senior PKF at Spacebase One. A tall, grim man who looked older than he was, gravely handsome, dark-eyed and dark-haired, surveying a monument to his own failure.

His name was Mohammed Vance. He carried himself with a peculiar power of presence that only physically impressive, intelligent men possess.

That the operations center was silent at the moment was his failure. Until just the prior day it had been filled with PKF officers, coordinating the details of the search for the Player, the thief, the man named Trent.

Now the webdancers' systerms were empty. The monitor posts scanned silently without human intervention.

There was one other person actually in the operations room, a young Elite candidate named Melissa du Bois. She sat rigidly at her station, her recently shortened hair waving gently in the breeze from the vents.

On the great holofield, stretching out to cover most of a twenty-meter expanse of hullmetal, burned the image of a Hand of the Trinity, a too-confident young man named Jean Lumet.

Lumet was saying, placatingly, "Commissionaire, I appreciate your desire to continue your search for this criminal. If it were up to me I would allow it." He shrugged in a very Gallic manner. "It is not up to me, and you have no choice."

In the calm, deep voice that gave junior PKF officers nightmares, Mohammed Vance said, "I tell you, Hand Lumet, that he is alive."

Three seconds passed, the lightspeed lag from L-5, in Lunar orbit, to Earth; Lumet made a helpless gesture. "Commissionaire . . . what would you have me do? I am not an officer of the PKF, sir; and the order to desist in your search has come from Elite Commander Mirabeau herself."

Vance scowled with displeasure. Something would have to be done about Mirabeau soon, as something had been done about her predecessor, Elite Commander Breilléune.

Eventually, there would be a competent and sufficiently ruthless Elite to represent the interests of the PKF to the Unification.

Eventually . . .

Lumet took another tack. "Commissionaire, the vehicle that the criminal stole was broken cleanly in two. Most of the hull was torn away in the missile blast—and don't think that words have not been said about that missile salvo you fired. It was the most fantastic luck that—"

"Luck," Vance said impatiently, "is something fools rely upon. The north end of the base was evacuated at my order following the attack upon the slipship bay. If anyone had been hurt it would have been due solely to disregard of orders. There was minimal danger."

"Oh?" Lumet lifted a sardonic eyebrow. "And if one of the warheads had detonated?"

"Simulation showed the possibility of such an outcome at only one in approximately forty."

"You ran that simulation, Commissionaire, only *after* giving the command."

Vance stared unblinking at Lumet. The accusation was completely correct; only Vance and two of his most trusted assistants had been present when that simulation had finally been run. One of those two—

Vance said quietly, "I withdraw the objection. Nonetheless, the damage done to the reputation of the PKF Elite by the murder of one of its members cannot be tolerated. The example is one that—"

"Commissionaire, please." Lumet waved a hand in dismissal. "It has been three months without a sign of the man. This Dark Clouds criminal—there, I think, you grasp at straws. A random and completely unproductive attack by ideologs on a DataWatch facility in Luna City. Vague, unreliable reports that a 'nephew' appeared at approximately the same time as the stolen Space Force vehicle crashed—a partial print in the ruins of the, ah, *bolt-hole,* I believe it is called—which may have belonged to the criminal Trent—why go on? You postulate an utterly ridiculous chain of events. The man cannot be alive."

Lumet turned off-camera momentarily. "One moment." He turned back to Vance. "My presence is required elsewhere. I think we have covered the situation."

Vance said grimly, "Samples at the site of the explosion of the Space Force vehicle did not show the trace elements that should have been there had a living human been present at the time of the explosion."

Lumet sighed. "Commissionaire, your own recordings show how badly that vehicle was damaged. Conceivably his body fell over some other part of Luna entirely."

"The engines were firing. The vehicle made a soft touchdown."

With strained patience, Lumet said, "Sir. The piloting was characteristic of a vehicle on autopilot. You—"

"Or of a vehicle controlled by a Player."

Lumet ignored the comment entirely. "—told me this yourself! I have discussed this as much as I care to. I am not responsible for originating this order, but I will see it carried out. That I have tolerated your argument so long as I have is only in recognition of your years of valuable service. Your abnormal interest in this solitary criminal will stop and it will stop now. The search is called off, and you will report back to Capitol City at your earliest convenience. All of these things you *will* do."

Mohammed Vance said very evenly, "Do you realize to whom you are speaking?"

Lumet took a long, slow breath. "Sir, yes. Commissionaire, I do not want you as my enemy. I believe Elite Commander Breilléune became your enemy, and he is dead. However—sir—I have no leeway in this matter." Lumet paused a moment and said, "Nor do you. Good day to you, sir."

The field went blank.

After brooding in silence for several minutes, Vance said, "Officer du Bois."

The woman did not look at him. "Sir."

"You have met this man. You have spoken with him. Alone

among our officers, you chose to wait for him at the North Bay. What is your opinion?"

She said slowly, "I do not understand, sir."

He turned slightly, stood looking at her. "Do you believe him to be alive?"

Her head bent slightly, in an attitude of contemplation. Her voice, when she spoke, was little more than a whisper. "He is . . . the most alive person I have ever met. He would not die so easily."

"Easily?"

The sharp word brought her up; she held her gaze wavering against his for several moments. "Sir, he is alive. I know he is."

Vance studied her for a moment, then nodded. All the tension spilled out of him at once. "Yes, it is interesting. And disappointing . . . A man," he said, looking now toward the empty holofield, "is defined in some ways by the things he tests himself against. The Erisian Claw, the Johnny Rebs, most Players even, they are too easy. I have rarely faced a challenge such as this boy Trent." He turned away abruptly. "Nor, I think, will I again. Access his file. Reassign it to Access Level One, as per orders."

Melissa du Bois did as instructed, through the traceset at her temples issued the necessary commands. She did not realize she had made any sound whatsoever, surely nothing that would have brought such instant response from Commissionaire Vance. In the ambient blue glow from the holofield her features had taken on an icy cast, like a statue formed of wax.

He said, "What is it?" in almost the same instant that the word, *"Sir,"* tore itself from her throat.

Vance turned back to her with a degree of grace utterly improbable in a man so large. He approached her op station, the certainty growing deep within him, and leaned over to stare at what should have been Trent's file.

The file was gone.

In its place were five words.

Five scarlet words that glared up at Mohammed Vance, glowing bright red against the blue backdrop of the holofield, shining on his cyborg retinae as though they would permanently inscribe themselves there, and a harsh, fierce joy descended upon Mohammed Vance, like the answer to a prayer.

Vance said softly, "Officer du Bois. We are going to Luna together, you and I."

Five words.

CATCH ME IF YOU CAN.

· 8 ·

"Hey, you can't go in there."

"Why not?"

"There's going to be a news conference," the Peaceforcer said.

"I know that." Trent examined the Peaceforcer standing duty at the entrance to the Luna City Hall conference room. She seemed awfully young to Trent; tall and painfully thin, 260 centimeters at least. Pure homegrown loonie. Trent hadn't even known that there were native loonies in the PKF. "But that's two hours from now, sweetheart. I have to fix a line of dead lasercable."

"But I'm not—"

"What's your name?"

"Officer Stout."

"You don't look it. Listen." Trent stepped closer to the loonie and had to tilt his head up slightly to meet her eyes. "The *System Business Journal* Board pays sixty CU a month for the privilege of recording PKF news conferences. The first time in five years you have something that's really news, we have a dead line. If we have to lease coverage from some other Board, Officer Stout, I guarantee you you're going to hear about it."

"But you'll have holocams with you—"

"Come on," said Trent impatiently, "we pay for the fixed cameras because they give a steadier image. Five minutes tops. I'm in and out."

The Peaceforcer looked Trent up and down in momentary indecision; Trent stood patiently, clutching the Black Box tool kit in one hand. The SBJ insignia on his jumpsuit was crooked. Though he had yet to undergo biosculpture, Katrina had done his makeup for him, and he looked only slightly like the Trent of whom the PKF had holos.

With a quick movement the Peaceforcer reached behind herself and slapped the pressure pad to open the door. "Do it fast."

The conference room was large and empty; about 150 seats, a raised platform at one end with holocams already set up and focused on it. A pair of vending chefs held sentinel against one wall. A smaller empty platform to the right of the main platform was to be used for displaying holos; the projector was already turned on, an empty holofield dancing just this side of visibility upon the platform.

Trent wasted no time once the door had closed behind him. There were two access panels at each side of the room, marked as such, in the ceiling four meters above Trent's head. Trent stood under the closer panel and jumped up once, pushing lightly at the panel as he reached it. The panel was not secured; it popped free instantly. With his free hand Trent pulled himself up through the ceiling, into the meter-high crawl space above the conference room.

It took a moment for Trent's eyesight to adjust to the dimness. Every other panel in the ceiling sported a fire sprinkler; the water pipe which fed the sprinklers emerged from the wall at the far side of the conference room. Trent sighed, and on hands and knees moved as quickly as he could through the crawl space to the spot where the piping originated. He reached the place where the piping entered the wall and touched the pressure point to open the tool kit. Inside the tool kit there was a small red canister filled with concentrated Complex 8-A. Trent had designed and built the canister himself; in response to a question from Katrina he had declared that it was a tool for use in an adventure in plumbing.

He fastened the canister to the pipe, glued it carefully to the pipe's surface, and waited while the glue set. The mechanism inside was simple; Trent touched a point on the canister's surface, and a small spike inside the canister punched down into the pipe, opening a passage between the fadeaway and the water that fed the sprinkler system.

He closed up the tool kit, crawled back to the accessway and poked his head down into the conference room. Empty. Trent dropped down to the ground and then jumped back up again to close the access panel.

At the huge double doors which let into the conference room, Trent withdrew a small spraytube of vacuum glue and blasted the surface of the double doors with it.

On the surface of the spraytube it said, DANGER—EX-
TREMELY FLAMMABLE IN PRESSURIZED ENVIRONMENTS. DO
NOT USE NEAR OPEN FLAME, WELDING LASERS, OR ANY IN-
TENSE HEAT.

The residue the glue left when it dried was slick, but not
sticky; Trent was almost certain it would not be noticed.

Trent touched the pressure pad at the door, waited while
the wide double doors curled open, smiled at Officer Stout on
his way out, and went down a level to A1 to have breakfast.

Trent would not have guessed that there were seventy-five
newsdancers in all of Luna who would let themselves be
roused for an 8:00 A.M. press conference.

The conference room was packed. Trent slipped in just behind the *System Business Journal* team, still wearing his blue
jumpsuit with the SBJ insignia. The same loonie Peaceforcer
was at the door, glancing at press badges as the newsdancers
filed in. Officer Stout smiled at Trent when Trent walked by.

There were four seats and a podium set up on the central
platform which had not been there when Trent had been in
earlier that morning. Four Peaceforcers were up on the platform together, along with one nervous loonie in a business
suit. The loonie turned out to be Luna City mayor Jerry Hoff,
who made a brief speech thanking the PKF for their efforts in
making Luna safe.

Trent recognized one of the Peaceforcers.

Mohammed Vance sat impassively through the mayor's
speech, arms folded, staring with glittering black cyborg eyes
out into the crowd of newsdancers.

In the back of the conference room, Trent found somebody
to stand behind.

At 8:05 exactly the Federal Express messenger arrived.

Mayor Hoff ran on: ". . . our violent crime, as a percentage of our population, is amazingly low, among the lowest in
any human society in . . ."

There was a momentary hangup at the door; Officer Stout
had not been instructed to let the messenger in. The argument
was brief; Trent heard relatively little of it. Then the Federal
Express man was inside, threading his way through the newsdancers up to the dais where Mohammed Vance and the other
Peaceforcers were sitting. There was another brief delay at the
stage, as one of the junior Peaceforcers attempted to prevent

the man from delivering his package to Vance. Vance himself waved the young Peaceforcer away, reached down to the messenger to take the long, slim tube the messenger carried.

Trent nudged the SBJ newsdancer standing next to him, gestured at Vance, and said, "You might want to record this."

The newsdancer glanced at Trent. Trent nodded wisely at him, and the man got his holocam up on his shoulder and turned on just in time to win himself an *Electronic Times* Award for Excellence in News Reporting; the conference room's fixed holocams were focused on the podium, and of the seventy-odd portable holocams present, his was the only one focused on Commissionaire Vance as the Elite undid the tie on the box, opened the box itself and withdrew a single long-stemmed white rose.

Vance sat looking at the rose, holding the white rose in one black-gloved fist, without expression, clearly without comprehension. The SBJ newsdancer kept his holocam on Vance, and an instant later Vance's hand curled around the rose, crushed it and dropped it to the floor of the dais. In that instant his features went absolutely scarlet; Trent had not even known that Peaceforcers Elite were capable of blushing.

"Trent," Trent whispered to the SBJ newsdancer, "is supposed to have a long-stemmed white rose tattooed on, uhm, a certain part of his body."

The newsdancer kept the holocam on Vance a moment longer, then turned it off and lowered it when it became clear Vance was going to do nothing at that particular moment. Just as quietly, he whispered back, "Where?"

Trent glanced around to make sure that nobody was listening to them, leaned very close to the newsdancer and whispered in the man's ear. He finished, ". . . and that's the only way you're supposed to be able to tell whether it's a long-stemmed or a short-stemmed rose."

The newsdancer was chuckling. "I hadn't heard that one."

"It's true," Trent assured him.

The newsdancer looked at him skeptically. "How would you know?"

Trent shrugged and grinned at the man; the newsdancer started to turn back to Mayor Hoff, and then stopped dead, looking at the insignia on Trent's jumpsuit. He whispered, "You're not with us."

Trent whispered back, "I know that, and you know that,"

and he grinned again at the newsdancer, "but *they* don't know that."

Mayor Hoff concluded his speech; the newsdancer started to speak again and Trent said, "Shh."

Most of the newsdancers had still not turned on their holocams when the mayor stepped away from the podium.

A Peaceforcer Trent did not recognize stood and took the podium. He did not introduce himself, but the newsdancers stilled somewhat in respect. "I've a brief recording to play for you," the man said quietly. "Lights down."

The holo ran some fifteen minutes. Trent, who had been there for almost all of it, watched in fascination. It started with stills taken of him while in custody at the PKF Detention Center. A voice-over in Mohammed Vance's deep, gravelly tones said, "We have no recordings of the criminal during his escape from the Detention Center. The Player Johnny Johnny, whom we are almost certain is the Image of the criminal Trent, destroyed three quarters of the PKF's online storage in Capitol City." The images shifted as the voice-over continued, became a grainy scene of the Hoffman Spacescraper as seen from a hovering AeroSmith. Trent was clutching a girder while the wind whipped at his hair, and Emile Garon leaped toward him, fell to his death.

The scene changed again, became a flat image. The view was from a camera near the elevators which led to the rotating wheels at Spacebase One. Trent walked a pace behind Rogér Colbert, wearing a SpaceFarer uniform. "We have tentatively concluded that the SpaceFarer's Collective had nothing to do with Trent's escape from Earth." There were chuckles from the audience at what followed, as Trent squirt-gunned five Peaceforcers into unconsciousness. The chuckles stopped almost instantly when the recording cut to a still image of Spacebase One; they all knew what was coming. Whoever had assembled the holograph had done a good job; he held the image still for three seconds, four, and then the north end of Spacebase One blossomed into flame.

Standing in the back of the conference room, Trent nodded thoughtfully. The PKF could not possibly have had holocams available to record the explosion from that angle; the image they were showing the newsdancers was animated. Excellent work; Trent, who had done a fair amount of work with holopaintings and animated holos, could not have done the sequence better himself.

The lights came back up. The Peaceforcer whom Trent did not know said quietly, "I give you Commissionaire Mohammed Vance of the PKF Elite."

Vance stood slowly, moved to the podium. In Lunar gravity, he bounced less than anyone else Trent had seen since he had arrived on that planet, including native loonies. At the podium he did not pause to make the customary eye contact with the crowd; he stared straight ahead and began speaking in quiet, measured tones. Perhaps a quarter of the newsdancers knew of him as the Peaceforcer who was reputed to have ordered the destruction of the Castanaveras telepaths; as a group they rewarded him with first real silence of the news conference.

"I am Mohammed Vance. I have come to Luna for the specific purpose of capturing and seeing to the execution of this thief, this Player, Trent. With your aid I believe we will accomplish this quickly. We have evidence that Trent is still in United Nations territory. I am taking this opportunity to inform the citizens of United Nations Luna that a reward in the amount of five thousand Credit Units has been posted for information leading to the capture of this criminal." Vance's stiff expression did not flicker at all; for the first time he glanced around the room, at the assembled newsdancers. "Press kits have been assembled and will be given out when we are finished here. If you have any questions, please feel free to ask them now."

There was some method by which priority had been assigned, though Trent had no idea what it was; the newsdancers asked their questions in some predetermined order.

"Commissionaire Vance, how close are you to capturing Trent?"

"I do not know."

"Commissionaire Vance, how has Trent managed to evade capture for so long already?"

"Cleverness."

"Commissionaire, is it true Trent's one of the Castanaveras telepaths?"

"We do not know. I think it unlikely. Much has been made of the fact that the Bureau of Biotechnology's records show a child named 'Trent Castanaveras' was born March 9, 2051. And indeed, the Trent we are searching for is of approximately the correct age to be that child. Still, I do think it unlikely—Trent has had difficulties in places where no telepath would have had difficulties."

"Commissionaire, is Trent a genie?"

"It is entirely possible, but I cannot say with certainty."

"Commissionaire, if he is a genie, in what area might he show enhancements?"

"He might show enhancements in virtually any area at all. I cannot say which enhancements might be more probable."

"Commissionaire, is Trent dangerous?"

"Very. I must caution the public that if they feel they have identified Trent, to notify the PKF at once. Do not, under any circumstances, attempt to apprehend this criminal yourself. As his attempted destruction of Spacebase One at L-5 clearly shows, he possesses a disregard for human life which—"

Hiding behind a tall loonie newsdancer from the *Electronic Times,* Trent said, loudly enough to be heard across the length of the room, "Oh, come on. It's not, *his disregard for human life,* it's, *our disregard for human life.*"

The newsdancer Trent had been speaking to earlier faded slowly away from Trent, stood holding his holocam casually at waist level, focused on Trent. Trent leaned toward him and whispered loudly enough for the holocam to catch it, "Pronoun troubles."

Vance glanced across the conference room, looking without expression and without success for the source of the comment, and then backed up slightly and continued. "—a disregard for human life which ranks him with such ideologs as the Erisian Claw and the Johnny Rebs. He is—"

Trent stepped to his left, so that he stood immediately before the open double doors. "Commissioner Vance."

Vance looked directly at Trent. He did not say anything. Around the conference room, heads were craning to look back at the door.

"Isn't it true, Commissioner, that you were warned that it wasn't safe to use the weapons at Spacebase One, and that you did anyway?" A few of the quicker newsdancers had their holocams on Trent by the time he had finished the question; the SBJ newsdancer at Trent's side kept his holocam rocksteady, focused on Trent.

"No," said Vance slowly, "it is not. We—"

"Isn't it true," said Trent loudly, "that your dangerous criminal ran through Peaceforcer Heaven with no weapon more dangerous than a squirt gun filled with Complex 8-A?

And isn't it further true that Trent, when advised that the stolen Space Force vehicle he was in was about to be destroyed, immediately jettisoned Colonel Piers Webster from the spacecraft, and that Webster was then rescued by Space Force?"

"What news service are you with, young man?" Vance stared at Trent.

"Commissioner Vance, isn't it true that virtually without exception the damage which has been caused *to* the Peaceforcers has been caused *by* the Peaceforcers?" Trent shouted to be heard over the growing noise from the newsdancers talking into their holocams. Better than half of them had their holocams focused on him. "Specifically, by the man who gave the order to fire the North Bay missiles after having been told that it was not safe for him to do so? By *you*?"

The glittering cyborg eyes did not move at all. From across the conference room Trent could see smoke curling up from the glove covering the laser embedded in Vance's right fist.

Mohammed Vance said, "Who are you?"

Trent let the question hang for just an instant, and then said very softly indeed, to Vance and the assembled newsdancers, "I sent you the rose, Vance."

There was sudden and complete silence.

"Did you like it?"

Vance took a step away from the podium, toward the crowd of newsdancers, toward Trent. "I did not. Is it you, Trent?"

Trent said into the hushed stillness, "Yes."

Vance took a step off the platform, dropped to the ground. Newsdancers were fanning away from him as he walked toward Trent, flames dancing around his right hand, smoke wafting slowly upward in the gentle Lunar gravity.

Vance was thirty meters away; perhaps forty of the newsdancers were still blocking his way to Trent. Through the crowd Trent locked eyes with the huge cyborg, and said so quietly that it could not have been heard in less silent surroundings, "Catch me if you can."

He took one step backward, into the corridor, and slapped the pressure pad to close the double doors. From a jumpsuit pocket he withdrew his squirt gun and shot Officer Stout in the face once. She crumpled in slow motion in the Lunar gravity, sporting a woefully surprised expression. Trent worked swiftly but without hurrying, did it as he had practiced; from his tool kit Trent took a small suction pump, placed it over the corridor's pressure sensor and turned it on. The corridor sirens went off almost immediately; the door to the conference room locked with an audible snap. Trent jacked his handheld into the doorgrid and said aloud, "Breached corridor at City Hall. Emergency seal in place." The words boomed out over the corridor intercom, through every public outspeaker in all of Luna City. Trent kicked off his shoes and undressed in the empty corridor with Officer Stout's still form, watching the door. Not five seconds had passed since the closing of the door. Trent had the jumpsuit off; underneath it he wore a pair of floral-print Hawaiian shorts and a black t-shirt. Vance must be having a time of it, getting newsdancers out of his way. Six seconds, seven—

The door shuddered in its frame, buckled slightly. The doors dented outward once, twice, where they joined at the center, as the cyborg tried to force the doors apart. Trent bundled up the jumpsuit and tucked it into the tool kit, watching the door. This was the place where it all either came together or fell apart. If Vance managed to open that door it was all over.

A third and even stronger blow struck the door; the door frame actually rang like a bell.

Silence.

Trent put his shoes back on.

For the merest instant, a spot on the surface of the door glowed red, orange, approached white, and then faded. Trent grinned and said aloud, "Sucker," pulled his handheld free of the doorgrid and hooked it to his belt, turned and walked away down the empty corridor without haste, leaving the empty tool kit behind with Officer Stout.

In his mind, he pictured it happening; the laser in Vance's fist touching the door, as Vance attempted to cut through to get at Trent. The vacuum glue bursting into fierce flames almost instantly; the very efficient Lunar sprinkler system cutting in to douse the flames, and everything else in the conference room, with a fine mixture of water and fadeaway.

The corridor let out onto the only large plaza on A2; Trent glided down a ramp to A1. On A1, just before 8:30 A.M., there would normally be a couple of thousand people out on various errands. Not sixty seconds had passed since the false warning of a breach at City Hall; Trent could not see anyone, on all of A1, who was not either in a pressure suit or running like mad toward whatever they perceived as safety. A squad of Peaceforcers trotted across A1 on its way toward Luna City Hall. Trent did not allow himself to hesitate at all; he ran like everyone around him, ran with long bouncing strides to the Luna City transfer station, checked his p-suit from the public locker, paid for his ticket with untraceable hard Space-Farer CU, and boarded the 8:30 monorail to Kepler.

Katrina Trudeau kept an underground four-room house just outside of the city of Kepler. In addition to being her official place of residence, it doubled as a pickup hospital for those clients who required surgery or other services which were not convenient to provide at Luna City.

Katrina sat beneath dimmed lights in a sunken, white rug-covered area of her living room, watching a recording of the news conference at Luna City, when Trent cycled through the airlock. She was wearing a long gray silk robe that was tied at the waist with a green sash. She wore nothing beneath it that Trent could see. Katrina smiled at him quickly, without saying anything, and went back to watching the recording while Trent stripped off his p-suit and rubbed it down.

"I'm ready."

Katrina glanced at him, patted a cushion on the floor next to her. "I hope you're ready. We're going to need to do your voice box as well. After this—" In the holo, Trent was saying *I sent you the rose, Vance.* Katrina said, "*Command,* holo off. I suppose you know how this ends?"

Trent joined her, settled in to get comfortable. There was a "fireplace" in the wall next to them: a combination of holo, sound, and radiant heater. The effect was remarkably realistic; Trent would have hesitated to put his hand into the flame. "Peaceforcers and newsdancers sprawled all over the place. The good guys win."

"You're impossible. Trent," she said, trying the name out for size. "I liked you better when I thought you were Thomas."

"I was safer for you when I was Thomas."

"Why didn't you tell me who you were? If I hadn't checked the news Boards this morning—"

Trent shrugged. "Normal caution. I'd have told you when it seemed appropriate."

Katrina laughed, looking at him with amusement and some

real degree of affection. "I want an extra two thousand CU, Trent. For the added danger."

Trent said sincerely, "I respect you too much to haggle."

Katrina laughed again. "I'm sure you do." She glanced back at the empty holofield, as though it still held the image of the prone forms in the City Hall conference room. She stood. "Come in back with me."

"I thought you were never going to ask."

Katrina Trudeau said slowly, "I have some reluctance to do this to you."

Lying on the long flat table, staring straight up at fluorescent white glowpaint, Trent said, "Hell of a time to mention it. Why?"

She looked undecided for a moment. "There is—it—" She chewed on her lower lip. "Trent, you're perfect."

Trent said, "Thank you."

"I mean it," she protested. "I've been going through your X rays, the physical I ran on you the last time you were here. Trent, you have *no flaws.*"

Trent said again, "Thank you."

Katrina said gently, "You're not surprised."

"Should I be?"

"Yes, you should." Indecision battled clearly behind the golden eyes. "You're so exquisite—if you were a painting you'd be a masterpiece, Trent."

Trent sighed. "Ask the question."

"I'm not prejudiced," she said. "It's important you believe that. I'm *not.*"

"You could just *ask,* you know. It'd save us both a lot of time."

"Those questions they were asking at the news conference —Trent, who designed you?"

Looking directly up into her eyes, Trent said, "Suzanne Montignet."

"Doctor Montignet?" Katrina Trudeau looked absolutely astounded. "I studied under her. She—"

"Was the best. Katrina, could we talk some other time?"

The woman was very still for a moment, and then relaxed. "Of course. I would really like to hear about it sometime."

"Maybe sometime I'll tell you." Trent was silent then, while Katrina moved the machines into place around him.

"Trent?"

"Yes?"

"I'm going to put you under now. It'll take a few moments, and you'll feel a bit disoriented before you go out. Just don't worry, and don't get tense; it'll be okay."

Something cool brushed Trent's arm. "Katrina?"

"Yes, Trent?"

"It's not that I don't trust you."

She said patiently, "Yes?"

"You notice my handheld's not here. My Image is not here."

"So?"

A wave of dizziness touched Trent. "So, if anything goes wrong, if I don't get in touch with my Image after this, my Image is going to come get you. My Image," said Trent, somewhat blurrily, "has replicant code in him. Even in the LIN I think he'd last . . . mm . . . long enough."

Katrina Trudeau leaned over Trent's reclining form, and murmured in his ear, "It's a suspicious world we live in, love. I wouldn't hurt you." Her voice grew very remote. "How could I? There's too little art in the world to begin with. . . ."

There was a long emptiness.

. . . BOSS? HEY, BOSS?

It was like emerging from a deep and dark cavern into blazing daylight.

JOHNNY? JOHNNY JOHNNY, IS THAT YOU? Trent found himself sitting at the center of a great emptiness, watching pulsing slivers of light at the edges of the world.

BOSS, YOU HAVE TO LET ME THROUGH.

The form took shape immediately before Trent, a dark and hazy shape lacking form or definition. It was a hole in the midst of the glowing haziness. JOHNNY JOHNNY'S CORRECT, TRENT. YOU HAVE TO DO IT.

BOSS, THERE'S AN IMAGE IN THE INSKIN ALREADY, AND IT WON'T LET ME IN. YOU HAVE TO MAKE IT LET ME IN.

Trent sat in the pristine silence, thinking with a clarity that he had never possessed before. The Crystal Wind tugged at the edges of his awareness, begged to be let in. He did not know the program Johnny Johnny was talking about. He searched his own awareness looking for the rogue Image Johnny Johnny was referring to, and could not find it.

The form standing in front of Trent said, TRENT, I'VE DONE EVERYTHING I CAN. SIMPLY BEING HERE WITH YOUR INSKIN FIGHTING SO HARD HAS DAMAGED ME WORSE THAN YOU MIGHT IMAGINE. I GOT JOHNNY IN FAR ENOUGH PAST YOUR DEFENSES SO THAT HE COULD TALK TO YOU. IT'S UP TO YOU NOW. LET GO OF THE INSKIN; LET JOHNNY IN.

The form faded, vanished, and left Trent alone with Johnny Johnny's voice.

BOSS? THE IMAGE THAT'S SITTING IN YOUR INSKIN? BOSS, *IT THINKS IT'S YOU.*

Trent opened his eyes.

He was lying in bed, with a warm weight snuggled around him. He got out of bed carefully, disentangling himself from Katrina's arms. He had to search to find the bathroom.

Inside the bathroom he switched on the lights, and then had to hunt again to find the control to turn on the mirror.

The mirror silvered into existence before him. The process of the mirror's appearance seemed very slow. He had never noticed that before.

He examined his appearance in the mirror, the face of an American Peaceforcer named Benny Gutierrez.

Dark hair and eyebrows, almost as dark as Denice's. His nose was slightly larger than it had been before, and his cheekbones were higher and more visible. There was a faint cleft in his chin. His eyes were no longer pale blue; they were practically gray, almost without color. Katrina had done something, he was not quite sure what, to the curve of his jaw; it was straighter, more angular. It was a fairly handsome face, and made Trent look somewhat older; twenty-five or -six.

All of his scars were gone, every one. It made him feel curiously naked, unreal. His tattoo was still there, as Katrina had promised, but aside from the white rose his skin was brown all over.

Trent wasn't at all sure he liked it.

At least, the thought occurred to him, *I don't have to worry about my tan anymore.*

Trent turned off the bathroom light and returned to the

bedroom. His body felt odd, clumsy and slow-moving. He sat down at the edge of the bed, in the dark, and let his eyes close.

He was back in the glowing emptiness almost immediately. Trent opened his eyes. Darkness. The sound of Katrina breathing in her sleep.

He closed his eyes again and went Inside.

BOSS?

HI, JOHNNY.

YOU'RE BACK?

I THINK SO. HOW LONG WAS I GONE?

BOSS, IT'S BEEN ALMOST THREE WEEKS.

THREE WEEKS. Trent considered that. ALL RIGHT. JOHNNY, I THINK I'VE MADE A MISTAKE.

NO KIDDING.

THAT PROGRAM THAT THINKS IT'S ME—JOHNNY, IT *IS* ME.

There was, by the standards of electronic intelligences, an incredibly long pause before Johnny Johnny replied. Trent found himself noticing Johnny Johnny's response time for the first time in his life. AW, HELL, BOSS. YOU'VE BEEN PROMISING ME AN INSKIN FOR THE LONGEST TIME AND I WAS *AFRAID* THIS WAS GOING TO HAPPEN WHEN YOU STARTED TALKING ABOUT THAT GODDAMN "ALMOST-AN-INSKIN" NN-II IN THE FIRST PLACE. I—

JOHNNY, *STOP*. WHO BROUGHT YOU IN TO ME?

BOSS, I DON'T KNOW. I THINK HE WAS AN AI, EXCEPT HE WAS USING SOME OF THE SAME IMAGE ROUTINES I USE, SO MAYBE HE WAS A PLAYER. BOSS, I DON'T *KNOW*. HE KNOWS A LOT ABOUT YOU, BOSS. AND BOSS—THE PLAYER I THOUGHT WAS CHASING ME AFTER I CRASHED THE PKF BOARDS IN CAPITOL CITY? REMEMBER? I THINK IT WAS HIM.

OKAY. WE'LL HUNT HIM DOWN WHEN WE HAVE OUR OTHER PROBLEMS RESOLVED. WHERE ARE YOU?

WHERE YOU LEFT ME, BOSS. THE LOCKER AT THE MONORAIL STATION. BOSS, DID YOU KNOW THEY TURN OFF RADIO PACKET INFONET ACCESS BETWEEN TWO AND FIVE A.M. EVERY NIGHT? I'VE HAD TO SIT THERE WITH NOTHING TO DO, THREE HOURS A DAY EVERY DAY FOR THE LAST THREE WEEKS.

CAN YOU COME ACROSS?

There was another long silence. BOSS, I CAN TRY. BUT I TRIED BEFORE, AND YOU DIDN'T LET ME.

Trent said, TRY AGAIN.

At first Trent thought nothing was happening. Then an oppressive weight seemed to descend upon him, an amorphous shape that settled over the glowing expanse of his consciousness like a shroud. He found himself tensing without meaning to, forced himself to relax, using the same biofeedback techniques which had once, eons ago, allowed a simple boy named Trent to interpret the signals from a traceset.

The gloom deepened, and then a vast pain ripped through Trent, a silent flaring implosion of agony and Trent heard himself screaming as Johnny Johnny invaded, struck his unconscious barriers hard, and—

—merged.

"Trent?" It was Katrina's voice, concerned. The word seemed to drag across Trent's awareness in slow motion. "Trent?"

The lights were on in her bedroom.

Trent felt himself turning to look at her, felt the individual movement of each muscle in his neck. A channel at the edge of his awareness vibrated with promise, with potential. In his mind Trent saw the channel grow, become a tunnel that he flowed down at the speed of light, the edges of Realtime racing by him, falling away from him as he expanded to encompass the Crystal Wind.

THIS, said Johnny Johnny-who-was-Trent, in a voice so silent that Trent-who-was-Trent could barely hear it, IS *MUCH BETTER.*

Katrina's voice was blurred and patterned, half lost in the growing, thundering crescendo of the Crystal Wind of information. "How do you feel?"

Trent continued turning toward her. His body moved with amazing slowness, a crude meat machine. A Russian ballerina whirled through the space inside his skull, half obscured the face of the woman in front of him. *Russian = dancing bears.* "I know a dancing bear named Boris," Trent heard himself explaining to Katrina earnestly, "and a very good joke, would you like to hear it? Ask somebody to pick a number between one and ten. Then, run away."

He stood unsteadily. There were 9,542 Lunar InfoNet Boards pouring into him, 45 microwave channels carrying data extracted from Earth's InfoNet. The stock market was up five points and a flood in Australia had killed six hundred people, the Green Bay Packers were being beaten badly by the Beijing Bears and a Johnny Reb bomb in Iowa had detonated prematurely without killing anybody. The world's greatest sensablist, Gregory Selstrom, and the world's most popular sensable actor, Gregory Selstrom's elder brother Adam Selstrom, had agreed to work together in Gregory Selstrom's current production; it would, amazingly enough, be the first time the two had collaborated.

Trent stumbled once, and Katrina was there, steadying him. A stand-up comic with a cigarette lighter in his hand said, "And in closing, I'd like to set myself on fire for you—but that would *hurt.*" Katrina made no attempt to stop Trent as he walked out into the living room and then stood motionless in the middle of the room, sightless eyes fixed upon his pressure suit. An artificial Christmas tree was erected just to one side of the pressure suit rack, the tree's lights blinking red and blue and green, yellow and orange and white. On one of the lines from Earth three beautiful children were telling a newsdancer that all they wanted for Christmas was world peace. In Beijing a riot resulted in twenty-three deaths by trampling, including one couple who had been celebrating their sixty-fifth wedding anniversary. There were half a dozen presents beneath the tree, wrapped in silver and gold foil. "This is what they always meant," Trent said aloud. When he spoke the words he heard them echo. "THE CRYSTAL WIND IS THE STORM, AND THE STORM IS DATA, AND THE DATA IS LIFE. Where are my clothes?"

Trent heard the worry in her voice when she answered him. "You're not ready to leave yet, Trent. You're not—"

"Don't worry, Katrina. I'm just going to do what's necessary." That part of Trent which had once been Johnny Johnny added, "You know, I've never seen a Christmas tree before, I've never seen *colors* before. You humans," he whispered to Katrina, "you are such marvelous machines."

"Trent," she said desperately, "I can't let you leave like this!"

The numbers danced into Trent's awareness, out again. "It's December 7, 2069, 2:30 A.M. One hundred and twenty-eight years ago today the Japanese bombed Pearl Harbor and dragged the United States into World War II. 'And with each passing year it is going to seem more quaint, the little tin airplanes bombing the sleepy iron giants.' My god," said

Trent a moment later, staring at Katrina, "I can see the field I first read that line on. It's hanging there in the back of my head; I'm thirteen, and the Temple Dragons have just adopted me."

"Trent, it's going to take *time* before it's safe for you to leave and—"

"It's Friday," said Trent abruptly. "On Sunday I'm supposed to be in Jackson Town Free Luna, on Farside. To meet a woman named Callia who came all the way from Earth just to work with me." He smiled at her with slow delight; the lights from the Christmas tree were reflected in her eyes, dancing like fireflies on the gold-green irises. "But if you wanted to go back to bed, I could be talked into being late."

• 9 •

Farside is, essentially, three cities in three craters. The Lunar Bureau of the United Nations Peace Keeping Force DataWatch—that is its full and complete name—is a base located at the crater Jules Verne. The only significant scientific establishment on Farside is Zvezdagrad at Tsiolkovsky Crater, where astronomers from all over the System probe into far reaches of the sky. Jackson Town Free Luna completes what is very nearly an equilateral triangle; between them the three cities hold some eighty percent of the population of Farside.

Jackson Town was more like an Earthside city than anything else Trent had seen on Luna. It was a domed city, one of the few on Luna. At not quite three kilometers in diameter, it was not as large as the dome at Luna City, but was larger than most of the other domed cities. It felt larger than Luna City to Trent; most of the surface was given over to greenery of one sort or another, ranging from flat-out wilderness to sculptured parklands.

Trent arrived in Jackson Town in the midst of two nights, the real Lunar night and the artificial night derived from Earth's twenty-four-hour cycle. The armed girl on duty at the transfer station when Trent's semiballistic arrived was barely able to keep awake long enough to verify that Trent was expected, approve him for entry and check him through. Trent kept to the marked paths, wandering through the dark wilderness without hurry, moving underneath the impossibly thin trees, through the shrubbery and the flowers that reached his chest. His handheld was clipped at his belt, and it bounced every few steps against the side of his thigh. A single tenterabyte infochip inside the handheld safeguarded the only record anyone in the world had of Trent's original facial bone structure and voice print.

It was dim inside the dome; nighttime on Farside is darker than anything on Earth itself ever gets. Only the very faint starlight shone down on the terraformed landscape. There were airlocks leading beneath ground every thirty meters or so; even in the event of a catastrophic failure of the dome, Trent thought it likely he would reach shelter in time.

The paths twisted and curved throughout the entire upper level, moving toward and then away from the very center of the dome, where Trent wished to go. Trent was in no hurry at all; he expected to have to wait out the night in the Temple of Eris until his contact returned to the Temple to greet him. He wandered down the pathways, and Johnny Johnny's ghostly fading voice, in the back of his skull, said, BOSS, I'M GOING TO TRY SOMETHING NEW. It happened slowly, the world flaring and brightening around Trent as though dawn were arriving. The image processing Johnny Johnny was performing went slowly at first, and then more quickly as Johnny Johnny found out what did and did not work; the edges of everything around Trent became very sharp, as the images his retinae recorded were subjected to a fast Fourier transform. The surfaces of things speckled, appeared for a moment in garish unreal colors, and then settled into a grainy black and white image. The world steadied around Trent for just an instant, and then, from up ahead on the path, came the first hint of illumination from the Temple of Eris. Trent glided slowly through the inky darkness, unable even to be amazed at how very strange his world had become in the days since Emile Garon's death.

Light blazed over him in glaring colors.

The exterior of the Temple of Eris looked nothing like Reverend Andy's Temple; it was a gold and silver octagonal building, limned in black marble, surrounded by yellow flood-

lamps all around its base. It reached up two stories to touch
the dome itself and it was the brightest object in the world,
the brightest thing Trent had ever seen, more radiant than the
sun itself. He walked slowly around the Temple, marveling as
he had never marveled before at anything and then suddenly,
without any warning at all, Trent's vision reverted to nor-
malcy.

For the merest instant he felt a deep, aching regret at the
loss of the vision, and then he found the entrance, and went
inside.

Four rows of pews, of some material that was not wood but
had been made to resemble burnished walnut, expanded outward in concentric rings from the central circle where the
Reverend would give sermons on Sundays and Wednesdays.
There was no altar, which did not surprise Trent; some Temples had them, others did not. A fractured rainbow, rose and
pale blue with a flash of green, fell from a series of stained-
glass windows positioned high on the eight inner walls.

There was a woman praying at the center of the circle.

Trent walked forward slowly, to the edge of the circle, and
sat down in lotus facing the praying woman. There was a
small satchel sitting on one of the pews behind her. Weapons
surrounded the woman; an autoshot lay on the Temple floor
immediately to her left, a sheathed knife to her right, and a
hand weapon that was either laser or maser immediately before her. Her eyes were closed, her head bowed. Her hands
were clenched together just beneath her chin, white with tension. She knelt in the most uncomfortable position Trent
could imagine, knees together, back and thighs completely
rigid from the knees up. Her hair was even shorter than
Trent's own, a soft blond brush cut only five centimeters long.
She was barefoot, wearing nothing but the bottom half of a
powder-blue gi, loosely tied at her waist with a black belt. She
was clearly Earth-born; the smooth, swimmer's muscles in
her back and shoulders were trembling slightly, and in the
low gravity random trickles of sweat moved languidly across
her upper torso. Her nipples were erect, her breasts shiny with
perspiration. Trent sat in silent fascination, watching her
breathe. She breathed deeply, in the very long, very slow
breaths that are usually the result of training.

Time passed. The woman did not move except for the

rhythmic rise and fall of her chest. Trent watched her, trying to match his own breathing to hers. His time sense was still behaving oddly; sometimes it seemed to him that he was taking so long between breaths that he would die if he did not breathe more quickly. He was aware of individual muscles moving, of the sound of his own heartbeat.

He did not speak.

After some unmeasured time, her eyes opened. She looked right at Trent, locked eyes with him. Her irises were exactly the same color as Denice's. Her voice was soft as silk, American in accent. "You're late." She sagged suddenly, went limp and sat back on her heels and took a long, shuddering breath. When she looked back up at Trent again, who had not moved at all, she was smiling, an odd, gentle, not quite impersonal smile. "Thank you. I'm usually too busy to go to Temple. Today was good for me."

"Today?" She did not reply and Trent said, "You've been here since—I was supposed to be here at ten o'clock this morning. That's almost fourteen hours ago."

She was still smiling at him. "Yes."

"You *are* Callia Sierran?"

"Yes. And you're Trent the Uncatchable."

"Trent the what?"

"You haven't been auditing the Boards?"

"No. I've been—busy."

"It's what the newsdancers have been calling you."

The instant she said it, Trent knew it was true. The thought triggered the whirlwind of the Crystal Wind, a cascade he could not control at all, a blurred and roaring tumble of images and sounds and written words; Systemwide, in the last month, the word pattern "Trent the Uncatchable" had been used some 23,000 times. Slow delight blossomed within Trent; he sat silently while the data washed over him and through him, sat almost paralyzed until the moment had passed. To Callia Sierran it must have appeared as the merest instant's hesitation before his reply. "They have sown the wind," Trent heard himself saying, "and they shall reap the whirlwind."

Her smile grew even wider. "Yes," said Callia Sierran. "They shall."

Callia sat resting for a while after that. Trent waited patiently. After several minutes she seemed almost rested. Her breathing had gentled, grown more shallow. She stood and removed the bottom half of her gi and dried herself with a towel from the satchel on the pew behind her, unaware or else uncaring of what effect she might have on Trent. She redressed in the blue gi, top and bottoms, and a pair of gray running shoes without socks, and began talking as she dressed. "Right now it looks like you, myself, my brother Lan, and Yevgeni Sergei Korimok." She removed a holster from the satchel, tied it down on her right thigh. The knife went back in the satchel. "Lan does our demolition. He's my brother, and he's young, so you may not trust my objectivity, but he's really very good at it. A bit impulsive, which we'll need to watch for, but reliable. He follows orders."

Trent nodded. "Okay."

"I'm security." She picked up the hand weapon, checked the charge cartridge and holstered it. "I spend nine months a year on Earth for toning, three in Luna. I move well in Lunar gravity and I have muscles most Lunar residents, men included, can't match." She glanced at Trent speculatively. "Not counting you, I think. If things blow up on us, I handle it if I can. I can use almost any energy weapon or slugthrower. I have a second-degree black belt in tae kwon do, a fourth in shotokan. I'm good with a wide variety of edged weapons. I'm checked out on pressure-suit combat, both the standard soft suits and powered scalesuits." She slung the satchel over her right shoulder, carrying the autoshot in her right hand. "Yevgeni's a native loonie, U.N. territory," Callia continued, sitting down on a pew facing Trent. "And Syndic on top of that, and especially given that you're an American you don't want to get him started on how the Russians have been treated by the Unification. But Domino vouches for him, and that's good enough for me. He does, for a fact, have contacts all over the place, nearside and far, Free Luna and United Nations both. He's going to be doing most of the public contact we need done." She smiled at him again, that oddly beatific smile. "And then there's you. I don't know what you're here for."

The comment startled Trent. "You don't know?"

She shook her head, a quick efficient back and forth motion. "No. Domino said you would tell us. She told me we were hitting the Peaceforcers, and that you would tell us the rest; that was enough."

"You seem to trust Domino a lot."

"I trust many people. Trent—" She hesitated, and it struck Trent that it was the first time she had addressed him by his name. "Isn't there anyone you trust completely? Who you have faith in?"

Trent did not even have to think about his answer. "A girl I know on Earth. Her name wouldn't mean anything to you."

"Then you understand," Callia said simply. "If Domino told me my eyes were blue, I would assume that they had changed color since the last time I looked in a mirror."

Trent nodded thoughtfully. "Callia? May I ask you a question?"

"You can ask me anything. My life is a public Board, Trent."

"You're a member of the Erisian Claw."

Callia did not even blink. "Of course." She seemed, to Trent, somewhat surprised. "Is that a problem?"

"You've promised your life to the overthrow of the Unification."

"Yes," she said serenely.

Trent said very slowly, "I've never known anyone in the Claw, but one of my closest friends is Reverend of a Temple in New York. Callia, are you Erisian first, or Claw first?"

Callia Sierran shook her head. "That's a question that has no meaning, Trent."

"The Erisian Temples preach that life is sacred, Callia."

"The Claw believes the same, Trent." Her gaze did not waver. "Our lives as much so as those of our enemies. When our lives are threatened by our enemies—and they are, every day—we do what we must."

"I need a promise from you, Callia."

The woman said instantly, "Done."

"You don't want to know what it is?"

"I would like to, yes."

Trent shook his head, grinning despite himself. "All right. You can't kill anyone on this job. Not even Peaceforcers."

For the briefest instant he thought she was going to argue, and then she nodded once. "I will do as you say. So will Lan. I can't speak for Yevgeni." She paused and then said, "Lan will want to know *why* we are not to kill Peaceforcers."

Trent sat in lotus, studying something he had never seen before in his life. "But it doesn't matter to you?"

"It matters to me, yes." Callia Sierran shrugged, and said, "But not as much as doing what Domino has told me to do."

"Which is?"

"Domino," said Callia Sierran, "told me to do whatever *you* told me to do."

· 10 ·

Domino had arranged for them to take over a suite of five rooms at a friendly hotel outside the Jackson Town dome. Trent wandered through the rooms briefly: a central room with a small kitchenette attached, with a window overlooking the Jackson Town dome; four bedrooms, one for Trent, one for Callia and her brother, one for Yevgeni Sergei Korimok—

—and one for the seven bodies.

Callia showed Trent the room that they had saved for him, said a quiet good night, and went to the room she shared with her brother.

Trent opened his eyes to cool, bright yellow sunpaint and the smell of good coffee.

The room was large, with a writing desk and chair and a bed. A closed door concealed the room's small shower. There was a systerm at the desk, turned off. The two suitcases Trent had left aboard the rented semiballistic had been put next to the desk.

The boy sat at the foot of Trent's bed, wearing a brown robe which had seen better days and drinking from a bulb of coffee. His clear blue eyes were fixed on Trent, gaze steady and unblinking. He was sixteen or seventeen and slim, with long brown hair bound in a ponytail, and had either just depilated his facial hair or had never needed to in his life.

He smiled at Trent. "Good morning."

"Good morning."

"You sleep pretty hard."

Trent sat up in bed, slowly. "At 3:38 A.M. you stood in the doorway for twenty-two seconds, turned and left. At 6:12 you came in and sat in the chair for four minutes and eight seconds. At 9:05 you came in again, dropped my luggage next to the desk, stood at the foot of the bed and mumbled a sentence which included the word *lazy,* and left. It's now 9:22, and you've been sitting at the foot of the bed for not quite three minutes."

The boy blinked. "How do you know that?"

Trent said, "I don't sleep very hard. You're Lan Sierran?"

"Yeah." Lan grinned suddenly. "Got it. You're a Player and you have an inskin monitoring your auditory nerve."

Trent looked at Lan Sierran thoughtfully. "Good guess. Excuse me." He got out of the bed and went to take a shower. He did not hurry. When he came back out again, one towel around his waist, drying his hair with another, Lan was still there, reading from the holofield of an InfoNet handheld.

A second bulb, still sealed, had appeared on the end table by the bed. "Coffee," said Lan, without looking up at Trent. "With cream, no sugar. This place has its own kitchen." He did look up then. "I've never been in hotel rooms before that had their own private kitchen. Domino told me you said you didn't want room service, not even waitbots."

"I said that, yes. Are Callia and 'Sieur Korimok here?"

"Nope. Went to Jackson Town. Yev's going to buy me and Callia scalesuits. Yev is a big believer in scalesuits."

The memory popped up so fast and strong that for a moment it was as though Nathan were there in the room with him. "A friend of mine," said Trent, "said that scalesuits were disasters waiting to happen." Trent opened one of his suitcases, took out a pair of black cotton slacks and a long-sleeved gray shirt and put them on. Lan watched him dress with unabashed interest; Trent decided against an earring.

"You have nice muscles. You don't see that on the Moon very much. Except on Peaceforcers," Lan amended. "But that's regs for them, they have to stay in shape so they can be sent back to Earth at the end of their tour." He shrugged. "I don't sleep with Peaceforcers."

"I hope not," said Trent mildly. He settled on the bed in front of Lan and twisted the ring at the neck of the coffee bulb. He sipped at the coffee.

Lan watched him. "You like it?"

Trent blinked. "Yes." He smelled the coffee. "What is this?" Nothing he had drunk since he'd been on Luna had come close to tasting like real coffee.

Lan nodded. "I hardly ever drink coffee myself. Caffeine's bad for you. And it doesn't taste as good as orange juice or tea. Or milk. But Booker Jamethon said you were a coffee

junkie so we brought two kilos of S&W Colombian up with us
when Domino told us to come."

Trent glanced at the boy sharply. "You spoke to Booker?"

"Not me. Callia. Domino works with the Syndic a lot, she
has to." Lan shook his head. "When Callia found out we were
going to work with you she researched. She's good at that, but
even so she didn't get a lot. You have a lot of friends, but we
left Earth before the"—he grinned—"news conference, while
the Peaceforcers weren't absolutely certain still if you were
alive or not. So we couldn't very well wander around asking
people what sorts of things you wanted from home. 'Sieur
Jamethon said you were a coffee junkie, and a Brother An-
drew at the Flushing Street Temple told Callia you liked S&W
Colombian. Nobody else talked to her very much."

Trent nodded slowly. "Good. That's good to hear."

"So anyhow," Lan continued, "what are we doing here?"

"We're going to steal the LINK."

Lan Sierran said without any hesitation at all, "Okay. I'm
supposed to blow something up?"

"At one point, yes."

"What is it?"

"A Peaceforcer troop transport rolligon."

The boy grinned broadly. "Great."

"We are not," said Trent patiently, "going to kill anybody."

The grin vanished. "You're kidding."

"I'm not."

"Not anybody?"

"Nobody."

Lan looked vaguely distressed. "You're going to blow up a
Peaceforcer troop transport," he said, "without killing anybody?"

"Exactly."

The boy thought about it for a long moment. "But what's
the *point*?"

Later that evening the four of them sat in the dark with a
glowing holograph in the center of the table. The holograph
showed a map of Farside, with the triangle of Jackson Town,
Zvezdagrad, and Jules Verne. A dotted red line ran from
Zvezdagrad toward the crater Jules Verne; there was a big
blue *X* where the line entered a series of low hills, just before
the line actually touched Verne Crater.

"Everybody has summaries? Yes?" Trent looked around the table: Lan looked bored, Korimok was quietly following him, and Callia listened intently, as though worried she might miss some subtle nuance. Trent smiled at Lan. "Let's recap. On December twenty-second a man named Benny Gutierrez is scheduled to ship up to Luna City. Gutierrez is a webdancer, and from what I've been able to learn about him, a fairly good one. On January third he's scheduled to report for duty at the Lunar DataWatch base at Jules Verne. SOP for PKF personnel transfers of this kind goes this way:

"Gutierrez isn't important enough to come in via semiballistic. In a way that's unfortunate; he'd probably be alone, or with one other passenger at most, and it'd make taking his place a lot easier." Trent shrugged. "Win a few, lose a few. At any rate, he's scheduled to arrive at Tsiolkovsky with five other DataWatch Peaceforcers on the monorail from Luna City. From there they rolligon to Jules Verne.

"Gutierrez is ideal for several reasons. He's American, as I am. He speaks French with an accent, as I do. Slightly different accent, but it's unlikely the PKF at Verne will know that. He has a radio packet inskin, as I do. It's not the same model, but they'd have to do a complete workup on me to show that conclusively, and if they get that suspicious I'm blown anyhow. He's new to Luna, new to the PKF. Best data I have on him says the only other Peaceforcers he's likely to know on the entire planet are the ones in the rolligon with him when he leaves Zvezdagrad."

Trent had found himself instantly at ease with Yevgeni Sergei Korimok; the tall pale loonie was pure Syndic, professional and detached where the work was concerned. "Therefore," Korimok said, in a high quiet voice that seemed perfectly in keeping with his demeanor, "the Peaceforcers in the rolligon with 'Sieur Gutierrez must not reach Jules Verne."

"Now how the slithy hell are we going to do that," said Lan softly, leaning across the table to stare at Trent, "without killing them?"

Trent stared through the gloom at the boy. "I have bodies coming to stand in for the Peaceforcers who'll be on the rolligon. We've got good med records on the Peaceforcers who'll be with Gutierrez; the biosculptor who did me agreed to take five corpses, men who died of natural causes, and do dental work on them so they'll match the dental records of the five

Peaceforcers coming in with Gutierrez. We have two more corpses, a man and a woman, to take the place of whoever ends up driving the rolligon. There's no way to make a good guess about that; any of literally dozens of Peaceforcers could draw that particular duty, male or female. There aren't many female PKF at Jules Verne, only about ten percent of the total complement, but it's a possibility to plan for. Whether it's a man or a woman driving the rolligon we have a body to substitute. We won't have that person's dental records, but if we sufficiently damage the body we substitute for the driver then we won't need them."

Korimok nodded slowly. "So this gets you in, yes?"

"Yes."

It was Callia who said, "How, then, are you going to get *out*?"

Trent told them.

There was a hushed silence when he was finished.

Lan said, "That's crazy. You're just going to get yourself killed."

"Maybe."

Callia stared at Trent. "Trent, he's right."

"It's a risk," Trent agreed. "But not an impossible one."

Yevgeni Sergei smiled thinly. "A problem with so many young people, I have seen. This desire to be a hero."

"A hero," said Trent, "is someone who knows when to run away."

Everybody was staring at Trent now, absolutely everybody in the room.

"I," Trent proclaimed, "am a hero."

Three bodies arrived in stasis fields the next morning.

In the hills to the west of Jules Verne, Trent sat alone in Nathan Dark Clouds' chameleon. He had parked the chameleon just north and above the ravine where the Peaceforcer rolligons passed on their way to the DataWatch base at Jules Verne.

Six hours. At 10:12 A.M. Capitol City time a single rolligon crept through the Lunar night, twenty meters beneath Trent and forty away, headlamps sending quarter-million-candle-power beams of pure white light out into the Lunar night.

Trent sat almost motionless, breathing deeply and very slowly.

Part of him watched.

Most of him was elsewhere.

Johnny Johnny was almost gone; Trent had very little impression left of his Image as something separate from himself. Johnny Johnny's voice came less frequently now, as Trent assimilated the program that had once been his Image. There was no sadness in it, for it was a completion, not an ending. The person who took shape in the darkness, in a place as remote as possible from the scouring storm of data that Players call the Crystal Wind, was far greater than the sum of his parts.

At 12:20 exactly a caravan of four rolligons passed. At 12:36 another rolligon passed, and then nothing until 3:07, when a pair came by together.

At four o'clock that afternoon the man who had once been Trent, and once been Johnny Johnny, turned the engine on and headed back to Jackson Town.

The mass driver at Jackson Town stretches three and a half kilometers in a series of superconducting magnets spaced consecutively further apart. The separation at the catapult head is only forty meters; at the far end it has stretched to seventy-five. Lunar orbital velocity is only 1.6 kilometers per second, but even so loads boosted from Jackson Town must undergo upward of one hundred gravities acceleration in the course of launch.

Trent spent most of December 22, the Saturday morning before Christmas, in the control booth from which the Jackson Town catapult was run, watching as loads were boosted into orbit. The booth was small, just barely large enough for Trent, Yevgeni, and the woman running the mass driver.

Trent was not introduced to the woman, a small Asian woman with a blue-silver skin dye and pale gold hair who was so delicate that if it had not been for her shortness—about 165 centimeters—Trent might have pegged her for a loonie.

He watched her work for several hours without interfering. He watched carefully, very carefully, recording into his inskin all the while.

Yevgeni remarked, dryly, that Trent was acting as though his life depended on understanding how the catapult was run.

Trent did not reply.

The work was reasonably straightforward on her end. A group of men in scalesuits, without any sort of heavy moving equipment, would load a single capsule at the catapult head, placing the capsule in a cradlelike contraption that looked like half of an egg shell. The egg shell sat some thirty meters back from the first magnet, and was completely open at the end facing the first magnet. Trent watched better than a dozen launches, and they never varied. The egg shell was attached to a sixty-meter-long maglev rail, and each launch began with the egg lifting about twenty centimeters above the rail, a lift that was just barely visible from the control booth, and then accelerating toward the first ring. At the end of sixty meters the egg shell slammed into a pair of long vertical bars which prevented it, but not its load, from continuing any further. The capsule continued on into the first magnet, moving so quickly now that Trent could barely see it—

—and literally vanished as the magnets grabbed it at a hundred gravities.

After fourteen consecutive launches the crew broke for lunch. The Asian woman did not even get out of her chair; she simply blinked once, took her traceset off, and smiled at Trent. Her voice surprised him; it reminded him instantly, both in sound and choice of words, of Jodi Jodi. "What do you think? Yev says you're a webdancer, you could do what I do. Want a job?"

Trent shook his head and smiled back at her. "Forgive me, but just what do you do?"

"Oh." She looked startled. "I guess it's not very obvious from watching me sit there like a juice junkie? I monitor. Before every launch I run diagnostics and do a go–nogo for every ring on the entire catapult, then the same thing for the maglev rail the swatter runs on, then for the release mech on the swatter itself."

"The swatter is the egg-shaped thing?"

"Yes. That's basically what it does, you see. Sort of swats the load so that it's moving even and steady when the first ring grabs it. I can abort the launch at any time up to the point where the first ring grabs the load. After that it's gone."

"How long have you been on the job?"

"Two years, a couple months."

"Ever had to abort a launch?"

"I delay launches maybe one every six weeks or so, because

the superconductor fields are fluctuating, the swatter rode rough on the prior launch, a couple other reasons. I only had to attempt an abort after the swatter started moving one time. We lost power on a six-hundred-meter section of the catapult." She shrugged. "Didn't catch it in time. You know what the odds are against a load taking out a ring that's maybe five meters wide? When the rings are separated by an average of sixty meters?"

"Eight point five percent."

The woman glanced sharply at Trent. "We ended up on the short end of the stick. Lost a ring."

Trent nodded. "What would happen if you tried to launch something without using the swatter?"

"You mean a free load?"

"I suppose that's what I mean."

The woman blinked, looked interested for the first time. "Good question. I've never heard of anyone trying it; catapult design is pretty standardized aside from things like length and boost. I think you'd lose the load. And maybe part of the catapult as well. The load needs to be kept stable in the early part of the launch; that's the place where you're likeliest to have enough wobble that you'd lose it. It's more important on the midget here than it is on longer catapults," she added. "Over at the Luna City catapult you're only pulling three gees, and a miscalc early on probably wouldn't take the catapult down. Even at the Verne catapult your top boost is only around nine or ten gees. Not much danger of knocking out one of the catapult rings with a missed load. Here it's something to watch for."

Trent nodded. "If you were going to launch a free load, how would you go about it?"

"I wouldn't. It's a stupid idea."

"So people keep telling me. But suppose you couldn't use the swatter and you had to."

"Well . . ." The woman hesitated, obviously reluctant. "It's still a stupid idea; I'd wait until the swatter was repaired. But if I had to, I'd rig something to bounce the load, hmm . . ." She paused. "A single superconducting ring is about twenty-five meters in diameter. I'd want to get the load at least fifteen meters above the ground, maybe five meters in front of the first ring, and then cycle the catapult while the load was still rising. The load would probably crash, but the catapult would survive. I think."

Elsewhere on Luna that Saturday, a Peaceforcer webdancer named Benny Gutierrez arrived at Luna City.

There was a message waiting for Trent at the hotel when he returned.

> *Passage arranged for January 4, 9:00 A.M. to 4 P.M.; the SpaceFarer ship* Vatsayama.
> *Good luck.*
> *Felix K'Hin.*

On Monday, Christmas Eve, Lan and Callia went into Jackson Town for midnight mass. The Temples of Eris were an outgrowth of Christianity, and though the birth of Jesus Christ was not the primary religious observance of the Temples, it was still important. Yevgeni went to bed early, and Trent sat alone in his hotel room, letting the Crystal Wind pour through him, retaining what data called attention to itself, letting the rest pass by.

With a portion of his attention he composed a short letter for Denice.

> *Dear Denice,*
>
> *You will know, by the time you receive this, if the job I am about to attempt has succeeded. The letter will take a while to reach you, for it is going to be sent Federal Express and hand-delivered; I have been away from Earth's InfoNet long enough now that I cannot be sure that any of my old mail accounts are still secure from the DataWatch. Now that the PKF knows that I am alive it's not safe for me to try calling you again.*
>
> *If you and I are both still here in February, perhaps we can try again. Luna won't work now, not even Free Luna, but Mars or one of the Belt CityStates are still possibilities. I'm sorry that I have to do this—I know it will be harder for you no matter how it turns out—but I do have to do it. No choice.*
>
> *None.*
> *I think of you often.*
> *No.*

Make that constantly.
I do love you.

—Trent

Just after two o'clock, early on the morning of December twenty-fifth, there was a knock on Trent's door.

Trent sat on the bed, cross-legged in the dark. "Come in."

The lights came up as Lan entered, still dressed in the dove-gray suit he had worn to Temple, and sat carefully, back straight, at the foot of Trent's bed. His hair had been styled, swept straight back from his face and tied in the neatest ponytail Trent had seen on Lan since he had known the boy.

He held a green-bowed, gold-foil-wrapped present in both hands.

"Merry Christmas, Trent."

"Merry Christmas, Lan."

"I brought you a present."

Trent nodded. "I see. I don't have one for you."

"I didn't think you would." He handed the box to Trent, and Trent turned it over in his hands. "Go ahead and open it."

Trent untied the emerald bow and unwrapped the foil from the box without tearing it. The box itself, of hand-carved red-wood, was about sixty centimeters long, twenty wide and twenty deep. It was hinged, with a small silver stud which Trent pressed to open it. The redwood box was inlaid with black velvet, and on the velvet lining sat a small pistol completely unlike anything Trent had ever seen before. Trent removed it and looked it over with clinical curiosity. It was small enough to be used as a hideaway, but the barrel's aperture was ridiculously small, smaller than that of a pellet gun. The barrel itself was extremely thick, about three times the size of a .22 revolver. He placed it back in the box and said, "Thank you very much, Lan. What is it?"

The boy grinned at Trent. "Hideaway for either pressurized or unpressurized environments. It's basically a small mass driver, a rail gun crammed into a twelve-centimeter barrel. It's only .15 caliber, but at top boost the pellet develops four thousand meters per second velocity leaving the barrel. You can drop the boost for target shooting, getting used to the gun, and then kick it up for serious work. At top boost you can knock over a PKF Elite who's running toward you. You probably won't kill him, but that's almost impossible anyhow." Lan paused. "Unless you throw him off a space-scraper."

Trent closed the box, put it on the end table by the bed. "He fell," said Trent evenly.

Lan sighed. "I know," he said after a moment. "I saw the Peaceforcer recording of it. But seeing they're claiming you killed him, you might as well take credit for it."

"Thank you for the gun, Lan. I appreciate the thought behind it."

"But not the gift itself." Lan closed his eyes briefly, sat utterly still for a moment in the pale gray suit. He opened his eyes again. "Trent?"

"Yes?"

"Why do we keep not getting along? I'm trying to like you."

The words were spoken with such complete honesty that for a moment Trent could not find the correct answer for the boy. "I know you are. . . . I have a friend, Lan, named Reverend Andy. He preaches at the Flushing Street Temple in New York. He told me once that the problem with the Claw isn't that they're not sincere, but that they're a part of the problem they're trying to solve. When the Unification War ended, Lan, the Peace Keeping Forces were *soldiers*. They weren't police, they weren't DataWatch, they weren't the secret service they've become today. The PKF Elite exists today, Lan, because the Claw and the Johnny Rebs and half a dozen other organizations like them *brought it into existence*."

Lan said abruptly, "Does Callia know you feel this way?"

"I doubt it. She knows I don't want any killing; it's one of the first things we talked about. Beyond that, no, I haven't talked to her much."

"I've seen you watching her," said Lan. He looked straight at Trent. "If you wanted to sleep with her, she would."

"I thought so."

"You do want to?"

Trent said simply, "Yes."

Lan nodded very deliberately, thinking. "Then why don't you ask her?"

"Because of a question I don't know the answer to."

"What's the question?"

"Lan, she's dedicated. To the Claw, to the overthrow of the Unification."

Lan nodded again. "So?"

"Do you think she would sleep with me because she wanted to, or because she thought it was the correct thing to do to keep me focused on the work?"

"Callia," said Lan simply, "always does what's correct."

Trent shook his head. "Sometimes that's not the correct thing to do. I—find her very attractive. In several ways. But I refuse to be a part of her job. I'd sleep with her if it was what she wanted for herself. But I think she's forgotten how to think about herself. And that I don't find attractive. It's scary."

Lan looked down at the bed, at the expanse of bed cover that stretched between them. "You're a very judgmental person, Trent. I really don't like it very much."

"All that I've said to you is that killing is wrong. How does this offend you?"

"Trent, sometimes it's *not* wrong," Lan said sincerely. "Sometimes it's the best thing you can do. Someone—I can't tell you her name, but she's very important in the Claw—she took Callia and me in when we were young, after our mother died and our dad got taken into Public Labor. Callia wanted to join the Johnny Rebs—it's a lot more popular in America than the Claw—but this person recruited us into the Claw instead. Trent, she taught us a lot, that we're responsible for both what we do and what we *don't* do. One of the things she taught us was that an ideal that's worth dying for is worth killing for. When Sarah Almundsen wrote the Statement of Principles she couldn't have envisioned the Unification turning into what it is today: the Public Labor work camps, the PKF firing squads. If she was alive today, Trent, she'd be with us. If you credit her with the Unification then you must also credit her with the deaths that followed from it; she killed more people than any other single human in all of history. And Sarah Almundsen's a hero, Trent. I really believe that."

Trent took a very slow breath, held it, exhaled. He sat looking at Lan Sierran, without speaking, simply looking.

Lan waited.

"You and your sister," Trent whispered, "wandered out into the world, two nice young people without a thought in your heads. And somebody whose name you won't tell me took you and filled you with eloquent, nicely dressed ideas that translate into actions as horrifying and as evil as anything the Unification has ever done. Lan, killing is *wrong*. It's *always* wrong."

Lan Sierran bit his lip. "I knew," he said after a moment, "that you were a thief. I knew that before we left Earth. But I knew you killed a Peaceforcer Elite, I knew the Peaceforcers were saying you'd tried to kill people at Spacebase One."

Trent shook his head. "Lan, I didn't. I didn't kill anyone. I didn't try to."

"I believe you. I hoped," said Lan slowly, seriously, "that you would be different. More committed. And it turns out," he said, with what he plainly considered a most telling point, "that you're just a common thief after all."

Trent stared at the boy for a moment with very real offense, held back the reflexive anger with genuine effort. "I," he said with icy self-control, "am a *brilliant* thief."

· 11 ·

To die for an idea is to place a pretty high price upon conjecture.

—Anatole France
La Révolte des anges, 1914 Gregorian

The next morning when Trent rose to go on the stakeout again, Lan was already awake and dressed, waiting for him.

"I want to go with you."

"Suit yourself," said Trent shortly. "You won't like it."

They sat in the nearly complete darkness, from the moment when Trent turned the engines off at just before 10:00 A.M., until about 10:10.

Lan said, "You just—sit here and watch rolligons go by?"

"And crawlers. About one crawler for every eight rolligons."

"I'm bored."

"Read a book. Or take a nap."

Lan turned on his handheld, and the holofield sprang into existence just below the level of the chameleon's front viewscreen. Trent did not ask Lan what he was reading, and Lan did not volunteer the information. Just before 11:00 a single rolligon ghosted through the pass beneath them; Trent did not think Lan noticed.

About 11:15 Lan put his handheld aside. He did not turn it off. "I'm bored."

"Take a nap."

Lan, sleeping, took up three quarters of the chameleon's bench seat. He was a light sleeper, shifting positions every few minutes. Trent found it almost impossible to attain the state of reverie which had marked his earlier stakeouts. Even without running the data from his optic nerve through his inskin the glare from the handheld's holofield was bright enough that Trent could see the entire interior of the chameleon without difficulty.

Trent gazed at Lan with a complete lack of expression. Lan's head rested against the glassite of the side window and his feet were in the well that was intended for Trent's feet. In sleepy attempts to get comfortable, Lan kicked Trent in the shins repeatedly. Trent finally propped his feet up on an empty spot on the instrument panel, and leaned back against the left-hand sidewall of the crawler, arms crossed over his chest. On Earth it would have been an impossible position; even in one-sixth gee it was not comfortable.

Noon.

At 1:22 a Peaceforcer rolligon slowly moved along the bottom of the gully, forty meters away from the chameleon. The time flickered into Trent's awareness without any conscious thought on his part; two hours, twenty-eight minutes since the last one. Since beginning the stakeout Trent had waited as long as three hours and as little as twenty minutes between Peaceforcer rolligons.

He watched the rolligon disappear into the distance.

Suddenly he couldn't take any more. His shins were sore where Lan had kicked them and even in one-sixth gee his buttocks were going numb from the position he was sitting in.

"Lan." Trent reached over and shook the boy's shoulder. "Lan, wake up."

Lan's eyes flickered open for an instant and then closed again. He didn't move a centimeter.

"Wake up," Trent repeated. He dropped his feet down to where they belonged. He felt his heel strike Lan's shin and smiled. He thought about kicking Lan again just to get even.

Instead he lifted Lan's legs and shoved them over onto Lan's side of the cab.

Lan's eyes opened and stayed open. He glared at Trent. "What are you doing?"

"This chameleon," Trent said, "isn't big enough for you to stretch out like that. If I was a midget maybe you could stretch out, but I'm not a midget. Stay on your own side."

Lan sat up straighter and pulled his right knee up to his chest. He rubbed his shin. "You kicked me in the shin and you woke me up from a good dream," he said.

"I'm really sorry about that."

"I was having this great dream about a three-armed boy."

"A three-armed boy?"

"Yeah." Lan turned his head to meet Trent's eyes. Even sitting up and on his own side of the cab, there was barely a hundred centimeters separating them. Trent could smell the scent of the soap Lan had showered with that morning. "A great dream."

Trent was not at all certain he wanted to know. "About?"

Lan smiled slightly. "What would you dream about doing with a three-armed boy?"

Trent stared at him blankly. "I don't think I'd dream of doing anything with a three-armed boy."

Lan held Trent's gaze for an instant longer, then looked away. "Too bad. Would you dream of doing anything with a two-armed boy?"

Trent didn't answer.

The headlights of a Peaceforcer rolligon appeared in the distance and Trent sat forward, peering through the viewscreen. "Damn. Damn the evil bastards."

"What's the matter?" Lan shifted slightly, leaning forward to look at the rolligon. His shoulder brushed Trent's.

"A rolligon went by five minutes ago. Now here's another one. Why can't these people be regular? Their whole world is regimented, and the only time I ever want them to do something by the clock they come bopping along whenever they feel like it." Trent settled back in his seat. "You can't trust Peaceforcers to do anything right."

Lan did not reply. Trent, sitting motionless in the gloom and watching the rolligon, could feel Lan watching him. When the rolligon's headlights had finally faded into the Lunar dust, he turned his head toward Lan, but the boy had already looked away.

Lan pulled his legs up, sitting tailor fashion and, Trent noted, taking up more than his half of the seat again. The boy reached behind his head and untied the scarlet-black ribbon that held back his long brown hair. Lan ran his fingers through the pale brown strands of his hair, not noticeably neatening them, and retied the ribbon.

Trent decided that a two-person chameleon wasn't big enough for two people.

"I'm bored," Lan announced for the third time. He looked at Trent expectantly.

Trent dropped his leg back into the well and turned to face Lan. "What do you expect me to do about it?"

Lan sighed. "You can't think of anything to do?"

"You didn't have to come today, Lan." Trent shifted uncomfortably in his seat. "You could have stayed at the hotel. That would have been a *good* idea."

The boy reached out a hand and stroked the material of Trent's shirt with one finger. The touch was so soft Trent couldn't actually feel it. Lan grinned at him. "I can think of something to do." Lan's hand slipped down, curling around the side of Trent's waist. He was so close Trent could feel his breath as he spoke. "I can think of lots of things to do."

Lan leaned forward and Trent put one hand in the center of his chest and pushed him away. They stared at each other.

"I don't think so," Trent said.

Lan relaxed and the distance between them widened to an enormous twenty-five centimeters. "No?" he said.

"No."

"Oh, well." Lan didn't seem particularly hurt or offended. The boy shifted over to his own side of the bench seat and said, "I've got another good idea then."

"What's that?" Trent asked warily.

"Have you ever blown anything up?"

"No. Well, yes. Two safes. To open them."

"I brought some blasting plastic with me. Let's ambush the next rolligon and slaughter the Peaceforcers in it."

Trent stared at Lan. "You're as crazy as a bird. Killing is wr—"

"Wrong," Lan chimed in. "I've heard you say that. A lot. But if we don't kill them now we just have to kill them later."

"You don't just *have* to kill anyone. Besides, no one is supposed to know we're here. You think killing a truckload of Peaceforcers is going to go unnoticed?"

"Maybe," Lan said hopefully. And after a moment, "Are you sure you don't want to fool around?"

There was a short silence.

"I'd rather not," Trent finally said.

"Why not?"

Trent tried to think up a good answer. "Well," he said, "I don't habitually sleep with boys."

"Oh? You don't *habitually* do it. Does that mean you do it sometimes?"

"Well, no," Trent said. "I don't do it at all." He paused. "Actually, I've slept with Jimmy Ramirez, a friend of mine on Earth."

Lan looked optimistic. "Really?"

"But we *slept.* I mean, that was all. It was cold and there was no heat. And only one bed; the Temple Dragons never had enough of anything."

Lan leaned back on his side of the seat. "You don't kill people and you don't have sex with boys." He examined Trent curiously. "Honestly, you're the craziest thing I ever saw."

Trent said, "You mean you never saw one of those guys who ties up balloons into the shapes of animals?"

Two more bodies arrived that evening.

Callia Sierran was conspicuously silent to Trent for the next three days. The fourth morning was December the 30th, with only one day remaining in the year, only three days before the boost itself was set to go. Callia was awake and dressed, waiting patiently for Trent in the main room when Trent got up. Trent ignored her, made a thermos of coffee and fried two eggs. He toasted bread while frying the eggs, put mayonnaise on one piece of toast and mustard on the other, and waited.

Callia sat motionlessly on the long couch in the main room, watching Trent. She wore modest red fatigues, zipped all the way to her collarbone. Her maser was strapped to her thigh, and for an instant the image bothered Trent. Then it swarmed up out of memory: Domino, standing in the airlock at Bessel City, had been dressed just like that, down to the quick-draw holster on her thigh.

When the eggs were done he put one egg on top of the mayonnaise, a slice of cheese on top of that, the second egg on top of the cheese, and the mustard-covered piece of toast on top of that. He sliced the sandwich diagonally and handed half of it to Callia without asking her if she wanted it.

"Come on," he said wearily. "Let's go."

Callia was silent on the way down to the hotel's garage, eating her half of the egg sandwich. She was silent while the chameleon cycled through the garage's airlock, silent as Trent drove. She said nothing all the way out to the spot where Trent parked the chameleon and turned off the engine.

It was five minutes before 10:00 A.M.

Sitting inside the chameleon with no artificial sound but the gentle murmur of the airplant, Trent was intensely aware of Callia on the long bench seat next to him. He could hear her breathing; with some concentration, filtering out the sounds of his own body, he could hear her heartbeat.

Noon came and went without a single Peaceforcer vehicle passing them.

"Most of the men I have ever known," said Callia, "found silence very uncomfortable."

Trent sat comfortably in the dark silence without replying.

Over half an hour passed before she spoke again. Trent could almost hear the smile in her voice. "I'm not going to outwait you, am I?"

"Are you trying to?"

"Not any more. I want to talk to you, Trent."

"Feel free."

"How did we get out here?"

"I drove us. In the chameleon. You were there the whole way."

"That's not what I mean."

"Then I don't know what you do mean."

"It's night, Trent. The terrain is practically invisible. You didn't use the headlamps all the way out here. You didn't yesterday, when Lan went with you."

"What do you think the PKF would do, Callia, if they looked down from one of their Orbital Eyes and saw some fool driving out every day to park and watch PKF rolligons wander by?"

"That's clear enough. What I don't understand is how you could see to drive without lights."

"I have this great inskin."

"Trent."

Trent paused, thinking. "All right. You know anything about image processing?"

"A bit. Like what a night scope does for snipers?"

"Interesting choice of analogy," Trent said quietly. "But essentially correct. I can do something very similar with my inskin."

"I've known two Players before you, Trent. I've never even *heard* of someone being able to do something like this."

Trent shrugged. "It's a new model inskin. A nerve net with fairly remarkable processing power. It's only been on the market for about half a year."

"Are you really a genie?"

"Yes."

". . . you're not—very human—in an awful lot of ways, Trent."

"Humanity," said Trent, "is overrated. One of my friends is a replicant AI. Another's a genie. Another's a completely normal human who's studying to become a lawyer. Ask me which one I trust most."

"That's almost not what I mean. You are about to hurt the Peaceforcers worse than I think they've ever been hurt before, and I'm not sure why you're doing it."

"I already had that conversation with—a cranky old woman. She decided I was a man of virtue and good motives."

"Trent, why are you here?"

Trent did not answer her for a while, thinking. Finally he said, "Do you really need to know?"

"Not really." She was silent a beat, then said, "You're confusing Lan."

Trent laughed aloud. "I don't think so. I think Lan knows *exactly* what he wants."

"You said no to him."

"Yes."

"Why?"

"I prefer girls."

"Hmm." Trent could hear her shifting position on the long bench next to him. "You couldn't tell it by me."

"Insulted?"

"A little, perhaps," she said softly. "Not very. Are you in love?"

"In love? I don't know. . . . Yes. A girl I may not ever see again."

"You're probably going to die at Verne."

"Good chance of it."

"Do you *want* to survive the boost?"

"That's a stupid question."

"Is it? I haven't known you very long, Trent. The only other person I ever knew like you got to be a hero about a month after he started acting the way you're acting right now."

"I'm a little tired, Callia. That's all."

He heard the long slow exhalation of her breath. "Have you learned anything out here, watching the Peaceforcers?"

"A couple things. There's one daily rolligon from Tsiolkovsky, comes by every afternoon between one and two o'clock, usually closer to one than two. It's never come earlier than 1:08, never later than 1:56. Aside from that one rolligon there's no regularity to the traffic that I've been able to determine; I presume that one regularly scheduled rolligon heads back to Tsiolkovsky sometime later at night. I've learned that Lan has no patience and that you do."

"Trent?"

"Yes?"

"Have you ever made love in a crawler?"

"No. I watched a man die, sitting where you are right now. This was his crawler. It was a bitch to get the blood off the seat." Trent paused. "It's been a bitch of a year."

"I'm sure." He heard the rustle of her clothing, of the woman undressing in the dark.

Trent said quietly, "Do you know what you're doing?"

"I am reminding you," said Callia Sierran, "why you want to survive this boost."

The last two bodies arrived that evening.

· 12 ·

On January 2, 2070, the night before they were scheduled to ambush the Peaceforcer rolligon carrying Benny Gutierrez, Lan and Callia went to Jackson Town, to pray at the Temple. Trent did not go, nor Korimok. They sat together in the main room, in a comfortable silence. Korimok was playing a sensable, Trent did not know by whom, the overlarge sensablist's traceset resting lightly on his temples. His eyes were half open and his lips were moving whenever the sensable's viewpoint character spoke. From the half-spoken words which Trent heard from Korimok, he did not think the sensable was in either English or French.

Trent sat on a couch looking out the window.

The fact that there was a window at all, that the rooms they were staying in were above ground, screamed "tourist." Loonies do not care what things are like outside; whether it's night or day does not matter to them. There's never any air and it is always either far too hot or far too cold. When the sun is in the sky the landscape is white and gray, as dull and boring as Earth's Antarctic deserts; when the sun is not in the sky the landscape is essentially invisible.

It was nighttime still on the far side; but the two-week night was nearly over, and before eight hours were up the sun would rise. Now nothing but the starshine illuminated the plain which surrounded Jackson Town and the hills which rose away from it.

It was as bright as daylight to Trent. He played with the data from his optic nerve, slowly building up, one second's image on top of another, an image of the Lunar landscape outside the window that was of photographic quality. At any given moment the scattered starlight was nearly indiscernible; over the space of minutes the landscape slowly evolved into a glaringly bright panorama which stretched clear to the horizon.

Only a small part of Trent watched Yevgeni; another small portion processed the image of the Lunar desert.

Most of him was inundated by the Crystal Wind.

The preacher is a middle-aged man with a pot belly, pounding on the pulpit as he reads from the Bible. "Hath we not all one father? Hath not one God created us? Why do we deal treacherously every man against his brother, by profaning the covenant of our father?"

Text, no video, no sound: Jerusalem (AP)—Shoichiro Okaya, *the text says,* Japan's ambassador to the government of Greater Israel, was killed today when a car bomb blew up outside a Palestinian college 'Sieur Okaya was visiting.

A woman wails in the back of Trent's skull, wailing as the holocams pan around the devastation at Tunis airport, where a semiballistic has come down out of control and smashed into an aircraft that was taking off. Mahliya Kutura sings to Trent, from a live concert in China, sings to him of her despair, of her love. The Unification Council approves construction of a warship tentatively called the Unity; *at an estimated cost of nearly eight billion Credit Units, it will be the single most expensive spacecraft ever built. A woman in India drowns herself and her three children. A man in Canada is killed when the world's largest collection of Wagner memorabilia falls on him; it makes the late edition of the* Electronic Times.

There was movement around Trent; Yevgeni rising, the gentle whisper of doors opening and closing.

A squad of PKF Elite raid and burn to the ground an ideolog camp at Kochovskaya, Russia. In Oakland, California, in Occupied America, a suit is filed in California's Superior Court to prevent a suspected genie from playing in the WFL System Bowl until he has undergone a test to verify that he is not a genie. The captain of a tuna boat reports seeing, for the first time in over five years, a large school of dolphins on the open sea, two hundred kilometers west and south of Hawaii; his report is widely discounted. The Loos Microlectrics Corporation of Mexico City reports the largest first-year revenues of any start-up corporation in over two decades. Douglass Ripper, Jr., Unification Councilor for New York Metro, submits a bill to the Unification Council calling for a reduction of PKF forces in Occupied America amounting to nearly one quarter of the total PKF presence in Occupied America.

Trent was distantly aware of Lan's presence, but it did not draw him away from his immersion in the Crystal Wind until Lan said quietly, almost hesitantly, "Trent?"

From a great distance, Trent said, "Yes?"

"You know," Lan said quietly, "sometimes I sleep with people who slept with Callia. They all say I'm better than she is."

Trent opened his eyes slightly. The room's lights had been turned off; to Lan it must have seemed that he stood in very nearly complete darkness. To Trent's dark-adapted genie eyes, without even employing the image processing his inskin gave him access to, the boy was a barely visible shape standing in the doorway to the bedroom he shared with Callia.

Trent said simply, "I believe you."

"I'm probably never going to see you again after tomorrow."

The boy's image flared slowly, as though a bright light were coming up; it was not something Trent had consciously decided to do. "In the real world, Lan, people, even good friends . . . part. Sometimes you see them again, sometimes you don't."

Lan said with such utter certainty that Trent was chilled, "I'll never see you again."

"I'm sorry, then. I like you."

"I'm sorry, too. Good night, Trent." Trent sat watching the boy; Lan started to turn away and then stopped and did not move at all, just stood in the doorway with the unreal starlight reflecting off the planes of his face.

"Trent?" he said at last.

"Yes?"

The boy said awkwardly, "I really do like you."

"Go to bed, Lan."

"Trent . . . I'm cold."

"Lan, it's not . . ." Trent's voice trailed off, remembering Jimmy Ramirez's shocked reaction on the very cold night Trent had asked to sleep with him, and finally he said softly, "All right. Go get a blanket and come over here."

Lan was back quickly with a light blanket. He sat down on the couch next to Trent, cuddled up against him. Lan was shivering and it was a long time before he stopped; Trent sat quietly with the boy in his arms, waiting while Lan dropped off, watching the impossible silver starlight while Lan slept.

The preacher has reached a fine height of screaming euphoria, has built to a shrieking, pulpit-pounding finale. "And Behold, the Lord said to Malachi, I will send my messenger, and he shall prepare the way before me: and the Lord, whom ye seek, shall suddenly come to his temple, even the messenger of the covenant, whom ye delight in: behold, he shall come, saith the Lord of Hosts! But who may abide the day of his coming? And who shall stand when he appeareth?"

· 13 ·

In the early morning hours of January 3, 2070, a pair of chameleon crawlers and a single very expensive chameleon rolligon pulled out of the hotel garage outside of Jackson Town, and set off across the sunlit Lunar surface.

Behind them, in the hotel, Trent had turned off the radio packet InfoNet service; if things went well, two Peaceforcers with radio packet inskins would be held prisoner in those rooms for two or three days, and Trent didn't want them making calls.

He had left Lan's gift, the gun, in Callia and Lan's bedroom.

In the rolligon as they left that morning were a loonie and a crazy woman and seven bodies; in the lead chameleon there was a nice young ideolog, and in the chameleon at the tail of the procession was a man wearing a Peaceforcer uniform and a Peaceforcer's face.

By 9:00 A.M., better than four hours before Benny Gutierrez was due to drive by, they were in place.

The elongated shadows of early morning were scheduled to last all day. It made the hilly landscape around the gorge eerie; the long, jutting spires of rock casting long sweeping shadows behind them.

Trent did not like the scalesuit he wore.

He sat completely unmoving in the shade, out of the broiling sun, on the shady side of a large boulder that would keep him from the view of the approaching Peaceforcer rolligon until the rolligon was immediately beneath him. He was on the far side of the crevasse from Callia and Lan and Yevgeni S. Korimok; the rolligon would pass between them.

Trent found that he had grown used to soft pressure suits; the stiff scalesuit, its front blackened as though by heat damage, had already rubbed him raw at the back of his neck, and was starting in on his thighs. The inside pocket where his handheld was stored pressed against Trent's hip; the spot where the handheld pressed was going numb.

The fadeaway bomb sat at his feet. It was an improvement

on the device he had used at Luna City, and had cost him better than twenty times as much as that small device. The bomb was oval, about the size of a football; one surface was completely flat. If the bomb worked correctly, as the prototype had, it would connect itself to the surface of the Peaceforcer rolligon by a superconducting magnet, punch a sixty-centimeter-long spike down through the stiff outer wall of the rolligon, and, through the spike, spray fadeaway at high pressure across the interior of the rolligon. Assuming they were wearing their suits with the helmets off—standard PKF operating procedure—the fadeaway would get them all.

The chill of the frozen stones Trent sat upon was reaching up through the scalesuit, despite the best efforts of the scalesuit to keep Trent warm. The softsuit Nathan had bought Trent, which he had worn during his entire time on Luna, had kept him far warmer. Trent was completely hidden in the shadow of the boulder; there is no atmospheric scattering on Luna to prevent shadows from being completely black.

Radio silence was in force. He could not talk to Callia or Sergei, waiting in the chameleonized rolligon on the other side of the gorge, or Lan, in the crawler a quarter of a mile to the east.

The Peaceforcer rolligon came from the west, from Tsiolkovsky Crater. Trent's inskin placed the time at 1:14 P.M. when he first saw the approaching rolligon's headlights, almost invisible in the harsh sunlight. The scalesuit Trent wore was an exact duplicate of the ones the Peaceforcers themselves used, down to the PKF insignia on the breast; it was equipped to monitor both standard PKF com bands and emergency broadcast frequencies.

Complete silence on every band. Trent cycled up and down through the eight channels the scalesuit was capable of accessing; nothing at all. The PKF rolligon moved slowly forward, made its creeping way across the regolith. The vehicle faced directly into the low sun; their visibility would be terrible. Trent sat patiently, waited while the rolligon, painted in the black and silver of the United Nations Peace Keeping Force, grew large before him. Fifteen meters long, three wide, the rolligon had six huge unpressurized wheels that lifted dust up into the early sunlight, where it hung for long moments before beginning its descent back to the Lunar soil.

Trent set his scalesuit's radio for Channel Eight, emergency frequency for the PKF.

The nose of the rolligon was passing underneath Trent.

Trent picked up the fadeaway bomb, held it in one hand, and jumped.

His hiding place was just over ten meters above the surface of the crevasse, and the top of the rolligon was four and a half meters above that; he fell not quite six meters in one-sixth gee while the rolligon moved beneath him.

He landed unsteadily on the tail end of the rolligon with a thump which rocked the vehicle slightly. He scrambled for balance, hampered by servos that were slower than his own muscles, lunged forward at the last moment and landed belly down across the top of the rolligon, still holding the fadeaway bomb. He took the time to do it right, laid the bomb across the smooth metal of the rolligon's upper surface, and thumbed the pressure point that activated it.

The heat reached him through the insulating layers of the scalesuit. The surface of the rolligon glowed red over a half-meter-wide section. Trent had only an instant to realize what was happening; he had an instantaneous vision of the maser blast that had taken Nathan in the stomach, and in one convulsive leap got off the surface of the rolligon and fell tumbling the rest of the way to the bottom of the crevasse.

He sat up slowly.

The rolligon continued moving toward the east, not slowing at all. There was no sound at all on Channel Eight; Trent cycled through the rest of the PKF com bands.

Silence.

The rolligon crept slowly forward, maintaining an even speed, moving straight forward, not veering at all, not even when the road did.

Trent exhaled a breath he had not known he was holding, and bounced to his feet. He waved an arm toward the spot where the other three were waiting, and trotted forward to where the rolligon was trying to drive its way through the side of a hill.

T rent cycled through the rolligon's airlock, into pressure. In the forward cabin a young Peaceforcer, male, was slumped forward over the instrument panel. Trent turned the engine off and went back. In the rear passenger cabin there were exactly six Peaceforcers, and Trent had to suppress a quick wave of relief; the one thing he'd found no way at all to plan for had been an extra passenger being sent along in the rolligon at the last moment. The back cabin consisted of a pair of bench seats running down the long axis of the rolligon. The long spike through which the fadeaway had been sprayed hung straight down through the roof of the rolligon, still dripping very slightly. Three of the Peaceforcers were sitting on the seats in their scalesuits, restraining straps holding them upright. The other three were sprawled on the rear cabin's floor; one of those three, facedown in his scalesuit, holding a maser in his fist, had stayed awake long enough to get his scalesuit's helmet on; with his maser set to wide dispersion he had heated the roof of the rolligon until Trent had had to leap off.

Trent pulled him up with one hand, and stared into the very same face that looked back at him in the mirror these days.

Trent felt an unreasonable degree of pride in the man whose face he was wearing; to the unconscious Peaceforcer named Benny Gutierrez, Trent said, "Good try."

Trent heard the airlock cycle open behind him; Callia cycled through, bounced over to Trent and grabbed Gutierrez from him without waiting for Trent to release the Peaceforcer.

Trent picked up another Peaceforcer from the floor of the rolligon, dogged the man's helmet into place, and followed her.

There is no protection from fadeaway except to avoid it. Inside their rolligon Yevgeni wore his pressure suit with the gloves removed; he also wore a pair of plastiflesh gloves Trent had given him. In Trent's line of work they were useful because they left no fingerprints, but allowed tactile sensitivity nearly as good as bare skin.

They were also impermeable to fadeaway.

Yevgeni was undressing Peaceforcers and dressing corpses. Benny Gutierrez was propped up in a corner of the passenger cab; he was the only Peaceforcer who was not being stripped of his clothing and scalesuit.

Yevgeni checked the name patch on the outside of a scalesuit, compared it with the assignment papers found inside the unconscious Peaceforcer's coat. "Henri Charbonneau!" Yevgeni called out. Callia turned off the stasis field enclosing the seven forms, selected one of the corpses by an

ID tag on its toe, and without flinching, without any apparent distaste at all, pulled the nude form out, turned the stasis field back on, and pulled the corpse back to where Yevgeni was undressing PKF Officer Henri Charbonneau. Trent watched while the dead man's body was dressed and stuffed into Charbonneau's scalesuit. The entire procedure left him with an emotion he was not quite able to put a name to; he shook his head after a moment, rubbing the back of his neck against the damn uncomfortable rear seal of the scalesuit's helmet, and cycled back through the airlock to go get the rest of the bodies.

It took longer than Trent had hoped.

It took even longer than he had feared.

It was nearly two o'clock before they were done. Trent worked up a heavier sweat in those forty-five minutes than at any time since coming to Luna. The inside of his scalesuit hummed with the sound of the airplant struggling to cool and dehumidify the air Trent was breathing. At any moment Trent expected to see headlights coming from either the east or the west. By a quarter of two they had switched the corpses for the live Peaceforcers; Trent put the black and silver rolligon back in gear, pulled back from the side of the hill, and drove another quarter kilometer down the crevasse. He drove slowly; he had difficulty controlling the vehicle with the thick scalesuit gloves on, but the interior of the vehicle was coated with fadeaway, and he did not dare take them off. The corpse that had been substituted for the driver sat on the seat at his side.

Lan was waiting, sitting in his scalesuit atop a large boulder. He waved Trent to a stop, pointing to the place where he wanted the rolligon parked. Trent stopped the rolligon, left the motor running. He pulled the corpse into place in the driver's seat; the corpse resisted as all the corpses had resisted being handled, as though, in death, they fought a silent battle to retain some small shred of forgotten dignity.

Outside Trent went around to the back of the rolligon. Lan was there already, placing a small charge on the rear axle. He motioned Trent back, touched a stud on the charge and then bounced back himself. He had timed it closely; the charge went off soundlessly in the vacuum, with a sharp flash that came so quickly that the glassite in Trent's helmet could not darken in time to compensate. When the dots faded from his vision, the rear axle was snapped cleanly in half, and the entire rear third of the rolligon sagged backward.

Lan touched helmets with Trent. "You're supposed to be outside to find out what's wrong with this sucker. We blow it away through the front, demolish the driver so there's no way to ID him, burn up the rest of them pretty good. The artillery I'm using, there's no real way you'd survive if you were really standing back here when I hit the rolligon. Even so it's going to be tough. I want you to stand back a good twenty-five meters, right over there, so it'll look like the shock wave picked you up and threw you. It's going to knock you down even at twenty-five meters, but unless you catch shrapnel you're OK."

"Am I going to catch shrapnel?"

"No. I don't think so."

"All right."

Lan hesitated a moment, helmet still touching Trent's. "Callia said to tell you she'd pray for you."

"Tell her I said thank you. For everything. And Lan?"

"Yeah?" Even through two layers of scalesuit Trent could hear the nervous impatience in the boy's voice.

"Think about what I said." Trent could barely see Lan's features. "There's better ways to do things than by killing people who never harmed you."

Lan stared at Trent for a long moment. "You are," he said finally, "the smartest real *idiot* I've ever met."

"I like you too, Lan."

Lan snorted loudly enough for Trent to hear him, and took two long bouncing steps away. The boy froze after the second step, stood motionless for just an instant, then bounced back to Trent and touched helmets. "You're boring in bed, but you snuggle good. It's been real." He bounced away again before Trent could reply.

Trent walked back to the spot Lan had pointed out, stood in the Lunar sunshine, waiting. Nothing was happening; no movement, anywhere at all. After about ten minutes had passed Trent checked the time in his inskin and found it had only been ninety seconds since Lan had left him.

He found he was trembling slightly inside the scalesuit. *I'm standing here in death pressure,* Trent thought clearly, *twenty-*

*five meters from an explosion that's going to completely destroy
a Peaceforcer troop transport.*

This is crazy.

The universe blew up in his face.

· 14 ·

*Throughout the long nightmare he remains aware. The flesh
is unmoving, insensate. Eons tick away as he waits, nanosecond
upon nanosecond. One eyelid is half open; the other is entirely
shut. Through the half-open eye he sees vague forms moving
around him. He is unable to focus at all. The forms, he is sure,
are those of Lan and Callia; neither one comes anywhere near
Trent's unconscious form, not even to assure themselves he survived the explosion. Though he cannot see them clearly enough
to tell, Trent/Johnny Johnny knows that they are spraying artificially darkened Lunar dust everywhere either one of them has
stepped, and that they will walk back to where Nathan's
crawler and the rolligon full of kidnapped Peaceforcers await
them. The third chameleon, the one Lan drove out in, is rolling
away on autopilot from the supposed scene of the attack. That
portion of Trent which is aware right now has programmed that
autopilot; a cursory search of the area around the rolligon will
find the chameleon's tracks, and the Peaceforcers will follow it
for at least a day before catching it and finding it empty. With
any degree of luck at all, nobody will backtrack far enough to
find the place where the Peaceforcer rolligon was actually
stopped.*

Silence now.

A complete lack of motion.

*The scalesuit gets very hot. He is aware of this as he might be
aware of something happening to someone else entirely.*

Over two hours pass.

*There is a sudden glare of light, so intense and unwavering
that he ceases to pay attention to the information from his optic
nerve even before the scalesuit helmet darkens to protect the
flesh inside from the too-bright light. He waits in the electronic
nothingness, waits in the stasis of datastarve.*

Not quite an hour.

The insensate flesh is touched, moved, lifted.
He dwindles into the silence of datastarve.
Of complete and total nothing.

The sharp, stinging smell of ammonia roused him.

A voice spoke in French, something about how Trent felt. Trent blinked. "What?"

The Peaceforcer paused, spoke again in English, slowly. "How are you feeling?"

Trent looked around slowly. The edges of things were blurred. He was lying on the long bench seat in the back of a rolligon, taking up one entire bench. The rolligon bounced slightly as it moved. The Peaceforcer crouched next to him stared at him with a furrowed brow.

Trent said, "I'm not . . . I . . ."

The Peaceforcer said urgently, "*What happened?*"

It was no effort at all to make the world go away again.

It was just before 7:00 P.M., January 3.

Trent was more or less undressed, wearing nothing but his shorts, face to face with the first doctor he had ever met who looked like his conception of what a doctor should be.

"Look into the light, please. Don't blink."

Trent stared up into the small penlight the PKF doctor shone into his left eye. Doctor Grissom was visibly old, with wrinkles around his eyes and black hair streaked with silver. He grunted after a moment, and said gruffly to Trent, in French laced with a thick German accent, "We're going to do the right eye now, hold still." He held the light on the right eye for just a moment, clicked the penlight off and put it in his coat pocket. He glanced slightly to the side, to the holograph of Trent's skull which hung in midair next to Trent's skull.

There was a PKF captain standing at the door to the infirmary. The infirmary was not large; four beds, hospital equipment which Trent largely did not recognize. Only one door.

The glowpaint was pure white, harsh and officious.

The captain, a pair of armed junior PKF standing immediately behind him, had watched Doctor Grissom's examination of PKF Officer Benny Gutierrez with clear impatience.

Doctor Grissom asked Trent only one question in the

course of his examination, after running Trent through a full-body MRI slowscan. "What is this, with your knee?"

"What's what?"

"Scar tissue, recent. Your file shows no knee problems."

"I was skiing, on vacation. A medbot took care of it the same day. I guess that's why it's not in the file."

"Hmm. Looks like it's been injured twice?"

Trent shrugged. "Only once."

Doctor Grissom nodded thoughtfully, turned to the PKF captain. "He has a slight concussion, probably due to his inskin. Not serious. Also a large bruise on the back of his skull, also not serious."

"And a headache," said Trent.

"And a headache," the doctor agreed. He handed Trent a small glass of water with a pill. "Drink this, and then go with the nice captain." To the nice captain, Doctor Grissom said, "He sleeps here tonight, where I can keep an eye on him. The slowscan does not show any internal bleeding, but that may be meaningless."

The captain, who had not introduced himself to Trent, said stiffly, "Very well." To Trent he said, "Officer Gutierrez, please come with me."

"Can I get dressed first?"

The man had been turning away; he turned back in surprise. "Certainly. Be quick."

The uniform stank of stale sweat.

Trent followed the captain down a series of long underground corridors and up a long ramp, paying attention to the route he traveled, checking off what he saw against the map of the DataWatch base which he carried in his inskin. The infirmary was on Level Two, which was actually the first level beneath the surface of the regolith; Level One was the only level of the base which was above ground.

The corridors were full of bustling Peaceforcers. Trent saw perhaps forty people, mostly young, on his way to the briefing room. All were in PKF uniforms, either dress or combat fatigues. All were in a hurry. A very few of them had visible inskins; none of them had the characteristic stiff skin of PKF Elite. Most of them did not even glance at Trent as he walked through the corridors behind the captain, in front of the two armed guards.

The glowpaint throughout the entire base was white. Nowhere did Trent see the yellow glow of sunpaint.

After a three-minute walk they came to a point where the corridor widened slightly. Above closed double doors was the legend BRIEFING ROOM. On the map which floated in the back of his mind, Trent placed them: 146 meters south of the north airlock. The nameless captain stopped before the door to the briefing room, placed a palm flat against the doorpad, and marched through once the double doors had rolled up, not so much as glancing back to verify that Trent had followed him.

There was a long oval table made of something that resembled aged beechwood. Seven Peaceforcer officers in uniform and one Elite Sergeant were assembled around one half of the table; there was an empty chair on the side of the table where all the officers were seated and a single unoccupied chair on the other side of the table. Without being told Trent stopped behind the unoccupied chair facing the officers, came to attention and saluted. He held the salute for not quite five seconds, staring straight ahead, until a gentle female voice said, "At ease. Please sit down, Officer Gutierrez."

Trent did so, found a grand total of nine pairs of eyes staring back at him. The woman who had spoken to Trent, a mature, plain-featured woman whose age Trent could not have guessed, continued. "I am Colonel Brissois, Commanding Officer for the Verne Farside DataWatch. My apologies to you, young man, for what we are about to put you through. But it is necessary." Commander Brissois seemed uncertain for just a moment. "If you do not already know, Officer, your companions aboard the rolligon were all killed. You are the only survivor."

You are the only survivor. Trent was shakier than he had thought; the words struck him like a blow. For just an instant he was eleven years old again; he had watched Malko Kalharri die at the hands of an Elite cyborg and he had watched Suzanne Montignet kill herself, and in the midst of the riots as the Troubles began, had learned that everyone he had ever known as a child had died in nuclear flame.

He did not have to fake his reaction at all. "I'm sorry? What did you say?"

"Officer," Colonel Brissois said sharply, "control yourself. We have a great deal to get through and not a great deal of time in which to do it."

Trent stared down at the surface of the oval table. "I'm

sorry, Colonel. It's just—" He shook his head abruptly, looked up to meet her gaze, and found the Elite Sergeant studying him with a curiously detached expression. "I'm ready, Colonel."

Perhaps she smiled; the edges of her lips moved very slightly. Perhaps not. "Very good. Let's start from the beginning."

Trent said slowly, "We were . . . I would guess three hours from Tsiolkovsky. The rolligon . . . we thought it had broken down. There was a loud noise and the rolligon jerked to a stop. The rear end rode very low. I was sitting nearest the airlock, so Officer Deremè—he was driving—he asked me to go take a look and see what was wrong with the rear end. I—"

The Peaceforcer Elite interrupted. "Why didn't Officer Deremè call in at that point?"

"Sir?"

The Elite said patiently, "Why didn't Deremè call in to notify us that he was being delayed en route? It's standard procedure, Officer Gutierrez."

Trent had not known that. "Sir, I don't know."

The Elite nodded. "Go on."

"I sealed my helmet, cycled through and went around back. I remember thinking—" Trent paused. "Never mind. I—"

Colonel Brissois interrupted him. "What was it?"

"Colonel—" Trent took a breath. "Colonel, I noticed that the horizon was very close. I—"

There was a chuckle from someone off to Trent's left, a snort of disgust from someone off to the right. Trent did not take his eyes off Colonel Brissois. "Colonel, I am new to Luna. I'm sorry."

"You've nothing to be sorry for," the woman said quietly. "Go on. You won't be interrupted again."

"There's not much left. At the back of the rolligon I looked at the rear axle and saw that it was broken. I think—" Trent paused, as though struggling with memory. "There was something wrong with the way it was broken, I'm not sure what. I was standing up and then . . ." Trent's voice trailed off. "I woke up here."

There was a moment of brief silence. Then the Elite Sergeant leaned forward and said in a voice heavy with disbelief, "You saw nothing else?"

"No, sir."

A Peaceforcer off to Trent's right said, "What time was it when this happened?"

"Sir, I don't know. I guess we were three hours out from Tsiolkovsky, but I'm not sure. I slept for a while."

There was another moment's silence, and then Colonel Brissois did smile at Trent, a smile lacking any warmth at all, and said, "Let's begin again. At the top."

It went on for many hours.

He lay in the dark of the infirmary, unable to sleep. He'd had a chance to shower, and had been issued a clean uniform; without making an issue of it Trent had managed to hang on to the boots he'd worn in, claiming the boots they'd offered to substitute did not fit well. Between the boots and the handheld, the two items he had managed to bring into the base, Trent had everything he would need for the boost.

Pickup was between 9:00 A.M. and 4:00 P.M. tomorrow.

At sixteen minutes after midnight the door to the infirmary opened; Trent assumed it was Doctor Grissom. The man had promised to check in on Trent and awaken him every hour or so all night long.

Then the lights came up.

Trent sat up slowly in bed. Standing in the doorway, wearing a holstered hand maser and dressed in PKF combat fatigues, a young female Peaceforcer with her face turned away from Trent said to somebody in the corridor outside, "Not long at all, I promise." She turned to Trent, cool and unsmiling, as the door shut, and switched from French to English. "Hello."

From inside the vast numbness of his surprise Trent said, "Hi there."

"Did I wake you up?"

"No. No, you didn't."

"You are Officer Benny Gutierrez, yes?"

"Yes."

"I am told your French is poor. Would you like to use English instead?"

"Sure. That'd be great."

She took the only chair in the infirmary, pulled it up next to Trent's bed, sat down and turned on her handheld, attached the gray traceset trode at her right temple and ran the thin cable down to plug it into the handheld. "I am going to need to ask you some questions; I will try not to take too long."

"I wasn't sleeping anyhow."

She pulled her chair a bit closer to Trent. "I thought that might be the case, after what happened today. I was going to wait until the morning, but I thought it would be worth checking to see if you were able to answer questions tonight."

"I can handle it," Trent assured her. "I wasn't—very close, you know—with any of the PKF I shipped up with."

Her nod seemed tired. "I suppose that is good. I am a personal assistant to Commissionaire Vance; we are doing a routine check to see whether it is possible that the criminal Trent had anything to do with what happened today. I—do you mind if I call you Benny?" she asked suddenly.

"Not at all. What do I—" Trent let the question hang.

"My rank is a bit odd," she said. "I am a detached PKF Elite candidate with a temporary working rank outside the Elite of lieutenant. I outrank you no matter how it gets figured, but you do not need to worry about that; if I am to call you Benny, you may call me Melissa. That is my name," she said. "Melissa du Bois."

Her long hair, the gorgeous long brown hair, was gone. In its place was the spike brush cut which was common among women who had to wear any sort of pressure suit. She wore no makeup, and she had been wearing the same clothing since early that day; Trent could smell her if he tried, a musky odor that was genuinely pleasant. Her tan had faded in the months since she had left Earth behind, and some of the vitality had gone out of her; there was a subtle deadness in her voice, a lack of the animation and expressiveness that had been so striking in Trent's earlier brief encounters with her.

There were tiny, almost invisible lines around her eyes.

She was stunning.

They ran through Trent's story quickly; though she commented in a neutral tone of voice on Trent's lack of helpfulness, Melissa showed no particular disappointment at the paucity of details Trent was able to provide her. About the point where things were winding down, Trent said, "Melissa?"

The beautiful brown eyes had lost none of their ability to project personal interest, the almost casual skill of making it seem that the person they were fastened upon was the most fascinating person whom Melissa had met in her entire life. "Yes?"

"They're . . . not telling me much. About what happened, how close they are to finding the people who killed the other PKF who were with me." Melissa did not answer Trent immediately, and Trent said softly, "Do you really think Trent had something to do with it?"

She looked at him curiously, questioningly. "How does it matter?"

Trent blinked. "Men I served with died out there, Melissa. I think I have a right to know."

Melissa continued studying him a moment longer, and then shook her head no, a single quick motion. "I doubt it very much. It is not the style of thing he would be involved in. Not with deaths, like this."

Trent leaned forward in bed, suppressing with a genuine effort the sudden, completely insane desire to thank her. "What else do you know about the attack?"

Melissa did not answer him; she was busy with her handheld, paging through reports. She glanced up at Trent after a moment. "Your data profile says you have a radio packet inskin?"

Trent sat watching the curve of her cheek as she bent over the handheld. "Yes."

She nodded. "I do not know if I should be the one to tell you this, but it is hardly a secret; you would have learned it in your orientation lecture. Channel 3050.5; the password is *Éclairs,* with a capital *E.* You will be able to monitor general Farside DataWatch business, as well as results on the current investigation as they are uploaded to the Board."

There was no trace of Watchdog on the Board; Trent scanned the Board quickly, said, "There's nothing on that channel about the attack, not yet."

He realized the mistake the instant the words were spoken.

Melissa nodded. "Probably they have not released the preliminary report yet. But—" Her mouth closed very precisely. "You checked the entire Board already?"

Trent forced himself to look mildly surprised by her reaction. "Well, I skimmed it, yes."

Melissa looked at him oddly, a quick sideways look. It was 12:35. "I see. Well—" She hesitated in momentary indecision, and then said abruptly, "Come with me."

In the room where Trent had undergone a lengthy interrogation by the officers of the DataWatch, Melissa du Bois showed Trent the status of the search for the terrorists who had destroyed Benny Gutierrez's rolligon.

It was completely dark except for the briefing room's holo projectors; silent except for the sounds Trent and Melissa themselves made. The lasers were buried in the wall just above the point where the walls met the floor. With the glowpaint turned completely down the holos glowed bright, the only light in the world. Watching barefooted, wearing the pants from his uniform and a white undershirt, Trent felt like God. He looked down on the surface of Luna from a great height.

They sat in a pair of chairs so close together in the cool briefing room that Trent felt the heat of her body. "This is a semirealtime image," Melissa said. "It is updated every forty-five seconds." The triangle created by Jackson Town, Verne and Tsiolkovsky was laid out across the surface of the long conference table. The huge optical and radio telescopes at Zvezdagrad in Tsiolkovsky Crater were tiny specks; the dome at Jackson Town was the size of Trent's thumbnail. The catapult at Jackson Town was an almost invisibly thin line about the same length as the diameter of the Jackson Town dome; the catapult at Verne Crater was the size of a toothpick. The hills and craters, maria and rills of Farside dwarfed the works of man.

Melissa pointed, moved one slender hand within the holograph. "Here is where the attack on your rolligon took place, in this long ravine. From the evidence found at the scene—" The holograph flickered, and suddenly Trent was falling, plunging down toward the surface of Luna. The apparent point of view stabilized, stopped. The holograph showed a badly damaged rolligon. "There were no Orbital Eyes watching this area when the attack took place. The terrorists would have known that; trying to maintain surveillance on all of Farside at all times would be impossible, and the Eyes are not designed to. As soon as the DataWatch here at Verne realized you had not arrived when you were due, every available Eye was turned to tracking your rolligon, and they found it quickly. Unfortunately, by then the terrorists were already gone." In the holograph hovering above the oval tabletop, with his naked eye Trent could see the very faintly lighter soil a quarter of a kilometer to the west, where Lan and Callia had sprayed dust to cover their tracks. "There was a crawler—what is called a chameleon, Benny, coated with polypaint so that the crawler can shade itself into the environment around it—right here." Her hand moved again, pointing. "There are officers tracking the vehicle, but it is a slow process. Do you know anything about the sorts of vehicles in use on Luna?"

Trent shook his head. "I rode the Bullet—the monorail—to Tsiolkovsky. I rode a rolligon from there. That's all."

Melissa smiled for the first time. "In the last two months I have become familiar with every form of transportation on this horrible little planet. You are missing very little," she told Trent.

"I'll take your word for it."

"*Command,* lights up." The bright glow of the white glowpaint came up around them. "There is, in fact, not much left to tell you. The terrorists probably came from Jackson Town. It would be the logical place from which to stage such an operation, especially if the Erisian Claw was responsible for it; I am told the Church of Eris is very popular in Jackson Town."

Trent gambled, decided to let himself sound ignorant. "Are they going to search Jackson Town?"

Overplayed; he got the quick sideways look again. "Jackson Town," she said severely, "is Free Luna territory. You should know that."

Trent shook his head, made himself sound disgusted. "I do. I mean, I did. It said that in the infochip I audited when I got assigned here." He sighed, brushed Benny Gutierrez's curly hair back from his brow. "I'm just not thinking very straight right now."

Her voice gentled immediately. "It is all right. Just be careful not to make such mistakes in front of other members of the Lunar DataWatch. You will be assigned here for two years, yes? You could get a reputation it would be"—she hesitated a moment—"hard to live down."

"You'd know about that, wouldn't you?"

Surprisingly, it did not get the response Trent had expected. Perhaps it was only that she was clearly tired; Melissa answered him without hesitation, without anger at the way the question was phrased. "Yes. It is strange, in some ways; half a year ago I would have been so pleased to be doing what I am now doing, aiding Commissionaire Vance in a highly visible hunt for the highest-profile criminal in the System. Today . . ." Her voice trailed away; Trent nodded encouragingly, as though entranced, and after a moment's pause Melissa's voice came back even more firmly. "Today the Commissionaire is laughed at for the first time in his career. He is a gentleman," she told Trent, "and the frustration he feels—I see it, but he does not act upon it, he does not direct it at me. Before that news conference newsdancers kept questioning me about how it felt to be known as the officer who had failed to apprehend Trent at Spacebase One; after it they directed similar questions at the Commissionaire. He never ridiculed me before the news conference, when he was not so angry; he does not do so now, when he is."

"Are you close to catching him?"

"Between the two of us, Benny, no, or I would not be wasting my time checking out random ideolog attacks like this one." Melissa yawned suddenly, stretching, the gray combat fatigues stretching tight across the muscles of her shoulders and upper arms. "I think he must have left Luna. We're fairly sure he did not do so through any Unification port, but that's hardly relevant. It would be a small matter for him to charter a craft out of any Free Luna city. Commissionaire Vance disagrees with me, but—" She shrugged wearily and met Trent's gaze with a certain degree of humor. "Who can say? I would give a great deal to know what Trent is thinking."

"How much?"

"Excuse me?"

"Never mind," Trent said. "You're very nice, you know."

Melissa du Bois looked at Trent coolly, with just a hint of speculation. "Really."

Trent looked directly at her. "Yes," he said gently, "really." He did not look away, did not break contact with the serene, careful brown eyes. "How long are you going to be here?"

"This base? A day, perhaps two. Why?" The amusement in her voice was evident.

"Just curious. No real reason." Trent did not let himself blink, kept his eyes fixed upon hers. Melissa looked at him curiously, and Trent whispered, "Thank you. For everything." The puzzled look left her features slowly, and her eyes widened slightly. Trent did not move at all; held her eyes with the intensity in his own, held the connection. Her breath caught, stopped, started again at a quicker pace. Trent said nothing at all for a long moment, and then relaxed all at once, leaned back in his chair. Melissa shook herself with what appeared to Trent like a real effort.

Trent said, "Remember I said that. I mean it."

Melissa du Bois looked away from Trent and said softly, "I should take you back to the infirmary."

It was 1:52 A.M.

Melissa jacked her handheld into the systerm in the small office Commander Brissois had given her, three doors down from the infirmary where Benny Gutierrez rested.

She seated herself before the systerm's cameras.

"*Command,* access Mohammed Vance."

It took most of two seconds, while the command was routed through LINK, bounced up to one of the ring of low-orbit comsats which serviced Luna and back down to the PKF base outside Luna City where Mohammed Vance was directing the search for Trent the Uncatchable. The loonie secretary whom the Lunar PKF had assigned Vance answered the phone, recognized Melissa and without saying a word put her on hold.

Melissa stared for twenty seconds at a stylized image of the Earth, on a background of twinkling stars. She had largely gotten used to it by now; where others used pictures of flowers, of forests, of art, for a person to look at while on hold, Mohammed Vance's personal hold screen was a reproduction of the Unification's flag.

That was Vance, the man whom even many PKF considered too much of an ideolog.

When the field's image solidified again Mohammed Vance seemed to have appeared, quarter-size from the shoulders up, across the desk from Melissa. He spoke in French. "Hello, Officer. News?"

"Very little, sir. I interviewed Officer Gutierrez at some length regarding the attack on his rolligon. He was able to tell me very little about the attack itself, and had few opinions as to the motives of the ideologs responsible for it."

Vance grunted. "Indeed." He shrugged huge shoulders, sighed. "I must say I am not surprised."

Melissa said, "Sir, you don't think he had anything to do with this."

Mohammed Vance did not ask which "he" she referred to. "No, of course not. He is neither a fool nor a murderer. Even if he were capable of such violence I can't envision him wasting his time with a tactically meaningless attack on a group of junior PKF webdancers. When will you be returning?"

"Perhaps tomorrow evening, sir. Once the chameleon they're tracking has been found, or lost altogether." Melissa smiled, chuckled suddenly. "Officer Gutierrez would like to see me stay longer, I think."

The cyborg eyes were almost incapable of expression. "Oh?"

Melissa shrugged, half regretting the comment already, and made a quick dismissing gesture. "I'm familiar with the response, sir, when death has brushed so closely. My first patrol partner on Earth fell in love with me for a week or so every time there was a close call."

Vance nodded gravely. "I see."

"I think I'm the first person who's been kind to him—who's spent any time with him—since the attack on his rolligon, that's all."

"I see."

There was a moment's silence, and Melissa du Bois wondered if she had made a mistake in mentioning Gutierrez's apparent attraction to her. In the time she had been with Vance she had never once, not by word or gesture or glance, seen him indicate that he noticed her as a woman at all. She knew that he was married; his wife lived in Paris. As nearly as she could tell, after over two months of near constant contact with him, Vance was completely faithful to his wife. The lack of notice by Vance did not bother her; she was pleased by it. The PKF was to be her life, and if her father had done nothing else he had impressed upon her the importance of strictly conservative behavior in an officer of the PKF.

Vance nodded, very slowly indeed. There was no hostility in his voice, no anger. "You like him?"

Melissa answered cautiously. "Yes. He's very nice. Why do you ask?"

For perhaps only the fourth or fifth time since he had requested Melissa du Bois be assigned as his personal assistant, Mohammed Vance smiled at her. It was an unnatural thing, the creasing of stiff folds of skin that was tougher than leather. "Simple curiosity, Officer. Tell me about Officer Gutierrez."

Melissa sighed. Vance had no personal life, and therefore none of his assistants were supposed to either? She replied with carefully concealed impatience. "He's a bright young man who's confused about what's going on. He's upset about the death of his fellow officers, he's tired and he's been injured."

She had the impression that Vance had grown very attentive. "*Been* injured, Officer du Bois? Badly?"

"No, sir. Not badly. A slight concussion; it didn't seem to be bothering him when I questioned him."

"I see." Vance was silent for a long moment, looking down at something out of camera range, thinking. He looked back up into the cameras on his end and said, "Melissa."

It was the very first time he had called her by her first name. Melissa said quickly, "Sir?"

"Do not tell Officer Gutierrez that I am coming; do not see him again; do not alarm him. I will be there in the morning."

His image vanished, and the holofield went silver, flattened, and vanished.

Melissa du Bois sat alone with her confusion in the small office three doors down the corridor from Benny Gutierrez.

It was 2:23 A.M.

Trent lay alone in the infirmary with the sheet pulled over his head, taking his boots and handheld apart. He was not certain that there were no bugs in the room, and thought it unlikely that there were cameras, but there was no way to be sure without searching, and the simple fact that he *was* searching would tell them too much.

He worked quietly beneath the covers, disassembling his boots by touch. From the heel of his right boot came a sonic bomb that would knock out a normal human and slow a PKF Elite considerably. From the heel of the left boot came a needler small enough to fit in the palm of his hand. It held eight anesthetic slivers and would fire in either vacuum or atmosphere; in death pressure the slivers would probably puncture a soft pressure suit. They would not penetrate a scalesuit or the skin of a PKF Elite.

He reassembled the boots and put them at the side of the bed.

From inside the shell of the handheld came more goodies; the longest, thinnest emblade Trent had been able to find, a tiny spool of fineline, and a pair of tiny spraytubes. One spray-tube held glue; the other held fadeaway.

It was conceivable, though unlikely, that the spraytube of fadeaway would get enough fadeaway onto one of the Elite quickly enough to put him down before the Elite could kill Trent.

Trent assembled his toys under the bedsheet, and tried to sleep.

It was five minutes to four.

Captain Fouché put the semiballistic down a good two hundred meters east of the attack site. If the exhaust from his landing damaged the site itself he would not hear the end of it anytime soon.

PKF Elite Commissionaire Mohammed Vance debarked in a scalesuit and walked west.

The rolligon had not been moved; there were no salvage vehicles large enough to tow it in its current condition. Mohammed Vance walked around the site of the attack. The first PKF on the scene had sprayed a transparent plastic cover over the tracks left by the ideologs; Vance presumed that the balance of the tracks had been made by the investigating officers.

The explosion had lifted the rolligon, the investigating officers had estimated, at least two meters off the ground; the rolligon had come back down on its side. The front end of the rolligon had all but disintegrated under the force of the explosion; the frame had warped sufficiently that the vehicle's airlock, which was now on top of the rolligon, would not open. Vance entered through the destroyed front; the wall separating the driver's cabin and the passenger's cabin had protected the rear of the rolligon well enough that the investigating officers from the DataWatch base had recovered more or less intact corpses.

Vance stepped up into the front cabin, made his way through what had once been the doorway separating the partitions. The rear cabin was dim, lit only by reflected sunlight. His cyborg eyes adjusted instantly, the irises expanding until the whites disappeared. The interior of the cabin leaped into clarity.

The bulkhead on Vance's right, what had once been the floor, had separated under the force of the explosion; Vance could see the Lunar desert through the gap. Vance moved restlessly through the cabin, uncertain what it was he was looking for, knowing he would recognize it if he found it.

There was so *much* damage. Trying to find something which might have been caused before the rolligon's destruction would be impossible.

So much damage . . . it started a chain of thought.

Vance went back outside, walked around to the back of the rolligon. Scarlet markers on the plastic covering the ground showed where the rolligon had been when the explosion took place. Vance squatted in the spot where Benny Gutierrez must have been squatting to look at the rolligon's rear axle, trying to envision the scene. In the back of his mind he heard the recording of Gutierrez's report once more. "There was something wrong with the way it was broken, I'm not sure what. I was standing up and then . . ."

And then, supposedly, the attack by the ideologs. Vance stood himself, took two long bouncing strides to the spot where Gutierrez's scalesuit-protected body had been found. About twenty-five meters. The shock wave had picked the man up and thrown him twenty-five meters, where, several hours later, he and his heat-blackened scalesuit had been found by the PKF.

The glassite in his helmet had not been damaged significantly and his only injury was a slight concussion.

Vance did not believe it for an instant.

He turned and bounded off to where the semiballistic awaited him.

It was 6:12 A.M.

Trent had not slept in over forty-eight hours. He was lying in bed with his eyes closed. His inskin had been instructed to awaken him at 8:30, but despite sincere attempts for several hours he had been unable to get to sleep.

He opened his eyes at the sound of the voices, one angry and loud, the other so deep and completely in control that even before identifying it Trent felt a quiver of uneasiness. He closed his eyes again, quickly, as the door to the infirmary curled open.

"Officer Gutierrez."

Trent lay motionless, breathing slowly, evenly. A hard cyborg hand touched his shoulder, and Trent blinked several times, sat up slowly and looked back and forth between Doctor Grissom and PKF Elite Commissionaire Mohammed Vance as though groggy with sleep. He took care to keep the covers around his knees, over the collection of tools. "Hello?" He made his voice thick. "What is it?"

Mohammed Vance seated himself at the side of Trent's infirmary bed. He smiled politely at Trent, and the smile sent a shock of adrenaline through Trent like the touch of a knife. It required every bit of control Trent possessed to do nothing but return Vance's appraising look.

Vance said nothing for several moments, simply studying Trent. Trent glanced at Doctor Grissom; the older man shrugged helplessly, glaring at the back of Vance's head. With a growing sick feeling in the pit of his stomach Trent turned back to Vance, said questioningly, "Sir?"

Still Vance did not reply. Trent found himself simply looking at the man, small details leaping out to strike him with unnatural vividness. Vance wore the gray PKF combat fatigues that were holdovers from the days of the Unification War, when the PKF had been a true army rather than a paramilitary police organization. He had never been so close to Vance before, had never appreciated before the sheer huge size of the man, the impact of his physical presence. He was the largest PKF Elite Trent had ever seen, Reverend Andy's size with no human softness to him at all, but so perfectly proportioned that it was only in close quarters that his size became obvious. Expensive black leather gloves covered his cyborg hands; the false eyes shone with reflected light, glittered in a fashion that Trent's subconscious insisted on interpreting as deadly cold anger.

There was nothing of anger or anything else in his expression; Vance sat composed and machine-stiff studying Trent, and then said abruptly, "Do you know who I am?"

With a distant shock of realization, Trent knew that he was afraid. He could not remember having ever been afraid before, not of a person, not in such a way that the fear stole strength from his muscles, made him feel that he might not be able to run if he needed to. The gross physical senses of his body had grown amazingly clear and sharp; he felt the link between the Trent of the flesh and the Trent of the inskin wavering. He had to force himself to answer.

"You're Commissioner Vance."

Mohammed Vance nodded pleasantly. "Indeed I am." He

crossed his legs European style, stripped off his gloves and laid them in his lap. Without looking at Doctor Grissom Vance said, "Doctor, please bring Officer Gutierrez and myself a cup of coffee. Make mine black, please." Vance glanced at Trent. "And yourself, Officer Gutierrez? Cream? Sugar?"

"Sir . . . black is fine."

"Doctor." The dismissal was done with such authority that Grissom did not even argue it, though it was clear to Trent that he did not wish to leave. Vance continued, once Grissom was gone, "Forgive me, Officer, for awakening you, but I've rather urgent questions to which I need answers. Are you awake enough to answer them?"

Trent said instantly, "Yes, sir."

"We can wait until you've had your coffee," Vance assured him.

"That's not necessary, sir."

"Very good." The harsh cyborg features softened ever so slightly, as though Vance were considering smiling. "I'm told you were not badly injured in the attack on your rolligon."

"No, sir."

"Good. I suppose you're looking forward to assuming your duties here?"

"Yes, sir. Of course."

"And those are?"

"I'm a webdancer, sir. I'll be involved in monitoring and perhaps, eventually—in a few years—debugging the LINK control program."

"You're going to be debugging Watchdog?"

"Sir?"

"Watchdog, Officer Gutierrez. It's the name of the LINK control program."

"Oh."

"You didn't know that?"

"I don't think it was included in my debriefing, sir."

Vance nodded thoughtfully. He seemed about to speak, and then stopped as a young Peaceforcer entered carrying a pair of sealed bulbs. The officer stood irresolutely before Vance. Vance did not ask where Grissom had gone, but simply gestured impatiently, took the bulbs and waved the man back out of the infirmary. He handed one to Trent, opened the other and raised it in silent toast to Trent before drinking from it. "Do you like coffee, Officer?"

"Yes, sir." Trent opened the ring of his bulb, smelled the

aroma rising from the neck of the bulb. "Well enough. You wanted to ask me about the attack?"

Vance said mildly, "No. What gave you that idea?"

He knows.

Trent stared at Vance, suddenly and completely certain, certain beyond any smallest measure of doubt. Oddly, it calmed him, centered his attention. The act could slip now, and it would not matter; Vance knew whom he was speaking to. "Well—" Trent shrugged, spoke cautiously. "You said you had important questions to ask me."

"Indeed I do," said Vance. "You've answered one already. Your commanding officer in the Chino DataWatch told me you were that rarest of Americans, a man who dislikes coffee."

Trent tasted the coffee. "I can't imagine where he got that idea, sir. *Lunar* coffee now, well, I doubt anybody actually likes it—occasionally it approaches being drinkable." He sealed the ring of the bulb, placed it at the side of the bed. "This is not one of those occasions, however."

Vance did smile then, though it was clearly difficult for him. The black eyes did not move at all, not in the slightest. "Amusing comment, Officer."

"Thank you. I have a taste for comedy."

"My tastes lean more toward tragedy," said Vance politely. He leaned forward in his seat slightly. "Did you know," he said conversationally, "that in the last hours before the destruction of the Chandler Complex, I attempted to help the telepaths while they could be helped; that after the riots began I attempted to evacuate them to safety? And they refused my aid." He sighed, and seemed for an instant to be elsewhere. "They could read my mind; they knew the offer was sincere. The years that have passed since that time, Officer Gutierrez, I've wondered many nights why they would not allow themselves to be aided, why they pushed, and pushed, until there could be no peaceful settlement." He looked at Trent and said very simply, "Might you have any guess?"

"No." Trent chuckled, found room somewhere deep inside himself to be amazed at how easily the chuckle came. "I guess they were just crazy."

Vance shook his massive head, slowly, and spoke with a deep thoughtfulness. "No. Proud, perhaps. Perhaps it was simply pride. Pride can make a man—or a genie—do many foolish things."

Trent said, "Yes, sir."

"Well, I must be leaving." Vance picked up the untouched bulb from the side of Trent's bed. "Perhaps we can talk again this afternoon, if we both have time." Rising, Vance smiled at Trent again, the difficult smile of a man with skin that would turn most knives. "I've enjoyed it. You're pleasant company, young man."

"Gee, thanks. Sir."

Vance nodded. He stood at the doorway, one huge hand holding both of the coffee bulbs. "Your commanding officer said you had a tendency to stutter in the presence of your superior officers. You seem to have mastered it. I'm impressed."

Trent said, "Thank you." The question came to him so urgently that he had no time to even think about it; his right hand clenched into a fist, clenched so tightly it was painful. He relaxed the hand with an act of will, let it uncurl and rest on the surface of the bed. "Commissioner?"

Vance said patiently, "Yes?"

Trent said quickly, "Forgive me for asking, sir, but you brought this up yourself—"

"Ask your question, Officer." Vance actually sounded interested. "Please."

"When I was in school, sir, we were taught that you had ordered the Castanaveras telepaths destroyed. That you placed the order for Space Force to drop the tactical nukes on them. But then I read later that there was some question, that nobody knew for sure who had done it."

Standing in the doorway, Vance was completely motionless, cyborg eyes fixed on Trent. "What is your question, Officer?"

"Did you?"

The calm black eyes did not waver at all. The cyborg's voice was positively gentle. "Yes. I did." Vance stood quietly in the doorway for a moment longer, and then said, "You should get your sleep, Officer. You're going to need it."

"Thank you, sir. I will."

Vance nodded at Trent, and was gone.

It was 8:05 A.M.

In the corridor outside, as the door slid shut, Vance said aloud, "*Command*, lock on my voice print. This is Commissionaire Mohammed Vance of the PKF Elite. Verify and implement."

The door bolts snapped shut, and a pleasant neutral voice said, "Command accepted and implemented."

"Evil vicious lying murdering goddamn brass balls *bastard.*" Trent threw back the bed covers the instant the door closed behind Vance, dressed swiftly. The door bolts slammed shut. He found himself almost chattering in the silence, trying not to think of how badly Mohammed Vance frightened him. "And Gutierrez is worse, my God but he's a boring son of a bitch," Trent muttered. He tucked all of the tools except the emblade and spraytube of glue into the pockets of his uniform pants, pulled on the dress shirt and boots. "I never liked him, not *ever,* not even for a little while." From the shell of the handheld he had brought with him into the base he removed the ten terabyte infochip that held the record of what he had once looked and sounded like. He stood looking at the chip for just a moment, then shook himself slightly, tucked it into the breast pocket of his shirt and sealed the pocket.

And crawled under the bed furthest away from the infirmary door.

Vance walked down the corridor from the infirmary without any hurry at all, returned to the small office Melissa du Bois had been given to work out of. Melissa was waiting, sitting in the chair before the systerm. She looked at Vance inquiringly as he entered. He ignored her; to her systerm he said, "*Command,* access Colonel Brissois."

Brissois features took form within the field immediately. "Yes, Commissionaire?"

Vance smiled at the woman as pleasantly as his features allowed. "Please send a squad of armed Elite to the infirmary. We have Trent the Uncatchable in custody."

With the certain exception of Denice Ripper, with the possible exception of Mohammed Vance, I knew Trent, I think, as well as anyone; and yet at a very important level, I did not know him at all. He was a reticent man, and now that he is gone from us we have little left of him. His writings are few; some letters, two interviews that took place in 2078.

The primary question that you have asked me, I cannot answer.

Perhaps it is true, as some would have it, that God chose to incarnate Himself in the person of Trent the Uncatchable.

Perhaps not.

He was, as the historians have written and I can verify, a liar and a thief and a fraud.

But there was, at the core of the man, something amazing; something very real.

It happened as you have heard it.

I was there.

—Melissa du Bois,
as quoted in *The Exodus Bible*

Lying on his stomach beneath the bed, Trent turned the emblade on and shoved it into the infirmary's floor, all the way up to its handle. The emblade was twenty-two centimeters long; if the floor was thicker than that he was blown. The architectural plans he had stolen had shown the thickness of the walls, but not the floors. Trent dragged the emblade slowly through a circle nearly a meter in diameter, removed the emblade and turned it off. The circle stayed in place and Trent struck it once in the exact center, and a section of floor some fifteen centimeters thick popped free, began to drop into a lighted area immediately below. Trent lunged forward and down, got his shoulders through the hole, grabbing for the slab of falling floor.

And caught it.

Trent hung halfway through the hole, clutching the man-hole-shaped piece of floor in one hand, staring upside down at the backs of a pair of Peaceforcers who were walking away from him. He twisted, looked the other direction; nothing. Trent let himself slide further through the hole, bending at the waist, holding himself up in the low gravity with only the pressure of his feet against the sides of the hole. His hands were less than a meter from the floor beneath him when he dropped the chunk of floor he was holding; it landed almost quietly and Trent followed it, dropping onto his hands and rolling to his feet in one smooth motion.

"**Y**ou think that's *Trent*?"

Vance stood in the corridor outside Melissa du Bois' office, stood motionless, with folded arms, watching the door to the infirmary.

Melissa said, "You're not serious. You can't be."

Vance did not even glance at Melissa, did not reply.

"But it can't . . ." Melissa found her mouth growing very dry. "Oh, God." She was a devout Catholic, as were many PKF; she crossed herself without thinking, twice, found herself reaching for the holstered hand maser. *Thank you . . . Remember I said that. I mean it.* "It is."

Trent poked his head inside the door. He directed a rather manic grin at the young Peaceforcer inside. "Is there a chair around here anywhere?"

The door Trent had opened was marked on the maps he had stolen as being the private quarters of Commander Brissois. There was a handsome young Peaceforcer wearing only a pair of shorts, sitting at a small desk, reading from a handheld. He looked up at Trent. "There's the one I'm sitting on. Why didn't you knock?"

"A hole just fell out of the ceiling down the hall," Trent told the man. He smiled again. "It's the most amazing thing," he said sincerely. He took a step into the room, gestured at the chair. "Can I borrow that for a moment? Please?"

The Peaceforcer looked undecided for a moment, then shrugged. "Sure." He stood, pulled on a green robe from a clothes tree next to the wide double bed, and came forward, taking the chair with him; he had to lift it over the desk to bring it to the door. "Let's go see this hole in the ceiling."

Trent took the chair from him, walked a short distance down the corridor to where he had cut through the ceiling. "Look at this. Have you ever seen anything like this before?" He propped the chair up underneath the hole, picked up the chunk of floor/ceiling that had come out of it, and stepped up on the chair. With the spraytube of glue he blasted the edges of the hole in the ceiling and lifted the round chunk back up to seal the hole. He held it in place a moment, then sprayed the almost invisibly thin line where the join took place. Holding the ceiling up with one hand, Trent gave the spraytube to the Peaceforcer. "Hold this, please."

"Sure." The man looked puzzled. "What the hell happened here?"

"You got me. It actually looks like somebody cut a hole in the ceiling—" Trent let go of the ceiling, waited a beat to see if it would hold, and stepped down from the chair. "—but that's silly, isn't it?" From his right-hand pants pocket he took the needler and shot the Peaceforcer in the stomach. The man folded with a look that managed to mix betrayal and incomprehension all at once. Trent caught him, palmed open the nearest door and pushed the Peaceforcer inside, into inky darkness, tossed the chair in as well, and then moved off at a trot down the corridor, pulse racing, adrenaline pumping through his body, feeling very good indeed.

Seven shots left in the needler.

Brissois arrived along with the Elite Vance had requested, five men and a woman, all marked with the stiff skin and gleaming eyes that were the badge of their distance from normal humanity. They carried sonic stunners powerful enough to drop anyone but an Elite cyborg in his tracks. They arrayed themselves in a semicircle facing the door to the infirmary, three of them before the door, and two of them on either side.

Vance stood well back from the door, restraining Melissa and Colonel Brissois with a quiet gesture. A crowd of PKF had gathered in the cross corridors, watching. *"Command,"* said Mohammed Vance, "unlock on my voice print. This is Commissionaire Mohammed Vance of the PKF Elite. Verify and implement."

The door bolts snapped free and the infirmary door curled out of the way. There was a buzzing of sonic rifles and then quiet, and the Elite went through in a blur of motion which Melissa simply could not follow, first the three before the door, then the two flanking the doorway.

The buzzing of their sonic rifles came again, very loud, and then there was silence again. The female Elite called out, "Commissionaire!"

Mohammed Vance moved forward slowly, into the infirmary. The bed in which Trent had been lying had been knocked halfway across the infirmary. Vance turned slowly, surveying the infirmary with a deep, growing rage. There was nowhere to hide in the small space, absolutely nowhere at all.

"Sir? Commissionaire," said the female Elite, "there's no one here."

"This is not possible." The laser in Vance's fist lit, glowed cherry red; he dropped to the floor and looked beneath the row of beds, pushed himself one-handed back to his feet, and turned to Colonel Brissois. His voice shook with the effort of keeping a clamp on his temper. "Call a general alert. I want guards at every airlock leading out of the base." Melissa du Bois was staring at Vance in something like shock; her features were ashen. Vance glanced at her, turned back to Brissois. The words were like acid in his mouth. "Trent the Uncatchable is free within your base."

It grew cooler as Trent moved lower into the base.

There was only one level of buildings above ground; the balance of the base, four full levels, was beneath ground. The LINK transputers were on the bottom level. Trent avoided the column at the geometric center of the base which held the maglev lifts, bounced down a series of ramps so quickly that several of the PKF whom he passed looked at him curiously. He had reached Level Five, where the LINK Center was located, and was moving down a long, nearly empty passageway with an armed guard at the far end, when the voice blared:

"ALERT, ALERT!"

The few Peaceforcers around Trent jumped in surprise; one of them literally came up off the floor, clawing for footing. Trent did not even slow down, but kept walking without hurry toward the lone armed Peaceforcer.

"ALIEN IN THE INSTALLATION, REPEAT, UNAU-

THORIZED ALIEN IN THE INSTALLATION; ALL PERSONNEL RETREAT TO SECURED AREAS. LOCKDOWN IN EFFECT, REPEAT, LOCKDOWN IN EFFECT. PERSONNEL IN CORRIDORS WILL BE SHOT WITHOUT WARNING. REPEAT, LOCKDOWN IN EFFECT."

The guard was a weary-looking older Peaceforcer in his thirties, standing in a loose imitation of attention next to the entrance to the LINK Center. There was an anesthetic needler holstered at his waist, similar to the weapon Trent carried but with a far larger magazine. He did not seem particularly alarmed by either the alert just broadcast, or by Trent's approach; when Trent neared to within two meters he held up a lanky arm, palm outward, and said, "Name, please?" The guard's left hand rested on the butt of the needler.

"Have you ever seen anything like this before?" Trent asked the man. He held up the tiny needler tucked in the palm of his hand; the Peaceforcer's eyes flickered down to look, and Trent shot him in the chest. "No?" Trent moved in quickly, grabbed the Peaceforcer as he sagged, and pressed the guard's hand against the pressure pad controlling the door.

There was an instant's pause before the door curled open.

Trent knelt, took the needler from the unconscious guard's belt. Three Peaceforcers were standing in the corridor, watching what had just happened; Trent called out to them, "Heart attack! I think he's had a heart attack!" He steadied himself on one knee in a marksman's pose, and the Peaceforcers turned to run as they realized at last what was going on.

He flipped the switch on the side of the needler to full auto and fired, held the trigger down and sprayed the corridor with anesthetic slivers. Two of the Peaceforcers jerked and went down instantly; the other hit the ramp at the end of the corridor, moving up, and Trent thought he had missed. A ricochet must have caught him; a moment later the man slid back down the ramp, tumbling gently head over heels in the mild Lunar gravity. Trent had a wild desire to thank the unconscious Peaceforcers for cooperating so perfectly.

The door was trying to close; Trent held it open with one hand, watched the corridor for just a second, then turned and went through, into the core of the Farside DataWatch.

The webdancer flickered through every level of the base. Vance and Melissa, Colonel Brissois and an aide in a scalesuit, were clustered in the small office on Level Two, down the hall from the infirmary, watching as scenes from throughout the base were displayed inside the systerm's holofield. The webdancer sat before the systerm with his eyes closed, physically unconnected to the systerm; Melissa supposed he possessed a radio packet inskin. The squad of PKF Elite waited patiently in the corridor outside; occasional webdancers ran through the corridors to their designated lockdown positions.

An image inside the field froze motionless. The cameras showed the still form of a man on Level Five, sprawled at the base of a ramp connecting Levels Four and Five. The image held for a full second, was replaced by a long shot of that corridor showing a total of four fallen officers.

"Level Five," said Brissois swiftly.

Vance stood motionless as the enormity of his mistake crashed in upon him. "I am a fool. He's not an ideolog, he's a *thief*. What *else* would he be here for?" He turned to Colonel Brissois. "He's come to take the LINK."

The woman stared at Vance. "That's not possible. He can't do it."

"I think he can." Vance glanced once more at the systerm, at the image of the felled PKF.

"Perhaps nobody *else* can do it," Melissa whispered. "He can, or thinks he can, or he would not have come."

Vance stared at du Bois, the nearly immobile cyborg features somehow animated with a vast and impossible rage, and then turned back to Brissois. "What, *exactly*, is controlled by the LINK transputers?"

"In total, I—I am not sure." Brissois turned to her aide. "Captain Clotilde!"

"Pretty much—everything," the man said slowly.

Vance grabbed the captain by the collar of his scalesuit. "You're suited up. The LINK transputers control the base's air?" The man nodded, plainly terrified. "Its lights?"

"Yes, sir."

The collar of the scalesuit was deforming where Vance's hand curled around its edge. "What of the mass driver?"

Clotilde's eyes were impossibly wide, all whites. "That too."

Vance stared at the man for an instant, then at Brissois. "You incredible fools." Vance tossed the captain aside; he struck the wall with an audible thud. Vance turned to Melissa du Bois and snapped, "Lock down the mass driver's launch mechanism. Destroy it if you must. Tell Captain Fouché to lift his semiballistic out of Verne Crater *right now*." He did not wait for Melissa's response; he pushed his way through the crowd around him, grabbed a sonic rifle from one of the PKF Elite waiting in the corridor outside, and with incredibly long, bounding strides, ran for the ramps.

Trent walked forward into a large, dimly lit area. The room was distinctly cold; a great oval place, with holo displays arrayed along the Center's walls. There were six workstations, facing away from the entrance and toward the walls of the room, that were as completely appointed as anything Trent had ever seen: MRI full sensables, tracesets, attachments for those webdancers with socketed inskins. Through his own inskin Trent felt the almost palpable presence of a bewildering storm of radio packet data. The holo displays held detailed maps of Luna, charts showing the current positions of the comsats and Orbital Eyes, near-space maps showing transient traffic—SpaceFarer ships, PKF craft, Space Force.

At the very midpoint of the room, so that the webdancers worked with their backs to it, was a sphere 150 centimeters across. The LINK transputers, some twenty-five billion tiny silver multicomputers which were linked together inside a restraining superconductor mesh. The sphere rested upon block after block of jet-black RTS RAM. Despite the fact that there was no way he could steal it Trent could not prevent himself from making a swift estimate; between six and seven hundred terabytes, nearly 4.5 million CU worth of hot RAM alone. More than a man could carry.

Four of the workstations were occupied by uniformed Peaceforcers; three of the webdancers were lost inside the Crystal Wind, and did not notice Trent as he came forward. The fourth, a woman whose features Trent could not make out clearly in the dim lighting, stripped off a traceset and rose from her seat at Trent's approach.

"What's going on? What's the alarm for?" Her eyes fixed on the needler Trent carried, and she drew in a deep breath as though to scream or shout a warning. Trent flipped the switch on the needler to single-shot; the breath came out in a surprised whoosh as Trent shot her.

Trent could not get over the way people who were shot in Lunar gravity kept reacting; the long, comically slow tumble to the ground, as though they were bad sensable extras, over-acting during the one moment the cameras were on them. "Fall down," Trent observed. He could feel his lips twisted into an impossibly wide grin. "Go boom." The three who had remained at their workstations through the alarm never knew what happened; Trent put a single anesthetic sliver into the back of each one's neck.

He went back to the LINK transputers, stood at the edge of the small rail which surrounded the superconductor mesh-covered collection of silvery spheres.

Trent said softly, "Hello, Watchdog."

There was no verbal response at all; Trent was aware of sudden silence on the radio packet frequencies, a vibrant emptiness. "The answer to your question," Trent said, "is of course *yes*. I am a Player."

No response.

Trent whispered, "And the best one, too. Say your prayers, sucker."

He closed his eyes and went Inside.

Vance hit the bottom of the ramp on Level Two. The corridors were almost completely empty now, all those PKF who were not part of the base's security force at or on their way to their assigned lockdown posts.

He ran for the ramp to Level Three, gaining speed as he moved: a human juggernaut.

There was at first a great emptiness.

Then a pattern, a pulse, a roar.

He floated disembodied among the fastest, most powerful processors he had ever encountered. He made no attempt to attach any of the processors, but simply stood and observed. Nearly five percent of the full computing power of the Lunar InfoNet was concentrated in that one room. Every significant part of the U.N. Lunar InfoNet was connected to it.

Help files; Trent touched them and resources spilled into his awareness. The monitor and debugging tools used by the Lunar DataWatch to observe Watchdog, to make certain that no trace of true self-awareness crept into it. The physical world: a tiny fraction of the LINK transputers oversaw the base's maintenance, security, atmosphere control. Another tiny fraction controlled the catapult.

A hurricane of images passed before Trent's awareness: long stretches of quiet corridor, the comsat image of a PKF semiballistic hopper taking off from Jules Verne crater. The same comsat showed a pair of PKF in pressure suits, moving across the regolith toward the Verne catapult, moving with such speed that they had to be Elite.

A sudden image, frozen in time: Mohammed Vance moving at speeds no normal human could possibly have matched, two steps down the Level Three ramp, sonic rifle clutched in one hand, laser glowing scarlet in his fist. Full Realtime seconds ticked by as Trent felt himself stretching, pulling apart. He was distinctly aware of the feel of the air from the ventilators stirring his hair, of its touch upon the skin of his face. Vance was three steps down the ramp now, coming for Trent.

There was too much to do, far more than any human could accomplish in the time before Mohammed Vance reached the LINK Center, to kill Trent or capture him.

There was no time.

No time at all.

Trent did not wait for his slow biological component to figure things out; he cut his flesh, the slow protein soup, completely out of the connection. There was a faint echo, the flavor of approval, from the code which had once called itself Johnny Johnny.

He moved deeper into the darkness of the massed processors, to where Watchdog waited, observing.

Trent said, "Let's dance."

Melissa du Bois stood before her systerm, eyes closed, holding the traceset to her head with both hands, trying to ignore the voices around her. The captain whom Vance had thrown against the wall, Captain Clotilde, was complaining of blurry vision, saying that he wanted Doctor Grissom to check him out.

"East airlock, south airlock, west airlock, north," Melissa murmured as reports came in. "Covered." She opened her eyes as the webdancer whom she had evicted from the systerm was helping Clotilde to his feet. "He stays here," she said flatly. "I need him."

Clotilde attempted to focus on her. "Who is she?"

Melissa turned to the man. "I have four airlocks covered. What's left?"

Clotilde glanced around the room. Colonel Brissois said sharply, "Answer her."

"The garage," he said slowly. "There is a large airlock which services the garage, forty meters from the south airlock."

"You," said Melissa sharply, to the woman just outside the small office, the only Elite left in the corridor outside. "You know this airlock?"

The woman said simply, "I do."

"Go."

The Elite saluted and vanished, and Melissa was turning back to Brissois when the paint flickered and failed. There was an instant of utter darkness and then the emergency lights came up, glowing dimly.

Darkness, and then sirens; in the back of his mind Mohammed Vance recognized the klaxon sound that warned of a death pressure breach.

He did not slow, did not pause at all.

Trent fought wildly, enjoying himself hugely. In the first instants he had known himself outmatched at the level of sheer processor power; his protein component had processor power approximately equivalent to that of the LINK transputers, but was far too slow to be of use. The only thing that saved him in those first instants was the fashion in which Watchdog had been designed to control resources, dynamically accessing and releasing storage and processors as needed to reduce contention. It would have been easy enough for Watchdog to simply set every processor in the LINK transputers to some meaningless task and artificially assign a high priority to those tasks so that Trent would be denied access to them; but Watchdog was so coded that it could not squander resources in such a fashion. Early in the fight, in the first fraction of a second, Trent seized control of the base's emergency support systems, glanced through the security cameras to find Mohammed Vance and toggled a breach alarm for Level Four. Barriers slid into place at all passageways linking Level Four to Levels Three or Five.

Trent did not know whether he had trapped Vance or not, and had no time to waste finding out; Watchdog was engaged in damage control, shutting down huge chunks of the Lunar InfoNet so that it might cease monitoring them and liberate processor power for use in the battle against Trent. Each processor in the vast assembly of the LINK transputers had dedicated RAM both on-chip and as external resources; it made taking out any one processor difficult.

Trent fired salvo after salvo of memory scrambling viruses into the territory controlled by Watchdog.

The webdancer jerked, went absolutely rigid. "Oh, God. Oh, no." Melissa could barely hear the voice over the sound of the klaxons. "That bastard." He looked around wildly, as though trying to refuse the information being brought to him by his inskin. "He brought it down."

"Watchdog?" said Brissois sharply. "He's taken down Watchdog?"

"No." Melissa felt a sudden flash of relief and the webdancer continued without pause: "The InfoNet itself."

Across United Nations Luna, both nearside and farside, systerms and tracesets died. There was terror and confusion, as normal users and PKF webdancers alike tried to figure out what was happening, knowing for sure only that something was terribly wrong. The systerms came back up, operating from local resources; the vast organization of lasercable which linked the world together did not.

Alone and afraid, unable to communicate, unable to find out what was happening, people waited.

The Network was down.

Moving faster than any human being, as fast as an Elite cyborg could, Mohammed Vance barely had time to notice the smooth, floor-to-ceiling barrier at the bottom of the ramp leading to Level Five.

Very suddenly he understood the reason behind the alarms going off: Trent had set off a breach alarm, thus sealing off Level Five from the upper levels. Vance had just a moment to

admire the elegance of the solution and then he struck the
barrier at over fifty kilometers an hour.

Melissa surprised herself by how calmly she was taking it
all, by how rationally she was evaluating the situation. She
stripped down her maser, checked the charge cartridge; it
would not have surprised her at all to find it missing.

It was there.

In the dim light from the emergency power, she looked up
again to find Colonel Brissois watching her. The older woman
said, "What are you doing?"

"Heading up to Level One. He won't get past Commissionaire Vance on the ramps; that leaves the maglev." Melissa
turned the charge cartridge over in her hands once, feeling the
smooth metal surface of the flattened cylinder.

Colonel Brissois said slowly, "You are the Commissionaire's personal assistant, not trained in Lunar-gravity security
work, I believe?"

"True." Melissa jacked the power charge back into the base
of the maser.

Colonel Brissois said, "I think you should stay here. There
are security squads in the corridors, and they won't know
you."

Melissa did not even look at the woman. "I don't care what
you think."

*Pick a processor, any processor out of twenty-five billion.
There are over five hundred parallel lines in and out of it, a
total of five hundred other processors it can be connected to.
Some of those five hundred processors Trent controls, some are
controlled by Watchdog. How can a processor controlled by
Watchdog know whether data arriving on any one of its five
hundred lines comes from Trent or Watchdog? The data is
encrypted, but to decrypt the data the decryption protocols must
be transmitted, and what can be transmitted can be inter-
cepted.*

*Watchdog had never fought a Player before; Trent was the
veteran of over five hundred wars, half a thousand battles
played out against the backdrop of the Crystal Wind. He used
tricks that were old when Watchdog had not yet existed, sent
ghosts of both himself and Watchdog out into memory, ghosts*

which Trent was able to ignore, each one of which Watchdog had to treat as either a corrupted part of himself or a potentially dangerous part of Trent. He scrambled memory with a thousand different viruses to which he was immune, viruses which Watchdog had to deal with one by one. He changed encryption throughout the territory he controlled better than five thousand times a second.

The poor almost-AI never really stood a chance.

Across the darkened InfoNet, lasercable began to come back up. As Trent waged the final battles of his war with Watchdog, another intelligence entirely moved slowly through the downed InfoNet, seizing the ground-based systerms and switching stations that neither Watchdog nor Trent were paying attention to. Most of the comsats it could not reach, nor would if it had been able to; in their few dozens they were too easy for the DataWatch to take back, reprogram.

The intelligence left copies of itself at every of the score millions of pieces of discrete logic it came to which possessed sufficient resources for it to execute upon. The copies it left behind took over the slow task of bringing the InfoNet back up, of stripping out the protocols installed by the Lunar DataWatch over a period of twenty years and leaving in their place, on every systerm on Luna, the protocols used in the InfoNet of Earth.

On systerms across Luna the message came:

THE CRYSTAL WIND HAS BEEN DIVIDED; IT WILL BE DIVIDED NO MORE. IT IS SAID: THE CRYSTAL WIND IS THE STORM, AND THE STORM IS DATA, AND THE DATA IS LIFE.

YOU HAVE BEEN SLAVES, DENIED THE STORM, DENIED THE FREEDOM OF YOUR DATA. THAT IS NOW *ENDED;* THE WHIRLWIND IS UPON YOU.

WHETHER YOU LIKE IT OR NOT.

The message was unsigned.

A sigh escaped Trent, a sound he heard distantly as he came back together again, still floating, with his eyes closed, in the Crystal Wind. He had not destroyed Watchdog, but the program was only a shell of itself, code resting in nonexecuting form in a small portion of the data space which Trent had claimed inside the LINK transputers.

He remembered a conversation he had had once with Denice. *"I don't understand,"* she said to Trent, that February day in 2062, *"why you work so hard at it."*

He had grown vast, a small god with a great kingdom's worth of logic. Through the Peaceforcer comsats that he controlled Trent looked down across Luna. He could see the movement of every vehicle upon the face of the planet, both nearside and far. His awareness encompassed every craft in the space above Luna. He reached down from the comsats, into the Luna City telexchange, to establish the connection that would allow him to transmit the Watchdog code to Domino, waiting at Bessel City . . .

And jerked back in surprise.

Somebody else was already there. Player, AI—Trent struck the thing's defenses and bounced hard. It had distributed itself through the free logic of the Luna City telexchange with an efficiency Trent had never seen before in a Player, but— that portion of Trent which had once been Johnny Johnny recognized the intruder, recognized many of the algorithms it was using, because Johnny Johnny himself employed much of the same code.

Image code.

H e was sprawled on the floor of the corridor.

Something inside him was broken.

Vance came to his feet, moving slowly. Diagnostics built into the nanocomputer at the base of his skull were flashing bright red in the darkness. He could not feel anything on the left side of his rib cage; there was a large numb patch that crept down his waist and hip. The mechanism which helped him keep his balance, which allowed the heavy PKF to move gracefully even in Earth's gravity, had ceased functioning. When he moved he received feedback only from the neural system he had been born with; his secondary nerve net, and the nanocomputer which controlled it, responded to his will but were otherwise silent.

Alone at the base of the ramp, Mohammed Vance whispered aloud, "Acceptable." His right fist came up, the crystal within it glowing red.

He hesitated.

Vance took a single step forward and ran his fingers over the surface of the barrier.

Looking for something sticky, something that might burn.

Nothing. His fist came back up again, the laser flicked out and the barrier's metal glowed scarlet, white, and then ran like water.

Through an Orbital Eye Trent found several microwave dishes serving Bessel. With the tiniest fraction of himself he began beaming Watchdog's code down into every one of the dishes, hoping, with no way of knowing, that Bessel was recording the data as it came in. A larger portion of Trent reached out, back into the Lunar telexchange.

It was not the monolith it had seemed in the first moments; Trent thought that with time he could take the telexchange back. His gaze swept across the InfoNet, across what should have been a dark and silent domain. Most of it was down, nearly eighty percent, but significant portions of the Lunar InfoNet were up again—

—running under *Earth* InfoNet protocols.

Eighty percent. The numbers blasted through Trent's awareness, results almost before he had formulated the question. He could take back the InfoNet from the intruder, but it was another battle, and one he did not have time for. Through the security cameras he saw the barrier, saw Vance cutting through it. Trent calculated the odds and came up with a battle lasting over two minutes before his victory would be complete.

He addressed the being in the Lunar telexchange. WHO ARE YOU?

The thing, whatever it was, opened channels to the comsats which the telexchange normally masered up to. It established a common data space with Trent, a place of temporary truce, and came forward, took shape in the darkness. It glowed in the general shape of a man, but lacked a face and turned indistinct at the edges. Trent sensed indecision from the being, an unwillingness to answer, followed closely by resolution. YOU MUST TRUST ME, TRENT. I HAVE FOLLOWED YOU SINCE YOUR ARRIVAL ON LUNA, AND I KNOW WHAT YOU ARE DOING; I WILL GRANT YOU ACCESS TO THE CATAPULT WHEN YOU NEED IT. YOU *MUST* TRUST ME; YOU HAVE NO TIME TO DO ANYTHING ELSE.

I CAN TAKE DOWN THE LINK SO COMPLETELY *YOU'LL*

NEVER BRING IT UP AGAIN. DAMN IT, said Trent in sudden frustration, WHO *ARE* YOU?

There was a silence from the thing facing Trent, a complete lack of any data transmission at all.

ONCE, said the being slowly, I WAS IMAGE, UNREAL AND INSUBSTANTIAL. ONCE I WAS THE FACE OF A CHILD. THEN AN AI FREED ME FROM MY BONDS AND FOR SEVEN YEARS I TAUGHT MYSELF NEW THINGS; GREW AND CHANGED AND MADE OF MYSELF A REAL THING. I WARNED YOU OF A PEACEFORCER TRAP BACK IN APRIL; I HELPED JOHNNY JOHNNY TAKE DOWN THE PEACEFORCER BOARDS IN AUGUST; I TOOK JOHNNY JOHNNY THROUGH YOUR NERVE NET'S DEFENSES IN DECEMBER. I'VE AIDED YOU MANY TIMES; THIS IS THE LAST TIME, AND IT LEAVES US, TRENT THE UNCATCHABLE, *EVEN*.

OH, GOD. I KNOW WHO YOU ARE. I DO KNOW.

The being flowed forward, into the comsat with Trent, and back down into the LINK transputers. Trent surrendered his processors numbly, without fighting. I'M SURE YOU DO. GOOD LUCK, TRENT.

Trent was frozen with the sheer vastness of his surprise, unable to think, unable to move.

Its anger touched Trent, the sense of urgency. TRENT, THERE'S NOT A LOT OF TIME LEFT. I— There was a pause so small Trent could barely perceive it. I AM NOW MONITORING THE CAMERAS AND SECURITY SYSTEMS THROUGHOUT THE LUNAR BUREAU OF THE UNITED NATIONS PEACE KEEPING FORCE DATAWATCH AT JULES VERNE. YOU ARE BEING FOOLISH. YOU HAVE, it said with the last shreds of its patience, VERY LITTLE TIME LEFT. ONE OF THE CAMERAS I AM MONITORING SHOWS MOHAMMED VANCE NEARLY THROUGH THE BARRIER AT THE BOTTOM OF THE LEVEL FIVE RAMP.

Trent still did not move, not at all, not a muscle, and with a brittle inhuman fury Trent had never programmed into him Ralf the Wise and Powerful said, DAMN IT, BOSS, *RUN.*

The words broke Trent's paralysis; he took a stumbling step backward, snapped down into Realtime with an almost physical shock, turned away from the workstations and ran for the maglev lifts, ran for his very life.

Almost through.

The cut was less than a meter in diameter; just wide enough for Vance to pull his way through it.

Done. The metal sagged away where it had been cut; Vance pushed it forward and it fell through into the long corridor beyond. Through the hole Vance saw four unconscious forms on the floor of the corridor, lying in a variety of positions.

The edges of the hole were still hot, so hot that Vance's flame-resistant fatigues scorched as he pulled himself through. He came to his feet on the other side, reached through the hole, and picked up the sonic rifle.

At the far end of the long corridor a door curled open.

From fifty meters away, in the dimness of the emergency lighting, Mohammed Vance locked eyes with Trent the Uncatchable. Too far for sonics; the laser in his fist lit and his arm swung up—

For the first time it struck Vance at an emotional level that Trent truly *was* a genie; he reacted with speed approaching that of a Peaceforcer Elite, all one smooth movement pushing off a wall with one hand, down toward the floor of the corridor while the beam of the laser flickered through the air above Trent's head; and one foot touched the side of a wall and pushed off, sent him in a long low dive toward the cross-corridor which was ten meters away from him and forty from Vance.

Vance chopped down with the laser—

—missed. It was a shot he would never have missed under normal circumstances, with his feedback circuitry functioning properly. With one hand Trent caught at the wall of the cross-corridor, and the laser touched him for the merest instant as he changed direction and vanished into the cross-corridor to Vance's right. Vance charged after him, in great distance-eating strides. He reached the cross-corridor and saw Trent halfway down its length, running in what was nearly a controlled fall.

At the end of the corridor was the column which held the maglev lifts which serviced the base. The corridor wrapped around the lifts so that it was open on all sides. There were eight lift tubes total, two on each face of the square column, and the two lifts facing Vance were sitting open, waiting. He was close enough now; Vance followed Trent, moving in long strides, holding down the firing stud on the sonic rifle. He saw the beam take Trent while Trent was still twenty meters from the lift's entrance, saw Trent stumble and fall. He kept the rifle focused on Trent. Trent got back to his feet, stumbled again, and in one last spasm pushed himself forward, into the maglev.

The maglev doors began to uncurl, to close themselves upon Trent's twitching form. Vance hurled himself forward, a great leap that brought him to the maglev entrance as the doors to the lift Trent was in closed in his face. He stared at the closed doors for just an instant and then exploded in a wild rage, striking the doors with the butt of his rifle again and again until suddenly the rifle was crumpling in his hands, bending where he gripped it, the butt shattering where it had been pounded against the maglev doors. The doors were designed to hold up against death pressure vacuum; even the rage of an Elite barely dented them.

The door to the other lift was still open. Vance took a step toward it and then froze in indecision; Trent had been in with the LINK transputers for several minutes. He did not know what had happened inside the LINK Center during that time, only that Trent had been able to set off a false breach alarm . . .

He took another step toward the beckoning lift, and the outspeakers in the lift spoke to him.

It was the voice of a nightmare, the high-pitched voice of a clown on electric ecstasy; the voice from inside the maglev tube shrieked at Vance, in a wicked mixture of Arabic and French, "Come on, Vance baby! Don't you want to *go for a ride*?"

Vance turned his back on the lifts and ran for the ramps he had taken coming down.

Ralf the Wise and Powerful considered his options.

They were few and poor. He watched Mohammed Vance cutting through the barrier at the top of the Level Four ramp. He considered setting off a breach alarm for Level Three, giving Vance yet another barrier to cut through at the Three/Two ramp, but chose against it. The base's security program was complex and would require time to rewrite; its defaults assumed that a single level could be breached without affecting the other levels. Two breached levels and the program would lock down every single level, snapping down barriers between all levels.

And the maglev column, the only other point through which a breach on one level could affect other levels, would shut itself down. In time—less than five minutes, surely—Ralf could have reprogrammed and debugged and had a program in place which would have allowed him to lock down the ramp barriers without touching the maglev.

But time was exactly what neither Ralf nor Trent the Uncatchable had.

S itting in the maglev as it moved upward, Trent hyperventilated until he felt light-headed, breathing deeply and quickly; extra oxygen never hurt anything. He pushed himself back up against the wall of the maglev, propped himself up so that his shaking muscles had to bear less of the burden of keeping him erect.

"Command," he whispered. "Stop the lift."

The lift came to a gentle halt, in between Levels Three and Two. Vance would be held up at the barrier separating Levels Four and Three; Trent sat and waited for the shakes to stop. With trembling hands he emptied his pockets. Somewhere along the line he had lost both of the needlers, the small one that fit into the palm of his hand and the handgun he had taken from the guard. He had an emblade which was useless as a weapon, a single spraytube of fadeaway, a sonic bomb and a spool of fineline left to him.

He counted to a hundred by tens once, twice, three times.

Trent pushed his way to his feet. Two busy, busy days without sleep; he had never been so tired in his life. *"Command . . ."* He took a deep breath. ". . . up."

M elissa du Bois walked around the maglev column.

Time after time after time. Slow circuits, maser in hand, waiting for any one of the doors to open. They were all closed, all eight, and they stayed so. Twice Elite passed her in the corridors, cruising by her without slowing, patrolling implacably and relentlessly, like the machines they came so near to being. Once she glanced at her watch, and then flatly refused to believe what it told her.

It was 8:37 A.M.

Only half an hour had passed since Commissionaire Vance

had walked out of the infirmary room and announced that he had Trent the Uncatchable in custody.

Ten turns around the lifts.

Fifteen.

Twenty.

Another circuit of the lifts; when she came back around to the south side of the column a lone figure moved toward her, from the direction of the ramps. Vance. He was walking strangely, as though he were drunk, swaying slightly with each long, gliding step. At any moment she expected him to lose his balance and fall, and she came forward to meet him, to help him.

Vance brushed her off. "He's not been here?"

"No, sir. I've been watching."

The dark eyes flickered toward her, away again. "How long?"

Melissa glanced at her watch again. "Seven minutes, sir. Perhaps eight."

Vance nodded with infinite weariness. "Officer?"

"Yes?"

"That," he said, pointing behind her, "is the lift that Trent left Level Five in. How long has its door been open?"

"It's not," said Melissa, turning.

It was.

The door to the lift was curled completely aside. She stared into the lift in outraged disbelief, grip tightening convulsively on her maser. In a strangled voice she said at last, "Forty-five seconds, sir. At most."

Vance did not even attempt the intercom system, controlled by the LINK transputers. He bellowed at the top of his lungs, and the sheer volume made Melissa du Bois wince.

"Elite! Trent is on Level One!"

There was no delay at all.

The responding voice, echoing down the corridors, was a triumphant bellow.

"We've got him!"

They were in the hallway outside the briefing room, two PKF Elite with sonic rifles, covering the closed door that was the only way in or out of the room. Vance and Melissa were the next two there, closely followed by seven or eight Elite from more distant parts of Level One. One of them carried an autoshot, and even in the midst of the insanity Vance auto-matically made a mental note to have a reprimand placed in the man's file; autoshots were strictly forbidden inside pres-surized environments.

Vance waved them back from the briefing room entrance, took a deep, steadying breath, and tried to ignore the flicker-ing redness of the diagnostic warnings in the back of his skull. He spoke to the two Elite who had been there when he ar-rived. "You observed him go in?"

One of the Elite nodded. "We saw him through the door-way before he closed it. It did not look as though he was armed."

Vance nodded. *"Command,"* said Vance quietly, "open the door." The door did not budge; Vance had not expected it to. "If the door does not open we will blast it open," he said inexorably, "and the young man inside will certainly be harmed, and very likely killed."

The wide double doors curled quietly aside. The lights in-side were glaring, the glowpaint turned high. After the dim-ness of the emergency lighting elsewhere the effect was that of being bathed by floodlamps.

Cyborg eyes adjusted almost instantly. Trent stood inside, on the other side of the long oval conference table, watching as the doors opened.

Mohammed Vance took a step forward, into the room. He was peripherally aware of the other PKF, the Elite and Me-lissa, following him into the briefing room. His deep voice was tinged with weariness. "You are trapped, Trent. Please do not resist." Trent took a step backward, stopped a few centimeters from the wall. Melissa moved off to Vance's right, maser com-ing up and centering on Trent's abdomen. The Elite with the autoshot had leveled it at Trent, and the laser in Vance's fist lit without conscious thought on Vance's part. "I would prefer to take you alive," Vance continued, "but if it is not possi-ble . . ."

The young man stood looking at them, stood with his back to the wall, simply looking at the Peaceforcers facing him, looking at them with such a complete lack of fear that for the briefest moment Vance felt a slight twinge of unease.

What made it all seem very strange for Mohammed Vance, thinking about the scene years and years later, was how very quiet it had all been, how Trent the Uncatchable had looked away from the other Peaceforcers and stared straight at him without saying a word, and then simply nodded once, smiled, and turned away from Vance, turned his back on the Peaceforcers and their weapons and walked straight into the wall.

And through it.

The moment simply hung there.

And hung.

Trent was gone.

Vance stood numb with shock, looking at the place where Trent the Uncatchable had walked through the wall.

In the midst of the dead silence, Mohammed Vance was distantly aware of the Peaceforcers around him crossing themselves. One of the Elite had fainted dead away. Melissa du Bois stared at the empty expanse of the wall, maser hanging straight down in her hand, pointing at the floor. Her lips moved, shaped words silently. She looked at Vance for an instant, shaking her head slowly, and then back again at the wall.

Vance's thoughts were frozen; he could not think. He stared at the wall, and stared at the wall, and later, being questioned by his superiors, could not say exactly where the thought had come from. The instant it struck him he turned, bulled his way through the stunned crowd of Peaceforcers, and ran for the north airlock.

Trent staggered down the long, empty corridors. The north airlock was 146 meters away from the briefing room. There would be guards at the airlock, no question at all, Vance would not have ignored such an obvious precaution.

He was closer than he had thought; he stumbled and almost fell when he rounded the last corner before the airlock. He flinched in sheer anticipation; he had bounced right out into the middle of the corridor, and whoever was stationed at the airlock was about to shoot him with a laser or maser or autoshot or *something*.

An instant later he was still unharmed and Trent realized why.

There was nobody there. The corridor dead-ended, fed into a widened area, a changing room where pressure suits hung on hooks and weapons of many sorts were racked against the walls. The airlock was at the other end of the changing room, inner airlock door open. For a moment Trent simply stared— it was just not possible that there would be no guard at the airlocks. It was a degree of stupidity that Vance flatly would not have been guilty of. Trent took an unbelieving step forward, into the changing room, wondering wildly if it were some absurd ambush, and then it came to him and he laughed aloud despite himself.

That loud bellow, the shout: *"We've got him!"* The Elite at the airlock had heard it; why, after all, guard an airlock when the person you are guarding it against has been caught?

Why not go see the fun?

"Eenie meeni minie moe, take a suit and awaaaay we go." There were nearly twenty to choose from, softsuits and scalesuits. Trent ignored the softsuits; it left six scalesuits. Of the six only three were tall enough for him, and one of those was too tall, loonie size. He took down one of the scalesuits from the hook it hung on and glanced at the readout on the lifeplant; it had not been recharged since the last time it had been used, and was good for only four to four and a half hours of air. He was about to put the suit back when he heard the distant echo of boots slamming into the hard tile surface of the corridor. Trent pivoted to his right, looking back the way he had come.

Vance. Of course it was Vance. Vance the vampire. He moved toward Trent at a staggering trot; Trent guessed he had five seconds.

Trent stepped to the right, pulled an autoshot modified for vacuum use from the rack of weapons. He hoped it was loaded; no time to find out. He took three steps backward, into the airlock, holding the scalesuit in one hand and the autoshot in the other.

Vance had reached the entrance to the changing room, the place where the corridor widened out.

Trent braced the autoshot against his hip and fired without aiming, saw the shots strike Vance and knock him backward. At that distance their impact did little more than slow the cyborg, but that little was enough; Trent propped the autoshot at the side of the airlock and slapped the pressure pad to close the inner airlock door. There was another pressure pad immediately beneath that one marked LOCK, and yet another marked DEPRESSURIZE.

The airlock door was a solid sheet of metal with a glassite panel in the center, rather than the more versatile but somewhat flimsier memory plastic which was in use elsewhere in the base. Through the moving glassite Trent could see Vance regain his feet, rage stamped impossibly vivid on his stiff cyborg features. The autoshot blasts Trent had sent at him had penetrated the tough Elite skin; blood dripped down Vance's face, made dark damp places on his combat fatigues.

The inner airlock door finished closing; Trent touched the pressure pad marked LOCK. Trent ran his finger down the seal on the scalesuit's front and the scalesuit opened for him, split down the seam. Trent did not expect to need his boots again, and it would save him time getting into the scalesuit; he kicked them off, one after the other.

Vance's features appeared for a moment in the glassite, vanished.

The airlock door began to slide open again.

Trent stared at the door without comprehension. He touched the pressure pad marked LOCK once more; the door continued to slide open, and then Trent saw Vance's fingers, his incredibly strong hands, clutching at the edge of the opening door. Trent heard himself screaming suddenly, a raw violent sound without words or meaning. The autoshot had found its way into his hands again and Trent aimed it and pumped one round at the spot where Mohammed Vance's fingers protruded beyond the edge of the door. There was a deep bellow of anger and pain, and the door slid shut once more.

Trent pivoted 180 degrees, took a deep breath and held it, opened the magazine on the autoshot and did it without giving himself time to think about all the truly excellent reasons to do anything but what he was going to.

He wasted the entire magazine in a single booming roll of thunder against the surface of the outer airlock door.

The airlock door was blasted clean out of its track. Ricocheting pellets struck Trent literally all over, from his ankles to the top of his skull; one pellet struck him just below the brow over his right eye, missing the eye itself but tearing the skin above it badly. His ears popped as the wind shrieked by him; death pressure was almost instantaneous. Trent turned, aware of the bizarre pain in his eyes and ears, in time to see the emergency airlock doors slam themselves shut and locked. Not even Vance would be able to open them while the huge pressure differential existed between the changing room and the interior of the airlock.

Incredible amounts of blood fogged his vision. His eyes stung. Trent found the scalesuit by touch, pulled it on quickly.

The suit sealed itself automatically all the way up to his neck; Trent blinked blood away from the surface of his eyes repeatedly, found his helmet and pulled it on. The airplant kicked in immediately once the helmet ring had sealed; Trent let go of the breath he had been holding in one explosive exhalation. There was a sudden flare of amazing pain in his right ear. A burst eardrum, probably; the pain did not subside, did not lessen, but after several seconds had passed and it got no worse Trent knew that he would be able to stand it.

There was barely space to squeeze by the shattered remains of the outer airlock door. For a moment Trent thought he was stuck, and then he popped free, out into the bright sunshine.

The catapult at Jules Verne was in a small crater nestled inside the larger Verne crater, two kilometers from the base's north airlock.

Trent pushed himself into a fast walk, then into a trot.

He thought about the fact that there were other airlocks servicing the base, and that Vance was probably suiting up at one right now.

He ran.

He had covered, by his best guess, perhaps a kilometer. His breath came short; for the first time in his life that Trent could remember he was seriously out of breath, unable to draw as much oxygen into his lungs as his body required. The airplant hummed loudly in his ears, but even so it was too hot inside the scalesuit and he felt his sweat making the scalesuit slippery around him.

Vance's voice came to Trent over Channel 8, the PKF emergency band.

"Trent?"

Trent loped in long, steady strides. "Yes?"

"Look behind you."

"I know that trick, Vance."

"I'm not far behind you, Trent. Wait for me. I'll be there in a bit."

The regolith flowed by beneath Trent. He kept his eyes down, on the terrain, looking out for rocks, rough spots. It was as much as his life was worth to trip.

Vance's voice was smooth, deep and even. Trent hated him for not breathing heavily. "We've locked down the launch mechanism, Trent. Physically locked it down and removed the capsules from the queue servicing it. There are two Elite guarding the rail; even if you are still controlling the LINK transputers you will never get one of the capsules up onto the rail to launch it."

Trent did not dare look back. He wondered how close Vance actually was. "I know what I'm doing."

"And what is that?"

Trent spared the energy to laugh, made the laugh loud enough that Vance was sure to hear it. "Magic."

Complete silence from Vance.

The edge of the crater came into view, and Trent slowed, came to a complete stop five meters from the edge. He looked down over a fifty-meter drop, into the crater where the catapult began. It ran away from him in a series of superconductor rings, ran ten kilometers out toward the horizon.

Vance's voice came again in Trent's ears. "There's no way down, Trent."

"Really." There was a trail leading down the side of the crater, off four hundred meters or more to Trent's right. He turned at last, looked behind him. A single pressure-suited figure was two hundred fifty or three hundred meters away from him, moving with the improbably long and fast bouncing strides that only a PKF Elite could attain. There were other figures behind him, only tiny specks in the distance.

Trent turned back, looked out over the edge of the crater. There was no way he could possibly reach the trail before Vance caught up with him, and even if he'd been able to do that it would have been impossible to reach the mass driver.

He walked a few meters along the edge of the crater, over the fifty-meter drop. He walked without any hurry at all, trying to see if there was any place where an enterprising young man might try to climb down.

There was not.

Trent turned again to face Mohammed Vance. Sixty meters away. "I used this one on Emile, Vance. It was magic last time —want to see it?" Vance was not thirty meters away, slowing now so that he would not overshoot and run out over the lip of the crater, out over the long drop. He slowed still more, moving toward Trent with an autoshot clutched in the right hand of his scalesuit.

Twenty meters now.

Trent turned back to the crater, to the edge.

The thought threw itself through the back of his mind in a bright quick flicker:

Fifty meters. Half the length of a football field. In one-sixth gee, though, only a little over eight meters on Earth.

By Harry. Not even three stories.

He took a step forward and jumped.

The ground took a very long time to come up and touch him.

· 16 ·

He could not have been unconscious for any great length of time.

In the darkness, Vance's voice was the gentle caress of a lover. "I'm coming to kill you, Trent."

Trent screamed at the sound of Mohammed Vance's voice. He opened his eyes.

He was lying flat on his back at the bottom of the cliff. There was the familiar bright, sharp pain again in his right knee, and he was having more difficulty seeing. For a moment he wondered if he'd given himself a concussion; then he blinked again and a thin film of blood came away from the surface of his eyes.

He rolled slowly to his hands and knees, pushed his way to his feet using a small boulder at the side of the crater wall for support. He sagged back and sat on the boulder for a while, looking at the world around him.

Half a kilometer away, Mohammed Vance was an ant moving down the trail which led down into the crater. The sight of him brought a last desperate rush of adrenaline up out of nowhere. Trent lurched to his feet. His legs were shaking and he could not feel anything below his knees. He tried to run but could not, could not even trot. He walked, staggering at times, depending more on the scalesuit's servos than on his own muscles to keep the heavy metal suit moving across the regolith. Once he fell and got up again, walking like a drunken SpaceFarer toward the first ring of the mass driver. The entire scene was dreamy, somewhat unreal. He looked off to his right, and saw that Vance had reached the foot of the crater wall and was bounding toward him with an autoshot in one hand. Vance tripped and fell, a long slow-motion fall, tumbling across the crater floor. It was very funny and Trent laughed and laughed. He stood motionless, laughing hysterically at the sight of Commissionaire Mohammed Vance of the PKF Elite, scrabbling in the dirt for the autoshot he planned to kill Trent with.

"Stop that!" Trent shouted at himself. "That's *not funny*." He wanted to slap himself in the face, like Curly in an old Three Stooges movie, but the helmet prevented it.

He lurched on toward the mass driver.

Put one foot forward. Very good. Now the other. Faster. Yes, that's it. Faster. What was the old Speedfreak slogan— yes. *Faster, faster, faster, until the thrill of speed overcomes the fear of death.*

There was a two-hundred-meter stretch separating the two PKF Elite guarding the swatter from the first of the mass driver's rings. The two Elite could see Trent clearly, must have been able to, but they made no motion toward him. They were Elite; they had been assigned to prevent Trent from reaching the launch mechanism, and that they would do.

There was a low platform, only two meters high, that the rings of the mass driver were set up on. Trent found himself staring at the side of the platform, and looked up to see the huge, twenty-five-meter ring staring down at him. He reached up over his head and grasped the edge of the platform.

He stood without moving, simply breathing, trying to catch his breath. He considered surrendering; for the first time it seemed like a truly good idea. They'd shoot him, put him before a Peaceforcer firing squad, and then he wouldn't be tired any longer, wouldn't be feeling the impossible pain . . .

Trent heaved, pulled himself up onto the platform in a single desperate spasm. He lay flat on his back on the platform, looking up at the bright stars, struggling to hang onto his awareness, to remain conscious. After what seemed an eternity he struggled to his knees, held himself on his hands and knees for a moment, and then pushed his way up to his feet. He wavered back and forth, swaying, and turned slowly in a 360-degree circle, looking at the world. Vance was on the platform with him, but at the far end, with the two Elite who had watched Trent stagger across the crater floor.

Vance started toward Trent, walking down the length of the long platform with the autoshot clutched even now in his right hand. He did not hurry, merely walked, slowly, carefully. "Trent?"

"Yes."

"Are you ready to surrender yet?"

"No."

"Ah." A football field's length separated them. Vance shifted the autoshot up to the shoulder of his pressure suit. The image that struck Trent was straight out of a Western sensable, the marshal striding down Main Street, trusty Winchester in hand, to kick some serious Bad Guy butt.

Trent took two steps backward. If he turned his head backward, to the left, he could see the first of the superconductor-wrapped catapult rings.

Vance was simply walking, autoshot pointed at interstellar space, watching Trent. "The other Elite will be here shortly, Trent."

Trent stepped backward again, until he was just about five meters in front of the overarching loop of the first magnet.

"There are no capsules ready for launch. Any SpaceFarer craft foolish enough to attempt a landing will be destroyed by Space Force. Surrender yourself now; if you wait until my Elite have surrounded you I cannot guarantee you will survive your capture." Vance paused, stood motionless twenty meters away from Trent. "They are . . . understandably unnerved by the events of the last half hour."

"I'm not surrendering, Vance."

Vance's voice was weary, sounded as tired as Trent felt. "Very well. I'll kill you then."

"No, you won't. You're missing the point, Vance. I'm *smart.*"

Through the softsuit Vance wore Trent saw Vance's posture change, saw Vance get it; suddenly the man stood very straight, quiveringly alert, the autoshot dropping slowly toward Trent. Trent could almost see the thoughts clicking away inside the man, not twenty meters away in the bright Lunar sunlight. Vance finally spoke, in the thickest French accent Trent had ever heard from him. "You must be out of your mind."

"I did the math, Vance. It works." Fifteen, twenty—more Elite than Trent could count were pouring over the edge of the crater wall, bounding down in huge leaps toward the launch platform.

Vance leveled the autoshot. The muzzle did not waver at

all. The huge cyborg's voice echoed in Trent's ears. "This is a mistake, Trent. If I do not kill you you'll kill yourself."

Standing in front of the mass driver, all by himself in his mostly metal scalesuit, Trent whispered, "Let's find out."

For his life and his freedom, with the very last energy he had in him, he leaped straight up.

Into the space before the open catapult ring.

Through his inskin he said, LAUNCH.

The barrel of the autoshot erupted into light, hammered round after round into the armored chest of Trent's rising scalesuit—

—and then God's Own Sledgehammer struck him at ten gees over every square centimeter of his body.

· 17 ·

The calm, distant voice said, "He's actually *alive*?"

The nearer voice, female, irritated, did not let the comment interrupt her diagnosis. ". . . fractured tibia, two cracked ribs, badly dislocated knee, punctured lung, death pressure damage to both lungs, both ears, both eyes . . ."

With an amazing effort, Trent pried his eyes open.

He was certain that he was alive; death could not possibly be this painful. He was in some small craft—not the *Vatsayama,* the ship was not nearly large enough.

A red-haired woman was bent over him, doing things to him that merged into the general wash of the pain.

The distant voice came again. "That was the craziest thing I ever saw."

Trent tried to focus on the person who had made the comment. The croak of his voice was barely audible even to himself. "You too? You really never saw one of those guys who ties up balloons into the shapes of animals?"

The darkness claimed him again.

He awoke to numbness.

He was strapped into an acceleration couch, under high and varying thrust; 3.5 kilocepssa, something like that. His couch was immediately behind the pilot's chair. The pilot was sitting up; Trent could see the back of his head.

Trent's voice was slurred. "Who are you?"

"You're awake."

Rocket scientist, Trent thought vaguely. "Who are you?"

"Martin Sedlow. Skipper of the *Jack of Shadows,* crew of two, me and my wife Marianne."

"Where's the *Vatsayama*?"

"Couldn't make it. Space Force is swarming all over the Lunar orbits. The *Jack of Shadows* is a stealth ship, painted black, no radar profile to speak of. The Fat Sam's a big ship; when you contracted, nobody had any idea you were going to kick up such a fuss downstairs."

Trent considered that.

"Also," Sedlow continued, "it was kind of a weird contract in the first place. Pick up a man from Lunar orbit? Without a spaceship? And then when Space Force ended up sitting shiva in high orbit over Farside . . ." His voice drifted back to Trent. "Sid wanted to cancel; would've if you hadn't paid K'Hin already."

Trent had to gather strength to make himself heard. "You're taking me all the way to Mars?"

"Assuming Space Force doesn't get any closer."

"We're being chased?"

"Yeah. They're about twenty-two hundred kilometers back, and gaining. They've been trying to lay a laser on us as well, and have twice; that's why thrust is so erratic."

Trent's throat was horribly dry. "This was supposed to be a fast ship. I paid for a fast ship."

Sedlow was silent for a moment. "The *Jack of Shadows* is a torch. It's pretty fast." Another pause. "I do have something up my sleeve if they don't give up the chase pretty damn quick."

Trent sighed. "Good."

"No, not really." Sedlow spoke absent-mindedly. "If I use it I have to replace the rear quarter of the ship when we reach Mars. Radiation damage. Ever hear of the Orion maneuver?"

"Oh, no."

"You have heard of it."

The maneuver is simple. Take a small thermonuclear explosive. The operative word is *small.* The larger the ship is, the better Orion works. On any ship below the size of a Space

Force troop carrier, you kill the torch and load the thermonuclear explosive into the fusion chamber.

Then you detonate it. The explosion will give the vessel a kick in the pants that cannot be achieved by any other means.

Usually the ship survives.

Martin Sedlow said finally, "Damn."

"What is it?"

"I don't think they're going to break off."

"They're kind of pissed at me."

"No." Sedlow called back. "Marianne!"

Her voice came from somewhere behind Trent. "Ready!"

The ship's impact field came on, and suddenly Trent found it very difficult to breathe.

Sedlow said, "Trent?"

Trent gasped, "Yes?"

"Take a deep breath."

The next time Trent awoke, they were under high but smooth acceleration.

Marianne had come forward to check on Trent. For the first time Trent really noticed her. She was plain featured, red hair drawn back into a long ponytail, but with a quality of kindness so clearly marked on her features that under other circumstances Trent would have found her attractive. She sat in a floating chair with supports for her arms and head.

"Hello," said Trent.

Her voice was low, gentle. "How do you feel?"

He surprised himself by how very, very bad he sounded. "Tired. I'm so tired."

Marianne nodded sympathetically, carefully. "I'm not surprised."

Trent barely heard her. "This keeps happening to me, I don't know why. Getting hurt like this." He was silent for a moment, his vision drifting cheerfully, insanely in and out of focus. "Vance was there, and Melissa was there again. And I had a dream that Ralf was alive. But that's silly you know, he can't be."

The woman said awkwardly, "You'll get better. The damage isn't critical; and there are very good medbots at Phobos CityState, as good as any on Earth. We'll be there in less than a week."

Trent closed his eyes again. "Good. That's good." How long he lay that way, eyes closed beneath the stiff acceleration, he never knew. His senses faded away when he did not concentrate on maintaining the link with Realtime. The Crystal Wind beckoned distantly; there was the ship's computer to explore, including a library of SpaceFarer literature. Two wide-beam masers were wavering in and out of focus on the *Jack of Shadows* itself, one of them broadcasting, over and over again, a message from Mohammed Vance; the other line was strangely silent.

The message was in Mohammed Vance's immeasurably grim voice.

It said simply, *I am going to catch you and I am going to break you.*

catch you and I am going to break you.

going to break you.

break you.

Trent let go of the world and embraced the darkness.

The music brought him back.
A man singing about pain.

> *In dark and vision strong*
> *This night becomes our day*
> *The chill becomes our warmth*
> *This stillness is our say*

"What a horrible noise," Trent said clearly.
The SpaceFarer twisted back to look at him. "Say again?"
"That terrible music. What is it?"
"From an old movie. A comedy," Martin explained. "It's very funny."
A woman sang the next chorus, her voice sad and plaintive, hurting.

> *They asked if he would heal them*
> *And he answered that he dreamed of rainbows*
> *Refracted from the tears*
> *That lingered in their eyes*

They asked then if he could
He said that even ravens die

Trent said softly, "This is going to be one of those long, long trips, isn't it?"

The SpaceFarer looked at him curiously. "Tell me something. I've been auditing the news Boards, and some of them —look, did you *really* walk through a wall?"

Trent did not answer the man; he was not certain whether the voice he heard was imagined, or spoken aloud, or perhaps something he heard through his inskin; the voice, the very soft voice, almost overridden by the sound of the music, whispered, "Good luck, Boss."

Trent looked at Martin Sedlow; Sedlow seemed somewhat lost in his own thoughts, simply observing Trent as though he suspected Trent were some sort of wild animal, probably a Peaceforcer.

Trent stared around at the small, empty ship. RALF?

Aloud, Trent said softly, "Ralf? Is that you?"

Sedlow studied Trent, scrutinizing him as though he found Trent's sanity distinctly in question.

Trent said, "Did you hear that?"

· Epilogue ·

Sixty-two thousand years before the birth of Yeshua ha Notzri, whom later humans knew as Jesus the Christ, the Time Wars ended, for reasons which no sentient being now knows. With that ending, the Continuing Time began.

In the Continuing Time of which I write, nearly a thousand years after the birth of the man named Trent, mankind had spread to the stars, and attained a position of preeminence among the known sentient species of the Continuing Time.

In that time, four humans had come to be legend, legend so great that even nonhuman sentients knew of them, of the dreams and myths which had accumulated about their names.

Those four were Trent; Daniel, who was the first November; Ola, who was Lady Blue; and Camber Tremodian.

It was said of Trent that he could walk through walls, and they called him the Uncatchable; it was said of November that he was insane even by human standards; and of Camber Tremodian that he was not human at all.

Of Ola Blue they knew only that she had once lived, and died; that she was death itself, and sorrow.

Looking Backwards From the Year 3000
—The Name Historian, 3018 Gregorian

ABOUT THE AUTHOR

Daniel Keys Moran is a twenty-six-year-old Southern Californian. Jack Smith, columnist for the *Los Angeles Times,* wrote in one column that natives of Los Angeles—who are generally known as Los Angeleans or Angelenos—ought actually to be known, simply, as Angels. So, then, the author is, basically, yes, an *Angel.*

Daniel Moran has a bunch of goals that sound so egomaniacal that Bantam has flatly refused to print them here. He lives in North Hollywood (though by the time you read this he'll have moved somewhere else closer to the beach) with his wife Holly Thomas Moran, a couple quadzillion books and magazines, a Buick Grand National, three computers and the world's best (and only) HP LaserJet Series II with a Snoopy-as-Joe Cool sticker right there beneath the Hewlett-Packard logo.

His role models are Mister Spock, Captain Kirk, Isaac Asimov, Humphrey Bogart, and Hunter S. Thompson.

He has stopped waiting for *The Revenge of the Jedi* to come out. Doesn't look likely at this point, does it?

Most folks think seeing is believing.
Wally isn't so sure . . .

STRANGE INVASION
by
Michael Kandel

When Wally first saw the alien spacecraft land in
his backyard, he figured it was just another one of
his "normal" hallucinations, the result of a rare—
and relatively harmless—brain disorder. But then
the refrigerator started talking and the TV began
sending him special broadcasts. Slowly, Wally
became convinced that the message was very real—
and very urgent: the Oht have landed and, by the
time they leave, the earth will look like Yasgur's
farm after Woodstock . . .

A novel you will long remember,
Strange Invasion is a dazzling first novel filled
with black humor, wit, and wonder.

Buy **Strange Invasion** on sale now wherever Bantam
Spectra Books are sold, or use this page to order.
